Praise for the Unparalleled Work of ANN RULE

DEAD BY SUNSET

"Fascinating material . . . Ms. Rule admirably recounts this labyrinthine tale. . . ."
—Walter Walker, *The New York Times Book Review*

"The similarities with the O.J. case are compelling."
—Dan Webster, *The Spokesman-Review* (ID)

"Rule provides a perceptive character analysis of a malignant, self-centered, charismatic con artist. It's a chilling, haunting portrait."
—*Publishers Weekly*

YOU BELONG TO ME

"Ann Rule delivers six tales of obsession and murder with the suspense and class we have come to expect from the author of *The Stranger Beside Me. . . .* Rule makes the story of each victim as fascinating as the pathology of the killer."
—Flo Stanton, *The Indianapolis Star*

"Each of these stories could be a book in itself, and each will cause you to creep out of your bed at night to double-check the locks and make your heart skip a beat at the next unexpected knock."
—Edna Buchanan, *Miami Herald*

"The cases [are] explored in chilling detail . . . compelling. . . . Rule [is] the ruler of the whole true-crime empire."
—Kate McClare, *The News* (Boca Raton, FL)

EVERYTHING SHE EVER WANTED

Books by Ann Rule

Green River, Running Red
Heart Full of Lies
Every Breath You Take
. . . And Never Let Her Go
Bitter Harvest
Dead by Sunset
Everything She Ever Wanted
If You Really Loved Me
The Stranger Beside Me
Possession
Small Sacrifices

Ann Rule's Crime Files:

Vol. 10: Worth More Dead and Other True Cases
Vol. 9: Kiss Me, Kill M : and Other True Cases
Vol. 8: Last Dance, Last Chance and Other True Cases
Vol. 7: Empty Promises and Other True Cases
Vol. 6: A Rage to Kill and Other True Cases
Vol. 5: The End of the Dream and Other True Cases
Vol. 4: In the Name of Love and Other True Cases
Vol. 3: A Fever in the Heart and Other True Cases
Vol. 2: You Belong to Me and Other True Cases
Vol. 1: A Rose for Her Grave and Other True Cases

Without Pity: Ann Rule's Most Dangerous Killers

The I-5 Killer
The Want-Ad Killer
Lust Killer

ANN RULE

POSSESSION

A NOVEL

POCKET BOOKS
New York   London   Toronto   Sydney

For information regarding special discounts for bulk purchases, please contact Simon & Schuster Special Sales at 1-800-456-6798 or business@simonandschuster.com

This book is a work of fiction. Names, characters, places and incidents are products of the author's imagination or are used fictitiously. Any resemblance to actual events or locales or persons, living or dead, is entirely coincidental.

"Our House" by Graham Nash. Copyright © 1970 Broken Bird Music. Used by permission. All rights reserved.

 POCKET BOOKS, a division of Simon & Schuster, Inc. 1230 Avenue of the Americas, New York, NY 10020

Copyright © 1983 by Ann Rule

Published by arrangement with W.W. Norton & Company, Inc.

ISBN: 978-1-4516-4432-6

First Pocket Books printing August 1997

19 18 17 16 15 14 13

POCKET and colophon are registered trademarks of Simon & Schuster, Inc.

Cover art by Don Brautigam

Printed in the U.S.A.

For

LAURA, LESLIE, ANDY, MIKE,
BRUCE, REBECCA, AND MATTHEW.

MAY THEY ALWAYS KNOW THAT LOVE
IS THE ONLY POSSESSION THAT MATTERS.

Acknowledgments

For their inspiration, patience, support, intelligence, and friendly criticism, I owe many thanks to the following:

Fred J. Horner, former Sheriff, Okanogan County, Washington; Paul Bernstein, former Chief Prosecutor, City of Seattle; Larry Nash, Chief, Puyallup, Washington, Police Department; Darrel Wilsey, Head Ranger, National Forest Service, Stehekin, Washington; Bill Wilsey, Betty Wilsey, Margie Wilsey, Stehekin Landing Lodge; Ernie Gibson, Chelan Airways; Miriam Giles, Barbara Easton, Gerry Brittingham, Lola Cunningham, Charles S. Miles, Maureen and Bill Woodcock, the late Sophie M. Stackhouse, and the Northwest Authors' B. and M. Society: John Saul, Michael Sack, Donald E. and Carol McQuinn, Ann Combs, Donna Anders, Margaret Chittenden, Terry and Judine Brooks, Jeanne Okimoto—and me too—a stalwart, if occasionally disorganized, group.

To my agents: Joan and Joe Foley, good friends.

And to Starling Lawrence, my editor,
whose pencil is as deft as it is ruthless.

Lureen Demich might have been surprised to know that her labor pains began less than a mile from where she had conceived the child. She had been with so many men for so many reasons in the year past that she could not be absolutely sure who the father was. Sometimes she let them do it because she was lonely, sometimes for money, and occasionally she had only been bored. But never once for love.

She moved on when the carnival's tents were struck and the caravans lumbered off to the next town, and the men blurred in her mind along with the cities along the circuit: Cincinnati, Moline, Ann Arbor. But she did remember one gangling, carrot-haired boy who'd been pushed into her trailer by some drunken fraternity boys, the kid who'd stuttered as he'd shoved a ten-dollar bill at her. He must have been a smart kid to be in college even though he couldn't have been over sixteen. She saw that he was a joke to the others, that they resented him for his brains, and she heard them laugh when his book smarts and fancy words failed him where it counted.

She'd taken his money and told him to hurry as his friends chanted cadence outside. And hurry he had. Never even really got into her before he spilled it all over her thighs. Then she'd laughed too and turned away to clean up the mess.

The carnival was a thousand miles away when she began to vomit.

Lureen had drifted aimlessly for all of her short life, planning nothing, and dreaming only impossible dreams. She always expected magic and begged the card readers to promise her a better life. But she had little aptitude for anything beyond attracting men, and when each one left

3

her, she always felt that things were a little worse than they had been before.

She was not yet eighteen when she crouched, terrified, against the cool metal wall of the Nashua trailer and felt her belly contract. She thought she might burst. She had been there all day and most of the night, attended by the blank-faced old gypsy woman who watched her with slight interest. There was no compassion, and no one to share the weight of Lureen's fear. The others had told her that the gypsy would know what to do, then left the two of them alone as if pestilence drenched the trailer house.

Lureen knew she was going to die; there was no way that she could push a baby out of her without dying. She turned her face away and gagged as the gypsy held a jelly jar full of whiskey to her lips, and then heard herself grunt deep in her throat. She bore down against the mattress beneath her hips. Her own sounds startled her; she sounded like an animal. The gypsy woman grunted with her, urging her down to darker tunnels of pain she had no wish to explore. She prayed that the baby was dead. She had never wanted it.

The gypsy woman moved toward her, blocking the window with her bulk, and Lureen closed her eyes and pushed with a shudder that shook her body. She felt herself split and something slippery and wet burst from between her legs.

For a moment, it was very quiet. She watched the gypsy rub the red and white thing with a rough towel, watched with a sense of complete removal. It *was* dead. Good. And then its mouth opened suddenly and she heard its cry bounce off the tinny trailer sides.

The old woman muttered with satisfaction and pushed the squalling bundle near her face. It lived, an ugly thing with a head drawn to a point, slick with her blood and covered with stuff that looked like cottage cheese.

She turned away, pressed her face into the mattress, and slept.

* * *

4

POSSESSION

In Coatesville, Pennsylvania—when her name was still Louise—her own mother had gone away, leaving behind one snapshot for her daughter to study. The little girl had been able to discern that Dorothy Demich had been pretty (as she was), full-breasted to the point of incredulity (as she would be), and young, very, very, young. Louise understood that Dorothy could not have survived long in the half-house she shared with Pete Demich and her grandmother, Lena. She understood it more through the years when she waited her own time to flee. The house smelled of painted-over dirt and old women. There was no dining room; her father slept in the single bedroom, and Louise shared a Murphy bed in the living room with the old lady.

Once she had longed for rugs, or even just one rug, to cover the linoleum that was so scuffed you couldn't tell what pattern it was supposed to have. She even tried to wash the gray lace curtains and found the old Easy Spin-Dri in the basement full of nothing but shreds after the water drained away. She finally accepted that there was no way to change the half rowhouse from what it was. The neighbors who shared the common center wall painted their side every five years; Pete never bothered.

Louise had tried to take friends home a couple of times, but when Pete worked all night at the Lukens steel mill, he woke in the late afternoon and walked through the house in his undershirt and shorts, scratching his testicles as if the girls weren't there, embarrassing her and frightening her schoolmates. When he worked days, Lena sat in the corner of the living room in the sagging, wine-plush chair and stared at them, her clubbed fingers spewing out lengths of tatting. What use there was for the strange knots that emerged Louise never learned. Lena refused to speak English in front of her granddaughter's friends, barking out comments in Polish to Louise. The other girls gathered up their paperdolls and went home to houses with mothers who baked cookies and hugged them.

Lena Demich had never hugged her, or kissed her, or even run a rough hand over her braids in a gesture of affection. At night, the old woman snored and farted, and

5

her great girth pulled Louise over to her side of the Murphy bed. Louise learned to sleep with one arm hooked around the bed frame.

Her grandmother was a presence. Nothing more. She seemed to have some attachment to the other old women who lived in the houses that clung to the hillside leading up from the valley floor and Main Street. Louise listened to their talk, trying to find some way to get through to her grandmother, but she never found the key. Lena and Pete communicated with single words over the supper table in the kitchen. They seemed to understand each other; Louise understood nothing.

She was not a bright child. Most of her teachers barely saw her small pale face in a sea of pupils. She neither caused trouble or excelled enough to be noticed. Over the years, an occasional teacher tried to draw her out, but there was never enough time, and Louise shrank from attention that singled her out. She was afraid they would find out that she could not read. Arithmetic was the same. What was it that other students knew that she could not learn? Why couldn't she learn?

Louise was passed from grade to grade along with the rest. As she fell further and further behind, her imaginary world insulated her from the frustrations that threatened to bury her. She fantasized that her mother would come back for her, that Dorothy would realize how much her child resembled her, that she had left part of herself behind. Louise was quite sure that her mother was an actress, really successful, who lived in a grand house somewhere. It was only a matter of time until they would be together. She lied about Dorothy at school, but no one believed her, and the popular girls in soft cashmere sweaters and coordinated skirts laughed at her. She could blink her eyes and make them go away.

Pete and Lena knew that Dorothy was never coming back to claim the strange, skinny child she'd foisted off on them. They knew Dorothy had been dead for three years, her body thrown away in an alley in Chicago by the man whose hands had closed around her neck until they left ten pale blue fingermarks in the soft flesh there. They had accepted the news of Dorothy's murder with stoicism; as far as they were concerned, Dorothy had died the day she walked out on the family, and her actual death neither surprised nor angered them. They hadn't sought vengeance, and no one was ever arrested for the crime. Pete and Lena had been relieved to have her gone, and they'd resented only that she hadn't taken her child with her. Her death verified for them their conviction that the wicked would be smitten down by the unyielding god they answered to.

They had seen no need to tell Louise that her mother was dead. Children always carried tales. When Dorothy's belongings arrived in a brown paper package, Lena picked through the clothing, papers, and bits of costume jewelry with distaste. She had always thought that Dorothy was a tramp, unworthy of a hard-working man like Pete, and the tight sweaters and flimsy undergarments confirmed her feelings. She lumbered down to the coal furnace in the basement and burned everything but the jewelry. Maybe she hadn't noticed the letter addressed to Louise; maybe she had. It didn't matter. Those who died out of grace had no right to send messages to the living.

Lena suspected that Louise carried the bad seed within her, and she watched her granddaughter closely for the signs.

Louise became Lureen in her own mind when she was fourteen, but she didn't tell anyone. There was no one to tell. She chose it for her own name, her *real* name, when she heard it in one of the Saturday afternoon movies she saw— something with Joan Crawford or Shelley Winters. Louise never identified with the main star of the movie; she liked to pick someone in the background, a young girl who was pretty and nice and always turned out to be happy at the end of the film. It might happen to her, when Dorothy returned, or it might happen when she grew up and was old enough to leave home. It couldn't happen where she was because no one could be happy there.

Louise-Lureen's body remained as slat-thin as a child's until she was almost fifteen, and Lena thanked God daily for that. But in the almost tropical heat of the August before her sophomore year in high school, the fact of her budding could no longer be denied. She lasted only a week in high school before she was called into the assistant principal's office.

"You'll have to wear a brassiere," the woman explained. "Or you can't come to school."

Louise was embarrassed to tears, and felt her skin suffuse with a wave of heat as it was pointed out that she "flopped" when she played volleyball in the gym.

"You must remember there are boys' classes on the other side of the gymnasium. There have been complaints."

Louise stared at the woman, confused. Who had complained? The boys? The other girls? The teacher? She had never really felt her own body; it had suddenly become as heavy as stone.

"You must be modest, Louise. You must show respect for yourself and for others."

The woman before her had no discernible breasts. How could she understand? Louise wished that she could have had a principal like Greer Garson or Maureen O'Hara, someone who might know that she had meant no harm.

"I'm sorry. I didn't realize. I guess I just suddenly . . . kind of . . . grew."

"A woman must be aware of her body."

"Forgive me."

"It's not up to me to forgive you, Louise. Try to be more careful."

She wore her coat for the rest of the day, feeling her face flame whenever anyone glanced at her, wondering which of them had been talking about her, wishing that she had had one friend who might have told her.

Avoiding her grandmother's half-lidded stare at the coat on a warm September day, she hurried to the bathroom and closed the door. The only mirror in the house was over the chipped basin, and she had to climb on the edge of the tub to view herself from the shoulders down. Balancing with one hand on the window ledge, she pulled up her blouse with the other.

POSSESSION

It was true. Her breasts had bloomed, plump pillows of white flesh, centered with salmon-colored nipples that seemed much larger than she remembered. They looked peculiar to her; she was so thin and they were so big. They seemed not to be a part of her body at all. She turned from one side to the other, getting used to them. In a way, she thought, they looked nice. Movie stars had big breasts, and nobody complained. Still teetering on the tub's rim, she pulled her blouse off and draped it around her, forming a vee of material in the center of her chest.

They did look nice. They looked like her mother's breasts in the snapshot she carried. She pulled the material tighter and two round half circles popped up over the top. She was amazed that they had grown so quickly, that she had barely noticed. She smiled at herself in the mirror. No wonder the boys watched her from their side of the gym. No wonder. She felt just the slightest sensation of power, something she had never felt before.

The bathroom door opened so quietly that she heard no sound at all. She didn't hear the old woman until she was beside her, spitting out a word of Polish that Louise didn't understand. Still, she felt the force of it, and the vehemence behind it. Her feet lost their tentative perch on the tub, and she fell, crashing against the toilet stool. The floor there smelled sharply of urine and she turned her head away, tasting blood in her mouth.

"Get up, and cover yourself. What you doing in here?"

Louise stood up slowly, lifting a hand to her mouth to wipe away the blood there.

"They said at school that I need a brassiere."

"Who said? Who thinks he has to mind our business?"

"A lady in the principal's office. She says I flop."

Lena jabbed a bony finger at her and poked her breasts.

"Ahh, she's right. You're as big as a cow. Come."

Louise followed her grandmother into the living room where the old lady pulled a flesh colored harness-like garment from the cedar chest there. She wrapped it around Louise's chest, tugging, pulling and lacing until Louise could barely breathe. She looked down at her breasts and

9

saw that they were flattened now, the bulk of them pushed against her ribcage and back under her arms. She tried to take in a lungful of air and couldn't.

"I can't wear this," she protested. "I look like a freak and I can't breathe."

"You wear it. I will go to Sears and buy you some brassieres. Now, you pull this very tight and your boobies won't stick out like you was a whore. You are like her, your mother who ran away. Big breasts. She didn't even feed you with them, too afraid they wouldn't be so big after."

Louise closed her eyes and turned away; she hated to hear Lena talk about Dorothy, hated the flat, closed look that passed over her grandmother's face when her mother's name was mentioned. She'd seen Lena naked once and had been horrified at the slack, empty breasts that hung down over her corrugated belly. She could not imagine that Lena had ever been a young girl. Lena avoided mention of anything having to do with the body, and she wondered if it was because Lena's own body was so ugly.

Still, having breasts seemed not to be as repulsive to her grandmother as having periods. Nobody had prepared Louise for the sudden rush of hot blood that had coursed down her legs six months before. That had been the worst day of her life. The terror. She had walked into the kitchen with her shoes literally full of blood and looked at Lena with a plea for help.

Lena had responded with rage, pulling Louise into the bathroom where she filled the tub with water. "Wash yourself. That is not clean blood. It is blood from the curse, and you have to wash it away."

What had she done to deserve such a curse? Lena had talked of evil spirits often, of things that happened in the old country, but Louise could not imagine what sin she herself had committed. Lena had not explained. Instead, she'd reached into the towel closet and brought out a length of flannel sheeting which she tore into squares and then folded into oblongs. Louise thought that the old lady had finally gone completely off her rocker.

"Now stand up," she'd barked. "See? See—this is how

POSSESSION

you do." Lena had lifted up her own black skirts and gestured between her legs. "It is to soak up the bad blood. You mustn't let anyone know. When the rag is full, then you wash it and hang it in the basement behind the furnace. You don't let your father see it, and don't let the boys smell the fish smell. They will know you are a bad girl. They will try to get you—to do the bad thing to you. The bad thing hurts. It is full of hurt; you must not let them close to you."

Louise had had no idea what the bad thing was, and boys never got close to her—no one did—but she obediently held the flannel rag between her legs. She'd been afraid to ask Lena for more explanation. She'd spent the next four days taking baths and washing the bloodsoaked rags until the skin on her hands peeled off.

The bleeding stopped then, and one of the girls at school told her about Kotex. She threw the soiled rags into the furnace. The next month the bleeding came again, and she realized that it would come and go and that it happened to all women, not just her. But the boys did come around her, like dogs who had caught a scent. Their sudden interest disturbed and fascinated her at the same time.

Louise felt some stirring that she had not felt before; she had always longed to have someone hug her, but what she felt was different. It felt good and bad at the same time, and she wondered what she could do to make it stop. It was like listening to a song she liked and then having the music end before it was time. She felt empty, with a compelling need to be filled. She knew it had something to do with the place between her legs. When she leaned against the washing machine, she could feel it in her belly too, and sometimes the machine's vibrations made her think that the elusive ending of the song was almost within her grasp.

Louise had not the faintest notion of the sexual act. If she had been able to read, she might have found out. The movies told her nothing; the characters kissed and held each other, and then the scene always dissolved, leaving her puzzled and frustrated.

Louise came home from school on a frozen January day when she was sixteen and found Lena sitting still as a rock

1 1

in the easy chair, her hands clasped around the spew of tatting. She was dead. She had been dead so long that she was stiff, and Louise could not release the chain of knots from her hands. She screamed for the old woman next door, and someone called Pete home from the steel mill.

Her father had fallen to his knees in front of his mother and begun to sob. Louise had never been more astonished, filled with wonderment at the sight of Pete rocking back and forth as tears made rivulets in the mill grime on his face. Her father had never demonstrated any emotion, nothing more intense than annoyance, and here he knelt in front of Lena and wept like a baby. Lena's laced black shoes were planted in a puddle of her own urine.

Louise began to laugh. She had never seen a man cry. In this house empty of feelings for all the years of her life she could not deal with this rush of emotion, and she could not stop laughing. She saw her father turn slowly and warn her with his eyes, and she laughed. Still kneeling, Pete raised his hand and caught her in the face. Then he fell sideways on the cracked linoleum, scrabbling at it with his hands and sobbed louder.

She ran. Past the arms raised to hold her back, beyond her father's shocked command, skittering down the ice-crusted ·porch steps, hardly touching them. It was only when she reached the sidewalk and drew a breath of crystalline air that she realized how nauseating it had smelled inside.

Old fool. The old fool was dead.

Louise felt no grief because she hadn't really lost anything. She wasn't sure what she felt, perhaps a renewed hope that her mother would come for her at last, now that there was no woman to care for her. Maybe it had been Lena who kept Dorothy away for all the years.

She could hear them inside, their voices rising and falling in choruses of mourning and indignation, punctuated by groans from her father, the keening of an animal left alone in the woods. She ran down the hill toward the Lincoln Highway, anywhere to get away from that sound and the smell. She would have to go back in there sometime, but not soon.

POSSESSION

She ran past the corner where the drugstore was, only vaguely aware of the whistles and catcalls from the high school boys who lounged against a window displaying trusses and surgical collars, pock-faced guys with duck's-ass haircuts and cigarettes hanging from their lips. The cold air froze her throat and hurt her lungs. A cramp seized her beneath her ribs, drawing her gut inward until she had to slow to a walk.

Her own bladder had been full to bursting when she had arrived home to find Lena dead. Now it demanded attention. The Day-Old-Bread-Store loomed ahead, windows steamed over. She ran inside, knocking over a stack of stale sandwich loaves, bouncing oblongs of red, yellow, and blue wax-paper into the narrow aisle.

"Hey!" the Italian shouted. "You! Girl!"

"Bathroom," she cried. "You got a bathroom?"

He was so close to her that she could see the pores of his nose, the stubble of coarse black hairs on his chin. He nodded and gestured toward the back of the store, as she dashed past him and slammed the door. The toilet was dirty, but she was past the point of caring.

The Italian looked at her curiously when she finally came out. He had pulled down the shades in the front windows, casting a greenish pall over the bread inside. The past-date bakery goods looked like bodies huddled on the white metal tables.

"You O.K., girl?"

Louise bent to pick up the bread loaves scattered around her feet. Wonder Bread. Wonder. Wonder. Her fingers felt numb, and she couldn't seem to grasp the slippery loaves. She looked up at the Italian and saw that he looked funny. But everything seemed different; the whole world had changed.

"Let 'em be. They're too old anyway. I'll give them to the pig man when he comes by."

"You're closing so early? It's only four thirty."

"It's a slow day."

She liked his voice; it was soft, and she was amazed that she had someone's full attention. She walked over to the counter and leaned against it. "You always close up at five. Every day but Sunday, you're open nine to five. See, I remember?"

"It don't matter. They don't come in by now, they won't be in. What's the difference in a couple loaves of bread?"

Vito Ferrano was thirty-eight, a bachelor not by choice but by circumstance, the grudging support of a senile father and a sister whose mustache discouraged serious suitors. Now the girls looked past him at the guys in their twenties, guys who still had hair and hadn't the girth that Vito had. He rubbed his hands over the white apron covering his belly and felt the growth between his legs; this girl always did that to him. How old was she? Eighteen? Maybe nineteen. Not a real pretty girl, but not bad either. She didn't carry herself like the ones who came into the store and teased him just so he'd throw in a free bag of doughnuts. She hunched her shoulders to cover up those breasts, or maybe it was just too much weight for her to carry up front.

He leaned forward over the counter, balancing his body on his splayed hands, hoping the apron hid the erection that he couldn't stop. There was something peculiar about the girl, but he couldn't figure out what.

"You got problems? Somebody chasing you?"

". . . I don't know. Maybe. She died . . ."

"*Who* died?"

"My grandmother. You know her. She comes in on Fridays and Tuesdays."

"Oh, yeah." He didn't know. One old lady looked just like the next to him. "That's too bad. You feeling real sad about it, huh?"

She bit her lip and looked down, poking her finger into the yielding white plastic package of rolls on the counter. She didn't feel sad, but she supposed she should. It was very quiet inside the dim store, and she could hear the man breathing.

"I just came from school and I found her. Just sitting there. Just dead. I didn't think people died sitting up."

He watched her, seeing the rise and fall of the white blouse over her breasts, the bones in her wrist so close to the skin that they shone through. He reached a plump hand across the counter and patted her hand. Her skin was as cool as water, and his own so hot he thought he would burn her with his touch.

"It's good when they go like that. They get old, and they just kind of stop. They don't feel nothin'; it's like you just turn out a light, you know? Just *click*, and then no more."

She nodded faintly. He took it for grief that she could not put into words. He moved around the counter and she leaned toward him, putting her head on his shoulder. He held his body back. He didn't want her to feel the bulge of his erection. What kind of a man gets a hard-on when he's supposed to be comforting a poor girl like this?

She smelled him, a yeasty odor, and his aftershave lotion. It smelled good. It got the smell of the house out of her nose. She leaned closer to him and he put his hands tentatively on the hip bones that pushed through her blue wool skirt, trying to hold her away from his lower body, but she pushed forward. She felt like a little rabbit to him, all bones, helpless, but her breasts burrowed into his chest, sending such shocks through him that he trembled.

"Don't cry," he whispered, although she wasn't crying at all.

"What's your name, girl?"

"Lou— . . . Lureen."

"That's pretty. You're pretty. A pretty, pretty girl." He stroked her hair. "This makes you feel better?"

She nodded her head and moved closer to him. She felt the hardness against her belly, and wondered what it was, and yet, not knowing, liked the feel of it. She worked herself closer to him, feeling the odd stirring that she'd never been able to explain. Her legs felt weak, and she clung to him for support. He lifted her onto the counter and stood between her knees.

"You call me Vito," he whispered. "You like being here with Vito, don't you? You forget about what's outside there. You forget you're sad."

He stroked her hair, her face, and let the fingers covered with silky black hairs trail down her neck. And then he touched her breasts, petting them as if they were separate beings. Stroking, kneading, rubbing them in a circular motion. She closed her eyes. This was the best she'd ever felt in her whole life. She could never remember being touched at all, and now she was being touched in a way she had never imagined. It was so much better than leaning against the washing machine.

"Little rabbit," he murmured. "Poor little rabbit." He opened the buttons on her blouse, and she made no move to stop him. Her breasts felt as if they had grown, as if they had to burst out of her blouse. She kept her eyes closed and gasped when she felt his lips on her nipples. He touched the erect pink flesh gently and then sucked, and she felt a warmth spread between her legs and into her hips and belly.

Suddenly, he moved away and she opened her eyes in protest. She watched, fascinated, as he untied the long white apron, and stood before her in a white T-shirt and dark trousers. He stared at her breasts and his face was so different, flushed with color, his lips parted. She could see the bulge in his pants and she watched as he unzipped himself and let a great blue-veined cylinder of flesh spring out. It seemed to have a life of its own, standing out from his open fly, the slit at the end of it touched with a drop of moisture.

He pulled at her shoulders, drawing her forward on the counter, and she spread her own legs farther apart, aware of dampness in the crotch of her panties. He was not gentle now, but fumbling and hurried as he tugged at her panties.

She knew that this must be the bad thing that Lena had warned her about, but she didn't care if it hurt. Grunting and panting, the man moved toward her, and she lowered herself onto the purplish probe, sliding down over it, wrapping her legs around his waist.

It did hurt, but only for an instant, and then Lureen felt, for the first time in her life, that the empty place inside her was filled up. She clung to him, and he lifted her clear of the counter, circling the room in a clumsy dance until at last he gave a cry and his arms lost their strength. He set her back on the counter and slumped beside her, his head on his arms, breathing so harshly that she thought he was sick.

"Vito?" She watched him with alarm. "Did I hurt you?"

"Huh?" He looked up at her and began to laugh. "Naw, you sure as hell didn't hurt me, little rabbit. You only just wore me out."

Relieved, she slid off the counter and began to look for her panties. She found them under a table and put them on. She watched him and saw him changed. He had been with her, touching her, surrounding her, enveloping her, and now he seemed so distant; he turned away and zipped up his pants, reached for his apron and tied it around him again.

"Vito?" she said quietly. "Do you still like me?"

He looked up, and his face was back to the way it always was. He didn't seem to know her. He grabbed a rag and started to wipe the counter.

"Sure, sure I like you. I like you fine."

"But you're different—than you were before."

"Well, it's always different after. You know . . ."

"No."

"Didn't you ever do it before?"

"No."

"Oh shit!"

"Well, I never did. But I liked it."

"Lureen . . . how old are you?"

"Sixteen."

He slammed one hand down on the counter and looked at her as if he hated her, and then he slumped and said quietly, "Lureen, I'm sorry. I thought you was older. I wouldna never done it if I knew."

"But I liked it."

"You gonna tell anyone?"

She considered that for a moment. "No. I haven't got anyone to tell. Can I come back again?"

"Sure. You come in anytime. I'll save you one of them pecan pies they send down from Philly."

He was walking her toward the door, his hand flat and insistent on her back, urging her out.

"No. I mean can I come back—like it was today?"

He pulled up the green shade on the door and surveyed the sidewalk outside, satisfied himself that it was empty of traffic, and unlocked the door. "Sure. Well, we'll see. You're O.K., kid. You're just a little young."

She turned against his pressing arm, trying to hold onto the good feelings, and yet seeing them vanish. "Didn't I do it right?"

"Kid. You did fine. I'll see you around. Right?"

Lureen was out the door and on the sidewalk. The ice beneath her feet looked clear on top, but she could see dirt and debris frozen into it where it coated the cement. She turned and headed slowly up the street toward the drugstore corner. It was so cold. Even the drugstore guys had gone inside. She didn't want to go home, but there wasn't anyplace else to go.

"Hey! Kid!"

Lureen looked back at him, standing outside the bread store. And she felt the loss that she would feel for the rest of her life. How could she have been so close to him just a few minutes before and be so separate from him now? How could people pull apart so completely? She had liked the "bad thing," despite Lena's warning, but she had basked in being held. Once it was over, there was no more holding. She made a half-step toward him again, but his voice held her away.

"I'm real sorry about the old lady. You take care now. Right?"

He didn't want her back. She walked away, wondering. There was something that made men want you close, and there was the thing they could do that took away the empty place, but you couldn't count on them to want you afterward. It didn't make sense to her.

She'd expected that Pete would shout at her when she got home, but he just looked up dully when she walked in. She went to bed all by herself—for the first time—luxuriating in being able to sleep in the middle of the bed, and in the silence.

* * *

18

POSSESSION

Lena's departure made so little difference to her that it was as if her grandmother had never existed. Pete went his own way, and Lureen rarely saw him. Sometimes she'd catch a glimpse of him downtown with a woman; it might have been just one woman or a series of women who looked so much alike that she couldn't tell one from the other. He gave her money once in a while and sometimes he brought groceries home. She existed on cokes and egg-salad sandwiches and Franco-American spaghetti, and used whatever money was left over for movies. Pete won a twelve-inch television set on a punchboard. She found it in the living room one afternoon. It must have been for her, she figured, because he was never home to watch it.

It changed her life.

Because she couldn't read, Lureen had drawn all her information from movies and pictures in books. She could not afford to go to the movies very often, but now she could spend hours and hours in front of the television set. The square plastic Philco centered with gray images was an education for her. The soap operas went beyond anything she had ever gleaned from movies; she could be part of them, live through each day's drama on "As the World Turns," and see what a family was supposed to be. It explained things she had never been able to grasp. She realized that Dorothy had not returned because Dorothy was suffering from amnesia. On television these people who had forgotten always came home eventually, and so would her mother.

Television became far more important than going to school, and she went less and less often. When she signed Pete's name to excuse notes, no one questioned her; the only class where she understood what was going on anyway was Home Ec. The things she really needed to know about were home on TV. She could spend a whole day and half the night curled up in Lena's old chair, the shades drawn against the sun. Sometimes she yearned to crawl into the set and be part of the life inside. Time telescoped and she was always amazed when the "Star Spangled Banner" and the nightly prayer came on.

1 9

"I Love Lucy" and "Queen for a Day" and the rest erased any memories of Vito Ferrano. She forgot what he looked like; the only thing that remained of that afternoon that Lena died was a rippling sensation, an awareness of her belly. It wasn't insistent enough to make her want the funny fat man to touch her again. If he could make her feel that way, then she suspected any man could.

There *was* a man she dreamed about, a man who walked with her day and night. *Elvis.* When she saw him for the first time on Ed Sullivan, she was stunned by his beauty. He was clean and pure, and yet he moved in a way she'd never seen a man move before. The audience roared and screamed when he moved his hips that way, and the cameras suddenly focused on his face alone. But Lureen felt so much more for Elvis than the audience did; he had such sadness about him. She could see it in his eyes and hear it whispering beneath the beat of his songs. She wanted to put her arms around him and tell him she understood.

Lureen knew that she would meet Elvis sometime, although she wasn't sure how or when it would happen. There were some things a person just knew. She knew that Elvis was good, and she heard on talk shows that he was a Christian and loved his mother, and that he'd been very poor. So he wouldn't make fun of her because of the way she'd been unpopular and lonesome and because she couldn't read. Most of all, she knew he would understand that she had to find her own mother.

Lureen didn't go to school the last Friday in April; she never went on Fridays because that was the day when something important happened on all the soap operas, something that you waited for all week long. She stayed in front of the set until 4:30 in the stuffy living room, the blinds blocking the breeze and daylight.

There was no food in the house, and Pete never came home until late on Friday because it was payday and he went to the tavern. There wasn't any money in the house, but she remembered that Lena had kept a jar of pennies and dimes on the shelf in the hall closet.

It was dark in the closet and the shelf was thick with dust.

POSSESSION

The coin jar was gone; she'd figured it would be. Her hand brushed against the candy tin where Lena had kept buttons and thread. Curious, Lureen lifted it down, the old eight-sided box, its daisies and roses barely visible anymore under the scratched grime on the lid. She carried it into the kitchen and turned on the hanging light bulb there. Lena could have left a few coins hidden under the buttons; she was surprised one of the old women hadn't taken the candy box away along with all of Lena's other things.

The tin was full of costume jewelry, and she recognized the pieces as if they were from another lifetime. It was Dorothy's jewelry; she had played with it years and years before. A double loop of dusky pink beads shaped like roses, claylike and still giving off the faint fragrance of the petals they'd been pressed from. A charm bracelet with an American flag, a "V for Victory," and an "E" from the steel mill—the kind they gave out during the war, the war when her father went away for a long time—a little cracked bell, and a funny little man with a big nose peeking over a wall. She picked out a flower made of colored stones caught in a tarnished metal ribbon. There were earrings. Dorothy had always worn earrings: tiny bananas and apples, red and white squares, purplish dulled sequins, silver half-moons with smiling, top-hatted ladies on them.

She picked up a watch, shook it, and heard a distant faltering tick. She wound it, but it stopped then, one hand falling inside the scratched face.

Her mother's wedding ring was there too, a thin band of gold where there once had been three small diamonds, now only three spaces with prongs sticking up hollow. She looked inside the band and could make out some writing there. Painfully, she spelled it out: "P.D. to D.D., 11-12-39, L.o.v.e."

"Love?" Boy, that sure didn't sound like her father. Maybe that's what they always wrote on wedding rings.

She'd seen every piece of the jewelry; Dorothy had let her play with it to keep her quiet. But Dorothy had loved jewelry. Why hadn't she taken it with her? Especially her watch and her wedding ring?

Lureen yelped as her finger hit the pin to Dorothy's favorite brooch, a large enameled dogwood blossom with a pink stone center. Sucking the drop of blood away, she carried the brooch to the bathroom mirror and adjusted it at the neck of her blouse. She could almost see her mother's face stare back at her from the mirror, remember how Dorothy had worn the pin just as she did now.

Puzzled, Lureen put the candy tin back on the shelf. She'd never seen her mother's jewelry around during all the time since she'd gone away, even though Lena had had her sewing things out in the living room often. So the pins and necklaces must not have been there before. If Dorothy had come home to visit, she would surely have waited to see Lureen. She wouldn't have gone away again without seeing her own daughter. It didn't make sense. Maybe Dorothy *had* left without her jewelry and Lena had hidden it from Lureen all these years, and then the old ladies had put Dorothy's things in the sewing tin after Lena died.

Trying to figure it out made her jumpy; she could reason it only to a certain spot and then her thoughts dissolved and she had to start all over again. She couldn't concentrate on the television. She poked around in the refrigerator looking for something to eat even though she didn't feel hungry anymore, but all she could find was an end of cheese with a fuzzy green patch growing on it, and a bowl of something she didn't recognize. She craved something sweet, like a "short-chocolate" at the drugstore. It wasn't a short-chocolate-something; it was just ice and milk and chocolate syrup. The girl at the counter had laughed when, wanting a double-size, she had first asked for a "large-chocolate," instead of a large "short-chocolate."

She dug down in the couch cushions and found a quarter and three pennies, and that was enough. There were probably more coins down there, but she needed to be outside quickly; sometimes, walking seemed to help her think better. But Lureen walked slowly along the Old Lincoln Highway—Main Street—and passed up the drugstore without seeing it.

She didn't realize that the blocks were melting away

POSSESSION

behind her. She had walked more than two miles in the failing light when she heard the sounds of the carnival. She looked up to see that the field next to the used car lot on the west end of Main Street was filled with tents and rides; a ferris wheel circled above the street, festooned with lights. Caught in the crowd, Lureen walked past the booths and the freak shows. It was so bright that her eyes hurt, and the music made her ears hum. Her vista on the world had been a twelve-inch screen for so long; now it made her dizzy to be shoved along the sawdust path of the midway.

Every stall seemed to have its own music, and a few steps past took her into another channel of sound. The night air smelled of fried onions, hamburgers, chicken corn soup (from the American Legion booth), submarine sandwiches, smoke, beer, and sometimes an acrid wafting of whiskey on the breath of men who nudged her shoulder as they passed. She saw people she recognized, faces from school, and some nodded. But no one stopped to talk to her. She was no one's best friend—not even anyone's second, third, or fourth best friend. It didn't matter; it hadn't mattered for a long time.

Male voices called to her as she was swept past the gambling booths, seducing her with their voices to come and win with the toss of one dime. She smiled at them, shook her head, and was carried on to the next coaxing pitch.

She stayed a long time in front of the freak show, wondering what it must be like for the creatures who stood on the rickety stage to be stared at. A bearded lady with hair on her chest, but with what seemed to be real breasts. A dwarf with a head bigger than any she'd ever seen, shuffling strangely on two tiny legs. A fat lady, sitting on a chair that looked like a throne. The fat lady had short curly hair and her eyes were almost hidden in a face whose red cheeks melted into her neck and her neck into her breasts, cascading flesh falling away from the polka dot, ruffled baby dress she wore. Her huge legs were planted like barrels beneath the baby dress, fat ankles pouring over little baby shoes with red bows.

It made Lureen feel suffocated to see the rolls and rolls of

2 3

flesh, and she touched her own waist lightly to be sure she could still feel her ribs there. The fat lady lifted a hand slowly and seemed to be beckoning to her with the perfect, star-shaped appendage, the red nails flashing. Lureen turned away and fled into the crowd.

She heard Elvis singing and she followed the faint thread of his voice, coming finally to a platform at the far end of the carnival grounds. "Heartbreak Hotel" played continuously as four women gyrated slowly before a gathering cluster of men. Lureen stopped, entranced, as they danced in a blue spotlight. They looked beautiful, although when she pushed in a little closer, she could see that they had on an awful lot of make-up.

"What you see here, gentlemen, is only a small sample of what those little ladies will show you inside. Every one of these dancers has been selected for her . . . er . . . particular dancing ability. This is not a family show; so we don't urge you to bring the little woman in. I'm not exaggerating when I promise you that you will never regret the price of one ticket. We're going to be full up inside; so I suggest you get in line now and get your ticket for the kind of show that you've never seen before."

Lureen studied the barker. He was slim, and he had brown hair with sideburns like Elvis. She thought he was kind of handsome, and he moved like he was full of energy or electricity. His white shirt was open at the neck and wet with sweat in his armpits. She liked his voice, and she liked the way he winked at the crowd. She thought it must be exciting to work in a carnival.

The dancing girls all wore satin brassieres and little skirts with gold fringe around the bottom. Their legs were encased in black net stockings with sequins that flashed when the light hit them.

"Now, Lila is going to give you just a short demonstration of what I'm telling you about, gentlemen. Show 'em what I mean, Lila." The barker smiled at the woman at the end of the line. She was older than the rest, and Lureen saw she had a soft layer of fat that was marked with a red line where the fringed skirt circled her waist. She stepped to the front

POSSESSION

of the stage and began to move her midsection so that you could see the muscles beneath her skin bunch and ripple up and down. It didn't seem quite right to Lureen to have Elvis singing for a dance like this one, but she did think the woman was pretty talented, even though she never smiled and chewed gum all the while she performed.

The men crowding against the platform didn't seem to mind; they weren't watching the dancer's face.

There was a scratching sound that made Lureen wince as Elvis's voice stopped, and "The Steel Guitar Rag" blared out. Now Lila put her hands behind her head and with elbows akimbo began to thrust her pelvis forward violently to the twanging music. The flesh at her waist quivered with each *Boom . . . Boom,* and the watching males sent out a kind of tension that made Lureen step back and cross her arms over her breasts. She'd seen a pack of dogs once circling a cat up a tree and the men reminded her of the straining, growling animals.

The music stopped in mid chorus, and Lila dropped her arms to her sides and stepped back into the line of dancers. All the life disappeared from her body; she didn't look at the crowd, but turned and walked back through the flap in the tent behind the stage.

"She wiggles, she jiggles, and she bounces, men. And she does more, but that's all for now. Line up over here and get your tickets. Fifty cents. One half dollar for a full show inside. Don't tell your wife, and don't tell your girlfriends. The show starts in two minutes; so have your money ready."

A couple of the men grinned with embarrassment and moved away into the constantly surging midway, but most of them dug into their pockets for coins and passed through the ticket stand. Lureen watched the last of the dancers disappear behind the stage and saw that there were spots in the sparkling net stockings that had been darned with heavy black thread.

She stood, hesitantly wondering where to go next. Part of her wished she had the fifty cents to go inside; she was curious about what more Lila could show the crowd that she

2 5

hadn't done outside. She wondered what it must be like to have so many eyes watching you when you danced, admiring you. And she wondered how you could make your stomach do all those rolling movements that made it look like that.

"Hey! You! Hey, girlie!"

Lureen jumped. The man in the white shirt who'd sold the tickets was leaning over his stand and calling to her. He smiled and she could see white lines in his tanned face as the skin pulled tautly across his cheekbones. She walked a little closer, and his eyes were so blue they were almost white. He was older than she'd thought—maybe about thirty, but she found him the best-looking man she'd ever seen in her whole life.

"You mean me?" she asked.

"Yeah, sweetheart. You." He jumped off the platform by placing one arm on the stage and vaulting over the footlights. His biceps stood out on the supporting arm, and his body moved as effortlessly as a leaf in the wind. He was short and that surprised her—hardly taller than she was. He stood so close to her that she wanted to step back. She couldn't.

"You with it?"

"What?"

"You with it?"

"I don't understand," she murmured, trapped by the clarity of his eyes.

"You with the show, I mean. You work here?"

"Oh. No—no. I was just watching them dance. I guess they have to study a long time to do that."

He laughed, a sharp rasping bark of a laugh. "Yeah. Oh my yes, a long time. You dance?"

"Not like that. A little—at school, and . . ."

"How old are you?"

"Sixteen."

"Naw," he drawled in disbelief. "You're kidding me. You're eighteen at least. You don't look like no sixteen-year-old girl."

"Really. I'm sixteen."

POSSESSION

"I'd say you're eighteen."

She couldn't look away from his eyes, and she shivered.

"I say you're eighteen, and you can dance like a dream."

She didn't answer.

"We've got a place for another girl. With your looks, and your figure, you'd be our star attraction. On-the-job training, free eats, free costumes, thirty-five bucks a week, and you get to travel all over the country. Get you out of this town. I mean some of our girls are on television now, in the big time."

"I can't dance like that," she murmured.

"Sure you can."

"Do you really travel all over the country?"

"You bet. Tomorrow Harrisburg. Pittsburgh. Detroit. Cleveland."

"Memphis? Do you go to Memphis?"

"Why not?"

She stepped backward, tripping over a snaking coil of extension cord, and he darted out a tattooed arm to steady her.

"I have to go home now," she stammered.

His eyes still held hers, and he was still smiling. He pointed to a silver trailer parked in the shadows behind the tent. "You change your mind, you come back, hear? You just knock on that door over there. You come back before 3:00 A.M. and I'll be waiting. Just bring your little suitcase, and you knock."

She didn't know what to say. He watched her as she edged away, trying to find a space in the flow of people behind her. Then she found one and slipped in.

"Hey, girlie!"

She turned and saw he was back on the little stage. He cupped a hand around his mouth and shouted over the din, "Memphis! New York! Miami!"

Lureen ran almost all the way home, and she kept seeing the man's eyes. She figured he'd been teasing her. She wondered if she'd look pretty in one of the costumes with the fringe and the net stockings, and then she was sure he'd been teasing her. Nobody was going to give a wonderful job

2 7

like that to her, except. . . . She stopped, winded, walked slowly past Piscoglio's Drugstore, the windows darkened now. It was a lot later than she'd realized. Except maybe it was the same thing as Vito Ferrano. Maybe it was because of the little bit of power she had with men. She wasn't sure she wanted a job because of that. And she probably wouldn't get to see "As the World Turns" anymore since most likely you couldn't have televisions in trailers.

The front porch light was out, but she could see the lamp on in the living room. She went up the steps quietly and tried to make the staircase inside without Pete's seeing her. He didn't care how late she stayed out, but she didn't like to talk to him when he was drunk, and he'd be sure to be drunk by this late.

"Where the hell you been?" His voice stopped her, and she blinked as she walked into the living room. The room looked different somehow, but she couldn't tell what was changed.

And then she looked toward the television set. It wasn't there. She darted glances around the room and she couldn't see it anywhere. She looked at Pete in bewilderment.

"So? What's the matter with you?" he said. He was really drunk, so drunk his whole face seemed squashed and the few strands of hair he usually combed over the top of his head were down in his eyes.

"Where's my television?"

"It ain't *your* television."

"Where'd you put it?" She felt panicky. "Did you put it in the kitchen?"

"It ain't here."

"Don't tease me. I want to know where it is. I've got shows I've got to watch."

"I gave it to Myrna. Hers is on the fritz and I said she could have it. Hell, I never watch the damned thing."

"*I* watch it!" she screamed. "I've got my shows. I watch it all the time."

"Well, you ain't gonna watch it no more because I gave it to Myrna."

Lureen sank down on the straight chair next to the

POSSESSION

hallway. He meant it. He wasn't going to bring it back. She started to cry, wiping her nose with the back of her hand.

Suddenly Pete was standing in front of her, weaving but standing. He grabbed at the dogwood pin on her blouse and pulled it off, ripping the thin material as the pin came away.

"What the fuck are you doing with this?"

"My mother left it. It was in Grandma's stuff. It's mine now."

"Your mother didn't leave one shitty thing here, dummy. She took it all with her when she waltzed out of here."

"It's hers! She must have left it. I remember when she used to wear it."

He held the brooch high over her head, making her jump for it as he staggered away.

"She took it when she run out," he shouted. "She took every damn thing but the silverware."

"Grandma had it," Lureen said softly. "She had all of Mama's stuff, and I found it in the closet. Give it to me!"

"They sent it back." Pete stopped, turned back to his chair and lifted his can of beer and drained it.

"What?" Lureen was in a frenzy. It was her fault. If she hadn't gone out, he couldn't have stolen her television set. If she hadn't looked in the closet, she wouldn't have found the jewelry. "Who sent it back?"

"No one." Pete studied the floor between his bare feet.

"Who sent it back? I'm going to find her. I'm going to ask her."

"You ain't gonna find her! Because she's dead. Dead. Dead. Dead."

"No!" Lureen screamed to drown out his words. "She's got amnesia. She can't remember how to get home."

"She can't remember because she's dead, you airhead. They sent all that junk back from some morgue in Chicago a coupla years ago. She left me, and she left you, and she wasn't nuthin but a whore. Shit! Shit, why'd you make me tell you? Ain't I taken care of you all this time? You just better believe she's dead and forget about her."

She looked at him without expression. She was more shocked than Pete was when she leapt on him, raking his

29

face with her fingernails, driving her knee into his hairy body. He covered his head with his arms as she beat on him, screaming, "Liar! Liar!"

He brought his arm back and knocked her halfway across the living room. She lay there stunned as he stood over her, blood oozing from the scratches on his face. He lifted his arm again, and then stopped. He could kill her. She would kill him if she had the strength. Her head ached where she'd hit the doorjamb.

She watched his chest heave, and then saw him lift his hand to his face and stare at it as it came away stained with his own blood. He turned and walked unsteadily toward the bathroom.

She was gone before he came out, everything she owned jammed into a shopping bag. She would never remember running back to the carnival grounds. There was no place to go back to, and no place else to run to.

She pounded on the door of the little silver trailer, saw a light come on inside, and then the man was there in the doorway. He was barechested and she could see he had a purple snake tattooed across his belly and over one shoulder. He smiled when he recognized her and stood back to let her in.

He looked at the shopping bag in her hand, and asked, "Now, how old did you say you were?"

She stared back with flat eyes. "Eighteen. I'm eighteen like you said."

After a few days, she saw that the baby wasn't as ugly. Its head had settled into a nice round shape, and they all came to see it and told her he was a pretty baby. Dolly Dimples, the fat lady, took care of her, bringing her food as the caravan hurtled through the nights and days, heading south. Her breasts filled with milk, and it was a relief when she nursed him. He was cute—like a doll—and he didn't cry very much. When he did cry, she discovered that she could quiet him with a teaspoon of whiskey. She didn't really want him, but she didn't hate him anymore either.

She decided to give him a really nice name, something

different. Duane—because that sounded good with Demich. And Elvis for a middle name, because she still thought about Elvis sometimes, even though they never got closer to Memphis or Nashville than Wilmington, Delaware.

When she had to perform, she either got Dolly to watch him, or she gave him a little extra whiskey and he slept in a cardboard box behind the stage.

He turned out to be a really smart little kid, and the roustabouts taught him to swear when he was two and everybody thought that was funny. She didn't know what the hell she was going to do with him when he got old enough to go to school, but the kid was a fact of life, and that's the way it was.

Sometimes she thought maybe she should adopt him out, but she never got around to it, and after a while he just seemed to take care of himself. She liked him when he was good, and when he wasn't, there was usually somebody who'd take him off her hands. She guessed she wasn't cut out to be a mother.

Lureen cried a lot. Just some little thing would make her eyes puddle up, and she couldn't help weeping. She tried never to think about Dorothy, not after that last night in Coatesville, but once in a while she just couldn't help it. She still dreamed about her mother and woke to find tears streaming down her face. Little things made her cry too; she couldn't bear to see the carcasses of cats and dogs that had been killed along the highways and left there as if nobody cared about them. Sometimes she cried because of things that men said to her and did to her, but that didn't last long because there was always another man in another town.

The baby hated it when she cried. He patted her face and cooed, "Poor Reenie," and she would hold him and rock him until her tears went away. It was a funny thing about that little kid; when he looked at her with those big eyes, it seemed like he understood everything, like he was the grown-up and she was the baby. The gypsies said that meant he was "born old," and it seemed like maybe he had been. Lureen was dumbfounded when she learned that Duane had taught himself to read when he was only just past four.

All that trouble she'd always had trying to figure out letters and numbers and her own kid could read better than she could. The gypsies said he was born under a Scorpio moon and that was why, but she didn't believe that; she'd seen them finagle too many suckers out of the gold in their teeth with all their spooky double-talk. Besides, Duane wasn't *that* smart. He got lost just like any kid and would stand in the midway bellering for her at the top of his lungs, crying till the snot ran down his face.

He always had a dirty face and wet pants, and he was afraid of the dark too. It was hard to figure him out. Sometimes he seemed grown up, and sometimes he was only a baby, clinging to her skirt and pulling on her until she felt like screaming.

Still, when she got to crying so bad and he looked at her and said, "Don't worry, Reenie, I'll take care of you," she just had to believe him. And she'd look right at him and say, "You do that Duane. You always take care of your mama and we'll both make out O.K."

Part 1

DUANE
September 1, 1981

1

He was as invisible as any living creature could be when venturing out of its natural habitat. Protective coloration. A tall man, all long bones, and yet crouched in what should be an excruciating position for even an average-sized man. He had trained himself to remain motionless for hours, a lesson learned from the yogi in the freak show who made the rubes gasp when he lay down on his bed of nails. He was shrouded behind a wall of trees and vegetation where humans could not see him, and the woods creatures skittered by him without fear or even awareness of his presence among them.

The huge rock he'd selected for his vantage point had been deposited by some glacier eons before. Its worn surface was baked hot where his toes gripped it, and the September sun above him seared the late afternoon and made the air smell of baked pine needles. But the man was oblivious to the sweat that oozed from his pores and snaked over his body and to the dusty membranes in his throat. There was a canteen he'd stashed beneath the lowest outcropping of his perch, but his mind was not on slaking his thirst. He felt no thirst. He felt no pain from the cramped muscles in his calves and thighs as he hunkered there, his long spine bent improbably forward, his elbows resting easily on his bony knees.

He used only one of his senses: sight. The binoculars pressed to his eyes lent him the semblance of a great brown frog alert for prey. He could see more keenly than any hundred men without glasses, but he had to be sure that this time she would be perfect. He had thought he had found flawless specimens before, only to find that they were shabby, deceptive imitations.

They had wasted his time and his energy and they had made him angry. He'd revealed himself to them, deluded by their lies and pretending, and so he had had to deal with them. God, how he hated the ugliness of it, but they each deserved it, and he had done what had to be done. Each time, for days afterward, he had trouble thinking clearly.

He couldn't have that now. His mind was one of his weapons. He'd known he was smarter than hell ever since he'd known anything, and he never made the same mistake twice; it was just that the sluts could put on so many different faces.

His mind had kept him alive. He had endured because of it, with no help from a goddamned soul. Ever.

His physical development had kept pace with his mind. Six feet, five inches tall, 195 pounds, with long, long femur and humerus bones supported by taut, functional muscles that gave him the strength some men coaxed and honed in gymnasiums and on playing fields. Sports were anathema to him, an odds-on threat to the only entities he was sure of—his body and his brain. He'd seen too many old boxers with stove-in faces and scrambled minds, reliving glory days that never happened; even Broadway Joe was walking around on legs with knees three times as old as he was. Stupid.

He had only the slightest of defects, and that had occurred before he was old enough to prevent it: a slight bowing out of his shinbones, the aftermath of rickets from a diet of french fries, Coca-Cola, snow cones, and never enough milk. Once he was big enough to steal or beg his own food, he'd eaten well, and become stronger than most men by the time he was twelve. He had just a vestige of hearing loss in his left ear; one of Lureen's boyfriends had knocked him across the trailer after he bit him on the leg, but that had almost been worth it—to see that fat turkey howling and jumping up and down on one leg.

He rarely thought of the raised scar that ran across his back from shoulder to shoulder like a bolt of lightning—bluish, smooth skin there, the keloid left when the burns healed. No feeling there, as if the streak of scar were full of Novocain. He couldn't remember pulling the coffee pot down off the two-burner gas stove, but he recalled the brilliant pain of the hot liquid cascading over his back and his screaming for Lureen who didn't come. He didn't blame his mother. He'd never held her responsible for any of the bad things; she'd done the best she could. Women liked to trace the slick-skinned path across his back, and he always told them he had been struck by lightning. Bitches who mothered him turned him off.

He'd had a mother. The only mother.

Lureen.

Her name whispered through the synapses of his brain cells and made his gut roll over. He missed her with a consuming ache, just as he'd always missed her. She was woman to him, and would be forever. Vague, tentative, frightened—too frightened to be with him all the times he needed her.

Sometimes when he visualized her face, he saw vertical bars superimposed on the image, and that had bewildered him for a long time, until he weighed the variables and realized he was seeing her through the slats of his crib. He could smell stale urine, feel the sodden lumps of his own feces in his full diaper. Nobody was supposed to be able to remember that far back, but "nobody" wasn't him.

He could not picture the men. He had seen them, but they were nothing to him beyond huge figures looming over his crib, or, worse, part of two locked bodies a few feet away, moving together in what had seemed to him a cruel struggle that surely hurt Lureen.

He'd sensed that some of those strangers had liked him O.K., and that others were pissed that they had to do what they did to his mother while he watched them silently, his little, useless hands clenching the crib's bars. He did remember his rage. He'd wanted to kill them before he had even known the word for it.

One of them took her away and never brought her back. He'd heard *dead* then, and whispered phrases that made him feel dead too.

He shut his eyes and blocked the memory.

The twitching in his arms accelerated, and he lowered the glasses from his brow and stretched, sending a family of quail fleeing in panic. He remembered the canteen, reached for it, and drained it of the hot, tinny-tasting water. He'd have to remember to get some salt tablets; the weather was much hotter than he'd expected. He'd always heard that Washington was cool and rainy, but that turned out to be the part around Seattle. All the sweating was making him lose potassium. Salt tablets would fix that.

He lay back on the rock, and the flat surface felt good under his extended spine. Tiny bits of sand and mica adhered to his damp skin, and he felt the difference in tactile sensation between the unscarred skin and the fibrous keloid. He would have to remember to wear a shirt to cover the scar; it made him highly describable to the law.

Research. Anything could be researched—legal or illegal —and understanding witness identification was one of his more meaningful projects. The dead didn't describe, but there were always others. He had a long head start on any adversary because of his intelligence, and he'd bettered his odds with information. He'd tried it on brains alone in the beginning, but the sheer number of cops, even bumbling along, outweighed his advantage. Most cops were stupid assholes who went by the book, never seeing subtle movement outside the pattern, but there had been a few of them who took the time to think and they'd blocked his path.

He'd done time for the little stuff—not a lot of it, but enough to let him know he couldn't stand to be locked up. Juvey hall, which was basically a joke. A month or two in one of their "training schools," but they'd never put him in the joint, and they never would. He was almost grateful to the smarter dicks because they'd taught him more unaware than they'd taken from him; he'd vacuumed what he needed out of their heads.

He knew how to change the way he was remembered. If he slumped, he could diminish his tallness by inches. The old fart in Denver who'd handed over her savings to the "bank examiner" had been adamant that he was under six feet and over thirty; she hadn't recognized him in the line-up, picked the off-duty cop standing next to him. The bunco dick had been pissed when he couldn't get the prosecutor to file. And Duane was out of Denver on the next plane. It was

POSSESSION

a disappointment anyway. Smog. He'd expected Denver to be clear and on a mountain and it was flat and smoky, full of pretend-cowboys and dull brick houses.

Washington looked like the calendars said it did. Seattle was surrounded by mountains, and it got even better when he'd crossed over them to the east. He liked the orchards and the brown hills that looked like giants fallen asleep in the baking afternoon, Gullivers who might wake at any moment to roll over and create an entirely new skyline.

Most of all, he liked the forest. He looked straight up at the trees above him. The firs and pines seemed to grow higher as he stared, their top-most branches turning to black filigree against the sun. There was a continuity here. They must have always been here, and they would always be here, reaching stoically toward the sky. It gave him a transcendent peace that only reinforced his choice of this place.

He closed his eyes against the sun, pale green eyes flecked with hazel. From the side the pupils were not the smooth concave half-sphere others had, but notched.

Lureen's image emerged now on the nether surface of his eyelids. He could see her little face with the regular features, her huge frightened pansy eyes, the faint dusting of freckles that touched her nose and cheeks in summer, and the mouth so soft. She had such a mass of dark flyaway hair, hair so fine that it curled in tendrils around her jaw and then became as evanescent as smoke haloed around her fragile skull. She'd hated her hair and tried to tame it with endless brushing that had only set it alive with electricity. Everything about her had been ephemeral, that tiny girl-woman as transient as a dragonfly.

He sighed. At twenty-four, he was already two years older than she would ever be. Still, she was always with him, waiting just beyond the limits of his peripheral vision. He sometimes felt that, if he could only turn his head quickly enough, he would catch her and draw her back to him.

He knew *that* Lureen was gone forever. But he also knew that she did not rest, that she still wandered lost and terrified in the world just beyond the tree tops and on the other side of the mountains.

His name was about all she had been able to give him, beyond life itself. Duane Elvis Demich. One of his cell mates in the reform school had pointed out to him what his initials spelled.

"You're dead, man," the stupid ass had chortled. "Get it? D.E.D. Dead. That ain't what you'd call lucky initials. Dee-wane Elvis. What the hell kind of pussy name is that?"

He had slammed the other boy back against the metal bunk and held him, dangling, above the floor until he just about peed his pants. Nobody ever mentioned his name again.

She had chosen that name, given him a name unlike any other. The only material things he ever bothered to keep were the warped 45 records she'd treasured so—Elvis's records. God, when the man himself dropped dead, it had been like she'd died again. He liked to think that Elvis was with her someplace, making it easier for her until he could set her free.

Sometimes he wondered why he couldn't have looked like her, and shuddered when he imagined her giving birth to him. How could such a tiny girl have delivered the great mass of him? Had she forgiven him the pain of that May night in Michigan? He'd found his creased, stained birth certificate and seen his birth weight: ten pounds, eleven ounces; it had made him wince to think of it.

"Mother: Lureen Dorothy Demich. Born: March 7, 1940. Birthplace: Coatesville, Pennsylvania. Father: Unknown."

His hair was light auburn, thick, and wavy. His eyes were green, or gray, or hazel, depending on his thoughts. His features were powerful, chiseled, defined, where hers had been so delicate. Viewed from the side, he had the etched-coin image of a young Greek god, just as her Elvis had had when he was younger. Seen full face, he had a slightly jarring appearance; the two sides of his face had come together and joined a few millimeters from true alignment. The off-center result was not enough to make him less handsome, and most people didn't notice it, but he wondered about it sometimes. His right eye slid off just a little,

POSSESSION

drooping when he was tired, as did his cheek on that side. Sometimes, he covered up one side of his face or the other and studied the portion left to view in the mirror. The left side looked angelic and calm, but the right was evil.

What the hell. He'd only done what he had to do. Survival is the law of the jungle, and the fittest don't regret what they do to stay alive. He had surmised that morals consisted of only what one perceived as right or wrong, and that what people said and what they actually practiced rarely coincided anyway. Most of the carnies he'd known in his first world took care of each other and ripped off anyone in the civilian world with impunity. Even cons had certain standards of ethical behavior. But the straight world—outside the tents and outside the walls, anything went. That's where the real animals were.

The tree darkness overhead devoured the sun and the wind lost its warmth, reminding him he was about out of time for the day. The massive rock had turned dank beneath him. He sat up and made a sweep of the two-lane road fronting the river's edge, looking for any sign of activity. It was presently empty of cars or joggers.

He had a gut feeling that this was going to be the place. He had always sensed vibrations of what was going to be propitious for him, and he'd been almost shaken with the strength of the signals he'd picked up as he had crossed the Cascades and seen the vista of eastern Washington spread out before him. What he sought waited here for him to discover.

He was a watcher, unseen, and he had an indefinable control over those he observed; they never knew he was near. Sometimes he prowled through lovers' lanes, padding silently up behind parked cars to see what was beyond the steamed windows, a woman struggling and sighing in the arms of some horny bastard behind the steering wheel, glimpses of bare flesh and tangles of arms and legs. He could get so close he could hear them rutting there, heedless of any danger.

Although he wasn't a voyeur, he couldn't stanch the

41

unbidden rush of blood to his groin, the erection that pushed at the fly of his jeans when he watched the fools playing at love. They had no comprehension of what real passion or commitment was, but they could mimic the act of love and trick his body to react instinctively. It annoyed him because that meant he'd have to find a place to relieve himself of the urgency in his genitals. He never thought of breaking into the cars and having the women he watched, nor did he consider having sex with the loud and pushy tramps who flocked into the Trail's End Bar back in Natchitat, sending out less than subtle signals to him with their self-conscious laughter, their compliant posture as they leaned against the jukebox pretending to make selections. Women always came on that way with him. They liked his bigness, his lidded stare as he watched them over a schooner of beer, but their made-up faces fell and their giggling faltered when he turned his back on them and walked across the gravel lot to his motel room.

He had no time now for any of that, and he was irritated at the betrayal of his own body, of that male response to anything female and young and soft, or anyone who looked that way in barlight.

The Big Apple Motel lacked a lot, but it gave him a base of operations. And it was cheap, a few steps up from the shacks furnished for migrant workers who flooded Natchitat when the crop neared fruition. The manager had assumed that he was part of them, a little better dressed, a little more savvy, but basically a transient willing to pay twelve bucks a night for a single iron bed, a toilet, sink, and a hot plate.

He'd stayed at the Hyatt Regency in San Francisco, the Brown Palace in Denver, and the Fairmont in Dallas, and had been charged more for one breakfast from room service than two days rent at the Big Apple. The Big Apple stank of sweat, spilled beer, semen, and Pine-sol, a permeating miasma that seemed to be ingrained in the asphalt tile floors and plywood walls. He could rid himself of the odor only by smoking and staying out of the dump from dawn until

POSSESSION

midnight. But it suited for now. Suited his medium-thick bankroll and suited his need for anonymity in Natchitat.

He had a couple of hundred bucks, and that was as low as he planned to get, and so he worked one of the minor scams available, nothing that would take much energy or much thought. It had taken him only a day to isolate the product most needed in Natchitat. The migrant shacks were a few miles outside of town, and few of the alkies had transportation into town. He saw they would cheerfully kill each other over a half-full bottle of Tokay but would not walk into Natchitat to buy the stuff for $1.19 a fifth at the Safeway. He could buy the cheapest vinegar-wine for $3.29 a gallon, and he bought ten gallons a day. Bottling was cheap; he paid one of the winos a buck to gather all the empties he could find, and he filled the dirty bottles with his Safeway supply. He made the rounds of the camps each evening with his Harley's sidecar filled with fifths of retread Tokay, and sold out quickly at two and a quarter apiece. His daily profit was $75.60—less the buck for the bottle man.

"A goddamned savior," one of his customers had called him, as he cradled a full bottle of Tokay. Two thousand bucks a month and he was a goddamned savior to boot. He'd made ten—twenty—times more than that as a bunco man, but that had taken full days of his time, and he needed time far more than money now.

The road was offering possibles infrequently; he was spotting mostly carloads of fishermen headed home. He stood finally and whirled his long arms to ease the strain of watching all day. He pulled the sweatshirt with *Ohio State* printed on it over his head, replaced the binoculars with mirrored sunglasses, and leapt off the rock.

He disliked this part of his day the most. He would have to eat, deliver to his customers, sleep, and rise tomorrow to begin again. He resented his need to eat and sleep as much as he detested the sexual embers that flashed into fire so often. Bodily functions delayed his quest, but he was ravenous now and could think only of a raw steak and cold beer.

The bike was safe, hidden by the fallen fir and the huckleberry bushes. Even a plane overhead would not be able to make it out. If the time came when he had to ditch it, he planned simply to send it roaring into the river. He ran his hand over the bulges in the saddle bag instinctively and relaxed as he felt the outlines of the guns inside; they were both there—the pistol and the dismantled rifle.

He was pushing the bike through the last copse of trees onto the roadway when he saw her. He blinked his eyes to clear the orange outline of the setting sun, but she was still there when he looked again, his breathing suspended by her perfection.

She ran alone, her breath sounds carrying back to him as he watched from the trees. Her jogging shoes slapped the asphalt steadily, but she ran like all women, arms flung out too far from her sides, breasts bouncing. The woman's hair was tied back with a red band around her forehead, wispy, fine, black, and faintly curly.

He must have made a sound, although he was not aware of it. For an instant, she turned her head toward the woods, and he saw her full face. Her large eyes looked . . . not frightened, but wary . . . and she ran past him, stepping up her pace.

He stopped himself from calling out to her; she would not recognize him yet. He had to expect that it would take a long time, but he felt the first ballooning of joy in his gut, the first wonder that it had come about. His knees trembled as he watched her run away from him, knowing it was only for the moment, knowing that she would never really run away from him again.

There was lettering on the back of her T-shirt. He raised his binoculars to make out what it said:

Natchitat County Sheriff's Office
Wives' Bowling League

And beneath those smaller letters, a name in flowing script:

Joanne

44

2

Danny Lindstrom watched the red and yellow lights dotting the dispatcher's panel and saw them blur, merge into each other, and then separate. He shook his head, as if he could jar the fatigue loose with an abrupt movement.

It was 4:12 A.M., and he was officially off duty, but it was always difficult to come down off shift—especially third watch. He chose to work the 8:00 P.M. to 4:00 A.M. shift, because it gave him his days with Joanne. But he knew also that the hours of darkness were when everything happened, and the sights and sounds and smells set his mind at a pitch where adrenalin flowed as a natural component of blood.

When it was hot and the moon was full, like tonight, almost every radio squawk brought situations laced with danger and excitement. He wanted it as much as he feared it. Hell, he sought it out; he was bored with routine police work and even after eight years he still got a kick out of flipping on the blue lights and jamming his thumb on the siren button. But it left him drained physically and emotionally and always with that fine edge of anxiety when it was time to pack it in and go home.

It was hard to let go.

He remembered now the hassle with Joanne. He hated arguing with her just as he was leaving for work, but she was determined to go out jogging by herself, no matter how many times he'd warned her that being a policeman's wife was no automatic guarantee against rape. And that had made her madder. Everything set her off lately. He knew what it really was; it was the same old argument about the baby, or, rather, the fact that there was no baby. Every time she started her period, she cried.

"You don't just pull babies out of a hat," he'd told her.

"No, you don't, Danny. At least, we sure don't. If you

4 5

could just see past your precious ego and go have those tests, maybe we'd find out what's wrong with our hat."

"*My* hat, you mean," he'd said, and slammed out of the house, and immediately felt rotten. What she was asking of him wasn't that much, but he couldn't bring himself to jerk off into a bottle.

He rubbed his eyes, trying to close out the picture of Joanne, her jaw set, her eyes furious. He hadn't even thought about her all night. Since he and Sam had reported in at a quarter to eight, neither of them had had time to think about anything, take a leak, or have a cup of coffee or a meal break. That was one way to avoid thinking about marital problems.

It had begun with a squaw fight at the Bald Eagle—two of them clawing and scratching over the sorriest buck of a man he'd come across in a long time. When it was over, there'd been blood all over the Bald Eagle, and enough spilled beer to float the whole place right down Main Street into the Columbia River. One of the old gals had her breast laid open from her collarbone right through her right nipple, and the other had fought and kicked and bitten them as they wrestled her into their patrol car. Sam was nursing a dead-center hit in his family jewels and their unit was missing a back window. The object of the ladies' jealousy had sat at the bar boozing quietly throughout the fray, never looking up. Hell, he'd been smart; *his* balls weren't hurting.

Danny glanced over at Sam who sat gingerly on the edge of the report desk, scribbling out the Field Investigation Report on the pickup they'd stopped right after midnight, an old beater full of bearded punks who'd given them a Seattle address and a lot of flak about being pulled over. Something was wrong about that truck, but they hadn't scored a hit on Wants and Warrants, and they'd had to let them go. They'd both figured the rig was a mobile cocaine stash, but they couldn't search it: no probable cause. The inviolate rights of the American citizen. Sure as hell, they'd get a call from the coast on that one in a week or so, but the old truck would be long gone by then.

POSSESSION

Danny sighed. He wondered sometimes why they bothered. Every time they made a stop like that one, they were flirting with having a .45 shoved up their noses.

The state cop—Richards, yeah, Richards—had bought the farm on the same stretch of highway last winter, just walking over to some vehicle he'd stopped. He and Sam had found the poor bastard sprawled face down in the snow with his ticket book still in his hand, his gun still holstered. Richards's body lying there wasn't as bad somehow as the imprint left behind in the frozen bank after the hearse left. Angel in the snow. The perfect outline of arms and legs and head there, and the great splotch of red where Richards's blood had melted the snow beneath his heart.

They'd thrown a great funeral, though. Cops from Spokane. Cops from Seattle, Wenatchee, Yakima, Ellensburg, even Puyallup, with a sprinkling of FBI guys, ATF agents, the Mounties in their red tunics, plus the whole damned State Patrol. Well, they should be good at funerals. Richards's was the third cop funeral in eastern Washington in a year.

A familiar bleakness rose in his gut, and he drew a deep breath. Sometimes he could see himself lying beside a road someplace, as motionless as a drunk, only not drunk. Dead. He wondered if Sam ever felt that presentiment of doom, if Sam ever felt that his time was running out. Danny never asked him; talking about fear was an unwritten taboo with cops. Don't say it out loud and it won't happen.

If either of them was living on borrowed time, it would have to be Sam. Sam was forty-eight, a veteran of two departments and twenty-seven years, survivor of two marriages, and with such a thirst for alcohol that his liver should have turned to stone years ago. Booze had gotten him booted off the Seattle Police Department, out of the homicide unit. Sam had made it on the street, on the bikes, and into the rarefied air of homicide. Danny wondered how it must be for him to be back in uniform now in a county car.

But that was something else they never talked about.

He studied Sam as he bent over the report, one hand splayed on the desk, his long, skinny legs dangling next to

4 7

the spittoon that had been there for forty years. Clinton looked as if he'd been born and raised in Natchitat County. His tooled boots were beat up but polished, just like every other deputy's were. His skin was as tanned and criss-crossed with frown and smile lines as any apple grower's. Danny couldn't picture him in the suit, white shirt, and striped tie he must have worn when he was a Seattle dick.

He stretched and said softly to Sam, "How's your balls? Maybe you better get home and pack them in ice."

Sam stood up painfully and grinned, showing the gap between his front teeth. "They're better than yours on a good day, Junior."

Fletcher looked up from the dispatch desk and laughed. "He's right, Clinton. You better get on back to your trailer and ice 'em down. At your age, anything that will make them keep, you better give it a shot."

"There's some things that go on forever, gentlemen," Sam said. "I may just drop in on Mary Jean on the way home, Fletch, and show her what a real stud can do—since you're stuck here playing radio."

Fletcher laughed.

"Mary Jean's working tonight, old buddy. You'll have to go over to the maternity ward and see if she can slip out to the broom closet with you, but don't hold your breath. I just talked to her and they're catching babies over there as fast as the mamas can squeeze them out."

"Full moon," Sam nodded. "You can count on it. I'll nail her next week."

"It won't be hard to catch her," Fletcher grinned. "That little woman is putting on weight. I think she weighs more than I do."

Mary Jean Sayers outweighed Fletch easily by eighty pounds, but Danny and Sam tactfully avoided agreeing with the little radio operator. Sam, in fact, envied Fletch, dreading the thought of returning to his own mobile home empty of any living thing except his old tomcat.

Sam didn't want to leave the sheriff's office; it was more home to him than anyplace else, just as all the department offices over the years had been. He belonged here, bull-

POSSESSION

shitting with Fletch and Danny and the deputies who wandered in and out. He liked the smell of the place: cigar smoke, dusty files, leather, gun oil, and drifts of aroma from the jail kitchen beyond the steel mesh doors behind the waiting room. Working graveyard, he could make the work time stretch, usually delay until the sun began to creep up on the other side of the hills before he'd finished his paper work.

Everybody else had someplace to go after shift, and someone to go to. Sam had run through everyone he'd ever had waiting for him, and he tried not to think about the women who had finally had enough of him. Enough of him, and liquor, and too much overtime, too many night call-outs, and his stumblings from grace with other women.

When Sam left home at twenty to join the navy, he encountered a seemingly endless supply of girls and more-than-girls who responded both to his open acceptance of them and his profound sexual force. Somehow, he could not keep them or they could not keep him. But until he was forty, until Nina, he had emerged unscathed beyond a fleeting depression. After Nina, he still liked women but doubted that any singular love might be his again. And he blamed only himself. Even sitting here in the office, nursing his bruises, he felt no animosity toward the Indian woman who'd landed the blow. She'd been hysterical over a real or imagined rejection by the runty cowboy at the bar. She hadn't wanted to go to jail, but he couldn't blame her for that. He'd been in a lot of jails, knowing he wasn't the one to be locked in, and they still gave him the feeling that his throat was closing up, that he could not expand his lungs fully behind the iron doors.

The Indian girls bloomed and faded quickly, like the morning glories that clung to the trellis outside his trailer. Their cheekbones soon blurred with fat, their burnished skin turned putty color, and their reedlike bodies became trapped in a burgeoning cocoon of their own flesh. The Indian men buckled too under the pressures of the white man's culture, but Sam didn't feel sorry for them the way he did for the women.

Wanda Moses hadn't meant to kick him personally; he'd just been part of the enemy. Tomorrow she'd wake up in the women's section of the jail with a grinding headache, puking, and she would have no memory of how she'd gotten there.

Danny's voice pierced his reverie. "You ready to split, pard?"

Sam slid the original of the FIR into the box marked "Undersheriff," and the carbons into the in-take file, and then limped toward Danny with the pretense of a man in excruciating pain. Danny laughed, and Sam wished for the thousandth time that there was some way to delay the moment when they'd head out on the highway in Danny's pickup. He loved Danny, as he'd loved all his partners, all the men who had stood between him and harm, all the men whose lives he, in turn, had felt responsible for.

Neither of his wives had understood the strength—the need—in that bond between males.

Penny had screamed at him once, "You care more about that goddamned Al Schmuller than you do about me! He gives you more of a hard-on than I do!"

That had been true, in a way. Not the last part. But Al knew where he lived and how he lived and what a tenuous grasp each of them had on staying alive when they worked the Tact Squad during the riots of the sixties. He and Al had faced ugly things together, and then drank together at the Greek's afterward. And three martinis barely blurred the memory of firebombs lobbed from roofs of old buildings at Twenty-third and Pine.

When he walked out, he'd thought that it would be temporary, but she'd never let him come back. Three days after the divorce, she'd married a civilian.

He'd thought Gloria would be different because she worked in the records section, and because she was a cop's widow. It had been O.K. as long as they worked the same shift. Had he loved Gloria? It was hard to remember. He'd loved her kid and had probably stayed with the mother longer because of the boy. But the marriage had started to erode from the moment he was assigned to second watch.

POSSESSION

When it was over, he missed the kid more than Gloria. And then there was only the job, and he was all right. He was good. He could concentrate and learn, and he went to every seminar he could sign up for: death investigation, narcotics, bomb search, even a weird demonstration of blood patterns when Englert, the expert from Oregon, showed up with the real stuff (and Lord knows where he got it) and explained how to tell from the spatters whether it was high- or low-velocity impact blood spray.

Sam found he could limit his drinking to a beer or two. When he moved into the homicide unit, it made up for a lot of his losses; it was what he was meant to do. It seemed as though he was always working, but nobody cared anymore if he was home at dawn or at noon. He had the knack. That it *was* a knack to see through the intricate puzzles of violent death did not seem strange to him. He reveled in his skill, and accepted the commendations from the brass and the respect of his peers casually.

There were women in his life again, women who wanted him, the thirty-five-year-old Sam Clinton who had it all together after the long bad time. Their faces blended into a mélange of sexual satisfaction and escape. He called them all "Sweet Baby," and he was neither committed to or involved with any of them, although he tried to stay long enough so that they were not one-night-stands in their own minds, and not so long that he might inflict harm when he left. He grew adept at knowing when to leave. He could no more have done without women than he could have gone without food, but too much closeness threatened him. He'd thought he could go on forever—tasting, enjoying, and moving on when he sensed the time was right. Each parting had torn something from him, but something so subtly damaging that he'd never felt the wound.

Jake Sorensen was his homicide partner—Old Jake, who at fifty-six was long since past voluntary retirement age. Jake hung on. Sam made him strong enough to get through the six-month evaluations. Sam made him look good. Together, they made a powerful team. Clinton-and-Sorensen, never referred to singularly and they wanted it that way. They drew the more difficult cases, worked them deftly, only rarely bringing in a loser to molder in the unsolved file drawer. Jake just missed being a joke in his rumpled leisure suits dappled with cigar ashes, his gut bulging over his belt, and his eyes magnified behind thick glasses. He dithered and wasted time and energy, but with Sam he was transformed into something better, into a working dick with thirty years' experience. They filled in the chinks in each other's armor.

When Sam met Nina, she caught him to her before he could see the danger. The others had been young, so young that their personalities could not harm him. Nina was lost when he met her; she'd been lost for a long time, and yet he was drawn to her by the sheer strength of her mind.

The homicide dicks steered clear of Nina Armitage, wary of a brilliant woman, vaguely resentful of a woman in a business rightfully peopled by males. They brought cases to her in the prosecutor's office only because they had to. Nina had climbed to the position of chief criminal deputy, not through her charms—for she betrayed none—but because she was one hell of an attorney. She worked three times as hard as any man, driving her slender, awkward body beyond what seemed the point of endurance, and kept on going.

She considered all policemen, including the chief, dumb cops, and even in court, even when they were on her side, she questioned them in a patronizing way. Behind her back they called her "the titless wonder," and worse.

Still, Sam was enthralled by her presence in the courtroom, never giving ground or depending on her femaleness to curry favor with judge or jury. She was as caustic as lye, her voice so husky it seemed she fought consciously to keep any feminine modulation from it. Her long, straw-colored hair hung in her face as she bent over the yellow legal pads, scribbling constantly, and she tossed it back with the impatience that was an integral part of her. Her skin was pale and freckled. True, she appeared to have no breasts, but Sam thought her long legs were sensational.

When they carried their cases to her so carefully catalogued, so neatly sprinkled with "probable causes" and good physical evidence, she got them their arrest warrants, their search warrants, and never seemed to differentiate one cop from another. They were all "Officer" to her—never "Detective." And, for her, they seemingly had no names at all.

Jake couldn't stand the woman. "Sammy," he muttered one afternoon after a two-hour session in her crowded little office in the courthouse, "you know how all blacks and Filipinos and Japs look alike to us? Well, all cops look alike to that skinny bitch. Put you and me and Cap and Little John and Big John in a line-up, and I'll bet you she couldn't tell one from another."

Sam laughed, but half agreed. He'd never seen her smile, and she never even looked up when he tried to banter with her.

"She never leaves that building," Jake said. "She just crawls into a file drawer at night and goes to sleep. You cut her and all you'll get is dust."

Sam had been as surprised to see her on a rainy Tuesday midnight in the back booth of the Golden Gavel as if he'd run across the mayor himself sitting there with four scotches lined up in front of him.

"Hey, you! Clinton! Have a seat," she called. "I'll even move so you can face the door. You're all paranoid about your back to the door, aren't you? You've seen too many movies about Luciano and Capone."

He'd sat down, staring at her. She was drunk, but alcohol gave Nina a softer look, a gentler mien, despite her smart mouth.

"I never thought you knew my name," he said grabbing one of her scotches.

"Now I have to order another." She lifted her hand and waved languidly to the bartender who appeared with one more scotch—neat.

"I know your name. I know all your names. The titless wonder never forgets anything."

He looked down at the rings on the table top, embarrassed.

"You thought I didn't know what you guys call me? I could tell you the others, if you like?"

"No thanks. For the record, I never called you any of those names."

"A genuine gentleman. But you don't like me any better than the rest of them do. You all have wives *and* girlfriends, and you all think women are supposed to cook and fuck and stay dumb, right?"

He stared at her. Her eyes were dark brown, wide and challenging, smudged with fatigue. She smiled at him, a wry smile—but a smile.

"I don't have a wife . . . or a girlfriend," he said slowly. "I can cook, and I wash my own socks and shorts. And I think you're the best working lawyer I ever saw in my life. So now what do you want to fight about?"

"Nothing. I want to celebrate. I won today. Joseph Kekelahni. He should have been 'bitched,' you know. Third felony conviction in ten years. Rape, oral sodomy, assault with a deadly weapon . . . and, oh yeah, burglary; he took all their purses after he was done with them. You know what he got instead of the Big Bitch?"

Sam nodded. "Let me guess. Sexual psychopath?"

"You got it. They slapped his little hands and sent him down to Western State so he can get in touch with his feelings. He'll be a real good boy for six months, and then they'll give him the key and a twenty-four-hour pass anywhere he wants to go—and he'll be right back at it. If anybody needs group therapy, it's the judge." She bent her head. "Oh shit!"

He started to answer, made a half move to touch her shoulder, but she looked up quickly and smiled again. "Wanta dance?"

She stood up and held out her arms and he held her, moving slowly around the tiny parquet dance floor to music from the jukebox. They were the only people in the place besides the bartender, who polished the long wooden bar and ignored them. Sam couldn't believe it; Nina Armitage leaning her head against his shoulder.

She was almost as tall as he was and she seemed to weigh

half as much. She danced well, but even intoxicated she touched him without touching him, holding back so that their thighs barely brushed. He was amused to feel that she did have breasts, and as embarrassed as a high school boy to feel his body react to her. She gave no indication that she could feel him.

They danced for two hours without talking, stopping only to empty the glasses the bartender kept filling. Sam realized that Nina had been here before, that she had a standing order.

She allowed him to drive her home. If he had pictured her living anywhere, it would not have been in the tiny houseboat at the end of the rickety boardwalk on Lake Union. She didn't ask him in, but he could see through the door, see into a rats' nest of books, plants, dirty dishes, and discarded clothing. A gray cat ducked through his legs and disappeared down the dock, and he caught a whiff of the animal's litterbox inside.

He stood, hesitantly, wanting, not wanting, to go in. She touched him lightly on the chest and pushed him into the rain.

"You can't come in tonight. But I thank you for the waltz . . . and the ride."

The door closed before he could answer. It was only as he walked unsteadily up the dock that he realized that she'd paid for all the drinks. That was a first. He grinned and ran up the steps to the road.

He meant to tell Jake about it in the morning—but he didn't. He hadn't meant to go back—but he did.

He had never been exposed to a really intelligent woman before. He had never approached a woman who seemed to care so little whether he showed up or not. And yet Sam found himself standing at Nina's door night after night, his head bent against the icy spray that whipped off the lake, feeling the boards beneath his feet creak and groan with the undulating swells of the water that cradled her floating home. The houseboat was in terrible shape, listing to port where the logs had rotted away, the eaves leaking rain on his exposed back.

She was always home, although she was slow to open the door. She admitted him with a shrug, letting him pick his way through the debris on the floor and clear his own spot on the old plush couch. She seemed to expect that he would come, but she showed neither pleasure nor annoyance at his arrival. She never fed him. Other women tried to coddle him with home cooking; he sometimes wondered if Nina cooked at all. Rather, he worried about her and brought her pizzas and greasy take-out chicken and urged her to eat. She ate pickishly, giving most of it to the gray cat, Pistol. She was never without a tumbler of scotch, laced sparingly with tap water.

Sam gradually stopped seeing other women, content to spend his evenings and nights with this intense woman who sat cross-legged on the floor with her elbows on her tender-boned knees and talked to him, listened to him. She understood the law and its intricacies in a way he had never grasped before. He had never believed that a woman might know more than he did; but he learned from her, reliving what had taken place during her long days in the court-house, understanding for the first time the dynamics of a trial.

He asked her suddenly one night, "Why do you want me here?"

"Who says I want you?"

"You let me in. You've unbarred your doors."

"Some of them . . ."

"Do you *like* me?" He was afraid to hear her answer.

She studied him solemnly and then touched his cheek. "Sure, I like you. You're smarter than anybody else over in your little Kiddy Cop Station. You think. You even think abstractly if I push you. I like your face; it doesn't hide anything. I like the gap in your teeth, and I like your dimples." She poked a finger in the indentation next to his mouth; he moved away and rubbed his face.

"It's a wrinkle."

She shook her head. "The rest are wrinkles; that's a dimple, Officer."

"Do you miss me when I'm not here?"

POSSESSION

"You're always here."

She stood up to fill her glass, gliding deftly through the piles of junk on the floor, effectively shutting him out.

But he worried it, following her, blocking her way from the cramped Pullman kitchen. He pinned her arms with his and forced her to look at him.

"I need to know that you give a shit whether I show up or not. I need . . . something. Hell, are you my girl or aren't you?"

She laughed. "Your *girl?* Why does that matter? Do you want to take me to the policeman's ball? Ahh, do you want me to be the policeman's ball? Is that it? You're angry because I won't sleep with you?"

He let her go. It was true; she wouldn't sleep with him, not even when she was so drunk she couldn't make her way across the room. And he wanted to sleep with no one else. He could touch her wrist and be as aroused as he'd been before with a fully naked woman beneath him, responding to him, but she refused him access to her the way a thoroughbred mare might deny a plowhorse. Sometimes she let him hold her, and she felt only of narrow bones and a heart beating in his arms.

It made him crazy.

"It's control, isn't it," he said angrily. "You have to have control over everything? You deny both of us because you need the control."

"But Samuel, I have no control. Or at least so little. Would you take that away from me?"

He left, slamming the door behind him, plunging onto the dock with such force that the houseboat deck was awash with water.

He always came back, and she showed no surprise at his reappearance.

There were some good times, enough to keep him holding on. Spring finally came—Seattle's green, water-washed spring with the sun breaking through the overcast only in late afternoon. They sat on her deck and tossed bread to the audacious ducks who ignored even Pistol. He brought her geraniums to replenish the dead foliage in the planters edging the lake, and she thanked him gravely. He painted the weathered siding and carried a pickup load of trash away.

He wanted to move in, but she was resolute that he could not.

"I need down-time. I can't have someone here all the time—not even you."

To his surprise and delight, she submitted her body to him finally, and the melding with her brought him to a place from which there was no return. Nina was as wildly responsive in bed as she was removed from him everywhere else, all mouth and hands and lips as soft as bruised roses. She sobbed and cried out and murmured obscenities, shuddering in his arms with a passion he had never encountered in more than two decades of sex.

He was never sure that he pleased her even then. When it was over, she rolled away from him and became as quiet as death. He had actually propped himself on one elbow to stare at her narrow ribcage in the dark to be sure that it still rose and fell from the force of living lungs beneath. He could not comprehend how their two bodies could move and breathe together at orgasm and only an instant later be further apart than at any other time.

He found the picture of the baby on a Saturday afternoon as he gathered still another load for the dump, a three-by-five hospital picture of a newborn infant with squinted eyes, a red face, and a tiny bow atop the thick dark hair. Beneath the swaddled baby form, there was a number and the words, "Baby Girl Armitage. 1-2-69."

Nina stepped into the room and saw him studying it, puzzled as he sat back on his heels. She took it from him and put it in a kitchen drawer wordlessly. Her skin, always milky, turned so white that the freckles seemed black in contrast.

"Whose baby is that?" he asked.

"Mine. She was mine."

"Where is she?"

"Dead. Dead these many years."

POSSESSION

"I'm sorry."

"Don't be. It was such a long time ago. Mr. Armitage was sorry too, at first. And then, after he quit crying, he decided it was my fault. He was sure that I covered her up too tight, or not tight enough, or betrayed some other great defect in what a mother should be. I wasn't the maternal type; he always said that. He never forgave me. He took himself off and married a *very* maternal type, a real mother hen, and fathered three more babies to make up for . . . for . . . Sari."

"But you knew it wasn't your fault."

"Did I? No, I don't think I did. See?"

She pushed up the sleeves of her sweatshirt and turned her wrists over to hold them in front of his eyes. He saw the fine drawing up of skin there, almost lacy with corrugated scars. He kissed the white lines and held her wrists against his face.

"Don't pity me," she said quietly. "If you ever pity me, I'll be gone so fast your head will spin."

"Is that why you drink?"

She looked at him with no expression in her dark eyes, and shook her head.

"No. I drank before. I always drank. I have a talent for it. You'd think it would kill me, wouldn't you?"

"Do you wish it would?"

She picked up the fat gray cat and held it against her, burying her face in its fur. Then she met his eyes again. "Of course not. Don't be ridiculous."

"We could have a baby. Would you try again with me?"

"Thank you. It's a most gracious offer. But I'm too old, and you're too old, and I don't believe in babies anymore."

God, how he'd wanted to save her. He'd been so convinced that he could rescue her and he'd never wanted anything so much in his life. His track record at making women happy was somewhat muddied, but he had never loved a woman the way he loved Nina. He felt sure that if he could only love her enough, she would have to love him back and be happy.

He began to drink with her. It brought them along

together through the long nights on the houseboat. Her mind—the mind that had snared him—continued to amaze him and let him think there was hope. He detested what liquor did to that intelligence and dreaded the inevitable progression to slurred words, the repetitions of half-ideas, and long silences. When he drank too, when she no longer made sense, it no longer mattered to him. They were together.

But he could not save her because she did not love him.

"Is it me?" he asked her once. "Are you ashamed of me? Downtown, you act as if I'm just another cop, someone you barely know. We could have lunch together. We could see other people together."

"No," she said. "It's me. Everything I touch turns to shit, Sammy." She cradled his head in her lap. "You'll see. You hang around here much longer and you'll see."

"You want me to go away?" He kept his eyes closed and tried to stop his ears against her answer.

"No—I don't know. But you will."

"I won't leave."

She sighed. "Yes you will."

And of course he had. Nina could handle the drinking. She could separate days and nights. She could put on day clothes and go to court clear-eyed and clear-headed and cogent. He couldn't. The change in his abilities was so subtle at first that he was the only one who perceived that he was missing details in a profession that demanded absolute attention to details.

And then one afternoon when they were working the fairly obvious suicide death of a downtown lawyer in the deceased's waterfront office, he caught Jake staring at him with a look of puzzlement.

"Why the hell did you put your cigarette out in his ashtray, Sam?"

"I didn't."

"Yes you did. You just fucked up the scene."

"Sorry." He scraped out the offending butt and slipped it in his pocket.

"Is it that woman?"

POSSESSION

"What woman?"

"Her. Armitage."

"What do you know about that?"

"I know. I'm an old detective, but I'm a detective. You've been leaving the same number for on-call too many times. I checked the reverse directory."

"It's no secret."

"It seems to be. You seem to think it should be."

"It's private."

"Your women were never private before. How come? She too good to share with Jake? She don't sit down to pee like any other broad?"

"She sits."

"Then for God's sake, enjoy her, but don't let it mess you up. Don't let it mess me up. I know you carry me. Everybody knows you carry me. I *can't* carry you; you're my last partner. You fuck up and we both go down."

He hadn't wanted to let Jake go down. He'd tried to cut back on the booze, but he couldn't be with Nina and do that. For the first time in his life, the job was less important than the woman, and they were both sliding away from him. He showed up drunk at a homicide scene at four one morning and it was all Jake could do to push him off into the darkness and pretend Sam was gathering soil samples. Sam was so damned shit-faced that he could only rock back and forth on his hands and knees.

Sam begged Nina to marry him and she laughed and turned away. He wondered if he hated her more than he loved her, but her hold on him was just as tenacious—more so—than it had ever been. She was killing him.

But it was Jake who died.

They were called out at six on a bitterly cold January dawning to work a scene that could have waited; the victim had been dead for a week and a few more hours wouldn't have made a hell of a lot of difference. The temperature cleared Sam's head for the first time in weeks, and that night-morning it had felt almost like the old days with Jake. He'd been anxious to enter a scene for the first time in a long time and call upon his instincts and skill to winnow out

6 1

what had happened. Jake had sensed it, and they'd bull-shitted with each other as if nothing had happened. As if Nina hadn't happened.

The patrol officer who'd responded to the first radio call was puking in the snow when they drove up, and Jake had silently handed Sam a cigar. It was going to be a smeller, reeking of putrescence that only a body left to decay in a winter-heated apartment could cause. They'd have to burn the clothes they wore when they finished, but the strong cheap cigars would let them work without gagging.

Up three flights of stairs, past the green-tinged officer who grinned at them with embarrassment as he leaned against the stained wallpaper of the upper landing, past the manager of the old hotel who seemed more annoyed than distressed. He'd heard Jake puffing behind him, but Jake always puffed and snorted if he had to walk up more than one flight of stairs.

The room was a morass of stacked newspapers, cardboard boxes, dirty clothes, garbage, and, for some reason, a dozen blank-eyed television sets. They had had to stand for a long time before they could even see the body that lay there in the flotsam of the last few years of the victim's life. And then they saw her, a great blackened, bloated balloon of what had been a human being, her skin stretched so tautly by decomposition gases that it had cracked in places. The stab wounds in her shriveled breasts gaped apart obscenely. An old hooker, who had probably lain down for a six-pack of beer, clad in torn lace panties and high-heeled, patent leather boots that still bore a Goodwill sticker on the bottom of one sole. As they puffed determinedly on their cigars, a rat jumped from the top of a pile of boxes and ran past them.

"Oh shit," Jake said. "Why do we get all the losers?"

But they had worked together that morning, attuned to each other, measuring, recording, snapping pictures that were going to make some jury blanch (*if* it ever got to a jury), bagging evidence from a seemingly unending pile of possibles.

They hadn't talked. Talking meant breathing without a

cigar to mask the miasma. Later, all the years later, Sam had wished that they had talked. He had felt *good*. Good for the first time in a long time, and never mind that a sane man should not feel good working around a body dead so long, amid trash that stank of that forlorn body. He'd been working and working well, and thinking only of the solution to the problem presented to them.

Jake had let out such a soft little sigh that Sam barely heard him, scarcely looked up. And then he'd felt the tape measure lead in his hand go slack and he'd turned to ask Jake to hold his end tighter. Jake was still hunkering down against the filthy sink, still clenching the cigar in his teeth, and his eyes were still open.

But he was dead—as dead as the prostitute who sprawled between them. Sam dragged him out into the hallway, screaming at the young cop who stood over them, transfixed by shock, to get the aid car. Sam pressed his mouth to Jakes's, willing the older man to take his breath and use it. He'd crashed his fist down over Jake's stilled heart, crushing the two cigars left in his shirt pocket; nothing changed what had happened. The Medic One paramedics with all their paraphernalia and radio-telemetry direct to the county hospital couldn't change it either.

Young men. Young men in dark blue uniforms with neat dark hair, mustaches, and flat stomachs. They worked over Jake for an hour and a half, piercing his chest with the long needle that made Sam wince, forcing air into his lungs and making him appear to breathe, letting Sam think that maybe it would be all right, that the new start they'd shared really had been another beginning after all.

They sat back on their heels finally and shook their heads, leaving Jake to lie on the frayed carpeting that jumped with fleas, his chest dotted with the white circles that held the useless defibrillator leads.

"Get him out of here," Sam said softly.

"I'm sorry," the tall young man said. "I'm really sorry."

"Get him the fuck out of here!" Sam yelled. "I don't want him here. This is no place for him to die."

They'd glanced at each other, confused by the vehemence

in his voice, at the lack of professionalism. They hesitated, reaching for their gear and slowly stowing it into their Life-Paks.

"I said get him out of here! *Now!*" Sam bent over Jake and tried to pick him up himself.

"Hey, man . . . sir." The young men stood up and reached for Jake. "We'll take him."

"Then do it."

Sam stayed at the scene until noon, doing it all himself. When he finally walked down the stairway, the snow was melting, sending eddies of water down First Hill toward the Sound.

He had lost his partner. He had never lost a partner before, and he vowed it would be the last time.

He didn't go to the houseboat. Instead, he drove to the apartment he still rented, the rooms unfamiliar now, filled with dust and stale air. He shucked off his suit and coat and left them on the bathroom floor while he showered for fifteen minutes, scrubbing long after the odor should have been gone. He dressed in old jeans and a T-shirt and he carried the reeking clothes to the dumpster behind the building, throwing them in along with his shoes. When he returned to his apartment, his phone was ringing, a nagging ring that went on for fifteen shrill alarms. He looked at it without interest. It stopped, then began again. He pulled the jack from the wall and the rings ceased, leaving only the sound of dripping water from the eaves outside the windows.

All Jake had ever wanted to do was to hang in as long as he could, and then retire to his cabin on the Skykomish River with his nice, fat, dumb, and faithful wife. Sam, who had no hobbies, no avocation, had never comprehended Jake's fascination with fishing, hunting, and endless Masonic meetings. Now Jake had no time for any of it, and Sam had more time ahead than he could ever hope to fill.

He shut his eyes, and the picture of Jake—dead—came back with such force that he choked, feeling bile rise in his throat. He made it to the stool in the bathroom and vomited until his eyes hurt and the veins stood out on his neck. He pressed his face against the coolness of the toilet lid and sobbed for the man he was supposed to take care of, the man whose inadequacies had been his responsibility to cover.

Then he drank himself into unconsciousness.

When he went back to Nina three days later, he knew that it was almost finished. She didn't question him about where he'd been, and she didn't try to comfort him about Jake; she waited, knowing that her presentiments of disaster had come to pass. She was calmer than he'd ever known her to be and drank less. He drank constantly from the moment he arrived at the floating home until he fell asleep. He woke sometimes to find that she was holding him so tightly that he could not tell whose breathing he felt, but he had no stirring of passion for her any longer. She had never talked to him about anything that happened in the deepest part of her mind, and he could not talk to her now.

They gave him another partner, one of the new guys, not yet thirty, who was a stickler for procedure and who had no wish to cover Sam's lapses or absences. Sam lasted two weeks before the lieutenant called him in. After ten minutes of embarrassed platitudes from the lieutenant and stony silence from Sam, he was offered a choice: sign into the alcoholic treatment program voluntarily or transfer back to patrol.

Sam stood up and began to empty his pockets.

"Badge. I.D. Call-box key. Oh, yeah—my free bus pass. I'll keep my weapon. It belongs to me."

The lieutenant had to push it. "Clinton, don't be an asshole. Six weeks and you'll be back here and nobody will remember it. That woman is behind it, isn't she? No woman is worth it. You're going to lose it all, and you'll be lucky if you get a security job at Pay-N-Save."

Sam stared at him with eyes as dull as smoke. "You keep your college-educated baby dicks and your admirable closure rate and stuff them all. I choose to keep my woman and my bottle and *fuck you.*"

He didn't keep his woman.

Nina watched him go as placidly as she'd allowed him into her life. She sipped scotch from a smudged coffee cup and watched him pack up. She didn't ask where he was going, or if he was ever coming back. She knew. She held up dry lips for him to kiss and lifted her cup in a last salute.

"You be O.K.?" he asked, and she looked back at him with the closed, blank look he'd seen so often. Then she set down the cup and picked up the gray tomcat.

"Take him. You'll need somebody to talk to. He always liked you better anyway."

He stood for a final look at the lake, the struggling cat under one arm, and a brown paper sack under the other. The geraniums were dead, blackened in their planter boxes. If she had said one word, if she had asked him to stay, he would have. But the only sound inside the tilted floating house was her stereo, tuned to high volume. He could see the back of her head through the door's window. She stared out at the water and let him go.

His old pickup was pointed east in the parking lot. As good a direction as any. Pistol sniffed the seat covers, and then curled up next to his knee as he headed across the Floating Bridge, through the eastside bedroom communities, and up toward the pass. It began to snow beyond Issaquah, white streaks darting straight at the windshield, road ice making the truck skid on the turns.

Six hours later, the truck ran out of gas. He was in Natchitat at two in the morning, the only creature alive in the clogged street, except for the cat. He had to piss.

He set Pistol down in the snow to relieve itself, and the cat looked at him outraged. Sam watched his urine make a yellow line in the snowbank behind the truck, and then saw that the cat was peeing too. He tucked Pistol under his parka and set out on foot to find a motel, startled to hear the throaty purr begin against his chest.

They survived the rest of the winter locked into self-imposed solitary confinement in the twenty-seven-foot trailer Sam bought from a widower headed for San Diego. Sam drank, and Pistol ate, and they watched the snow melt and the apple trees bud out and blossom.

POSSESSION

At some point, Sam realized that he had to decide whether to live or die. A thousand times, he thought he would call her, but he never picked up the phone, and it never rang. By May, it had a thick mantle of dust, and Sam knew that he was going to live.

The Natchitat County Sheriff's Office welcomed him, and few questions were asked. His record was clean, he waived medical coverage because of his age, and his former Seattle police associates were generous in their reference letters. He fit into the department as easily as he slid his service revolver into his shoulder holster.

He took Danny Lindstrom as his partner.

Off duty, Sam and Danny walked away from the office into the first light of dawn. It would be hot later, but it was cool now and the sky just above the mountains' ridges was the color of peaches and plums. They stopped silently to acknowledge the day before getting into Danny's pickup.

The town was still asleep; the guys who'd just come on watch could coast for a couple of hours. Sam leaned back and enjoyed the ride past the closed stores on Main Street, and then the neat streets lined with single-family residences, their yards square patches of green bordered with petunias and zinnias kept luxuriant by careful watering in this parched season. The citizens inside seemed safe from harm at this time of day, safe and loved and happy. He closed his eyes and let his head rest on the seat behind him, the leather cool and lightly damp from the night in the parking lot behind the jail.

Danny glanced over at him. "Tired?"

"Yeah. It's hell when you get old."

Danny laughed and pushed the gas pedal toward the floor as they neared the town limits and started up the hill where the orchards began, trees pregnant now with fruit, their branches supported by props, endless rows of them.

"You coming over for supper?"

"That would make three nights already this week. I think Joanne's getting tired of the sight of me."

"Never happen. She likes you."

"She likes all stray animals. She's a natural-born patsy for the homeless and forsaken."

"Do it for me then," Danny said. "She's in a better mood when you're there. She's antsy lately. We fight. We never used to fight. She's bored, I guess. She hates me working graveyard. And she's still not pregnant."

"Seems like you could fix that," Sam offered finally.

"Seems like I can't. What if it's my fault?"

"So what if it is? It's not like you can't get it up. It shouldn't matter whose fault it is. I hear it can be fixed."

"It matters to me," Danny said. "It matters a hell of a lot, and I don't want to find out if it's me."

Sam shifted in embarrassment; the functioning of female organs was not an area where he had any expertise or any particular interest. The vast majority of the women he'd known had been more concerned with staying un-pregnant than in conceiving.

Danny and Joanne were a happy family unit, not young enough to be his children—but almost. Their farm was a place to go when Pistol's company failed to fill the void he still lived in off duty. His partner's marriage was something to take quiet comfort in, however vicariously. There was no envy in his soul over Joanne; he found her delightful, winsomely pretty, the matured image of the cheerleaders he'd yearned for in high school. She was a nice little woman.

Danny. Danny he would kill for. Danny was his partner.

"She still running?" he asked.

"Who? Oh . . . Joanne? Yeah, she's out there running her little buns off."

"You should go with her. Get rid of that tummy."

Danny sat up straighter as he turned into the trailer park, sucking in the suggestion of fat at his waist.

"She doesn't want me to. It's her thing, and running five miles is the last thing I feel like after supper."

Sam crawled out of the truck cab and stood with his elbows leaning on the open window. "Take her on a vacation," he suggested.

"Got no time."

POSSESSION

"You got time. Take her on a vacation, spend about three days in bed together, with no pressure. Make a baby."

Danny laughed, shifted into low, and pulled away with a wave of his hand. Sam watched the truck until it was out of sight, caught in a cloud of road dust. Then he turned and walked through the sleeping park, feeling rather than seeing Pistol's soft body against his hins.

The trailer was cool and smelled of full ashtrays; his daveno bed was rumpled from the morning before, and three days' newspapers covered the floor beside it. He caught a whiff of gas from the leaking pilot light on the chipped green stove and cracked the windows in the living room of his metal box. Pistol made hungry sounds; Sam reached automatically for a can from the stack of tins on the counter and ladled out the fishy substance. He leaned against the wall and watched the old cat eat, feeling a twinge of arthritic pain in his left hip.

Sam grabbed a can of beer for his own breakfast. Pistol leapt onto the daveno, tired from his tomcat prowls in the night, ready to sleep the day away with him. He drained the can, crumpled it, and reached for another, watching the park outside come awake. Then he eased his body into the couch and fell into an almost dreamless sleep.

3

The entrance to the lane leading up to the Lindstroms' farmhouse was placed so exactly between the orchard rows and was so overgrown with weeds that as many times as Danny approached it he had to look carefully to spot it. He liked it that way; the spread looked like only an orchard and not a homestead. He'd deliberately mounted the mailbox a hundred feet beyond the turn-in, just as he'd vetoed Joanne's suggestion that they name the farm and put up a carved sign and arrow where the rutted lane began. He had to leave her there alone so often, and he felt easier knowing that the squat shake buildings were invisible from the county road. Townspeople knew they lived back there, just below the far rise in the lane, but strangers driving by couldn't glimpse even the peak of the roofline.

His truck jounced through the last wisps of ground fog, brushing against the dew-laden heads of wild wheat that leaned over the lane, and Danny smelled the sweetness of a recently mowed alfalfa field nearby. It was his favorite time of the day, coming home to Joanne, knowing she slept soundly in the old house. He listened for the hoarse welcome from his old dog, Frank, and then felt a keen pang of loss. Jeez. He *was* tired, and out of it. Frank wouldn't be waiting near the shed; he was buried out in back of the barn and had been for almost a year. He still missed the old Lab, especially in the early morning like this. He knew he had to bring himself to get a pup, but it was hard. Frank had been with him for half of his life, and you didn't find many dogs like that one. He'd found Frank, left behind when the migrant families moved on, when he was fourteen and Frank a pup barely able to walk. They'd looked each other in the eye and known they had the right combination. That dog had seen him through an awful lot of pain. Danny sighed, and thought of Sam's frowzy old tomcat who seemed more like a pain in the ass than a companion, but there was no accounting for taste.

The pickup hurtled over the rise in the rutted road and Danny saw the house was still there, safe and drowzy, its window-eyes closed with drapes. Joanne had left the back porch light on as always, just as his mother had when he was in high school.

He'd been itchy to get away from Joanne last night, free from her anger and depression, but it didn't seem important now. He only wanted to be with her again and hold her against him for the few hours they had to share in bed. It was no wonder they argued; they hardly ever saw each other, with his graveyard watch, and then sleeping all day. All they really had was suppertime, and he wanted those few hours to be peaceful and happy instead of a continuation of her harangue about babies, and sperm counts, and whatever the hell else Doc had been filling her head with.

Danny eased the truck into the shed, and walked stiff-legged toward the house. He tensed, alert, at the approach of the creature who waddled with wings spread warningly, from behind the sagging grape arbor. It was Billy Carter, a better watchdog than Frank had ever been. B.C. recognized Danny in mid-hiss, and lowered his wings, locking step with Danny. B.C. was Joanne's and only suffered Danny's presence grudgingly. Danny suspected that the goose didn't really sleep at night when he was on duty and was probably relieved to have him take over. The big man and the strutting fowl passed Joanne's kitchen garden, a blighted effort where only zucchini thrived.

"She's got a brown thumb, B.C.," Danny said companiably, and then laughed when the goose darted a look of what passed for disapproval at him. "Maybe *you* can survive on zucchini and sunflowers and worms, but she ain't no earth-mother."

The sunflowers were Joanne's triumph. Twelve-foot stalks with flowers as big as dinner plates edged the entire rear wall of the house and dwarfed the straggly petunias beneath them.

Danny paused as he always did to gaze across the now sere winter wheat field behind the house, and then to the gorge beyond where the river cut through the rocky canyon. The river was running shallow; he had to stop breathing to hear it now, but in a few months it would be filled with glacier run-off and snow from the Cascades and it would roar again.

Even in Natchitat where life moved along so languidly that changes were almost imperceptible, things did change. But not the river, nor the farmhouse where he was born. His father's going off to Korea had hardly touched him; he had his grandfather, his grandmother, and Anna, his mother. He'd only been two years old and his memory scarcely formed. When his father didn't come home, his own life went on unchanged. His mother had cried, but Danny had wept only because her tears frightened him. Like all children, he assumed that his life was blessed, that the tragedies that consumed others would not come to him. And then both his grandparents had died within a week.

Doss Crowder was fire chief then, and father to the frail little girl that Joanne had been. Doss was over at the farm a lot, helping Anna sell off some of the acreage she could no longer manage, somehow taking his granddad's place for Danny, and Danny couldn't remember if Joanne came because Doss was there or if it was the other way around. She was a pest, following Danny around like a shadow, asking stupid questions and getting in his way. It was years before he saw her as a young woman so pretty and soft that he ached to touch her, and quaked at the thought of Doss's wrath if he did. But by then, Joanne was so popular that he had to stand in line to date her.

God, he had been so jealous and so filled with frustration, secure only in athletics. Watching the river had comforted him during those years—until the day an aneurysm lying dormant in his mother's brain had burst and flooded that vital tissue with a sea of killing blood. She was dead before he could get there. She was forty-six years old and Danny was seventeen, and there was no one who could assuage his grief. He'd hated the river for continuing to flow, and the apple trees for daring to blossom that spring.

He refused to leave the farm, and he and Frank batched it while he finished high school. Joanne was the only one who could break through the anger that consumed him, and she'd given up going to college on the coast to marry him. Then the farm was a home again and after a while he even forgave the river. But he never took anything for granted after that, knowing that what seemed safe and permanent could be taken away in an instant. Doss too. But when Doss died, he had Joanne and she had him, and Danny was a man finally who could take care of his own.

Danny reached down absently to stroke B.C.'s crooked neck, felt the peck coming without seeing it, and jerked his hand away. "B.C., you're an old son of a bitch. You ever hear how easy duck soup is? Well, think about goose soup." He laughed and walked into the kitchen.

POSSESSION

As always, he walked softly through the dim rooms to glance into the bedroom. She was there, curled on her side, her dark hair curtaining her face, her arms hugging the pillow. She lay on the edge of her side of the bed as if she'd fallen asleep determined to be untouchable even when he wasn't there. The room was morning cool and Joanne was covered with a sheet. He pulled the spread up over her, but she didn't move. He watched for a moment to see if she was really asleep, and then relaxed to see the steady rise and fall of her ribs beneath the quilt.

Danny shut the bedroom door gently and flipped on the kitchen light. Except for the new stove and refrigerator, Joanne had insisted that the kitchen stay just the way it had always been. It was a good kitchen. Suddenly fashionable again, the old oak table with red-and-white-checked oilcloth still stood in the middle of the room. The wood stove, seldom used, was there too with his grandmother's rocker beside it. Even the pitted sink with the pumphandle you had to prime to get water. He'd put in real faucets years ago, but Joanne wouldn't let him take the funny old pump out.

The day she'd walked into this room as his bride, she'd touched everything in it lovingly, and then smiled at him.

"I used to come over here to get warm a long time before I thought of you as anything more than a smelly little boy. You thought I had a crush on you, but I came here in spite of you, old Danny. Your mom. Your grandma. They always had time for me, and, if I got something dirty, they didn't act like I'd just walked in with shit on my shoes. My mother spent her whole life wiping things down with Lysol. Even me probably. I shouldn't say that—she tries so hard."

Danny had hugged her. "She turned out a pretty good little girl, although Doss was more than half of it. She is what she is and we'll go have dinner with her every Sunday night and act proper."

Joanne had glanced around the kitchen and frowned. "Everything's still here, but you and Frank have pushed it a little beyond casual living, haven't you? Don't worry. I'll fix it."

And she had. She'd vacuumed out bushel basketsful of

dog hair, scrubbed the sticky linoleum, and made new curtains, but she hadn't really changed anything. She'd given him his home back and loved him.

The table was covered now with jars and jars of jam that she'd canned while he'd been out patrolling stinking taverns with Sam. He wondered if she hadn't plunged into a flurry of canning more out of anger than anything else; she did this sort of thing more and more lately.

"I have nothing but time on my hands," she told him flatly. "I have no one to take care of but you—and you're never here, and if you are here, you're asleep."

His sense of serenity vanished. She was changing, and he couldn't deal with her. He'd heard that women grew more and more like their mothers as they aged, and wondered if he was destined to end up with another Elizabeth Crowder instead of the wife he'd married.

Danny was more bewildered than angry; he'd wanted kids too, but he'd never thrown it up to Joanne when she didn't get pregnant. He'd never pushed her into Doc's office, and he'd gone along with her plans to go when she wanted to, but he felt sick at the idea of putting his manhood on the line, of having Doc or anyone else know if there was something wrong with him. She didn't understand what she was asking of him.

He looked under the breadbox for his note. There was always a note—something silly or sexy or teasing. He ran his hand under the tin box but came up empty. And there were no cookies or sandwiches on the counter either, nothing to indicate that she was glad he'd come home to her.

He turned on the radio on the windowsill and listened to the weather and the farm report while he ate a bowl of cold cereal. He didn't give a goddamn about the weather or the price of hogs, but the familiar drone of the announcer's voice filled the empty kitchen. He put the cereal bowl in the sink and ran water over it so the Wheaties wouldn't stick and harden, turned off the light, and walked down the hallway, unhooking his gunbelt and hanging it over the halltree. Joanne didn't like to have his service revolver in the bedroom, and it was close enough if he needed it.

She lay exactly as she had before, turned away from him, and she didn't stir as he padded through the room to the bathroom. He urinated, flushing the toilet as noisily as he could, letting the water run full force in the sink as he washed his face, hoping she'd wake up and reach out for him when he came to bed. And then he saw the familiar square blue cardboard carton that held her Tampax. The top was torn raggedly, and two of the white paper-wrapped cylinders were missing.

Again. Without wanting to admit his anxiety about it, he'd been counting the days crossed off on her calendar and noted that she'd been five days overdue. And now she wasn't overdue anymore, and she'd blame him. There was just a brush of dried blood on the toilet seat when he flipped it back down.

He'd laughed when Fletcher had a vasectomy and Sam kidded him about shooting with an unloaded gun. Well, he wasn't laughing now. Danny leaned on the sink with both hands and stared at himself in the mirror. O.K. O.K. Damn it to hell. He'd go and do it, but he wouldn't tell her. He didn't want her to know for certain that she'd married a eunuch.

Joanne wasn't asleep. She'd heard the truck coming up the lane, and said a prayer, as she always did—thanks for Danny's being safe. She'd sent him off in anger, and she'd gone to bed without leaving one sign for him that she cared if he got home or not. If anything had happened to him, it would have been her fault for sending him off that way.

She was barren. Barren. It was the loneliest word she'd ever heard; she'd never done anything worthwhile, been anything worthwhile, and now she never would. Danny could be proud of his job, and he had friends who understood him. He saved people, for God's sake. And she canned plums.

Without moving, she watched him through half-closed eyes. He hung his uniform shirt carefully over the chair by the dresser, creased his pants and draped them over a hanger, lined up his boots, and she thought he was beautiful. The tanned broad shoulders and back, and the white buttocks that made him look like a little boy. He wasn't the slim, perfect Danny she'd fallen in love with, but the trace of a belly only made him dearer to her. She fought the rush of love. She had to be stubborn, as stubborn as he was, because if he wouldn't do this one thing she asked of him, she knew they were lost.

No, *they* weren't lost. She was lost.

She had never wanted anything more than to be like everyone else, to be accepted, but if it hadn't been for Sonia Hanson—Sonia, square and broad-faced and stump-legged, but full of confidence and loyalty—Joanne wouldn't have had a girlfriend in high school. Walt Kluznewski had adored Sonia ever since first grade, and if he'd looked twice at Joanne, Sonia would have blamed him and not Joanne.

She'd asked Sonia once, "Sonie, why don't they like me? I mean, they act like they like me when we're all out there leading cheers, and then they just walk away after, like I wasn't even there."

Sonia had snorted in disbelief. "Joanne, you're so *dumb!* You look like Elizabeth Taylor, and every single bitchy one of them would gladly kill to look like you. Besides, at least half of them are panting after Danny, and he's nice and polite to them, but he belongs to you. They're so jealous they almost wet their pants, so they try to make you miserable. Just ignore them."

"I can't help how I look."

Sonia laughed. "Neither can I, and I'm lucky big old Waltie doesn't mind. He likes me and I like you and Danny loves you, and high school doesn't last forever. Before long, we'll all be fat, jolly married ladies with babies and nobody will remember who did what at Natchitat High."

It worked out for Sonia. She married Walt and had three kids in three years, and Walt Kluznewski ran his Standard station with a big grin on his face in hot summer or icy winter. All the really smart girls in their class went off to college and then settled down in Seattle or Spokane. The rest of them got married and turned into housewives who seemed to accept Joanne. She ran into them at the Safeway, most of them pushing one baby in a shopping cart, and carrying another one under their belts. She was invited to baby showers and Tupperware parties, but Sonia was still her only friend.

Nobody wanted a thirty-one-year-old cheerleader. She was never the one anybody called when they needed a shoulder to cry on. She never really pleased anyone—not even Danny. Sooner or later, he would look at her and realize how dull she was, his pretty little wife who cleaned his house and spoke sweetly to his friends, and was afraid to ask him why he cried out in his sleep. She knew it was important to him that she be in the farmhouse waiting for him when he came back from his other life, but that was only for now. Maybe not even for now; maybe there was already another woman out there who was alive and vital. And not barren.

She shifted slightly and felt a gush of warm blood between her thighs. She had tried so hard not to bleed this month, willing herself to breathe gently, to handle her body as if it were breakable, not even running for a whole week of mornings and evenings—when running was all she had that belonged only to herself.

"You awake?" Danny whispered, and she lay silent. "Hey, babe, you awake? I'm home."

She was resolute, drawing her body so tightly into itself that she barely touched the sheet beneath her, breathing deeply in a semblance of full sleep. She felt the bed sink under his weight, heard him sigh, and smelled his faint male sweaty odor, and stronger than that, shaving lotion that he must have just splashed on. She had fantasized long ago about being in bed with Danny, but it had never been what she thought sex was supposed to be. If she'd ever had an orgasm, she hadn't recognized it as the powerful sensation she'd read about, or heard other women hint at. Danny was so quick, treating intercourse as an athletic event where the swiftest won. Sometimes she had a glimmer of what it might be, a curious tickling buzz, but Danny was already past her response before it could grow. He always came with a last triumphant thrust, and he dismissed her a moment later with a friendly pat on the shoulder before he turned away and fell asleep.

His beautiful hands, the hands that were so delicate in woodworking and fly-tying, were clumsy when he touched her, and he seemed to have no idea where the center of her sexual feeling lay.

"Tell him," Sonia said. "Tell him what makes you feel good. All those ex-jocks are like that. They can romance a football but they wouldn't know a clitoris if it bit them on the nose—and it should." And Sonia had dissolved into giggles.

"Oh, I couldn't. Sonia, I just couldn't. That's *awful*. It would hurt his feelings, and what if I didn't like it either?"

"Don't knock it unless you've tried it. You have to think of it as teaching braille to a blind man. De-klutzing therapy. Joanne, you keep assuming that men are more than ordinary human beings. They aren't. You have to give them some kind of roadmap."

"Doesn't Walt get angry?"

Sonia laughed. "He stomps and fumes, and once he put his fist through the wall in the bathroom, but he eventually gets the point. See, we talk to each other. He doesn't have to guess what I'm feeling or thinking, and I don't go around resenting him."

Joanne looked up sharply. "I don't resent Danny."

"No? You resent the hell out of him, but you won't admit it. You're still trying to be the Ideal Couple of 1967, but you're blowing it, kid. That was fourteen years ago. We're all grown-ups now, and you're still trying to be perfect and you're losing yourself in the process."

"Then I'll lose him too. I couldn't live without Danny."

"Oh yes you could and stop being such a wimp. Look at me. Take a good look." Sonia stood up and twirled around, displaying her ballooning figure, barely squeezed into a T-shirt and red shorts, her thick ankles rising out of black oxfords and encased in Walt's white socks. "If *I* can ask for something for myself and still keep Waltie racing home to me at night, *you* certainly can. Danny's nuts about you. Just try him."

It sounded so easy when she was listening to Sonia, but Sonia believed in Sonia, and Joanne still felt like a shadow.

She was happy that Danny was home, relieved that he lay beside her in the big bed that felt so empty when he was gone at night. She felt him roll toward her, and then his heavy arm slide across her ribs, his hand caress her breast. She stiffened.

"Joanne? Honey?"

He pulled her against him tightly, his body curving around hers, urging her silently to soften to him. His penis, half-hard already, pressed her buttocks.

"Danny, I can't. I started my damn period. I can't do anything."

"I know. I don't want that; I can't help getting excited when I touch you. I can't control that. Just let me hold you while I fall asleep. Just let me kiss you."

"I taste awful. I haven't brushed my teeth, and I'm all sweaty and yucky." She felt her body relax against his; she didn't want to be angry and alone.

"You always smell good to me, you always taste good, and I need you. We had a hell of a night, and I just kept thinking about being back here with you." His hands moved over her, as if he were gentling a flighty horse. "Sam got hurt— but he's O.K.—and your goddamn goose bit me, and you didn't even leave me a note, and I was afraid you'd run off with the milkman."

"You fool," she whispered, turning over. "We don't even have a milkman. We have a cow."

He made her laugh, and she couldn't stay angry, picturing Billy Carter attacking him. She rolled over and kissed him on the mouth, tasting cigars and toothpaste, feeling the thin sheen of perspiration on his chest, and his penis nudging her belly. He forced her hand around it, and his breathing grew harsher.

"Baby, Joanne, do it for me?"

She kept her fingers still, tried to move them away, but he held her wrist firmly. "Do it, please?"

"I hate that."

"No, no, it's O.K. Just for a little while. Just slow . . ."

She grasped him more firmly and moved her hand tentatively up and down, feeling the silky foreskin slide over the end of him. His breathing accelerated, and she felt him slip away from her, become oblivious of any part of her but her hand servicing him. She shut her eyes against it, removed herself from it.

"Faster . . . do it faster, babe." He lay supine, his back arched. "Make me come."

Something in her mind balked. She didn't want to be back in his '64 Chevy, doing what he asked of her, helping him spill useless seed. She didn't feel guilty as she had then, only tired. And alone. She took her hand away from his penis, and she heard him swear softly before he bolted out of bed and headed for the bathroom, slamming the door behind him. She couldn't hear him in there, but she knew that he was masturbating himself because she'd failed him.

She heard the rush of the faucet, and then his tall shadow walked back to their bed. He patted her on the shoulder, as if she'd been with him when he came, and then he was asleep, sprawled over most of the bed. Her eyes hurt as she watched the sun slide down the bedroom wall like hot butter, bringing with it the heat of another long day.

She couldn't sleep now, and she slid beneath his heavy arm and stood up. She stripped off her gown and panties and tossed them into the bathroom sink, sluicing cold water over them. The dark blood and water swirled together in a pink froth and eddied away. She didn't cry until she was in the shower where he couldn't hear her. She wasn't even sure what she was crying about—the blood that meant another chance gone or the man who lay asleep in the room beyond.

She shrugged into her jogging clothes and felt under the bed for her Adidas. Danny slept fitfully, fighting whatever demons haunted him. She put a hand on one heaving shoulder and he practically leapt off the bed, and then quieted as she stroked his back. She shut the bedroom door quietly and left him to his day's sleep.

It didn't matter now how hard she ran, and the road

beneath her pounding feet felt resilient and supportive. The cramps in her belly eased, her muscles stretched, and she ran, leaving it all behind her.

The morning was hers, still cool but with edges of heat. Down in town, her mother would be going through her familiar morning rituals, preparing for the faculty meeting before the school year. She still taught, and she was still a model no daughter could ever hope to emulate. Elizabeth would drop by the farm after her meeting, carrying a basketful of produce, grown in her own garden, tended with gloved hands that never showed a bit of soil. Without seeming to, she would check out Joanne's housekeeping, frown at Joanne's wasted garden, and evince just the slightest disapproval because Danny slept the day away, no matter that he worked all night.

She ran harder. Slap. Slap. Remember not to flail your arms. Keep them tight against your chest. Breathe deeply. Smell the pine sap. Smell the river.

The road ahead veered away from the river bank and climbed upward through the fallow pasture-land. The muscles in her calves ached and her breath seemed to draw only from the top half of her lungs, but she couldn't slow down or rest, not at this spot. She knew the desiccated shell of the ruined barn was just to her left, and she tried not to look at it. She knew though, knew the very moment she passed it. Maybe no one else even noticed it anymore, the dead fingers of silvery-black wood poking up through so many years' growth of rye grass, the agonized spears of twisted metal, all of it covered over with a funeral blanket of field daisies and Queen Anne's lace. It was a more fitting memorial to Doss than the flat bronze plaque on the firehouse wall.

What made her run this route morning and night? Penance maybe—or defiance? Danny wanted her to run in town where she'd be safe, and she was damned sick of being safe. This was the last place she'd ever seen her father alive, and while this forlorn field filled her with a wave of melancholy and dread, she felt compelled to pass it twice a day; it was her commitment to Doss.

Her running wasn't working this morning; the anxiety that she usually managed to keep just behind her crept up and paced her stride for stride. She ran faster, and it pulled at her shirttail and whispered in her ear, its voiceless message sending little balloons of fear through her veins to her gut.

I am not afraid. I am not afraid. I . . . am . . . not . . . afraid.

She raked her mind for song lyrics and couldn't remember any. Did anyone else feel this way? Was anyone else as afraid as she was, and afraid of nothing? If she could put a name to it, then she wouldn't fear it, but it was transparent, unidentifiable, impossible to ward off.

Her heart jolted in her breast at the sound from behind the grass-clogged barn skeleton, a sound she couldn't identify. Not a rabbit's panicked leap for cover, or a garter snake sliding through dry wheat. Nor a grouse flushed at the sound of her thudding feet. It was more of a whistling sigh, as if someone terribly old had called out to her from behind the pile of charred timbers.

She stopped and felt the tiny shivers ripple across her exposed neck and arms, aware that something alive was watching her.

But there was no definable presence, only the tentative wind whipping the tall grass around the jagged boards and beyond the flattened barn a stand of poplars half asleep in the early morning.

She fled, pumping her legs so violently that she was thrown off stride and tripped, catching herself awkwardly just before nearly falling headlong on the gravel road.

A dusty pickup raced from behind her, throwing up a rush of pebbles that stung her legs, and the driver leaned out his window and catcalled, "Keep 'em bouncing, Jugs!" and then fishtailed around the curve ahead.

She didn't recognize the truck, couldn't make out who the driver was, the back of his head obscured now by two rifles mounted on the gunrack behind him.

Her fear distilled to blank rage and she stood in the

middle of the road and raised her middle finger at the spot where the truck had been.

"Fuck off!" Her voice echoed like a siren in the morning air. "Just fuck off you crummy bastard!"

4

Now that he had finally found her, it seemed as if it had happened perfectly. Duane was convinced that this time he had found the right woman. His relief that the search was over was profound enough to merit a small celebration. He had allowed himself the steak dinner—and not one of the cheap minute steaks that emerged leathery and sawdust-tasting from the microwave at the Trail's End Tavern, but a sixteen-ounce T-bone with mushrooms and onion rings at the Red Chieftain Hotel, with three martinis beforehand and Grand Marnier after.

The liquor had plunged him into a stuporous sleep despite the lumpy mattress, and he was filled with sweet dreams of the running woman, her exquisite face turning again and again to his, full of adoration and no guile, hardening his penis as he slept. The almost-forgotten sensation of oneness flowed through him. He murmured and smiled in his bed, tracing her breasts with his fingers, thrusting himself against her.

And then something woke him, a grinding of brakes from a truck outside, a drunken shout from the Trail's End maybe, and he snapped fully alert, his nerve pathways crackling with electric buzzes. The image of the running woman vanished, and he felt a jolt of apprehension he could not identify. He watched the shadow patterns on the stained wall and tried to isolate the cause of his anxiety.

And did.

The other women. They had seemed perfect too at first. Not as perfect as she was. No, they hadn't come close, and he'd realized too late that they'd been put in his path only to delay him. Most of them would be bones now, their wicked flesh melted into the earth and water where he'd hidden them. But even dead they mocked him and tried to make him doubt his selection. Sluts. They were jealous of his joy, their stupid ghosts trying to make him remember them.

He would not remember them clearly; he would only recall where they lay rotting, and remember that because he had to be aware of places where he must not return—on the off-chance that someone might have found them. Their faces were gone from his memory and gone in reality because he had been careful to obliterate them. They were no longer women, only crosses on a map. Warning signs.

He concentrated on the map in his head and fixed on the crosses.

El Paso. The one who'd gotten into his car as he headed down from Amarillo. She'd pretended to be sweet and good, and then she'd exposed her tattooed breasts in the pale moonlight that washed the Franklin Mountains, as if she were proud that other men had marked her and disfigured her. She was under the rocks in the mountains now, shut off from both the moon and the sun forever.

Niagara Falls. The American side. The college girl who thought she was a goddamned shrink, who told him he had a . . . a what? . . . yeah. An Oedipus Complex. The bitch went off the edge of Goat Island, screaming and tearing at him while the rapids swallowed her voice.

Someplace in Iowa. Council Bluffs. He couldn't remember anything more than they'd been on a train heading for Chicago, and then she wasn't on the train any longer and he was alone and happy she was gone.

Where else? He couldn't think of where because they were all alike. Wait. Yeah. L.A. So many broads got snuffed in L.A. they hardly kept count there. He remembered tearing up ice plants along a canyon road to get to the ground where he could dig a hole to plant her. And the sticky purple flowers bleeding all over his hands.

He didn't want to go through the rest, but he forced himself through the roll call. There were six. No, seven. El

POSSESSION

Paso, Niagara Falls, Council Bluffs, L.A., and . . . Klamath Falls in Oregon right off the I-5 freeway. Cut Bank, and waiting a long, long time to get a hitch that took him out of Montana. And one more . . . *Where?* He blanked on the seventh one; it was so long ago, before he was even nineteen. It was winter that time. Frozen ground and the wind pushing at him. Someplace in the north.

He lit a cigarette and went back through the litany, and it spilled into his consciousness easily, as if he was reciting a poem by rote. Bemidji! Paul Bunyan country. She was under the ice of a lake, floating with her hair like seaweed and her eyes staring up through the blue-white crypt, even though she couldn't see anymore.

He had never read their names in the paper. It was probable the cops still didn't know where they were, but even if they did, they sure wouldn't connect him with any of it. He knew the value of moving on, and never going back.

Now, it was O.K. *She* was here, waiting for him. She'd be pleased when he told her about getting rid of the others, the false ones.

He'd found her, and all he needed was a plan. In an hour, he had it, a solid matrix where each component fell into place like tumblers in an intricate combination lock. Euphoria seized him. He had never experienced such a sense of rightness. He knew how he would find her again and show himself to her.

But there was no rush. There was no tearing hurry for anything.

He forced himself to go through the daily routine of the wine pickup at the Safeway, the rebottling in the moldy bathroom of his room—not because he needed the money that badly, but because he was superstitious enough not to break the patterns that had brought him to her.

When it was done, he felt free to look for a bowling alley. The bowling alley was a good omen: every hick town in America had a bowling alley with a blue neon bowling pin instead of a glowing cross. St. Brunswick, the Divine. Come unto me all ye with bad backs, beer bellies, and empty

8 5

minds. He stood on Main Street and saw the beacon calling to him above the buildings.

It was open for business. He stepped inside and walked unerringly past the counter and the smell of fresh donuts and stale hamburger grease, the sound of lumbering balls and crashing pins familiar music to his ears. There it was: the trophy case. The glass was smudged and dead flies lay parched and still on its faded velvet floor. And, of course, the framed photographs were there, recording championships wrested over a long time in Natchitat, row upon row of grinning, vacuous faces.

He almost gasped out loud when he found her, saw her small wonderful image gazing directly at him. A flower shining among the ordinary. She knelt on one side of the massive trophy, one arm extended across it and touching the shoulder of a fat, red-headed woman with a foolish smile on her face. The others were grouped behind her, all of them wearing the same T-shirt she'd worn last night. His hand trembled as he traced the printing beneath the photo.

Natchitat County Sheriff's Office
Wives' Bowling League

And in smaller printing, the names. "Front row, left: Joanne Lindstrom."

She had given him the sign; there was no question about that, even if she hadn't realized it. She could have worn anything else when she ran past him, but she had chosen the shirt that would tell him where to find her.

He fumbled in his shirt pocket and pulled out the small spiral pad and his gold Cross pen. For the first time he wrote her name, printing the letters carefully. *Her* name.

He forced his eyes away from hers and scanned the rest of the group shots, carefully now. He knew he would find the other picture because it would not have been this simple to find her unless he was meant to find the next information he needed. The men's picture was bigger and on the shelf above. Two rows of cops. He could spot cops if they were walking down Main Street naked; he could smell them.

POSSESSION

They carried themselves as if they had a poker up their asses. Self-important pricks. And they went to seed and fat quicker than other men, full of the free meals and courtesy liquor.

He played a game with himself. There were nine of them in the photograph, all dressed in dark trousers and white shirts with red embroidery snaking across the right shirt pocket, broadcasting their names. He would pick the husband without checking the surnames spelled out below.

Not the old one with his bald head painstakingly covered with long hair combed across and plastered in an attempt to make it look like it grew there. Not the two fat, moon-faced ones who looked like Tweedledum and Tweedledee. Not the really young ones.

Duane leaned closer, shading his eyes with one hand to cut the glare from the bare overhead bulb, smiling a little to himself because the winnowing out process was so rudimentary. It sure wasn't the little guy in front, so short he'd never have made it in a big city department. There were two big men on each side of the dwarf, clowning for the camera with their flattened palms resting atop the head of the midget. Cocky sons of bitches.

It couldn't be the taller man with the gap-toothed grin and deep wrinkles around his eyes. He was too old. Had to go fifty—maybe more—and she could do better than that.

The other one. Yeahhh—it had to be him. Not a bad looking guy, but a stereotyped, dull kind of handsome. Brown hair cut cop-short. The regular facial features softened as they fell away to the chin that was threatening to duplicate itself in fat. He guessed there were twelve to fifteen overweight pounds padding the athlete's body, broad shoulders, thick neck, and the big thighs of a linebacker. The guy didn't look really out of shape, but on the verge. He was sucking in his gut, self-consciously, an ex-jock surely who was packing in the calories as if he was still turning out.

His eyes followed the flourish of the embroidered name on the guy's breastpocket. "Donny—no, Danny." Shit, the guy looked at least thirty, and he was still walking around with a kid's name on his chest.

He would enjoy eliminating the cop.

He glanced around to see if he had attracted attention, and was satisfied that he had not. The woman behind the counter looked hung over or bored as she made ineffective swipes at the Formica with a stained towel. The manager was smoking a cigarette and staring out of the window, as if something on the street beyond fascinated him.

Leisurely, Duane copied the deputies' names into his notebook, adding cursory descriptions to remind himself which was which. The date on the men's picture was "Fall, 1979" so there was a good chance they were all still employed by the Natchitat County Sheriff's Office. When he had filled two of the blue-lined pages, he walked over to the pay phone booth just inside the front door and turned to the front page of the thin directory.

There were three Lindstroms—Ole, Walter, and, of course, Daniel. City cops never listed their names and home addresses unless they used their kids', wives', or even their dogs' names, but the pigs in little burgs were too dumb to expect reprisal.

Dumb Danny had his address right there: 15103 Old Orchard Road. Duane noted that and the phone number, and then added the number for the Sheriff's Office. He slid the notebook back into his pocket and dialed the last number.

The voice that answered was laconic, touched with just a shadow of a drawl, "Sheriff."

Duane let his voice falter and he spoke in a thin nasal tone. "Yes sir, I was trying to locate Deputy Lindstrom."

"Not here. Anyone else help you?"

"No sir—I guess I better talk to him. Could you tell me a good time to call back?"

"Be in about 7:30. You wanta leave a number?"

"No sir. I ain't got a phone at my place. Thank you sir. I'll call him tonight."

"O.K." The phone went dead, the desk man unaware of how much help he'd been.

In fifteen minutes Duane had learned Joanne's surname, her husband's name, their address and phone number, and

Danny's shift; 7:30 check-in meant third watch—which meant Danny would be gone from home from then until dawn.

Perfect.

Duane walked out into the morning sun, filled with the joyous blessing of the bowling alley; the light and the way had been pointed out to him, and he had endless corridors of time in which to develop his procedure and carry it out.

He knew the Old Orchard Road; he traversed it every day with the full wine bottles chunking together in his saddlebags. The dirt road crossed the blacktop edging the river where he had his vantage point in the woods. He had found it unerringly as if an inner voice had led him almost to her door, sensing without knowing that she would be close. He believed in no god beyond himself, but he was convinced there were forces unseeable that had propelled and buffeted him in his quest, and the sheer gift of this realization hit him now, relaxing all his taut muscles so that he almost stumbled as he walked toward his bike.

5

Sam dreamed that he was walking across a desert wearing a fur parka hauling his injured leg behind him. A red bird circled over his head—a vulture—screeching at him in annoying cadence, but he couldn't move fast enough to get away from its raucous cry. In his dream he fumbled with the zipper of his parka, struggling to pull the heavy garment off so that he could run.

Pistol, sprawled across his master's chest, took umbrage at the rough treatment, struck out with one unsheathed paw and caught Sam across the chin, leaving a dotted path of blood.

Sam swung and reared up in the same motion, swearing at the scarlet bird that had just attacked him, and sending Pistol off the daveno to skid against the wall. He was awake now, his mouth as parched as the desert he'd just escaped, the afternoon's ninety-five degrees threatening to bake him alive before he could stumble to the door and kick it open. Pistol spied the opening and was gone in a blur of disgruntled gray fur. The bird became a phone and continued to shrill at him.

His bad leg almost buckled under him.

"HELLO! God damn it—"

"Hello yourself, little Mary Sunshine," Danny laughed. "Did we disturb his little nappie?"

"What the hell do you want?"

"This is your wake-up service, sir. You asked the desk to call you at four so you could get the preacher's wife out of your room before vespers."

Sam relaxed against the counter, rubbing his leg with one hand and holding the black earpiece with the other. When the leg could bear his weight, he used the massaging hand to reach into the refrigerator for a cold beer. He rubbed the can over his face and chest before opening it, slowly coming back to the reality of the afternoon.

"She left at noon. Said she couldn't take any more after the fifth go-round. They don't make women like they used to—at least *I* don't. Now could you tell me why you're calling at dawn?"

"Joanne says supper will be ready at five-thirty, quarter to six, and to get your ass out here."

"She didn't say that. She talks nice." Sam ripped the tab off the beer and took a deep draught. "You sure she wants me out there tonight?"

"I'm sure. Mother-in-law cruised by and left yesterday's harvest. There's enough to feed the whole department, but we thought we'd start with you. Corn, beans, tomatoes, and steak."

"Mother-in-law ran over a cow, did she?"

"Only the front half. You comin' out?"

Sam glanced around the trailer; it was so hot inside he could almost see heat waves emanating from the debris he'd meant to pick up when he woke up. "Oh hell yes. What can I bring?"

POSSESSION

Danny paused for a moment and Sam heard him cover the phone with his hand and call something to Joanne. Another pause.

She says nothing—but I'll take a couple of beers if you want to stop by and get some."

"I'll stop. Mother-in-law still there. Maybe I better get a case—I know what a lush she is."

Danny laughed at the thought. "Halfway under the table already, and she's panting to see you. The woman's insatiable. Naw, really—she left after the produce run. We'll see you in a while." He hung up before Sam had a chance to change his mind.

Sam's head felt thick from his day's sleep in the heat of the aluminum trailer. He grabbed another beer on his way to the shower and enjoyed the cold spray against his chest as he opened it; it was cooler than the shower would be. He was grateful he had someplace to go. He could stand staying in the trailer just long enough to put on his uniform—but no longer.

His truck, parked for forty-eight hours with locked doors and closed windows under the tin-roofed lean-to, breathed fire when he opened the door. He held his breath as he leaned across the hot vinyl seat and rolled down the passenger window, knowing he'd have to drive five miles before enough air could circulate to make the cab bearable. Before he could suppress it, his memory tricked him and raced back to find a cool place, and he was on the deck of the houseboat again with the rain sluicing down his neck. He could feel his hand on her doorknob, see through the steamy windows to where she sat cross-legged on the floor staring out at the water.

He felt better once he was out on the blacktop, moving away from his bleak thoughts and cloying memories. He was not lost; he had someplace to go, someone who waited for him, and a job he was damned good at. It was O.K. now, and he drew a breath of air that was, if not cool, at least bearable.

Natchitat was always two different towns to him; in the morning light, the dawn light, no matter the season, it was

9 1

clean, kind, almost surrealistically pure, all imperfections softened by the plum velvet shadings of summer and the blue-pink of winter skies. But late afternoons brought a harshness, an unforgiving searchlight that weathered facade and exposed an underlying ugliness. If it were possible, he would have avoided Natchitat in daylight and stayed in the hills beyond town.

Sam wheeled into the Safeway parking lot, relieved to see that the evening shopping crush hadn't begun yet in earnest. For a moment he thought about locking his truck but dismissed the precaution, unwilling to face the furnace again. He stepped into the store and felt the ice-water air piped there. His uniform pulled eyes, sparked curiosity even among the most languid of shoppers. When he moved easily toward the rear, nodding at the Fast-Check-Out clerk, the one with orange hair and shelflike breasts that obscured her view of the cash register, the shoppers relaxed—half-relieved, half-disappointed, that it was to be an ordinary day after all.

He grabbed a six-pack of Coors, and then realized it wouldn't look good for him to buy only beer while he was in uniform. He picked a half-gallon of Safeway Snow Sparkle Almond Crunch ice cream, and spun around toward the quick-check line. He watched the checker—Beverly—yeah, Beverly—and saw a thin trail of perspiration ooze its way toward her cleavage.

"You find everything you want, Sam?" Her breasts seemed to have a life of their own, and they vibrated as she spoke. Sam looked up, caught. She smiled.

"Seem to have it all for today, Bev. You have a special I missed—giving anything away free? I forgot my coupons." There was no desire behind his banter; it came as automatically as breathing. She was very young, and her round brown eyes reminded him of a calf's. She liked him, but, God, what was she? Twenty-three? Twenty-four? He had nothing to say to her, or she to him. Even so, he smiled back, his eyes aimed directly into hers.

"You, Sam, don't need coupons." She reached across for

the beer and ice cream, leaning just off balance enough so that he knew it wasn't accidental that her breasts brushed his tan-clad arm. He kept his hand flat on the check-out counter, pretending he hadn't noticed.

"You going on duty? Or off?"

"On, sweetheart. Can't you see I'm not sweating yet? Graveyard, like always. We're ships that pass in the night. You work days; I work nights, and you'll be tucked safe in bed long before I get off. My bad luck."

She looked away from him, jabbed at the cash register with improbably long scarlet nails. Twenty years ago, he would have thought about her as he rode through darkened streets. Now, she slipped from his mind like smoke before he was even through the automatic door to the parking lot.

The Harley parked next to the vapor light pole caught his interest. His own bike had been a Harley. This one had no distinguishing marks at all, just a few nicks and scrapes in its black hide, scuffed black leather saddlebags, and Oregon plates. And all alone. Harleys generally moved in herds, but this one was a maverick. Probably belonged to some businessman with a midlife crisis. Sam moved on, but the bike registered someplace deep in his mind, the cop part, a programmed chip full of vehicles, faces, distinguishing characteristics, M.O.s and peculiarities, most never needed again.

He eased the pickup through town and floored it when he hit the blacktop, passing the trailer park again without glancing at it, and a mile farther on, turning onto the dirt road that led to Danny's place.

He didn't see the black dot in his rearview mirror until it grew large enough to fill the mirror. It was the Harley, going too fast for the unstable surface—almost close enough to destruct on his rear bumper if he chanced to stop suddenly. Irritated, he tapped his brakes and the hog pulled back, controlled easily by the big man who rode it. Sam pegged him certain for a stranger; his old pickup was familiar to almost everybody in Natchitat, and no punk around town would have the balls to play games with him. He gunned the truck again and the bike pulled up closer. He tapped the brakes, watching the rider in his mirror. The bike shimmied, slid off-course a few degrees, and seemed about to tumble into the ditch before the rider rammed his booted foot into the gravel and skidded to a stop. Sam laughed and picked up speed, sashaying the old truck's rear end in a mechanical put-down. The biker's helmeted head protruded from the froth of the road dust and his silver-rimmed goggles glinted in the sun, making him ageless, unidentifiable—a disembodied, round-headed mask.

Sam lit a Marlboro from the crumpled pack on the dashboard and tasted stale tobacco flakes on his tongue, annoyed with himself because he'd forgotten to buy more at the Safeway. Now he'd have to wait until he got to the machine in the office or give in and accept one of the rotten cigars that Danny smoked occasionally.

He heard the bike roar behind him again just as he reached the lane up to the farm, where he concentrated on avoiding the weed-choked ditches on either side of the narrow entrance, his truck crawling a few miles an hour. He waited, only slightly curious, for the Harley to pass, turning his head to catch a glimpse of the black hog with its tall male rider. Jeans. A black T-shirt and the white helmet. Caucasian. The rider's right hand left the hand grip for just a moment, jutted in Sam's direction and the middle finger raised in obscene salute.

Sam debated backing the pickup out and giving chase. He would enjoy seeing the slow recognition on the Harley rider's face as he unfolded his uniformed frame from the pickup, seeing the turkey's bravado seep out of his features when he realized who he'd been playing with. He debated too long, torn between the welcome waiting up at the top of the orchard road and the satisfaction of writing a ticket for the fingerman. The hell with it; he'd have all night long to find assholes. No need to run one down now when his stomach growled for something to eat and his mouth watered for a beer. Besides, the ice cream would melt.

He pulled in behind Danny's new red GMC and headed

for the back door, boots silent on the mowed lawn behind the house. He could see them inside, unaware of his presence, only a dozen feet away from him through the open window but caught in emotions that did not include him.

Danny stood, back to the refrigerator, arms folded over his chest, a closed look on his face—not angry, but cautious. Sam had seen that look a thousand times, that protective facade while his partner waited for someone else to speak, to telegraph weakness. Joanne was at the table, her hands full of silverware, her face turned toward Danny. Her shoulders, bare above the flowered sundress, were bent, almost supplicatingly, toward her husband. Sam could not let them speak because if they did, he would be able to hear every word, and they would be very private words, not to be shared with him or with anyone else.

He banged on the door, and their startled faces turned toward him, veiled almost immediately with smiles.

"Hey, can I come in before I get goosed by the goose?" he said too loudly. "He thinks he's in love."

Danny strode toward him through tension that still hung heavy in the kitchen and held the screen door open, grabbing for the Safeway sack with his free hand. "What the hell took you so long? I've been reduced to drinking lemonade."

Joanne took a beat longer to shake the dark mood, and then she laughed and brushed his cheek with a half-kiss. "He just got out of the shower, Sammie. If you'd got here any sooner, you would have had only me to talk to."

He looked at her, seized as always with pleasure at her genuine prettiness, and wondering at the same time what in hell they *would* have found to discuss without Danny in the room to share the banter.

"And that would have been my good fortune," he lied. "I have heard everything the kid here has to say too many times already. And he didn't know that much to start with."

He accepted the beer can that Danny held out to him, raised it in a mock salute to click with Danny's can, and began to relax. Even solid marriages were given to argument;

he had simply blundered into the middle of one. And yet, he couldn't shake the memory of his own failed marriages. Gloria had put it bluntly, "Bad marriages need spectators, Sam. It helps you pretend for a while longer that everything's all right. I'm acting and you're acting, but if we can convince somebody else that we like each other, maybe we'll believe it ourselves."

He watched them—Danny standing close to Joanne, his big hand dwarfing her waist, holding her tight against his hip, giving her sips of beer while she struggled half-heartedly to get free.

"Let that woman go, man," Sam laughed. "Can't you see she's panting to cook, and I'm starving?"

Danny released her, and then pulled her back and gave her a resounding kiss. "So cook, woman." He turned to Sam. "You may be sorry. She's into zucchini; it's a kind of fetish. We've got zucchini bread, zucchini pickles, zucchini stuffed, fried, baked, and fricasseed, and—except for you— we'd be eating zucchini ice cream. Everything's full of little green specks."

"Don't believe him, Sam. We don't have *baked* zucchini. I didn't want to overdo it. Sit down before you faint from hunger."

He sat at the table, feeling good again, with the small rush of beer in his system, part of this little family who were now easy with each other. The table was covered with bowls of corn on the cob, sliced tomatoes, green beans, boiled potatoes, and Jell-O. Danny forked the steaks onto each plate with a grandiose flourish. Fried steak. Nobody in Natchitat broiled steak. He shut his eyes for a moment and the aroma brought back his mother's harvest meals.

"Joanne, if I could find a woman who cooked like you do, I'd marry her in a minute."

"Liar." She looked at him accusingly. "Every woman in Natchitat County can cook like I do—and better—and I haven't seen you racing to the altar with any of them. I suppose it's my fault. If I quit feeding you, maybe they'd have a chance."

"Ahh—there you have me. It's not your cooking at all

POSSESSION

It's your sensuous beauty that keeps me coming back. Lord knows, I've tried to fight it. . . ."

She giggled. "I can't hear you with your mouth full."

Danny sat at the head of the table, watching them with a look of pride on his face. It was a good time, with the first streams of cool evening air blown off the river stirring the ruffled window curtains, the muted lavender dusk throwing the corners of the room into shadow. Sam knew his limits with the small woman across the table. She belonged to his partner, and yet he knew Danny took some delight in watching Sam flirt with her. He felt a surge of affection for each of them, willing them to be happier.

Joanne bent over the table, slicing the brown spicy-smelling loaf with a serrated blade. A slice fell away and Sam laughed, seeing the bright green flecks in it.

"See," Danny said. "I told you. Zucchini. She spent all day grinding it up. I understand it's an aphrodisiac. Three slices of that and you'll be a frothing maniac."

Sam looked at her delicate hands on the knife, seeing the dusky blue veins that glowed beneath the skin of her wrists and pulsed in the soft places in the crooks of her arms. He could not imagine Joanne running five miles. He could not even picture her running one. She seemed to him to be the softest woman he'd ever seen—not fatty soft, but somehow crushable. Nina had been fragile on the surface, but with a resiliency that he could not find in Joanne.

"Sam? . . . Sam . . . ?" He looked up, pulled out of his reverie. Danny dangled another chunk of steak over his plate and he nodded, pushing beans and Jell-O aside to make room.

"So then, Joanne," he began. "What did you do all day while we were sleeping? Besides cooking and grinding up zucchini?"

She drew a breath, and the flowered material over her breasts expanded. She traced a line in the tablecloth with her fingernail.

"Well . . . I ran this morning, before it got so hot. Along the river road and up over the cut behind Mason's warehouse." She darted a glance at Danny who continued to cut his meat, staring down at his plate. "I guess that's about six miles going out and coming back."

"Six miles!" Sam forced a heartiness into his voice that sounded patronizing, even to him, but Joanne didn't seem to pick up on it. "Honey, you're going to have calves like Babe Zaharias!"

"*Who?*" She looked mischievous. "Is that one of the waitresses at the hotel? The one who's so crazy about you?"

Danny choked on a laugh and turned away from the table, coughing into his napkin.

"No. That's not a waitress at the hotel. It's—oh, forget it. I keep forgetting that we're from different generations."

"You've got it wrong," Danny cut in. "The waitress at the Chief has little skinny legs, and it's Sam who's crazy about her, but she won't give him the time of day. She likes younger men."

Sam had to work to keep the conversation light, aware that it veered dangerously close to sensitive areas, and he felt his gut begin to tighten again. Joanne was talking to him, and Danny was talking to him, but neither of them was speaking to the other. As long as he kept them all together with inane humor, they might just make it through the meal without a slipping back into words that could not be easily forgiven.

He took a deep breath. "So you ran your little fanny off—and then what?"

"Then what? Not much, Sammie. There's not much for me to do around here. I washed dishes and a load of laundry. Then I folded the laundry, and then I read another book, and then I babysat for Sonia while she took the older kids in to get vaccinated, and then I came home and cooked supper."

"Sounds like a full day to me," Sam said weakly, willing Danny to open his stubborn mouth and join the party. "I mean—all Danny and I did was sleep all day."

Joanne stood up, and began scraping her plate. Her movements were brisk, tight little sweeps of her knife across the flowered crockery.

God. How many women had he seen angry like this?

POSSESSION

He gave it up, and joined Danny. The two of them ate silently, working through the pile of food on their plates, and he tried to pretend he didn't notice that Joanne was pissed with both of them. Danny looked at his watch and pushed his chair back. The meal was over, thank God, and Sam yearned for the freedom that beckoned beyond the screen door. The shrilling cadence of the phone broke whatever awkwardness remained. Danny picked it up on the third ring, and bellowed, "Halloo—we're on our way in, Fletch. Get off our backs, would you—"

He held the phone away from his ear, shook it, said "Hello" again, and then hung it back on the hook.

"Who was that?" Joanne asked.

"Nobody. Wrong number probably. Or our lousy phone system."

Danny hugged Joanne, kissed her averted cheek, and they were out of it, into the darkened yard with its lone circle of yellow light from the porch bulb.

Sam backed his truck out without speaking, hoping that Danny wouldn't speak either. He fumbled in his shirtpocket for a cigarette, remembered that he had none, and reached for the sun-baked pack on the dash. There was one bent white cylinder left, and he lit it without much hope; it tasted worse than he'd expected. He concentrated on the road, and Danny stared ahead too without talking.

Fletcher was pointing at the clock and grinning when they walked in.

"Fifteen minutes late, kids."

"Don't nag, Fletchie," Sam laughed.

"Wanda Moses is being a real bad girl, Sam. She threw her supper back at Nadine, and she's screaming for ciggies."

Sam bent over the cigarette machine and fed quarters into it. He pulled the knob below the Marlboro slot and waited.

"Damn it, Fletch. Is this thing fucked up again?"

"Romance it a little."

Sam whacked the machine with the flat of his hand and three packs of Marlboros let go. He slid one into his shirtpocket, one into his back pantspocket and handed the third to Fletch.

"Here, take this back to Wanda, and mind your face. She scratches. Mind your cojones too—she kicks."

"She ain't gonna be that grateful."

Sam swung the little deputy by the armpits and put him on the counter and chucked him under the chin. He was the only guy in the department who could do that and leave Fletch laughing.

"You better quit giving Wanda presents," Danny warned. "I think she's single."

"Ain't they all, pard? Ain't they all?"

6

Duane let the receiver slip softly back into its cradle, neither frustrated nor particularly annoyed that his call had failed, again, to connect. The few failures in his life were failures of patience, and he had learned from them. He was curious about the sound of her voice. He expected that it would be breathy and delicate, but he could not be sure until he actually caught her fast at the end of the phone's wire. He had got the man on the first call. Say it. Her husband. He looked at the summary in his notebook: "7:51 P.M.—male answered. 8:15—busy signal." He added "9:20—no answer."

"Hey Ace," a muted voice intruded on his thoughts. "You gonna stay in there and pick your nose or what?"

He turned to see the broad, blurred face under the cheap cowboy hat with its band trailing fake feathers. The man was half-drunk, showing off for the skinny woman who clung to his arm. Neither of them would remember him, the time of day, or their own names. He hit the fold in the door and pushed past them, catching a blast of beery breath.

"It's all yours, champ," he muttered. "Sorry about that."

"No problem. No problem. Didn't mean to hassle you."

He weaved his way through the cluster of tables that surrounded the ridiculously small dance floor, and sat at the far end of the padded red bar. The bartender wore western garb too, his belly pushing at the mother-of-pearl buttons on his red plaid shirt. Everybody wanted to be a cowboy.

"Beer?"

"No."

"So, what?"

"A Dirty Mother."

The bartender looked offended. "What the hell is that?"

"Kahlua and cream."

"You mean a White Russian."

"No. I mean a Dirty Mother. Vodka makes me vomit, and you've got such a class act crowd in here, I'd hate to disgrace myself."

He was talking too much. He looked directly at the bartender and flashed his most ingenuous smile. "No offense, friend. I've just got a bitch of a stomach problem."

The man measured him, took in his size, and gave the smile back. "Tell me about it. Stress. Makes your gut bleed if you don't let it roll off your back. Kahlua and cream. Gotcha."

"Great. I appreciate it."

"Work around here?"

"Naw. Passing through. Gotta make Spokane by tomorrow noon."

Somebody bellowed for beer from the other end of the bar, and he was left alone to observe. The Red Chieftain Hotel management had obviously redecorated in the recent past. Walls carpeted halfway up with red and orange patterned in black cattlebrands, and above that, festooned with steer skulls and horseshoes. The pretzels on the bar were offered in dried and salted bull scrotums. Nice touch.

Tacky as it was, the Totem Room was the best of all places to get a look at Danny Boy. Cops never showed up at the Trail's End Tavern unless they were summoned, but here there was always a patrol unit or two parked out in front.

The pigs wandered in all day to sip free coffee and jaw with the waitresses. Short of parking across from the sheriff's office, Duane couldn't find a better vantage point. Once he had a look at the husband in the flesh, made sure he was really on duty, he had all night to check out the house.

He sipped his D.M. and watched the coffee shop door, while he made a mental inventory of his cash situation. Once he had her, they would have to hole up for a while and that would take a thou, maybe two. Credit card slips—yeah. The marks guarded their little plastic rectangles like they were gold, but they threw away the receipts with all the magic numbers. Waste baskets were full of them, and he could get into any bank machine for all he'd need. By the time the bills came in, he and Joanne would be long gone.

He smiled, thinking of it, and the dumb barkeep smiled back, sure he was going to get a big tip.

Fat chance, turkey.

It was after ten when Joanne left Sonia's and Walt's place and headed out the blacktop for home. She dreaded driving home after dark, but she'd dreaded more the long evening alone on the empty farm.

On the last dirt road even the moon disappeared behind the trees. She would not let the dark frighten her; it was the same road she jogged along in the daylight, the trees were the same trees, grotesque and lowering only because they clawed out into the headlight cones, gnarled and crippled by shadows. If she didn't have the guts to drive home alone at night, she'd be dooming herself to isolation. Still, her heart beat too fast, responding to her thoughts. To work around it, she escaped. She was not herself; she became someone else, someone who drove along an unfamiliar road with no particular destination, safe in the Celica-cocoon.

It got her up the lane and safely into the shed. Twenty steps to the back door, with the night noises rustling behind her. Then her key found the lock and slipped in, connecting just as the darkness crept closer and shrunk the yellow sphere of the porch light.

The phone began to ring before the door was fully open,

and she hurried toward it across the black kitchen. Two rings—two more. It was their line. She didn't see the chair in her path and it caught her hipbone with its oak-knobbed back, sending thrills of pain through her belly, more intense because of the cramps. It paralyzed her through three more double rings. When she finally picked up the receiver, she heard only silence and the blank buzz of nobody there.

The back door was still open, and she felt the cool draft, started back to close it, and felt something slide across her thigh, pressing insistently. Her throat closed and the back of her neck shrunk with horror. Something behind her fluttered and clicked.

There was some living presence in the room with her, and she forced herself to turn slowly to face it.

The goose eyes reflected a slice of moonlight, and even as she recognized Billy Carter, she couldn't stop the scream that rose in her throat. The gander's wings flared wide and he waddled toward the door hissing indignantly. She slammed it behind him and slid the bolt across, realizing that if the scream had been for real no one would have heard her.

Duane had been about to hang up when she answered, and she sounded just as he thought she would—soft, frightened. It was all he could do not to speak to her. He waited, letting her repeat "Hello . . . Hello . . ." a few times before he pushed the lever down gently, breaking this first link between them.

Later. Just a little while longer, Joanne.

As he turned, he saw them walking into the coffee shop. Lindstrom and the old guy, sauntering into their territory, straddling stools and leaning forward on their elbows as the waitress fluttered over.

He took his time. He added the notes: "10:27 P.M.—Heard Joanne. 10:31 P.M.—D.L. and—(he squinted to read the name pinned over the old guy's shirtpocket)—Sam Clinton, coffee break at hotel."

The fucking waitress was falling all over herself, laughing when the old guy kidded her, bringing them slices of pie, filling their cups. The dumber the broad, the more impressed by a uniform.

He left a buck-seventy-five on the bar and moved closer to the counter, but he couldn't hear what they were saying. He was close enough to see the triangles of sweat under their arms, close enough to smell them. Close enough to grab their skulls in two strides and slam them together, or to slip the .38's out of the holsters where they dangled and pull the triggers before they got their noses out of their banana cream pie. Blood and brains on the polished glass. . . .

He forced his rage inside. He had not come so far after so long to lose it. The husband was big enough but not as big as he was, and the cop was smug. You didn't see a hell of a lot of cops sitting with their backs exposed to a window. The old guy was clearly a country hick, over the hill. Duane had beaten a lot better. A lot better.

Sit there and slop up your pie, Danny. I'm gonna have your wife and teach her things you never thought of.

Her voice had turned him on; his groin still throbbed with the soft looseness he'd heard in her. She already belonged to him. She would do all the things the other women had balked at. When they were alone. When they were alone, he wanted her naked all the time so he could touch her heavy breasts and the secret, moist folds of her whenever he wanted, rub himself all over her and make her beg for it. And he would give it to her until she was so sore she couldn't walk. She'd waited long enough for him, and he would make it up to her.

The cops had finished their pie. The old guy slipped a buck into the waitress's apron and Duane heard her giggle. They ambled out the back door, toothpicks sticking out of their mouths. He watched them drive away before he took a stool at the counter.

"Miss?" She wasn't a "Miss"; she was well over forty, but the old ones loved being mistaken for young meat.

She smiled at him and bent lower, showing the dry wrinkles between her breasts. "What's yours?"

"I'll have what old Danny had. Looks like great pie."

POSSESSION

"Oh, it is. Fresh every day." She set a conspicuously large portion in front of him. "Real whipped cream."

He ate a mouthful of the sweet mess, and signaled to her with thumb and forefinger.

"You like it, huh?" He'd got her with the first grin; she was going to watch him eat every sticky crumb of it.

"Always eat where the cops eat. Some people say truck-drivers, but it's really policemen who know where it's at." He smiled again, and let his eyes drift down the front of her as if he was hungry for her too. She liked that.

"You a cop?"

"Me?" He laughed modestly. "No such luck. I'm blind in my left eye. Vietnam. Old Danny and Sam though, they've got it made."

He could see her study his eyes to see if she could tell the difference.

"They work hard though," she offered. "You're probably better off. You a salesman?"

He shook his head slightly and gave no direct answer. "Dangerous too. They take a lot of chances, but I still envy them."

She bit. Spilled her guts, trying to keep his attention. "Danny's gonna take some time off. Old Sam talked him into it. You know how they are. Danny looks up to him, takes his advice, kind of like father and son."

The news wasn't what he wanted to hear, and he had to keep his voice calm so she wouldn't pick up on it. "Take time off?"

"You know Danny—usually just goes elk hunting in November with the guys, but he's gonna take his wife on a vacation. Old second honeymoon treatment and all."

His voice was O.K., but his pulse was spinning free. "Vacation, huh? Labor Day and all? Seems like that's their busy season."

She shrugged. "Women like Joanne—they get what they want out of men. Never have to work and go home with sore feet like I do. She wants a vacation; she gets a vacation. You aren't eating your pie. Is it really O.K.?"

105

He forced down two more bites and smiled at her. "The best. What time do you go home?"

"Three A.M. Pretty late, huh?"

He looked her up and down again. They all went for that; you could practically see them get wet. "For tonight. I have an appointment—business stuff. Where's Danny taking off to?"

"Didn't say. Sweetie, I wouldn't care *where* it was if somebody offered me a trip, you know? I'd go to Tacoma or Humptulips or wherever. . . ."

"Somebody told me you and Sam were pretty tight. Ask him to take you."

"Who said that?"

"Gee, I can't remember, but all I can say is he's a lucky man. You sure you two aren't engaged or something?"

She was still chuckling to herself, and trying to figure out what the old deputy could have said about her when he walked away.

In the lot behind the hotel, he slammed his fist into the Harley's leather seat. Take her away. Damn them! Never. He would not allow it, not now, not ever. He would watch her every minute of every day, and if they tried to take her, he would . . . He sat down on the old, scarred bike and closed his eyes. In a few moments the tension drained out of him and his mind was clear again.

Run, Danny. Take her and run as far as you want, but when you stop, I'll be right there.

Joanne dreaded the sound of the phone late at night when Danny was on duty. The voiceless presence could not have been Sonia; she and Walt were on their way to bed when she left. When Danny called her, they had a signal. Two rings, hang up, and then call again so she'd know it was he who called. Maybe the first two rings had sounded as she ran from the car; maybe she hadn't heard them. She dialed the office and Fletch assured her that everything was all right, that Danny and Sam had just gone back on the air after their coffee break. She called her mother, woke her, and heard the familiar impatient little sigh as she apologized.

POSSESSION

Joanne told herself that she was quite safe; nothing real had been taken from her. She was alone, but she was inside the farmhouse with her doors bolted. Her anxiety was familiar; she shouldn't be afraid for herself—only for Danny, riding somewhere out there in the dark, circling the county. He was a target, not she. Her rooms were safe behind drawn curtains and locked doors.

Joanne uncapped her vial of Librium, counted that there were sixteen tablets left, and allowed herself one—the first in a week. Maybe the phone call had just been a mistake.

In bed, with the drug already beginning to soften the sharpest points of worry, she drifted into a half-sleep but it was marred with echoes of Danny's words, the words cut off when Sam knocked at the back door. "Let me breathe, Joanne. . . . Sometimes I can't breathe without you wanting to know why. . . . I can't breathe. . . . You're so scared, you're making me scared."

Something—wind in the trees outside, a tapping against the house—roused her slightly and she turned over, looking for sleep on the other side of the wide bed. And remembered that she had sent him away again, puzzled and frustrated by her sullenness. A branch cracked and she heard it as a shot. She saw Danny falling dead. Again and again, his hand held out to ward off a bullet, a last agonized look on his face as he fell. She closed her eyes tight to strike the image, and another rushed in. She heard the impact as his squad car crashed and saw the brown-and-white unit reduced to crushed metal trapping her dead Danny.

Now Danny wasn't dead. He was only injured, and she was being rushed to the hospital to be with him. She would bring him back through her love and tender care. She would not leave his bedside; she would will him to be whole again and warm his skin back to life with her own.

She thought she could actually smell the hospital odor, and Danny's muscular arms were dark brown against the bandage and bedsheet white. Lying there like that, he seemed very sexy, and she felt a tickling beat in her crotch, an insistent heat there.

She was not asleep and not awake, but aware enough to glance toward the shade and see that it was not flush with the bottom of the window. She sighed and switched off the little light by the bed and then got up and pulled the shade all the way down and checked to see that the bedroom door was locked.

She lay back in bed and pictured the scene again. Danny, injured but alive, and herself sitting beside him, his hand clutching hers, holding onto her as if he would fall away forever if he lost touch. She could smell the bandages and iodine again, see his arms flex, and then, slowly, a small tent rising from the sheets where his erection pushed.

She leaned across to stroke his shoulder, and she felt his mouth nuzzling blindly against her breasts. She opened her blouse and put his mouth on her tingling nipple, cradling him as she let him suckle, knowing that she was keeping him alive.

Her fingers tugged and circled her nipple's rubbery hardness as Danny nursed at her in her mind, and she let one hand fall lightly between her legs, feeling how warm and moist she was. It wasn't bad if she didn't let her hand move; it was only daydreaming.

Danny's eyes were still closed, but his penis poked at her, fighting to get free of the knitted sheet. Still suckling his eager mouth, she pulled the cover away and saw his huge and dark hard-on trembling beneath his hospital gown, the eye of it wanting her mouth. Outside their white room, nurses and doctors were walking back and forth; they could come in any minute. She didn't care. She massaged his penis and he groaned and whimpered against her breast. She let him suck on her finger as she moved down in the bed. He tasted quite sweet where she licked him and drew the silken head into her mouth.

She wanted him so much that she felt swollen, and she couldn't stop. She mounted him, letting herself slide over his straining cock, feeling it push up. And then she rode him wildly, letting her breasts whip back and forth across his face, letting her own hand move fiercely over the pink nub between her legs.

POSSESSION

She saw the shocked faces at the doorway, saw them raise their hands to warn her away from Danny, and still she bucked on top of him triumphantly. When the feeling grew to bursting, the lover who had been dead beneath her except for his mouth and his cock threw back his head and shouted, and his voice shimmered up through her belly and down her thighs in waves that made her legs shake.

Joanne lay back and sobbed, horrified at what she had done, and still knowing at last what had been waiting at the top of the hill she'd never managed to climb. She walked shakily to the bathroom and bent over the sink, scrubbing her hand in the dark.

Duane padded around outside the farmhouse in the dark. He knew she was in there because he heard rustles of sound—a door slamming, the floorboards or maybe the bed creaking, and, finally, a sound as if someone inside wept. Maybe. It was hard to hear through the walls. He tried each window, quietly so that no one could possibly hear him, and found them all locked. He'd expected that the doors would be and they were. He could break in, shatter the glass to get to her. But that was risky; she might have enough time to get to the phone. He couldn't cut the line; it came down from the pole and entered near the roof, too high over even his head.

He wanted to smash and force his way in, but his common sense prevailed. Tomorrow, he could find her along the road, alone, with no walls between them at all. He would have to sleep outside in a close watching place to be sure he didn't miss her—or them, if the husband took her away. His sleeping bag was already on the back of the bike, and his saddlebags were packed now and ready. He didn't even have to go back to the crummy room.

He could see into the kitchen with its single dim light glowing, but no matter how he tried, he could not see into the room where he believed she slept. Reluctantly, he turned to leave and his foot pressed against the soft feathered body.

He took the bird with him, its fractured neck flopping

crazily over the saddlebags as he coasted down the long driveway.

He tossed it into the ditch below, and saw it disappear beneath the long grasses there.

She slept so soundly that she heard no sounds at all outside her window.

Part 2

STEHEKIN
September 4, 1981

7

The Lady of the Lake, broad-bowed and gleaming, bumped impatiently against the long, narrow dock and tugged at her lines. Beneath and around her, Lake Chelan mirrored the blue of the sky, so calm and flat that it seemed painted, the thick wash of it brilliant against the umber hills.

By 8:15 A.M., Joanne and Danny waited in line with a hundred other tourists behind the chain blocking the gangplank. Joanne saw the tension in the set of Danny's shoulders. He didn't really want to be here, and it had been Sam who'd convinced him to go, hurrying them both through immediate departure, as if their chance to leave would vanish if they didn't seize it. She'd packed in one day, wondering now what she'd forgotten to bring.

Joanne thought about the nights on the trails ahead, where she and Danny would curve around each other like spoons to shut out the cold, and was glad they had somehow managed this trip. She hooked her arm through Danny's and leaned over the rail to watch the sinuous forms in the shallows below them. Fish slid darkly beneath the surface and duck families circled, their necks craned expectantly for crumbs from above. They made her think of Billy Carter's disappearance, but she didn't want to bring that up again.

"Look honey," she pointed. "See how tame they are."

He wasn't looking. He was turned away from her, staring at the next dock where a sheriff's launch idled, spitting gray-brown smoke under the gap-planked pier. Everything in him seemed to pull away from her and he didn't notice when she released his arm. She watched him without hope, almost expecting him to walk away and start a conversation with the Chelan county deputies in the boat.

They moved into the seating area—green vinyl upholstered chairs, nine abreast, railed with white iron lattice work. She hesitated and Danny pulled her toward a window seat.

"You want a beer?"

"No. Not yet."

"I need one. How about coffee?"

"Sure. Great."

She looked up at his face bending over her, caught in bas relief by a shaft of sunlight. She could see a puffiness under his eyes, the creases in front of his ears, and a kind of fullness in his cheeks she had never noticed. With a jolt she realized she had not seen him close up in daylight for a long time, and now she saw that her husband was growing older. Not really old—not like the men she'd been watching in the line—but older. He wasn't the Danny she'd married; that one had slipped away without her knowing it. He bent his head, and she saw the sheen of his scalp through the hair at his temples. She reached out to touch his arm.

"Danny?"

"Yeah?"

"I love you."

He looked around, embarrassed, and grinned finally. "Me too."

The good moment stayed in the air even after he moved up the aisle. It was going to be O.K. They had come close to the edge of something, but they hadn't fallen over and they weren't going to now. He had come with her along the dark roads of morning, without sleep after his night's work, and they were on their way to a better place. A second chance.

The Lady of the Lake pulled out sluggishly at first, turning to port, past her sister ships, and then more smoothly as she eased past the "76" pump. Even after a hundred years of civilization, the town of Chelan here at the lake's edge looked tentative, threatened by the sere brown hills that lowered over it, muting the bright colors of houses with the sheer depth and breadth of brown, brown, brown. Close by the water, the land came alive in the rich green swaths of orchard after orchard.

Danny looked back at Joanne from his position on the

deck. She was playing with a kid in the seat in front of her, hiding her eyes with her fingers and then flashing peek-a-boo. The kid was laughing and jumping up and down. She should have her own; he owed her that much because she'd never broken even one promise to him. She didn't flirt, she didn't chippy, and she tried so damn hard.

He moved forward to the prow of the boat, edging past the tall man who stared up at the hills through binoculars and who grunted at his "Excuse me." The hills seemed greener now, but the water was slate blue and smooth, deeper as they plowed ahead. A transport that looked like a weathered wood catamaran headed toward them, its deck full of cars and an antique pickup. The boatman tooted and waved as the *Lady* sluiced by.

Danny thought about Sam—Sam who had pushed him into this trip by an invitation for a tour of his pit of a trailer. Sam had wiped out all of his own illusions; he had shown him what happened to cops who fucked their badges and lost their wives. The man didn't have *anything*. Heroes weren't supposed to evaporate like that—they weren't supposed to make you bleed for them. If Sam had lost it all along the way, where the hell was *he* going? Well, Sam had made his point, made it in spades, convinced him to go into Doc's office and try for half an hour to ejaculate into a glass beaker. He'd finally managed, handed the damned jar to Doc, and escaped. He still felt like a fool about it. And worse about seeing Sam's loneliness.

Danny couldn't shake his vague depression, and something more menacing that came with it, something that should not be part of the bright morning. The mountains ahead of them fell one upon the other, triangle against triangle, and their ridges were sharp and cruel. There was no end to it; when he expected to see the lake's furthest shore ahead, there were only more of the steel blue triangles, as if the boat they rode on was chugging steadily toward the end of the world.

He walked back to where Joanne sat, pretending that he had not left her alone for half an hour. He touched her hair and she leaned toward him, smiling too intensely.

"Hey babe, come on out on the deck with me. We're coming into Manson."

She shivered. "What an ugly name for such a pretty little town."

"How much farther?" he asked. "I thought you said it was just a little boat ride, and we're already in the middle of nowhere."

She looked at her watch. "A long ways. Three hours and fifteen minutes. I told you it was the end of the world."

He had thought it, and she had said it now. Probably that's where it had come from in the first place. They were committed to the water that stretched ahead, gliding past the looming, blank-faced rock walls.

There were no more clusters of houses, only a few cottages and trailers along the lake edges. The water was olive green and opaque and the fir trees had relinquished the hills to hardier pines. The landscape was crumpled and humbled by the grinding glaciers that had formed it, and it still bled streams of rock slides, boulders big enough to crush a man. Even the last telephone lines warned of danger; the black wires across the channel were strung with orange balls to alert seaplane pilots.

Danny had not slept for almost twenty-four hours and the fatigue made his eyes grainy, filled his muscles with lead. He should have slept a day before they started out; the effort of being cheerful and interested fatigued him more. He longed to lean against Joanne's shoulder and let his eyelids drop. Instead, he bought two beers and a mammoth homemade ham sandwich from the pleasant woman in the snack bar and carried them back to where Joanne sat.

The P.A. system buzzed, and the young pilot's voice boomed out, saving them from the effort of conversation.

"Welcome aboard *The Lady of the Lake*. Lake Chelan is fifty-two miles long, the deepest lake in the continental United States, formed by glaciers many, many centuries ago. This canyon was created millions of years ago when the Cascade Mountains were formed, and the lake dropped. River gravel and sand has been analyzed and confirmed seven to eight thousand feet above the present lake. The towns of Chelan and Manson rest on a natural earth plug."

"Fascinating," Danny muttered, and Joanne poked him. "Sorry."

"Indian tribes wintered over at Bitter Creek at Stehekin almost two hundred years ago; they called the lake 'bubbling water.' With the arrival of the white settlers, the Indians were moved to the Columbia Reservation. Prospectors moved in in the late 1800s—but Holden's copper claim was the biggest. The mine was closed in 1957; four to five hundred people live in the Lutheran camp there now. Some of you folks will be getting off at Holden Village for your retreat. The camp will have a jitney there waiting for you.

"When the white man arrived here, the lake level was 1,070 feet above sea level. It was raised 21 feet in 1927, for the power plant, and the Chelan Power Station and dam was the first in the state of Washington. Forty-eight streams and one river flow into Lake Chelan at all times, and there is one million, two hundred thousand acre feet of water outflow a year. This is a cold lake, ladies and gentlemen, and a clean lake; you can see thirty feet down. Below thirty feet, bodies will not rise to the surface. Otherwise they float after three or four weeks."

"That's cheery, too," Danny commented. "At least you know you won't rot if you fall in."

She turned toward the window, wondering why Danny's response to the mention of death was always sarcastic, and then knowing—as she always knew—that it frightened him.

". . . copper, lead, zinc, gold." The speaker continued. "M.E. Fields, the postmaster of Stehekin, built the Fields Hotel where the Stehekin River ran off the lake in the late 1800s and worked a package deal with the Great Northern Railroad to have *The Belle of Chelan, The Clipper,* and *The Stehekin* bring wealthy tourists in. M.E. put in crystal chandeliers, velvet drapes, grand piano, all as grand as Chicago and San Francisco—and all brought in by barge and boat. The hotel was covered over by the lake in 1927."

Joanne shivered. Despite the scenery, nothing of human endeavor and enterprise seemed to have lasted here: the Indians uprooted from their bubbling water, the mines deserted, and the hotel covered over. She wondered if it still existed under the lake's surface, with only ghosts playing its grand pianos for the silly girls coaxed into the wilderness by rich old men who promised them lobster and champagne and nights of dancing, and then wanted payment. She told herself she read too much fiction.

The big boat nudged the decrepit dock at Holden's Camp and the Lutherans on board debarked, decimating the passenger list. And then the mountains closed in tighter. The water was deep aqua and viscous, and the sun disappeared into the rock.

Danny looked at the lake and wished they had gone to Tahoe or Vegas.

The mountains came straight down into the water with no handholds out of peril. A drowning man, his blood chilling with hypothermia in the icy lake, would have as much chance of crawling out as someone in a glass-walled pit. The rock face went up and up and disappeared into storm clouds thousands and thousands of feet above. He thought he could see a harbor in the distance and checked his watch. Less than an hour to go and all signs negative. He cursed Sam silently, closed his eyes, and fell asleep immediately.

Up on top of the boat, the red-headed man with the binoculars smiled as he focused on the moving white form high above the water and watched a mountain goat tread a clearly impossible path.

8

Danny woke—minutes, hours, days later?—his face pressed against Joanne's bare arm, his mouth dry and bitter tasting. Her flesh was tender now, accepting him, cradling him as she held one of his hands in hers. They would make it up—they always did. He sat up, wiping his mouth and stretching in the same movement, bringing one hand down to caress her neck.

"We here?"

She smiled at him, but her eyes were hidden from him behind her sunglasses. "We're docking now. There's the lodge."

He had expected a village, a colorful settlement cut deeply into the mountains at the lake's end, but the wilderness had given only grudgingly of itself, allowing perhaps three hundred feet from the shore to the firs and pines that loomed over the half-dozen structures. A foothold, but nothing more. The building directly in front of them was long and rectangular, its southern wing two-stories, and topped with a corrugated metal roof. In front of the lodge, a planked deck guarded with a fence made of staggered one-by-sixes was dotted with picnic tables.

He was disappointed; he'd pictured a rustic log cabin lodge, and he saw buildings that reminded him of a small-town motel built in the 1950s. There was a broad apron of concrete at dockside that appeared to be the dead end of a road that snaked along the woods to the north to accommodate, presumably, the motley vehicles parked in front of the lodge: old cars—fifties cars to match the architectural style of the lodge—and Forest Service pickups and vans, motorcycles, bicycles.

The whole settlement seemed to be temporary, nothing more than a slight irritant on the flank of the mountains, the forest so dense that it looked like a gently undulating black-green sea.

He did not want to go into that maze of trees and trails and climb straight up toward the dead blue sky. He knew it was too late to change his mind. They had come too far. Danny envied the tourists who would eat their lunches on the deck, buy souvenirs, and be back in their own beds by nightfall.

His legs still heavy from sleep that was not really sleep, he moved to the open hold door and retrieved their backpacks.

The crowd milled with subdued expectancy, the bulk of them city people who seemed awed by the mountains, a few of them obviously skilled hikers who grabbed their gear and moved to wait in line for the vans that would carry them uptrail to begin their ascents. The boatmen finished unloading suitcases and packs and turned to crates of liquor, meat, produce, and clean laundry for the lodge.

Danny, seeing Joanne walk confidently toward a white Samoyed standing in the back of a Forest Service pickup, started to shout, "No!" but relaxed when the dog allowed itself to be hugged and nuzzled. She trusted too much. Damn. One day she was going to get bitten; she assumed the whole damn world would respond to love and kindness.

"Danny! Come over here and meet this fellow. Isn't he neat?"

He reached out his hand to the dog, who reared back, distrusting some scent on it, and then yelped.

The ranger grinned at him.

"He likes ladies best—and kids—but he's not too sure about men."

Danny held out his hand. "Danny Lindstrom, deputy from down in Natchitat. You guys the law around here?"

The ranger shrugged. "What there is of it. We don't have the kind of problems you guys do. Keep track of the hikers and make sure they come back or make it over the top to the North Cascades Highway. Not much crime up here—too hard to get out."

"That figures. No place to run, I guess."

The ranger laughed. "Oh, we had one poor slob—robbed the post office over in Malott and headed over here. He liked to starved to death, finally killed him a deer, but he practically threw himself into our arms when we found him wandering around in circles."

Danny smiled absently, staring beyond the buildings at the blue-gray mountains. "What if somebody gets hurt?" he asked, turning back to the ranger. "How in hell do you get somebody out in an emergency?"

"Ernie Gibson can get up here from Chelan in his float

plane in twenty minutes if he pushes, and there's a landing strip toward High Bridge for a regular plane to take off in a pinch. We've been lucky though—haven't had anything we couldn't handle. The Chelan county boys have their launch docked down lake, and they can run the lake a lot faster than the *Lady*. You on vacation?"

"Yeah. The wife put her foot down. Said I was working too hard?"

The ranger looked at Joanne appreciatively, and Danny put a proprietary hand on her hipbone. She nodded and smiled.

"This is your dog? He's beautiful."

"Thanks. He's called McGregor after that mountain over there." He turned back to Danny. "You going backpacking?"

"Tomorrow. The wife's got it all plotted out—up to Rainbow Lake, camp out there, and head back here probably. How's the fishing?"

"Fishing's good. Mosquitos are better. You got some insect repellant?"

"Hell, I hope so. She packed *everything*. You know women."

The men laughed, and the ranger moved toward the door of his truck. "Be sure you sign in at our office over there before you head up—so's we know where to find you if you don't come back."

"We'll do that."

Duane had a coke and a burger on the deck, watched Danny leave the Forest Service office, and waited until he'd disappeared into the lodge. He strolled over to the office, pulled the register toward himself and pretended he was about to sign it. When the ranger on duty turned away, Duane read down the list and saw "Lindstrom, Danny, Joanne: Rainbow Lake. Est. Ret: 9-7-81." He closed the book and grabbed a handful of maps and trail guides.

He knew where they were going, and he could study how to get there. Lucky he had his sleeping bag, and there was a little grocery store to stock up. He would not have to wait for them and follow them; it would be better if he went on ahead to reconnoiter. It would give him the advantage. When he walked out, he saw Joanne and Danny climbing the steps toward the lodge office, and felt the pang of knowing that she would be with the other man for one more night at the very least, closed in behind shingled walls.

It could not be helped; he would not think about it.

He caught the shuttle bus with the summer baby-ranger, jammed in with hardcore hikers eager to start up and make camp before nightfall. Three miles to the trailhead. He could have just as easily walked—and should have, damn it. Duane was out and turned away from the rig when the kid called him back, "Sir?"

He turned back, keeping his expression bland and free of the annoyance he felt, the slight apprehension.

"We need your destination, sir. If you'll sign this, put in your name, where you're headed, and when you're due back, I'll let the head ranger know."

"Sure. Fine. But I'm not coming back in. I'm going over the top and pick up the trail to the highway. What do you figure it will take me?"

"Ten hours—depending. Watch out for the rattle-snakes."

"Thanks." He scribbled on the clipboard held out to him: "David S. Dwain, Portland, Oregon. Destination: North Cascades Highway."

And it was true. That was his initial destination, a hop, skip, and a jump from the Canadian border, and once over, endless freedom. He liked the name Stehekin, liked its meaning: "The way through." He always found a way through, no matter how narrow the opening or how difficult. If the body could not insinuate itself through blocked passages, the mind always could.

His pack was light, his elation diminishing the weight on his back. He was alone, with the river rushing behind him, the empty trail ahead.

* * *

POSSESSION

Danny watched her unpack, carefully putting away the jar of instant coffee, powdered cream, sugar, eggs, and bacon in the kitchen that was as equipped as their own at home.

"Joanne," he teased. "You call this roughing it? We've got a bathroom with a shower and a tub and a goddamned flush toilet! We've got electricity and a smoke alarm."

"Only for tonight. Tomorrow: the wilderness."

She bent over to look under the sink, and he moved behind her, his arms encircling her waist, pulling her back against him.

"He wanted you," Danny whispered into her ear.

She held her breath. "Who?"

"Who? That guy."

He forced her against the hard sink, one hand holding her buttocks, the other on her breasts, reassuring himself that he owned her.

"You mean the boatman? Or the kid who brought the sheets? That's who, right? The kid who brought the sheets?" She laughed but it came out hollow; she didn't really enjoy this game.

"The ranger. He thought you were some kind of woman."

"The dog liked me too."

She twisted around until she was tight against him. "Does that turn you on? Is that what it takes?"

He stepped away from her, startled. "What does that mean?"

"What if I was ugly? What if nobody else wanted me? Would you still want me?"

"Come on, Joanne. I came over here to be a little bit friendly, and you—"

"I should be enough by myself; you should be able to get turned on without seeing me reflected in some guy's eyeballs."

"That's kind of sick, Joanne."

She walked over to him and put her head on his chest, tugging his arms around her. "I'm sorry, Danny. I guess I'm nervous. It seems like a honeymoon. Remember how nervous I was the first time? I'm sorry."

"Just don't take offense at everything I say. O.K.?" He brushed her hair away from her face and looked at her, and she thought that it was all right again.

"O.K. Kiss me?"

"You got it."

His hands moved down to her buttocks and he pulled her close to him, responding to her.

"Wait. Let me just take a quick shower."

"I like you the way you smell now."

She pulled free of him carefully. "Just a few minutes. Wait right here for me."

"You're not going to slip into something more comfortable, are you?"

She grinned. "I'm not going to slip into anything at all."

"That's more like it."

"Stay right there, and close your eyes."

"You close your eyes. I'll be looking."

She showered for a long time, trying to wash away the awkwardness and her feeling that she was only playing a part. Wanting to let go, and be what he seemed to want. Naked and feeling slightly foolish, she stepped out into the living room.

He was asleep, fallen on his side on the plaid couch, his legs sticking out through the maple arms, one cushion held viselike against his chest. She tried to wake him and move him into the bedroom where he would be more comfortable, but he only groaned and she gave up. He deserved to sleep undisturbed; he had to be exhausted.

The room, so recently bright with sun, had darkened and she felt cold. She wrapped herself in a blanket and crouched by the window watching the sun lose itself behind the clouds eating up the mountain peaks. Lightning darted jagged tongues into the lake, and moments later the building shook in sympathetic vibration with the thunder that followed. Danny jerked in his dreams, but slept on.

She wondered about the hikers who had headed uptrail when they docked. Were they up there now seeking shelter under a rock ledge or a mass of fir boughs? Were they

POSSESSION

frightened, sorry that they'd left the safety of the lodge down below them? No. They would be prepared for storms or they wouldn't be up there. She was grateful for the roof over their heads. She had not expected that the mountains would be so high or the forest so thick that the sun died in it.

She shivered; a rabbit had walked over her grave.

Joanne wondered if she asked Danny to stay with her in the lower valley if he would. Not likely. She'd heard him tell the ranger they were going up and maybe over the top, and his pride wouldn't allow him to change his mind even if he wanted to. They would be out there by tomorrow night, somewhere on the mountain in a place hidden now behind the clouds, beyond returning.

She turned on the kitchen light and the illumination made the room look normal and safe again: white enameled stove and refrigerator, linoleum in the same pattern as her mother's kitchen, red-and-white checked curtains, a bunch of wild sweetpeas in a water glass in the window. The light warmed her and she made coffee and a bologna sandwich, chewing and sipping in deliberate movements as she pored over the pamphlets on how to stay alive and healthy in the wilderness.

The storm drained itself of fury, leaving only a soft rain that picked at the roof and then pattered gently into the ferns and berry thickets outside. He did not wake, and she left him in the dusky living room and carried a paperback novel into the bedroom, reading in the narrow light of the bedside lamp. She was caught up easily in the story of the gothic heroine who worshipped the cruel, brooding wastrel son of a wealthy English family. The heroine came together with him every twenty pages or so, but the sex was only vaguely erotic. There was nothing for her to match herself against and come up lacking. Crashing waves and shooting stars and heaving breasts. She wished it was really so easy.

Without expecting to, she slept—through the evening and into the night, lulled by the rain. When she woke near dawn, Danny was beside her, still dressed in his T-shirt and jeans. She molded herself against him and fell softly asleep

1 2 5

again. When she woke, it was daylight. Good strong daylight, and Danny was in the living room checking out their gear. The strangeness of yesterday had evaporated with the raindrops.

9

The shuttle bus hurtled north along the Stehekin River Road toward the High Bridge turnaround, apparently without shocks to cushion the jolting, bucking ride. The driver, a young temporary Forest Service employee, kept up a steady monologue.

"That log cabin there on the right is the grade school, fifteen students up to grade eight, and the little cabin out back—well, that's just what it looks like. They got some flush toilets in there but the ecology guys won't let them use them. The Field Hotel was over there, but it went when they dammed the lake in '27. The Golden West Museum back by the lodge still has some of the wood from it. Over on your right—that's an organic vegetable garden. The guys who run it sell to the restaurant at the lodge and they bake the pies too. Boysenberry this week. Great pies. You eat there last night?"

Danny shook his head. "We meant to, but we overslept. Have to give it a try when we come back down, unless we decide to go on over and into Okanogan County."

"Food's good. Now, look back there to the right, way back in there behind the trees there. That's all that's left of the Rainbow Falls Lodge."

They looked and saw only what looked like a pile of weathered boards and a sagging roof. Joanne had a momentary flash of the dead barn at home and heard the sighing beyond it again. She shut her eyes and it washed away.

"Old gal named Lydia George ran the Rainbow Falls Lodge in the early 1900s. Her brother—forget his name—

POSSESSION

was a miner, lived there with her. Winter of 1909–1910, it snowed and snowed and snowed. They finally had to use thirty-two lengths of stovepipe to clear the snowpack on the roof. Kind of took the heart out of Lydia's business."

"What happened to her?" Joanne asked.

"Don't know. Must be dead by now."

Danny laughed. "Unless she's 110."

Joanne looked back at the sad little pile of timber, wondering what lost dreams Lydia might have had. "Do they have a cemetery up here?"

"Someplace, but only the old-timers know where it is. People die up here now, they take them out on the boat and bury them in Chelan or Wenatchee." The boy was so young, a college boy from Indiana or Ohio, and she could see cemeteries were of little import to him. He was pointing to trees on the left of the road, hard by the river. "Notice how they're all charred black on the south side? A firestorm blew through the valley in 1889 and took out most of the timber. The ones that survived still have those burn marks on them, but they kept on growing just the same. The Indians say there'll be a forest fire every ninety years. Always has been; always will be. When it comes down the valley, it takes everything in its path."

"Then you're due for one," Danny said. "Is that why they never built up farther into the trees?"

The driver shrugged. "Might be. The only way out would be the lake."

The shuttlebus slowed and stopped, and the driver climbed on top of it and threw their packs down. He gave his instructions to Danny.

"You've got eleven miles up to Rainbow Lake. It's not easy, but it's not too rough either. Watch for the signs and be careful of rattlers and rock slides. If you go on over, it's seventeen miles to Bridge Creek. Be sure you hang your food up when you make camp. You can't just put it up a tree; the bears will shinny up and have it. You have to suspend it ten feet up and five feet between the trees on a rope—that frustrates them."

"*Are* there bears?" Joanne asked.

"They're up there. Black bears mostly. They won't bother you unless you get between a she-bear and a cub; so don't ever do that. There might be a few grizzlies left, but the last verified sighting was in 1965. We haven't seen *any* kind of bear down in the lower valley this summer, so I wouldn't worry about it. Just follow normal precaution."

They started up, with Joanne leading the way. Yesterday's rain might never have fallen; it was dry and rocky underfoot on the steadily upward trail. They passed a reservoir and she worried at leaving it behind, although their canteens were full. She tried to concentrate on the vegetation, all of it proof that living things had defied the fire and the animals and rockslides: ferns, bracken and fiddle-head, elderberry, daisies, butter-and-eggs, mock orange, salmonberry, wild sweetpeas, wild phlox, kinnikinick, and flowering moss. They moved easily as their muscles warmed and their breathing coordinated, although Danny puffed more heavily than she did. She felt happier, and then simply happy.

The trail switched back and the incline's angle was steeper now. They stopped at a knoll and looked down, seeing the tops of evergreens below and the lake, blue as cornflowers between the mountains that held it. He draped an arm lightly over her shoulders.

"You had one hell of a good idea, kid. We're on top of the world."

"Not yet. Look behind us."

He looked over at the trail still ahead and groaned, flopping down on the grass, pulling her with him.

"I'm going to tell you two secrets—if you promise never to tell anyone."

She nodded her head and realized he had never told her even one true secret.

"One. And no 'I told you so's.' I am not in very good shape. My legs hurt. My back hurts. My goddamn *butt* hurts." He held up his hand to silence her. "Two. I am afraid of snakes. I am fucking terrified of snakes. Not just your rattlers that you're exposing me to. Garter snakes. King snakes. Corn snakes. Blue racers. Rubber boas. Anything that slides through the grass or out from under rocks and sneaks up on me. Are you going to laugh?"

"No." She reached for his hand. *"No.* I wouldn't laugh. I'm glad that you felt you could admit it to me. I'm afraid of so many things, and I thought nothing frightened you. I'm glad you're afraid of snakes. Most people are."

"Are you?"

"What?"

"Afraid of snakes?"

She pondered it. "No, I don't think so. I used to have pet garter snakes when I was little; I carried them around in my sweater pockets and fed them chicken livers."

She moved closer to him, reluctant to let the moment go. "Do you want to know what I am afraid of? Really afraid of?"

"Sure. Lay a few of them on me. I earned it."

"O.K. Let me think." She looked away from him, concentrating on the lake far below. "Well, I'm afraid of being dumb—"

"You're not—"

"Let me finish. I didn't interrupt you, and if you stop me, I might lose my nerve. So, by being dumb, I mean that I was never expected to be anything but pretty and nobody has ever shared anything with me that called for a serious opinion. People talk over me and around me. It takes me longer to verbalize what I mean—and then the chance is gone. What I say is of little value."

He started to speak and then said only, "O.K. What else?"

"I'm afraid of being alone. I'm afraid of losing you. And . . . I'm afraid of ghosts."

"Ghosts? Ghosts in white sheets?"

"Are you teasing me now?"

"No."

"Ghosts that watch me. Ghosts that wait for me in old buildings and lonely places as if I owed them something— as if there was something I should have done and now it's too late."

He was quiet for a long time and their breathing was

louder than the forest noises. "I felt something when we were on the boat—something like that. I wanted to turn around and go home."

"Why didn't you say something?"

"It was nothing real; it was just a feeling."

"Feelings are real. Do you want to go back now?"

"No." He rubbed her back with the palm of his hand. "It's gone now, whatever it was—probably just felt guilty leaving Sam back there working alone."

"He was the one that talked you into coming away with me, wasn't he? How did he do it?"

He could not tell her the feelings he'd had in his partner's dirty, empty trailer. It would be a betrayal.

"He said I was lucky to have you, and if I didn't watch out you'd be running away with the Fuller Brush man."

She laughed at the old joke. "He's misinformed. It's the milkman I want."

"Well, something along that line. 'You don't realize what you have until it's gone.' Sam's not one of your great philosophers. He just said to get my ass out of there and spend some time with my wife."

"I owe him."

"Yeah."

"But I *love* you," she said quietly. "And I'm greedy for all the time I can get."

He held out a hand and pulled her to her feet, holding her against him. And then they were climbing again, the high noon sun focused on their exposed skin, making them sweat with the heat of it as well as their exertion.

The trails were well marked and they made the two miles to the juncture with the Boulder Creek Trail within the hour. They detoured a half-mile to a point above the falls, hearing the roar of the endless cascade long before they saw the falls themselves tumbling for hundreds of feet down the mountainside in hypnotic continuum. Joanne moved toward the spray of suspended droplets in the air, and Danny held her back.

"No."

POSSESSION

"But it feels so cool. I want to take off my clothes and let it touch me."

He held her still. "And I'd like to see that. But the ground could give way and you'd be part of it."

She pulled her eyes away from the plunging water and followed him back to a safer vista. "It's dangerous up here, isn't it? Everything looks so beautiful, but someplace underneath it, you know it could kill you."

He led her back to the hot trail and they hiked steadily without speaking, the big lake diminishing behind them. There were no other hikers; they might well have been the only humans on the mountainside. The trail was capricious, punishing them with a maze of switchbacks that tried the muscles of their aching legs, and then turning suddenly into meadow paths choked with valerian and daisy-mimicking fleabane, Jacob's ladder, everlasting, and creeping phlox, a vista like the fairy gardens in children's storybooks. They stopped in a meadow and ate the last of the bologna sandwiches, drank warmed water, and kissed like high school lovers.

Duane had traversed it all before on stronger legs, but his first night on the mountain had been miserable. The storm had drenched him in his sleeping bag, and insects rose from Rainbow Lake to sting and bite his exposed face and hands moments after the rain ceased. And in the black black just before dawn he became anxious. What if they had taken another trail? What if the storm had kept them away from the mountain?

He waited until noon, hearing the call of the loons and high wind in the pines. He headed south over his own tracks, searching for them. Up. Then sharply down past the trilling of the small falls to a place where he could see the spread of meadow. He crouched there, watching, for most of the afternoon. The sounds came before sight, laughter bouncing off trees and multiplying its vibrations back to him, before he could make out their images in his binoculars. What if they weren't alone? If a party of four or more crossed the meadows, the challenge for him would be increased ten-fold for each doubling. He held his breath as he saw them emerge from the wall of pines—the woman first, and then the man. Only two. And he knew them even before their features were clearly defined, recognized her movement from all the hours he'd watched her, graceful as only slender, fragile women are. The man moved stolidly and betrayed fatigue.

They did not see him in his watching place, secure in their belief that they were alone, their eyes cast down upon the trail as they walked toward him.

He watched for as long as he dared, reluctant to lose her in his glasses, and then he turned and ran silently back to the green lake and the hidden camp he had chosen for himself a hundred yards beyond the favored campsites. Sunset was still hours beyond. He would watch to see their exact location of encampment, and then sleep easily in his hidden blind and regain the hours he had lost to the night's anxiety, sleep with the sun orange on his shuttered eyelids, while his gear dried out and his body warmed for the things he would demand of it.

They crouched next to the fire Danny had built and battled the onslaught of mosquitos, clouds of stinging gnats. Joanne dotted 6-12 on her face and hands and then anointed her husband with the greasy liquid. The sun was gone, leaving a fluorescent glow in the western sky where the treetops were black tracings, the air as chilled as pebbles in a creek bottom. Their shirts were pulled over their hands and their pants tucked into their socks as much for warmth as to form a barrier against the mosquitos, and she moved closer to Danny to let the heat of their bodies combine, realizing that they were truly in the wilderness. They had come to the place hidden behind the storm clouds she'd watched yesterday; their legs had carried them five thousand feet above the big lake and eleven miles from the shelter of the warm rooms behind them. She was not afraid, but subdued by the way the mountain changed when the sun left it. Even the sounds were different.

POSSESSION

On every side of them—rustling, scrabbling, a swishing as if something glided through the grasses, and somewhere, far into the trees, a crashing of brush. The birds no longer sang, but she could hear the beating of wings occasionally above them. She looked at Danny, and he seemed not to hear the hidden life around them; he gazed into the fire and puffed on a cigar, fascinated by the flames.

She was tired, exhausted really, and her legs trembled still from the day's exertion, but she was not ready yet to trust enough to crawl into her sleeping bag and sleep. Something could come for her while she slept, and she would not know her enemy until it was too late. At that moment, a woman's scream sang through the woods, leaving a silence that seemed endless. She threw both her arms around Danny's neck and buried her face into his chest, and then was startled to feel his laughter rumble against her face.

He held her against him and whispered, "Hey, babe—that's nothing that will hurt you. It's a cougar—a *lady* cougar—with the hots. She's not looking for us; she's after a mate. I hope it turns him on, because it's not doing a thing for me."

"Are you sure?"

"I'm sure. If we freak over every sound up here, they'll have to come get us and take us to the Home for the Bewildered. I thought you said you wanted to go out in the wilderness and rough it—so this is it. Too rough for you?"

She drew away and shook her head. "No, but you'll have to admit it's different. I guess we should have camped out in the backyard at home for a while to get used to it, kind of ease into it. I know what—let's sing."

"You're kidding."

"No. That's what we always did at camp around the campfire." Her voice quavered and then grew stronger. "I love to go swimming with bow-legged women and dive between their legs."

"Joanne, you didn't sing that at Girl Scout camp, did you? No wonder you grew up to be such an animal."

"We sang *terrible*, filthy songs every time we had the chance. We put rubbers in the counsellor's make-up kit, and

133

ran Kotex up the flagpole—only nobody ever accused me because I was such a good little girl."

He sang with her while the night settled over them, obliterating first the treetops and then everything except the fire and the moon's silver quarter. "Yellow Submarine," and "Eleanor Rigby," and "Fight On for Natchitat High." He was an awful singer; she understood why he never sang in church. Their voices floated over the dark lake and drowned in it.

She sang alone for him, no longer afraid, in a high sweet soprano. "Our house is a very, very, very fine house with two cats in the yard. Life used to be so hard; now everything is easy 'cause of you—"

He moved so suddenly, his hand into his backpack and emerging with the gun, that she was singing when she heard him say, "Who's th—" with the song still in her throat and spilling out unheard. She turned from him and saw the figure loom behind the fire. The creature-thing was so large and it had crept up on them even as she sang for her husband, its face black as the night around them, the shape of it blurred and part of the night too. When it spoke, she was astounded to discover that it was human.

Danny did not relax, but stood in one fluid movement, the gun in his hand part of him, and a part of him that she had never seen. The man across the fire slowly raised his arms.

"Easy, friend. I'm no Sasquatch. Just a dummy who ran into a bear and hightailed it into the woods. Put your torch on me. I'll keep my hands up."

Danny grunted at her and she felt along the ground for the flashlight she'd used earlier and pushed the switch forward. The cone of light swept over her husband first, and she saw him holding his revolver in both hands, legs wide, his attention entirely on the man before him. She moved her wrist toward the stranger's voice and he appeared, a big man, inches taller than Danny, his eyes glowing red as a fox's in the beam. His hands were open and quite empty. Danny hesitated, and then slid the gun into his belt.

POSSESSION

"Sorry," he said. "You startled me. We thought we were alone."

"I thought I was alone," the man answered. "Scared the shit out of me . . ." He glanced at Joanne and said, "Sorry." He lowered his hands deliberately and stood, seemingly embarrassed, waiting for an invitation to come into their space.

"How long have you been up here?" Danny asked, and she could hear his voice was normal now; the impulse to attack washed away from it.

"Hell—sorry—I don't know where I am. I came up on the boat yesterday and lit out for the hills, got caught in the storm last night, and started out for Early Winters this morning. Then I met a she-bear and two cubs on the trail. Spent half today up a tree, and the other half trying to figure out where the hell I was. When I heard singing—a woman singing—I thought I'd either died and gone to heaven or round the bend. Hey, I'm sorry to butt in."

Danny took the flashlight from Joanne and shone it into the man's face, and the last trace of tension left him. "You came up on the boat we were on—right? Saw you up top. Come on in, buddy. Joanne, give the man something to eat."

"No, thanks, ma'am," the stranger said softly. "I ate some dried stuff when I was up the tree, and frankly, I guess I've been too scared to have an appetite."

Danny added logs to the fire and the embers exploded into flames that cast yellow light over them, letting her see the man completely for the first time. He was younger than Danny and taller, a red-looking man. Coppery hair that the firelight turned magenta, red eyes, animal eyes, and the kind of skin with blood vessels close to the surface. He was quite handsome, but she did not like looking at him; his redness made her feel faint.

He held out his hand to Danny; he had barely glanced at her. "David Dwain," he said. "From Portland. How come you're carrying a .38? Most guys come up here with a rifle— if they can sneak a gun in."

1 3 5

"Would a plumber go camping without his plunger?" Danny laughed. "I'm a cop—feel naked without it. Almost took your head off too, creeping out of the woods like that. Name's Lindstrom, Danny—we're from Natchitat, and this is the wife, Joanne."

The stranger looked at her without interest, and slid his bedroll off his back. He grinned at Danny.

"I came up here to get away from it all, but it looks like you can't shake it. I'm a cop too. Multnomah County Sheriff's Office." He turned finally toward Joanne. "So you're pretty well protected, ma'am. You got yourself two lawmen to scare the varmints off."

He lies. The thought bloomed and then disintegrated. Of course he was a cop; he had the look. She had only just gotten Danny back, and already he was slipping into his man-man thing, urging her to wait on the stranger, pulling his pint of whiskey from their supplies. She ladled reconstituted beef stew out of the kettle and saw with some satisfaction that it was lukewarm now as she poured it on a plate for him. He took it from her with an absent nod, his whole attention fastened on his conversation with Danny.

A mosquito stung her cheek and she slapped it away dead, felt the pop of its blood-filled sac on her cheek. She moved closer to Danny, and he put his arm around her, but his mind was on the red man. He was always like this when he met another cop; they had their own language and they were like dogs sniffing each other, checking out mutual acquaintances, and then settling happily into war stories.

She stared sullenly into the flames and heard only bits of their conversation.

"You got a real antique of a jail down there, I hear," Danny was saying.

"Rocky Butte? It's better than it was—since they filled in the moat and closed the dungeon. Our offices are some better too. They moved us out of the courthouse and put us out on Glisan by the airport. Don't have any windows, but they painted it before we moved in."

"You like Checks?"

"Let's say it's a challenge. Some of those paper hangers

are smarter than hell. We had one person—and I mean a really, gorgeous person. Bounced them at I. Magnin and Meier and Frank's Designer Shop so fast, she was out of town before they ever hit the bank. I picked her up in San Francisco and she was livid. Outraged dignity until she saw I was really going to put the cuffs on her. Then she flings her arms around me and starts sobbing and offering what you call sexual favors."

"You're shitting me."

"Naw. In other circumstances, I would have gone for it, but. . . . So I pull away and she's still hanging on and shaking—and her wig fell off and I like to shit. She's bald. Only it's better than that. She's not a *she*—she's a he. One of the best-looking broads I've ever seen, and it's not even female. He started to cry and kick and the motel manager says to me, 'You shouldn't be so rough with a woman'; so I grab one tit in each hand and pull and they end up around the paperpusher's hips, and you never saw such a look as that manager's face. Hell, I had to buy the guy straight clothes to bring him back on United. All he had was dresses."

Danny was loving it. Joanne had to urinate; she tried to ignore the pressure in her bladder, but it only got worse. She whispered to Danny, and he turned to her impatiently: "Well *go,* baby. You've got the whole woods out there."

"Danny." She tugged at his sleeve and felt like a child. "I'm not going out there by myself."

"We'll be right here. You don't have to go very far. Take the flashlight."

"Danny." She was embarrassed and she hated the interloper with a passion that startled her, hated Danny too. "Come with me."

"O.K." He turned toward the stranger and laughed. "The wife's got to take a whiz. Scared of the woods. We'll be back."

"Don't go too far in," he warned. "I don't think I've come that far since I ran into the bears; I've got a feeling I've been circling. Holler if you need help."

They moved away from the clearing and Danny pointed the flashlight toward a fallen log. "Go on, babe. Hurry up."

"Well don't shine it *on* me for heavens' sake. He can see me."

"He's not looking. Dammit, Joanne, go ahead and pee; it's freezing out here."

She squatted just beyond the perimeter of the circle of light and struggled to hold her jeans away from the stream of urine, her buttocks vulnerable to the cold air and whatever was beneath her. She heard a splattering sound from Danny's direction. Everything was easier for men; *they* didn't risk getting poison oak all over their private parts—all they had to do was haul it out and go. She pulled up her jeans now and felt the wet spots at the waist already turning cold and clammy. If he wasn't so damned impatient, she wouldn't have missed.

"You done?" He wasn't waiting for her; he'd already turned, ready to go back.

"Danny!" It was a hiss, furious.

"What now?"

"Come here! Stop a minute."

"What?"

"I don't like that man. I don't want to camp with him."

"Joanne. . . ." His voice was heavy with annoyance. "Joanne, we've got no choice. You want me to boot him out and send him downtrail when it's pitch dark? If the animals didn't get him, he'd fall off the mountain."

"There's something wrong with him."

"What?"

"I don't know. He just sneaks up on us, and you welcome him like he's an old buddy, but he makes my skin crawl. How do you know who he is, really?"

He sighed. "Joanne, he's O.K. He knows who he's supposed to know, and he talks the language. Besides, I saw his I.D."

"When?"

"When you were cooking. You think if he was some kind of pervert he'd be up here? It's not exactly your prime stalking grounds."

POSSESSION

"Maybe it is."

He turned away from her and then said, "I think you're mad because things aren't going just exactly the way you want. You're acting like a spoiled little girl, and you'd better learn that people have to adjust to circumstances. He'll be gone when it's daylight."

"I don't like him."

"Then don't like him. I'm going back. Are you coming with me?"

He walked away, taking the light with him, and she ran to catch up. The stranger was running her supplies and cooking gear along a rope he'd tied between two fir trees. Danny grabbed the end of the rope and held it taut as the big man positioned the canvas sack equidistant between the trunks.

"I know I'm spooky," he grinned at her. "But after today, I think we'd better be extra careful that we don't make ourselves an attractive target. I hope you don't mind?"

She shook her head, wordless, and she would not return his smile.

"This wasn't my first encounter with old Brer Bear. I was in Glacier Park in 1979, when one of the lodge girls was killed." He paused, and his voice was tight when he continued. "I was in the party that found her, and it was . . . an . . . ugly thing. Grizzly took her arm and half her head . . ."

"Hey," Danny said, jerking his head toward Joanne. "Maybe we better talk about that in the daylight."

"Sorry."

She would not let it go. "Why do you hike then, Mr. Dwain? Why don't you stay down in Portland where it's safe?"

She had asked the question, but he looked at Danny when he answered, dismissing her. "I guess I don't like to think any creature can stop me from doing what I like, don't like to be scared off. But it's made me cautious. Anyway, the girl in Glacier had a dog with her and was sleeping in a tent with her supplies. Broke all the rules."

"So she deserved what she got?" Joanne's voice was hard.

"Joanne!"

"Nobody deserved that, ma'am. I'm sorry I made you nervous. I shouldn't have brought it up."

She bent down and grabbed her bedroll, picked at the knot that held it in a tightly-packed sausage. "I'm going to sleep now. It's late." She waited for Danny to say he was coming with her, but he had turned away and was pouring whiskey for the red-headed man.

She lay six feet from them, watching their silhouettes against the fireglow, hearing fragments of conversation about guns and sex and arrests, their voices deep and rumbling and then bursting into laughter that seemed drunken. She watched the moon move across the sky. It was very, very late when Danny turned to her, fumbling at the zipper to her sleeping bag. He was singing in slurred, sibilant phrases.

"Please come down and let me in, please come down and let me in. Please come down and let me in. I'm Barnacle Bill, the Sailor—"

She turned on her side and pretended sleep, but he was persistent, sliding the zipper down slyly, letting icy air creep under her shirt and up her spine like a snake. She pushed his hand away and pulled the zipper back up.

"Baby?"

She stayed silent.

"You mad?"

"I'm asleep. Go to sleep."

"Let me in. It's cold, and I can't get my fucking bedroll untied."

"Cut it. Bite the cord in two. You're a big, strong man."

"You're mad at me. Joanne's mad at me, and it's cold out here. Come on, honey, don't fool around. Let me in."

"Go sleep with Pistol Pete from Portland."

"He smells."

She laughed. "So do you."

Even drunk, he saw that she had weakened and he played on it. "But you're used to the way I smell. Joanne . . . Joanne, remember how I said I was afraid of snakes. Well, for God's sake, let me in. I'm scared to mess around with my bedroll."

POSSESSION

He made her remember the good time on the trail, and she let herself think that tomorrow would be better.

"O.K. But no fooling around."

"Absolutely not. It never occurred to me. I'm just so fucking cold I couldn't get it up anyway. I swear."

She let him enter her canvas capsule and felt that he was naked and hard. He was on top of her, pinning her backbone to the pine-needle-carpeted turf beneath her.

"You *lied.*"

"I know," he giggled. "I'm a rotten, filthy, stinking liar."

He pawed at her jeans, managing to slide them off her hips and down somewhere to the bottom of the sleeping bag.

"Danny, we can't. Where is he?"

He kissed her mouth and ears, gluing his face to hers as she tried to turn away from him. "Him? He's to hell and gone over by the lake. He can't see anything. Couldn't see anything anyway. We're all covered up inside here, safe as a bug in a bug, pardon me, a bug in a rug, two bugs in a rug."

"You're sure he can't see us?" She felt herself responding to him. "Be quiet for a minute. Be *still!*" He stopped moving, and they listened, hearing nothing but a few last pops and hisses from the dying fire.

"See," he whispered. "He's way over there, sound asleep, and we're not going to let him spoil our good times, are we? I'm sorry I yelled at you because you had to pee, because all God's little girls have to pee, don't they? Now, just lie there real nice and still, and nobody will know what we're doing."

She let him enter her, feeling his penis strangely cool from its exposure to the frigid air.

"I thought you couldn't get it up if it was cold?"

"It wasn't easy."

It was quite good for her; she held him long after he had finished with a muffled groan, long after he had slipped out of her, held him like a child against her breast, his head heavy with sleep, loving him fiercely and protectively.

She opened her eyes at last to chart the passage of the moon toward dawn. And saw the big man's face above them, leaning over and staring down at them without expression. She shut her eyes in horror, and instantly opened them again to see nothing but the crescent moon and scudding fingers of cloud. A dream. A half-dream born from her suspicion and the fear of discovery. He could not have been there watching; she would have heard his feet crushing the spongy ground as he fled, and she had heard nothing.

After a long time of listening for something beyond Danny's heavy breathing, she relaxed and curled herself around her sleeping husband and dreamed with him. The she-cougar screamed again, but she didn't hear.

10

Joanne woke to sunlight, morning light—not yet full of heat, but pale lemon drifting down through the treetops, speckled with motes. Danny had been with her in the night, but he was gone. She sat up quickly, and zipped herself free of the constricting bedroll.

"Danny!" Her voice, distorted, bounced back at her from the wall of the forest. "Danny! Where are you?"

She heard crashing noises then and footsteps approaching.

"I thought you were going to sleep all day." It was Danny, and he was alone. "Don't move fast; there must have been rocks under all that moss, and it's going to hurt to stretch out."

She jumped up and laughed at him. *"One* of us was in shape, my darling, and *I* feel wonderful."

"Then I must have been on the bottom." His eyes lidded with the memory of their mating. "I didn't start out on the bottom, though."

She remembered then the fleeting glimpse of the stranger standing over them, or when she had seen him there in her mind, and remembered too that they weren't alone. "Where is he?"

"Dave? He's gone downtrail. He said he'd probably take off when it got light. Nobody's over there now, and his gear's all gone. You weren't very nice to him."

"He gave me the creeps but you were nice enough for both of us. Oh, let's forget him; I guess I was pretty bitchy. You hungry?"

"Do bears shit in the woods?"

He'd answered her that way a hundred times, a thousand times, but it jarred now. "Couldn't you have said, 'Do birds fly?'"

"I'm hungry. O.K.? I want eggs and bacon and pancakes and biscuits and gravy."

"Dream on, and shinny that pack down for me and I'll see what your choice is."

He brought water from the lake that seemed safe enough, and she made coffee with it, and mixed it with dried beef stew, fried eggs, and wrapped canned biscuit dough around a stick to bake it. They ate together, silently.

"You want to go over?"

"Over where?"

"Into the Okanogan country. If we do that, we go on up north over Bowan Mountain, and then it's five and a half hours to the Pacific Crest Trail."

She handed him her plate to finish.

"Do we have to decide now?"

"Nope. That's the beauty of it. We're free, and we don't have to decide anything. That's finally beginning to come through to me."

He looked years younger; the puffiness under his eyes gone away, the tension lines ironed too after two good nights of sleep. She reached out to him and touched his hand. "You know something? And I think it's all right for me to say this now, and I don't know why I know it's all right. I think I might just walk off this mountain with a baby started."

He stared back at her, and seemed to be weighing something unsaid. And then he lifted her hand to his lips and kissed it, and she felt his love unfettered by desire. She leaned against him, trying to make the moment last as long as she could.

The gunshot spat out somewhere along the trail.

Danny still held her fingers to his lips but the gesture was automatic and deadened. There were two more shots. He stood up, sheltering her with his body as he gazed toward something he could not see.

"What is it?"

He answered without looking at her. "I don't know."

"Hunters?"

"No. It's out of season. Target shooting maybe. We're not the only people up here."

"Should we do something?"

When he turned toward her finally, the tension creases were there again in his face, and she saw him reach toward the pack that held his gun; it was an unfinished gesture—his hand stopped before it closed around the checkered grips.

"No. There's nothing to do; it's got nothing to do with us."

But it had.

The red stranger came back; she saw the sun glinting off his hair and turning it into a torch among the leaves as he approached. He was running, easily and fluidly, and she felt not danger *to* him, but danger *from* him. She lifted her hand in warning, but Danny wasn't looking. The big man was so close to her that she could see rivulets of sweat oozing from the auburn hair that curled around his ears, but he was shouting not at her, only to her husband.

"Grizzly! My God, it's a grizzly!"

11

She waited. High in the pine tree where the men had boosted her, her arms encircling the thick trunk, slippery fingers laced together. She feared falling; her legs trembled and the limb beneath her feet bent toward the ground. With the slightest movement, it creaked and shed showers of drying pine needles to earth. The gummy sap smeared her face where she pressed against it and she thought of blood. She could not see where the men had gone, and heard only crashing far off in the woods that grew fainter each moment, leaving her as isolated as she had ever been. She had clung to her husband, pleaded with him not to go away with the stranger, but he had shaken her off as if she were only an irritant. Then both of them had lifted her with their huge hands and pushed her into the branches. Danny had said, "Climb! Damn it. Climb!" And she had cried out to him, "Come with me. Come *with* me!" even long after he had disappeared. She knew nothing of guns, but she doubted the power of the blue-black, snub-nosed gun he'd held, or of the weapon in the other man's hand. They were children's toys against the thick pelt and hide of a grizzly. Together, the three of them, they could have waited the animal out in the trees until someone came to help them. She felt frustrated rage at both men for deserting her, for risking everything in her world.

She prayed. She offered up sacrifices to God if only He would allow Danny to come back to her. Her own life. She agreed to die at fifty—then at forty—if she could have him again. She would be a better person, please God, and see that they tithed everything they had. She vacuumed all her sins up from her mind and cast them out. Gossip. Pride. Pettiness. Avarice. Jealousy. She *was* jealous; she would be no longer. *Please God—Please God—Please God—Please God.* She repeated the litany aloud, unaware, until her mouth was dry and her lips started to crack.

She did not know how long they had been gone; her watch was someplace down on the ground with their supplies. She tried to count seconds and chart minutes, but it seemed senseless anyway because she had no idea how far they had had to go or what they meant to do if they ran into . . . *it*. It seemed an hour to her since she'd settled into her perch, and there were nerve buzzes along her arms from lack of circulation. She tried to change position, but her foothold dropped farther toward the ground, and she could picture herself sliding down the limb helplessly, her hands clasping air and dry needles.

Nothing had really changed. That was the important thing to remember. Danny had gone off with his gun to do something. Danny went off with his gun every working day, and the only real difference was that now she knew the moment of his approach to danger. Their gear on the ground below her was somehow comforting, familiar possessions, the coffeepot still breathing a small geyser of steam. The tube of Danny's sleeping bag resting next to hers. The frying pan, its dregs turning hard and crusted with the last coals of their campfire. She would have to soak that or scrub it with sand to get it clean. Tonight, she could fry fish in it—if Danny caught any.

If he comes back. Don't think that! Thoughts could become real if she let them. Prayers skittered and fell away before she could hold onto them, but the fear stayed.

There was a soft rustle in the weeds below her and she looked down and saw a tiny mottled brown and white bird rise, its tail feathers clean as new snow, a ptarmigan. The birds were all around her, taking flight from their hiding places and winging to the branches high above her. But one bird flew straight to her as if she had called it aloud and settled on a branch a few feet away.

She took it for a sign of hope.

There were two men out there. Big men—with guns and branch-clubs, competent to scare off the bear; wild creatures ran from humans if they had an escape route and there was all the mountain for it to flee. The beast was probably already gone, and Danny and the stranger were waiting only to be sure it was well gone before they came back for her. She tried to picture them beyond the pale of trees that cut her off from them, resting now, lighting cigarettes or cigars, laughing at their victory.

But she did not believe it. The hopeless dread that consumed her was familiar. When Doss died and his flesh mingled with the burning barn timbers, she had watched from the gravel road. She did not know at that moment which of the canvas-jacketed men was trapped inside when the roofline sagged as if melting and then imploded on itself, could not have known that the anguished, too-late shouts of warning were for Doss. But she had felt it in her stomach and in her heart's thudding.

Our Father who art in Heaven—Yea, though I walk through the valley of the shadow of death—And when she could not call forth any other prayers from her numbed mind, *Bless this food, oh Lord we pray* and *Now I lay me down to sleep.*

The little birds came closer to her, almost a dozen of them waiting. If she dared unclasp her hands, she could reach out and touch the soft breasts. But with the first booming shot they lifted off their perches and left her alone. With the second shot, its blast treading on the echo of the first, she felt warm urine sluice down her legs and heard it patter on the needle carpet beneath the tree. Her hands slipped from the branch and she fought to hold on against a dark tide of dizziness.

They were not as far away from her as she had thought; the shots seemed to come from just beyond the first bend in the trail.

There was a time that was quiet again, stiller than before, or maybe it only seemed so because the shots were so loud. She held her breath and listened to nothing. And then there was a kind of thrashing sound but she was not sure if it came from where the shots had, and that was followed by something screaming that seemed neither animal nor human. A yelp that grew and grew until it split the air, and finally diminished to a choked whimper. She thought that it could not be a man's sound; a man's voice could not reach that pitch. It did not come again.

She had to go to them. She could not be safe when something awful was happening to Danny. Maybe to Danny. She prayed that the red man had screamed and not Danny. But she could not move. Her hands would not let go now; the flesh between her fingers had grown together, hand-to-hand like a vise. Vomit crept up her throat and pushed over her tongue, filling her mouth until she leaned almost lazily away from the trunk and spat it out. If she leaned just a few inches further, she would fall. She wondered if she could hope to die if she fell, or if she would need to climb higher so that she could be certain of it. And yet she could not seem to move at all.

There were no more sounds. The birds came back and the sun rose higher in the sky as if the world were still alive. Everything was the same as before Danny had walked away from her.

Any minute now, he would come back. She watched for him so steadily that she forgot to blink, and her eyes burned.

Someone was coming back to her. The faintest break of snapping twigs first, and then steady footfalls on the trail bed and crackles of underbrush. She kept her eyes on the trail and concentrated on her husband's face so that she would know him when he appeared. She thought first that she did indeed see him, and then the sun touched the red man's auburn hair, and she saw that it was not Danny at all.

He walked easily, neither hurrying toward her or away from something dangerous behind him. She would not look at him, but kept her eyes just over his left shoulder so that she could see her husband when he too rounded the trail, but he seemed to be a long way behind. The big man searched the trees quickly until he spotted her and he ran toward her in loping strides and climbed next to her, standing on the same branch and enveloping her body in his. His chest was damp against her bare back, and she remembered the red-red-red on his T-shirt that she had meant not to see while she was watching for Danny.

His mouth bent down and whispered against her hair.

"Mrs. Lind . . . Joanne . . ."

She tried to move away. "No. I don't want to talk now. I don't want to listen to you."

"It was bad, Joanne."

"No."

"I got back to you as soon as I could."

POSSESSION

"No. I don't want you here. I want you to go back and get my husband."

He waited a long time before he spoke. "I can't do that."

"Then I'll go. Let me down. Don't hold me. Don't touch me. I'm going to get him." A voice was screaming, and she did not recognize it was her own.

She tried to slide free of him, and he held her faster, pinning her against the tree's trunk.

"You smell," she said. "And I don't want to be here."

"I'm sorry. I can't let you down because it's very dangerous and I have to keep you safe."

He was suffocating her. She pushed back hard against him with her buttocks and heard him grunt, but he still pinioned her fast.

"Let me go. Let me go, you fucking bastard!" *She never said that.* "You filthy, lousy, stinking fucking bastard. I'll kill you if you don't let me go, and I don't want to listen to you or see you or ever see you again."

She saw his hand splayed out next to her face, thick brown fingers with tiny red hairs on them, and something else that seemed bad to her—dried brown segmented streaks like broken worms that flaked away when his fingers moved. She could not remember the word for it. She turned her head and sank her teeth into the heel of his hand and he shouted and slammed her forehead into the tree, and she remembered the word was *blood.*

She bit him again and again and each time he knocked her head forward until she was exhausted and bright red blood streamed down his wrist. She leaned her cheek against the bark and closed her eyes. His voice was a buzz, full of metallic sounds that were not words.

When she finally understood him she wished she had not.

"He's gone."

"Where did he go? Where? He should have come back for me."

"No. I mean he's gone. He's dead."

"No."

"I shot the bear, but I don't think I killed her."

1 4 9

She was silent.

"Did you hear me? Did you understand?"

"He needs me." Her words were very careful now because if she could speak clearly, he would let her go to find Danny. But he was insane and had to be dealt with cautiously. "You see, he belongs to me and I have a right to go and help him. And then we'll let him rest and we'll all go down the mountain together and it will be all right. But you have to let me go because you're too strong for me to fight."

"He's dead, Joanne. Believe me, I checked him very carefully before I came back here. It was very quick and he doesn't feel any pain now."

"You don't understand." She tried to be patient as she would with a child or a retarded person. "We came on a vacation together and we were having a really good time until you came. I don't mean to be rude to you, but you don't belong with us. I forgive you for banging my head, but you have to let me down now."

"He's dead, and you can't go down there until I'm sure it's safe."

"No."

"He's dead."

"No."

"Dead."

"Please don't talk to me anymore." Her voice was so weak that most of it was lost in the wind that stirred the limbs around them, and then she was silent.

He waited for her to move or to say something more, but she was frozen, immobile as the tree itself. It was an hour before she began to weep, softly at first and then with ugly retching sobs that were more animal than human. He held her tenderly high up in their green-blue thicket of pine needles; she seemed unaware of his erection, his groin pressing against her buttocks. When she had cried her throat raw, he told her that it was finally safe for them to climb down to earth. He steadied her and helped her place her nerveless feet and hands and then lowered her to the ground as gently as a leaf's dropping, dangling her with one hand. She seemed weightless. She sagged and rocked quietly while he gathered up their gear.

She knew, finally, that there was no place she could go where she might find Danny, and there was no use to fight the big man, and no use not to. There was simply no use for anything. She was tired, more tired than she knew a human could be, and she was amazed that she could stand and move when he signaled to her that it was time for them to go. Her legs had no strength but they obeyed her brain's command to move forward.

She had forgotten his name. There was something. What was it? Something she had to ask him. "Stop," she called. "Stop, please."

He turned his large head to her, waiting. "What?"

"Do you know me?"

He seemed not truly surprised, but a bit off balance. "What do you mean?"

"Do you know me?"

"I met you last night, remember?"

"Oh—yes. Last night, we . . ."

"Is that what you meant?"

The tree-green kept coming at her in waves, and then pulling back and it was hard to focus on anything and keep it bracketed in her vision. She was confused. She looked down at her own body and was surprised to see that she was a woman and not a child.

"I don't know why—" She stopped and tried to find words that fit together correctly. "When I was little . . . you know, when I was a little girl, I always needed to know that. There were so many tall people, but that's only because I was so small, and they talked to me as if they knew who I was—probably because of Doss. But you don't know Doss, do you? Never mind about that. The thing is I had to know if they knew who I was because I was frightened. I'm very frightened now, you know, and you're very large and you don't know me and I'm afraid you are going to hurt me."

"No." He was talking to the child, very softly. "No, I wouldn't do that."

"Is Danny really—oh, I don't want to say it. Is he really?"

"I'm sorry."

But he wasn't sorry; the edges in his voice told her that. He was glad.

"You killed him, didn't you?"

He walked back to her and knelt on the ground in front of her, taking her chin in one hand. "Of course not. But you can't understand now. You mustn't think about it. You're very tired now, and you're in shock and I need to take care of you."

The tree-green and the color of his eyes blended together and spun around like a kaleidoscope picking up black particles until there was only black on black on black. An instant before she fainted, a little door in her mind shut tight and locked the horror behind it because it could not be dealt with. She did not feel him as he picked her up in his arms and carried her farther into the woods. She breathed and her heart beat on, but her mind was hiding somewhere back in the black.

He looked down at the white face bouncing against his chest, at the delicate, veined eyelids, and the mouth with the vestige of vomit dried in the corners. He smiled tenderly. He had told her all that she would have to know.

Her husband was garbage now, and she belonged to him, and they were all alone in the woods. He couldn't have planned it better if he had set out to have it this way. He'd had to tie up some of the others and gag them and rough them up, and even when their bonds were loosened, they'd cried and fought him.

She wasn't fighting him now. Maybe she already knew who he was. Maybe she only realized that she had no way out without him. It didn't really matter because he would have her with him when it was dark, and she would do anything he wanted. This time, she wasn't going to go away and leave him.

He smiled down at her. This part, the first part, was almost his favorite part of the game.

12

Joanne had lost all measure of time and place; she was only vaguely aware of being carried. She could feel her arms around a strong neck, and feel the slight shock as step, step, step hit the earth. For the briefest moment she thought she *was* a little girl again, back in Doss's arms being carried from the old '47 Studebaker to her warm little bed. Then the picture disappeared. That was wrong. She was someplace else, moving through the fading light of another day. Was it still Sunday, still the endless day she clung to the tree? Or was it a long time after? She seemed to remember following the big man through the forest for a long time, and then waking from a drowsy shock-sleep from time to time after that to find that he was carrying her, not through the trees but along a lake shore edged with thin ice. It was dusk now, but which dusk? And which meadow was this?

She caught a whiff of a metallic smell, and saw his shirt against her cheek, its hardened, crackling surface stiffened by something dark red. She moved in his arms and looked up into his shadowed face. She closed her eyes and opened them quickly so she could see clearly. He looked exhausted. She thought it was good of him to carry her because she must have been injured by something she couldn't recall. Danny should carry her for a while and let the other policeman rest. She remembered that Danny couldn't do that but the fuzziness in her head prevented her from understanding why. It was peculiar, this blankness where she lost whole segments of recent memory and yet still sensed something just beyond her thoughts, something better not pursued. She would think of it later.

"You can set me down. I can stand."

He lowered her carefully to her feet, but she couldn't stand; her knees buckled and she knelt in the long grass and alpine asters, surprised to find the ground still warm below the chilled air. He shrugged off the backpack he had carried for all her lost time. He kneaded his cramped shoulders and swung them in arcs to bring back circulation, grunting.

"Do your arms hurt?" she asked finally. "Did you carry me a long way?"

"Not that far. You're not that heavy anyway."

"Are we going back to the lodge?"

He shook his head.

"We must be. I think I remember this meadow. I think this is where we sat yesterday."

He stared over her head, sweeping the forest beyond them with his eyes. "We can't go back to Stehekin. I couldn't risk it."

"No, you see . . ." It was so difficult to talk to him. She was so tired. "No, it wasn't that steep; the trail was safe."

"I didn't mean the trail."

"Then, why?"

"She might still be waiting—the grizzly. Some of those animals are cunning. They set their own traps."

Her mind focused on the terrible knowledge. She moaned.

"Where's Danny?"

"You remember. We had to leave him."

"But I didn't want to."

"But we had to. You mustn't cry again. You cried for a long time this morning, and it made you sick."

"Did I talk to you after? I remember the tree and then the woods."

"We're safe here for a while. Tomorrow, we'll go up over Bowan Mountain and then down toward the Pacific Trail."

"Danny said that was what we were going to do; so that's good, isn't it? That's what he'd want me to do. He always knows what to do."

Her constant harping on the other man irritated him, and he had to remind himself that it had only been eight hours, that she would forget soon enough. He turned away from her to unroll the sleeping bags.

"What's your name?"

"Have you forgotten again? It's Duane. Duane Demich."

POSSESSION

"Why did I think it was David?"

"Beats me. They both start with D."

"So does—did—Danny. Which is it?"

"That *was* his name."

She hadn't moved from her kneeling position, and she swayed as if she had lost her center of balance.

"Why couldn't you have saved him? Did you really try to save him?"

He moved to her and let her rest her head again on his shoulder, feeling her whole body vibrate with fatigue and shock. Then he held his right arm up for her to see the long deep scratches that ran from his wrist to his armpit.

"I almost had him free of her. She like to took my arm off and I had to back off. Somebody had to come back for you. You would have been all alone up here and you couldn't have survived. I had to make the choice between letting her kill both of us and your survival. He would have wanted me to take care of you."

She nodded against him.

"Can you eat?"

She gagged and turned away from him at the thought, and then slowly stood up. Her bladder was bursting, and she wondered how bodily functions could go on when nothing mattered any longer. What was she going to do? She was terrified of going into the dark trees alone, but she couldn't urinate with the stranger nearby.

"I have to go to the bathroom," she said softly.

"Do you want me to go with you?"

"Oh no!"

"Then go on over there behind those larch trees. You'll have your privacy and you won't have to go far in."

She walked carefully away from him, aware that his eyes followed her, and she went deeper into the blind of trees than she wanted to to get away from his watching. It was so dark now, and she could make out only pillars of black as if the sun had never penetrated the spaces between them at all. She wondered how far he had carried her away from Danny. Maybe only a little way. There was still a chance she could get back to him, find him waiting for her to come and

155

help him because it was not possible for him to be truly dead. Danny was too strong to die in a few minutes.

But there were no trails; if she tried to find the way back, she would be lost forever on the mountain and ferns would grow through her skull when spring came. She crouched and emptied herself. Something nearby scuttled through the dry leaves, but she couldn't tell if it was coming toward her or going away from her. She held her breath and listened for its breathing. The creature too had suspended breathing, waiting as she was.

She had hated the big man before—yesterday? Today? And she wished herself away from him forever. She wasn't strong enough. There was fear here and fear ahead of her and fear back with him, all around her, waiting for her in the darkness. He seemed the least of it.

He held the sleeping bag for her to crawl into it, and she was so cold, deep into the insides of her bones, dead cold where sleep might promise no awakening. She did sleep, almost immediately, tumbling into a pit of nothingness where even dreams had no substance and spun themselves out before she could catch them.

When she woke, her eyes snapped open and she felt her heart beating too fast. She had forgotten again where she was, but the image of death consumed her and she reached above her head to touch the cover of her casket to see if she had been buried alive. Her hands rose high, touching air, and she could see stars and an opaque slice of moon behind clouds. She heard a man breathing next to her. Thankful that the nightmare was over, she reached out to touch Danny.

Then her hand froze in mid-air as she remembered.

My husband is dead.

She accepted it with complete lucidity, with such a pang of hopeless loss that she felt her heart break.

The man—the stranger—David?—no, Duane—caught her hand and held it fast. She thought he had done it in his sleep, and she tried to pull free, but he would not let her go.

"What is it?"

He didn't answer.

POSSESSION

"Please let go."

She could not tell if he was awake or asleep still, but his breathing was different, faster. She tugged at her trapped hand, and his whole body rose up and he rolled on top of her. She tried to squirm out from under him, and he drove the lower half of himself against her and pinned her to the ground.

His eyes were wide open, light and luminous as a fox's. Crazy eyes.

"What?" she whispered. "What's wrong?"

But she knew.

"No!"

"You belong to me now."

"Please—"

It was no good talking to him. She began to cry because she couldn't help it.

"Don't do that. You're going to enjoy this. You're going to like being fucked. Say it."

"What?"

"Say 'I want you to fuck me.' "

"No."

"I want you to say it."

"No—"

He hit her in the face so swiftly that her head twisted and smashed into the ground. She tasted blood in her mouth.

"Say it."

She spat at him and he smiled while her spittle ran down his cheek. Then he slapped her again, holding her chin with one hand so that she couldn't roll away from the force of the blow.

"Say it."

"I . . . want . . ."

"That's good. I knew you wanted it. Say it real nice for me."

"I want you . . . to . . . fuck . . . me."

"That's better. Now, I'm going to touch you all over, and I want you to keep telling me how much you like it. See, like this—"

He rolled off her, lay beside her, and unzipped her

157

sleeping bag. Freed to run, she scrambled away from him, but he caught her with one leg and held her in a scissors hold.

"Don't try to fight me. It only makes me angry. I don't want you to make me angry. If you do, we'll have to start all over again or something bad might happen to you. Can't you understand that?"

"I'm so cold. My teeth are chattering."

"I'll make you warm. See? Doesn't that feel good?"

His hand moved over her skull first, and she thought he could crush it if he chose to. Massaging fingers poked into her ears and around the edges, and then over her eyes, her nose, and into her mouth. He did not kiss her; his fingers touching her teeth, her tongue, were worse than his mouth somehow.

She stiffened as he trailed over her throat with his huge hand, encircling it and squeezing, testing to see how much pressure it took to make her cough.

"Your air even belongs to me. Say that. You can't breathe unless I say so."

"My air belongs to you."

"Let me see your breasts. I want you to show me."

"Oh . . . Please—"

He pressed her throat and took away her air. "Show them to me."

She could not feel her own fingers, but somehow she managed to unbutton her shirt, her eyes closed so she could not see his own glitter above her.

The hand on her throat moved down and yanked at her brassiere. She felt it rip and fall away, and then the hand circling and massaging her nipples, kneading, flattening, playing with her. He buried his face between her breasts and wallowed there, licking her with his tongue so that the air chilled his saliva. She shivered.

"You like that, don't you?"

She shook her head, but he wasn't paying attention; his control was sliding away, and he nibbled at her in a frenzy, hands and mouth moving over her breasts and down her belly. He crooned and growled and sighed. He was going to devour her.

"Do you feel me, Joanne?"

". . . yes."

"See how hard you make me? See what I've been saving for you? You must be so happy. Touch me." He released her to expose himself.

She lay still, her hands across her breasts.

"Touch me."

She couldn't do that. She could not touch him.

"I said touch me. See how big I am. Put your hands on my dick."

She rolled and managed to get on her hands and knees and crawl before he snaked out a hand and grabbed her ankle. He flipped her like a wrestler would and nailed her hands to the ground, his weight on her wrists so that she could no longer move at all. She thought he would kill her now, but he only smiled at her as if she had somehow pleased him.

He seemed to enjoy playing with her, letting her crawl just far enough away so that she thought she might be able to run into the trees, and then drawing her back to him and laughing. There was no way to escape him.

She could not fight him. She could not run. She felt bruised in all the places where he'd caught onto her to drag her back. He was going to do it anyway. She watched him, panting, submissive and only wanting it over with.

"That's better. Now say it again. 'I want you to fuck me.' "

"Iwantyoutofuckme."

"That's not good enough. You have to sound like you really mean it. You sound like you're doing me a favor, and I don't like that. You're not ready yet, are you?"

He stood above her and shucked his jeans, preening for her. The first fingers of dawn light had crept from behind the trees, and she could see his pale solid flesh and the terrible jutting penis. He was immense. Monstrous. He would split her cleanly in two with it and leave her bleeding in the meadow to rot in the sunlight, just as Danny lay rotting somewhere behind them in the shadows. Danny had died with more dignity. She was a thing now, something for the red man to play with.

She shut her eyes tightly and waited for him to do it to her. She felt him turning her body as if she were a doll. He was taking too long, folding her clothing carefully and laying her things in the weeds. She felt him looking at her.

He was touching her again with his thick fingers.

"You're sweating. You're getting hot."

A finger moved beneath her breasts, sliding across the cold perspiration and then down, circling her navel and poking into it. Over the flare of her hipbones. She felt him turning her over and panicked.

"No . . . please—"

His hands cupped the cheeks of her buttocks, and then the awful tracing started again. There was no part of her that would belong to her when he was finished. Nothing. The finger moved deeply along the crease and prodded, trying to enter there. She held her breath, too terrified even to pray.

Finally, the hands turned her onto her back again, and she thought that now—

"You're not wet enough. You're holding back from me."

". . . no."

"Don't lie!"

He was between her legs, his hands almost lazy. Touching, rubbing. He stopped for a moment and she opened her eyes and saw that he was staring down at her crotch, his mouth open and slack. He caught her looking at him and smiled.

"You like this. You love it, don't you?"

She shut her eyes.

"I'll bet you taste sweet."

"No . . ."

"Oh yes, you do." She felt his lips and tongue violate what had been her private center. Danny had never done this to her. The red man made some noise, some humming growl against her most vulnerable flesh. He seemed about to

160

bite into her and leave her bleeding. "You do taste sweet. Taste."

He plunged one finger deep into her and withdrew it, bringing it up to her lips. She clenched her teeth.

"I said *taste it!*"

His finger forced its way in, past her lips, cutting her teeth, and she tasted blood and a muskiness that must have come from herself.

"See?"

"Yes. Just do it if you're going to. Please."

"Beg me."

"Please . . ."

"Say, 'I'm begging you to fuck me.' "

"I'm begging you . . ."

"To fuck me."

". . . to fuck me."

"On your knees."

"I can't move."

He yanked her by the hair and her body rose up to its knees. She repeated whatever he wanted to hear.

"Where do you want it?"

"What?"

"Where? In the mouth? In the ass? In the pussy?"

". . . in the . . . pussy."

He hurt her more than she had ever been hurt, at first a tearing pain in her pelvis, and then something shattered inside, and she could no longer tell where the damage was centered. She heard him gasping out words against her ear, but could not grasp their meaning and did not want to know. It went on for a very long time, until she was sure that he was killing her; all she knew for certain was the pain.

He drove himself into her rhythmically and then faster and faster, his face a set mask—so red from the sun that shone directly into her own eyes—and there was finally no sound except for the slap, slap, slap of his thighs against hers and the screaming in her head. Suddenly, he whimpered and gasped, and stopped, rolling off her in flopping motion.

She did not turn her head. She could see the sky and a hawk sliding on the wind above her, could feel some insect creeping in the sweaty furrows of her neck. The red man gulped for air and sighed to himself.

She knew that she would kill him. She would find some way to smash him and smash him until he was no longer recognizable. And then she would go to Danny and lie down beside him and wait for death to cleanse her.

He leaned over her and she flinched, but he only kissed her cheek and patted her shoulder. Did all men do that, even rapists? She felt hysterical laughter bubble up, but it emerged a sob. He let her crawl away now without protesting or grabbing for her and she searched through the grass until she found her clothes. She dressed with her back to him, but he said nothing.

She saw that he was asleep, his face soft and open. He was not afraid of her, and he didn't move at all when she walked away. If he woke, she would tell him she had to go into the woods to pee, and he would believe that. She had to find a weapon. His guns were somewhere in the pack underneath his head, and even if she could get to them without waking him, she didn't know how guns worked. Danny had tried to show her so many times. Why hadn't she paid attention? She could not kill him with her bare hands. It had to be with something that would stun him as he slept. If he was conscious, he would kill her. He was going to kill her anyway when he was done with her.

She couldn't find a club. The fallen boughs were either too big for her to carry, or so rotten that they crumbled in her hands as she lifted them.

The rocks were too round, with no true cutting edges, and they were covered with moss. After a half hour she found one rock, heavy—but liftable—and chipped cleanly on one side, sharp enough perhaps to sever an artery. She cradled it against her breasts and carried it back toward the treacherous meadow. Killing him might possibly wash him out of her body and her mind. She could still smell him; his semen drained out of her and she shuddered. She would not be clean if she bathed for days.

162

POSSESSION

The rock was warm and solid and the feel of it calmed her and her rage calmed her, but her legs trembled.

He was still asleep, on his back now, one arm flung across the place where she had lain. He did not hear her approach, or perhaps he only seemed not to hear her and was listening. Animals did that and he was only an animal. He was ugly.

She looked down at him and wondered which part of the head must be smashed. She assumed the forehead, but if she missed, the thudding stone would alert him. Her preference was the face itself. She wanted to see his eyes and mouth lost in bone chips and blood. But she knew he would still be able to rise and strangle her, even with his ruined face and blinded eyes.

She would have to chance the forehead, crack the skull-plate hard enough so that the brain beneath would bruise and bleed. Danny had told her people died like that, quite easily. The brain bounced around inside the skull like a balloon as it crushed itself on every unyielding plane of bone it hit. And brains controlled life—not hearts or lungs. She should have paid more attention to Danny's stories of murder. She had never killed even a spider or a mouse; she had avoided hearing about the killing of humans.

He stirred in his sleep, and she raised the rock higher, casting its shadow over his face. She could not do it, hesitating not from mercy but because she was afraid. Life was no longer important to her, so she should not fear dying. But she feared more pain. She dreaded the violence that would fall upon her if she could not render him helpless with her first blow. And she was ashamed. If she could be assured that she too would die in an instant, she would not be afraid, but she could not endure another long time of hurting.

Her arms ached from supporting the rock over his face, but her hands could not let it go, any more than she could put it down. If she let him live, he would rape her again—and probably worse. That was one choice. If she succeeded in destroying him, she would die, but at a leisurely pace in the wilderness. She did not know which way they had come and therefore knew no route out. Either way, she was dependent on him. Living or dead, he controlled her existence.

There was God to consider. If she killed the red man first, would God forgive her—or was murder murder, no matter?

Her hands shook and bits of dirt broke free from the rock and bounced off his sleeping face. She willed herself to let go of the weapon, but she could not. Then she saw his eyes flutter and open. He watched her for a moment. She had expected fear in him, but there was only a flicker of surprise. She raised her arms higher and he moved like a mongoose, the side of his hand catching her behind the knees so that she fell heavily across him. She still clutched the rock and it crushed her fingers against the ground. There was an instant of numbness, and then her hands flamed with pain.

He was on his feet, and all her tenuous advantage was lost. She waited for him to hit her. Instead he crouched beside her and took her hands in his, turning them to see where she was cut.

"What were you doing?" He seemed genuinely puzzled.

"I was going to kill you."

"Why?"

She pulled her hands away from him and sidled back into a sitting position against a stump. "Because you raped me. You had no right to touch me. You told me you were going to help me."

"I am going to help you."

"You hurt me."

"I didn't hurt you. You fought me. You may have hurt yourself."

"You raped me. You destroyed something that was very precious to me."

"I don't understand you. You need me."

"I didn't need rape. I didn't need . . . what you did to me."

"You were slipping away. I had to warm you. I had to make you part of me so that I could give you some of my life."

"You're a pervert—"

164

POSSESSION

His hand covered her mouth. "You don't understand, but you will. You'll remember why I'm here and you'll be sorry you talked like this. You have to live. You will have to eat and sleep and walk when I tell you to because I'm the only one who can save you."

He took her cut hand in his and watched her blood seep into the marks her teeth had left in his palm. They were part of each other now.

"Will you promise not to—not to touch me that way again?"

"I don't have to promise anything. You don't know what sex is. You don't understand at all. I will show you that sex is a way to keep from dying. I gave you life when you were trying to throw it away. You were allowing yourself to die. You didn't want me, but you will."

"Never. I will never want you, not like that. Not in any way, and I will kill you the first chance I get."

He stood up and gathered their gear, ignoring her. When he had shouldered it, he turned back to her. "It's daylight, and the days are growing very short up here. We have to get over the mountain summit while we have the sun. You can come with me or not. If you stay here, you're going to die and there won't be anyone to help you. If you think that she-bear has given up, you're mistaken. She's out there right now tracking us. She can smell exactly where we've been when the ground fog lifts. I had to kill her cub, and she won't forgive me for that. She's big. Bigger than you can imagine; she could take your whole head in her mouth and crush it until nobody would ever recognize you. Is that what you want? To be nothing but pieces of bloody meat?"

She covered her head with her arms to shut him out.

"I'm going now. Are you coming with me?"

"Go away."

He sighed, and she heard him throw one of the backpacks down, and then the sounds of his feet moving away from her through the meadow. When she looked up finally, she could see only the back of his head and his shoulders disappearing fifty yards beyond where she sat, heading down into the apricot haze of larch, and then she couldn't see him at all, only the meadow itself and the walls of trees on every side. She could hear far-off noises behind her, something moving through the way that they had taken, and she knew she wasn't brave enough to die alone.

He turned and looked back toward the meadow. He could see her weaving through the weeds, looking for his trail. He could shout to her and tell her the way, but he stayed silent and let her fumble her way along. She had been ungrateful and hostile to him. She needed humbling.

He leaned against a boulder, shutting himself off from her sight, and lit a cigarette.

She would come.

13

It was almost noon when he stopped in the shade of a rock cliff, and handed her two protein bars. "Eat them," he said. He had not acknowledged her at all when she'd caught up with him, had pretended she wasn't walking behind him.

She forced them down, chewing with jaws clenched unconsciously for too long. She felt leached of any kind of feeling at all, save a stubborn resolve. He would pay, and she would be free of him.

He reached to take her pack, and she shook her head; she wanted nothing from him except escape and the satisfaction of seeing him arrested. And she asked nothing of herself beyond the physical stamina to maintain his pace along the trails. She thought she could do that. All the hours of running had prepared her to climb and hike and cling to the narrow trail with an efficiency of effort that few women—few men—could match. She could not think of Danny or ponder why he was dead and the red man lived.

There was an awful thought that she'd tried to block

before it bloomed fully. Was it possible that Danny was dead because of her, because this crazy stranger had wanted her and knew that the only way to have her was to kill her husband? If that was true, and if she had only suspected that, she would have lain down for him. Anything to keep Danny safe.

She hadn't flirted with the stranger; she hadn't even liked the stranger. She'd been bundled up in layers of shirts and jeans, without make-up and with greasy, tangled hair. She could not be the cause of it. She had to push that explanation away each time it crept toward her, or it would mean that she had killed Danny. No, he had raped her as an afterthought, because she was female and helpless and *there*.

They were climbing toward a summit, and she tried to gauge their direction from the sun. It seemed that they were heading north, but she wasn't sure of it and she would not ask him. His self-control seemed erratic, as if his surface calm might splinter at any moment and catch them both in the madness beneath. As long as they kept moving, she felt safer. For the moment, she was more afraid of the mountain, revealing itself now as bare rock, deeper and deeper hues of stone where nothing could survive beyond the clinging lichen, a few tenacious bellflowers, and the thickening larch trees, evergreens that were not evergreens but stunted, burning bushes caught in a last fiery display before winter left them naked. Another time, she would have been awed by their splendor, but now they looked like the flames of hell.

She thought they had been moving steadily upward for almost a mile, and that his leg muscles must be screaming in pain as hers did. It was a clean pain and she almost welcomed it. He betrayed not the slightest slackening of effort. She followed him six paces behind, her boots slipping on the rocky scrabble that scaled off the boulders. His sweat soaked his armpits and formed a wet V on his shirt from his shoulders to the lower point of his spine. It was a different shirt; she wondered what he had done with the bloodied green shirt.

It was odd how her mind jumped as if it had to skitter away from dark places where it would be trapped. She tried to dull its sharp edges with safe thoughts, the way she did at home when she couldn't sleep, when she built a little house in her mind, with her own safe room where rain danced on the roof and she lay swaddled in soft blankets. She could create the exterior of that cottage now, but she could not find the safe room. The stairs leading to it became the mountain trail with nothing certain at its end.

Just as she knew she could climb no farther, they reached the top of the pass. He stopped and waited for her.

"There. Look."

She gazed where he pointed and felt sharp disappointment; there was only more wilderness below them, nothing that promised freedom. The trail down was so steep that she gasped aloud. Dropping, dropping, and snaking around a sheer rock face. One misstep and death waited just out of sight, over the edge.

"Rest here," he panted. "Then down through that forest, into the meadows, and out to the trail. Five hours. Six maybe."

She didn't speak, but accepted the canteen he passed to her and drank until he took it from her.

He gazed down into the meadow. From this angle he looked boylike and, when he closed his eyes and leaned back against the rock face, almost angelic. Lucifer. Fallen angel.

Sometimes all men looked like boys—in sleep, or in grief, or in moments of exuberance when they dropped their armor. He sensed her watching him, even with his eyes closed, and he turned to her and smiled, the first open smile she had seen on his face. It transformed him, making it almost impossible for her to believe that he had raped her. She felt suddenly dizzy.

He stood up and stripped off his soaked shirt, his back to her, and she saw the scar that flashed brilliant on his shoulders. At some time he had been terribly burned. She spoke without intending to. "How did you get that?"

"What?"

POSSESSION

"That burn scar on your back."

"That? I was just a little kid, and I pulled a coffee pot down on me. I was screaming, I guess, and the old lady in the next trailer put lard on it and wrapped it in a sheet—wasn't supposed to do that. Some nurse had to peel it off and my skin came with it."

"Where was your mother?"

"Working. My father took a hike before I was born."

"Does it hurt?"

"Nothing hurts anymore. You ready?"

He didn't wait for her answer, and she had to scramble to catch him. They worked their way downtrail now, the brunt of the pull on different muscles, making her ankles ache and strain against the laces of her hiking boots. The larch trees were close, but not close enough to stop her if she began to slip. Then the forest pulled back and there was only the rock shoulder of the mountain. She slid often and felt a thrill of fear erupt from her stomach and tingle in her arms and legs. He held out his hand and she took it instinctively, letting his power steady her.

"We're dropping a thousand feet in a mile," he said. "Put your feet sideways if you start to slide. Don't panic. I can stop you."

Halfway down the slope he paused, so suddenly that she could not keep from bumping into him. He put one hand back and propped her against him. She followed his eyes and saw the avalanche meadow far below them. She could see the short grass and forest edging it. Some of the great trees had been wrenched from their hold on the earth by avalanche, their roots dead or dying in the cold air, but she could see no way out. No trails at all. She turned to ask him which way they would go, but the waterfall spewing out of Bowan Mountain filled the air with a roaring din that absorbed human sound.

She trusted that he knew and trusted him in that way only. She followed him again through a forest that expanded from stunted, struggling fir, pine, spruce, and the changed larches to tall trees that blocked the meadow view.

169

Miles and miles of it, closing her in with him. She was close enough to smell his odor, to see the jagged scar stretched even tauter by the movement of his free skin, and the barely healing scratches along his arm. She saw that he had bite marks on his hand, purple indentations too small to have come from the huge bear teeth he'd described. She wondered about them, wondered who—or what—could have bitten him.

Halfway down the damned mountain, he should have been able to spot the trail, but he hadn't seen anything ringing the meadowland but trees. He was more annoyed than alarmed. He had studied the relief model in the ranger's office and read the guidebook they sold for three bucks. The route was clear from both those sources. But the trail wasn't there. He couldn't find it when they were in the meadow either. The book said to look for cut-ends of deadfall trees, but there were so many of the giant pick-up sticks, and none of them pointed the way out.

But he had *her,* and that was good. She was already depending on him to save her. Just like Lureen, unsure of herself, looking for a man to rescue her. She was only acting mad because she was scared—just like Lureen did when she had her temper tantrums. She was physically stronger than Lureen, but even so she was slowing them down. It was midafternoon. If he didn't find the trail in an hour or so, they would be trapped by night. He paced the perimeters of the grassy plateau, searching for a channel through the trees while she sat in the meadow plucking the little daisies that grew around her.

Her chin lifted defiantly at his approach and her eyes were dark with fatigue and indecision.

"You're not a policeman, are you?"

"No."

"And you're not from Oregon either, are you?"

"No."

"And you're going to kill me, aren't you?"

He dropped beside her and slowly unbuttoned her blouse,

letting his fingertips touch her breasts lightly. "Why would I kill you?" He pressed his lips to the vein that beat frantically between her breasts and felt her breathing stop. "I won't kill you. I love you. You've always belonged to me. You belong to me now. You're my possession."

She realized then that he was quite insane.

She didn't fight him or beg. She lay back and let him touch her. She felt his penis slide over her eyelids and circle her mouth, poke into her ears, and move over her body as if he was anointing her with it, and heard him chanting "Your eyes belong to me, and your mouth, and your breasts. It all belongs to me—all of you." It was all a dream, and she was not really part of it. She was no longer inside of her own skin, but stood somewhere away from it, watching but not feeling. She moaned when the red man told her to, and she parted her legs when he burrowed between them. When it began to hurt, she let the woman on the ground absorb the pain.

He held her afterward, rocking her in his arms, stroking her as if she were a rabbit until her breathing quieted. When she tried to pull away, he pressed his thumbs against her throat and choked her again, and she made herself be still. He seemed pleased with her.

She tested him later, pulling away just an inch or so at a time, and he allowed her to slip away from him. She put on her clothes and he watched her.

"You are the most beautiful, most perfect woman in the world. I will protect you and keep you safe. I didn't hurt you. You didn't fight me. It was the way it should be. You're part of me now."

She walked away from him, toward the edge of the wood. He made no move to stop her, but he watched her while she pushed into the foliage. She tried several places, willing the trail to be there. When she found it, she would run and if he caught up with her, she would find someplace to jump off. Some high place.

She looked for a long time, but she could find nothing that looked like a trail; it was all choked with woods and underbrush. After a while she walked back to the meadow and lay down, curling herself into the smallest possible ball. He walked over to her, but he didn't touch her; he only cast his shadow over her and then he went away and she slept.

14

Sam turned his pickup into the lane and headed up to the farmhouse; it was raining again and the weeds seemed to have grown a foot in four days, his fenders catching them wetly and then flopping them back away in a shower of water. No one had answered when he called at seven, but that was cutting it close. Their boat should have come into Chelan at six, and the drive south would take a good hour, barring Labor Day traffic. 7:45 now, they should be back. He was disappointed when he pulled into the yard and saw that Danny's truck was not in the shed. He lit a cigarette and waited for Billy Carter to waddle up in full attack, but the gander didn't appear. The farmhouse had that lost look of all empty houses. The grass was tall here too, and Joanne's sunflowers bent like old women's heads from their weight of water. He finished the smoke, lit another, and listened for the distant throttle of Danny's truck coming up the hill. He heard occasional tire-on-gravel sounds from the road itself, but nothing nearer.

It occurred to him a little before eight that Danny might have left him a note. But the little cedar house with a notepad attached hadn't been opened for a long time; there was an old cobweb across the latch. If Danny was really running late, he'd probably taken Joanne to her mother's and gone straight to work; he had a spare uniform in his locker. Sam felt for the key they always kept under a loose shingle over the porch. It seemed important to go into the house—just to see if there was some sign that they had been home at all.

He walked into the silent kitchen. The ticking of the old

gradeschool clock on the wall the only sound except for his own steps. The room smelled stale—cigar smoke, dust, and a faint trace of garbage—two plates left sitting in the sink with moldered toast and hard yellow egg bits. A row of canning jars sat on the counter, and he ran his finger along one and he saw the mark left in the thin veneer of dust. They were labeled in Joanne's neat hand: Peaches—September 3, 1981. He smiled; she'd been canning right up to the last minute. It must have bothered her to have to leave dirty plates behind.

He walked to the phone and dialed the office. "Fletch?"

"You better get your ass in here, Sammy."

"Danny show up there?"

"Negative."

"I'm out at his place, and they're not back here yet."

"Probably got held up in traffic. Everybody waiting until the last minute to head home."

"Yeah, well—I'm coming in. Tell him to wait for me if he comes in before I get there."

The trip out to Danny's place had fouled up Sam's timing, placing him in the squad room with the under-sheriff, Walker Fewell—or, more likely, Fewell had cooled his heels waiting for a deliberate confrontation. Fewell was a short, well-muscled martinet of a man who looked like a Marine DI shrunken and preserved—which he was. He'd squeaked into the Natchitat County Sheriff's Office through a loophole in the civil service qualifications list. Everything he knew about police work could fit into a shotglass with room left over; perhaps worse, he realized it. So he made up for his inadequacies by demanding absolute respect, spit-polished boots, and perfectly creased, spotless uniforms. He brown-nosed the press, and he nit-picked everything Sam did because he couldn't stand a deputy who simply refused to acknowledge his existence. Sam always stared somewhere over Fewell's right shoulder when the under-sheriff addressed him.

Walker Fewell sat now in his little office with walls plastered with certificates and awards for work not done, behind his clean desk, and worked over Sam's field reports from last night, marking out and changing Sam's round printing with the prissiness of a schoolteacher.

Sam eased past his door, and signaled to Fletch to toss him the keys to his unit, but Fewell called out in his high, nasal voice.

"Deputy. Deputy Clinton. Would you step in here before you leave?"

"He's gonna check to see if your shorts are ironed, Sam," Fletch whispered.

"Hell, I'm not wearing any."

"Then Lord help you. Sam—don't get him riled up. He's been going over the time sheets and he saw you were late three times last week. He'll have you sweeping up the jail if he can work it."

Sam leaned into Fewell's office, his hands splayed on either side of the doorjamb, dwarfing the under-sheriff where he sat in his little chair at his huge desk. His expression was respectful, but Fewell either recognized or imagined mockery in Sam's eyes.

"Clinton, you're not indispensable."

"No sir."

"You were tardy several shifts last week, and you're seven minutes late this evening. Is punctuality a problem?"

"No sir. I've had some trouble with my truck."

"Then you should make other arrangements."

"Yes sir. Is that all, sir?"

"We're a small department, but our standards are as high as any in the state. You know the pride I take in running an efficient, productive organization?"

"Yes sir."

"This follow-up on the incident last night with—er—a Mrs. Alma Pavko." He tapped the yellow sheet in front of him with the bowl of his unlit pipe. "Deputy Clinton, this comes across as a very crude comedy routine. We do not use the word 'shit' to refer to human excrement. They'll read your FIRs and follow-ups into the record in the courtroom, you know, and 'shit' and 'bare-assed' show an appalling lack of taste."

"I have testified in court a few times, sir. I am aware of

the use of the reporting officer's follow-ups. I doubt that Mrs. Pavko's case will go into litigation. I would expect she's somewhat embarrassed today."

"Perhaps it won't—but I think you take my point."

"Yes sir."

"Where's your partner? Is he late too?"

"He took some comp time, sir. The Lindstroms have evidently been held up in traffic. I'm sure he will check in the moment he gets to town."

"That's all. You're dismissed—but I want to see Lindstrom when he shows up."

"Thank you sir." Sam moved out of the doorway, and then leaned in quickly, catching Fewell picking his nose. "And have a good evening, sir."

He called Fletch so many times during the shift, checking to see if Danny had checked in, that even Fletch got exasperated. "If he calls, dammit, I'll let you know. Now get off the air and earn your salary."

15

She woke slowly, surfacing through layers of tension, and when she broke through the top of her sleep, her terror was as bright as the sun that stabbed into her eyes. She knew now that Danny was truly gone, and that there was no going back to save him. That tomorrow and next month and Christmas and next year, and all the years of her life lay ahead without him. The knowledge was more than she could bear.

She turned her face into the rushed grass and tried to shut the world out. She was alone.

She was not alone.

He crouched above her, pulling at her shoulder. She moaned and burrowed herself more deeply into the carpet of grass, deep enough to feel the grave-cold earth beneath it. There was no comfort there; there was no comfort left anywhere. She stood and began to pace with tight little steps, wringing her hands. That spot of meadow seemed safer. No, this spot. No, the terror was inside of her; there was no place to run to.

"What time is it? What time is it? Time? Time——" Her voice was a chant.

"Almost five."

"Morning five? Night five? We have to go. I have to get away from here. Hurry. Hurry. Show me which way."

"It's afternoon. You slept a long time. I let you sleep because you were worn out. The meadow is soft, isn't it?"

"It's cold. The ground is cold. We have to leave. We have to go down the mountain and tell someone to come and get Danny and take care of him."

"He's dead."

"I know——I know——I know. But he has to be in a clean room, a place where——oh my God——nothing can get at him. We have to tell someone."

"We can't go tonight. It's too late and the forest is too dark. Things in the woods——at night——they follow you and find you and you don't see them. You don't have any warning. They come for you."

"You did, didn't you? You came in the night and you crept up on us and you changed everything. You killed everything."

"No. I warned you. I came and warned you of the danger. God put me there so that I could save you. You believe in God, don't you?"

"I did." She had forgotten God the moment He failed her.

"You still do. Nothing happens without a reason."

"What reason?" She was screaming at him. "What reason for my husband to die instead of you?"

"I don't know. I only know that I'm here for you, and that you must trust me."

"Why?"

"Because you don't have anyone else."

He was mixing her up. He was not God's emissary; he was

176

POSSESSION

Lucifer, using God's name to confuse her. But what if she was wrong? He hadn't killed her yet, and she had expected that he would. He was probably crazy but she was not sure now if he was bad-crazy or good-crazy. She was quite sure that he had raped her, but whenever one memory segment became clearly defined, other recollections blurred. Was she remembering sex with Danny or with him?

She watched him bend over the fire to stir something, and she smelled food.

He smiled at her. "You have to eat. You must be strong because I've found the trail. It was right there behind those deadfalls; I found it while you were sleeping. In the morning, after you've eaten and slept, we will follow the way out. I promise you."

"Why did you rape me?"

He smiled at her again. "Is that the way you remember it?"

"Of course that's the way I remember it."

But in fact she only remembered their bodies moving together and the moon above or the sun—and then his face. No, that was with Danny. What did she remember?

"Do you read the Bible?"

"I used to read it a lot."

"Then you know that a man is responsible for his dead brother's wife; it is given to him to care for her and to hold her in love because his brother cannot."

"It was too soon . . ."

"The time is not important. It was inevitable that we should be together in love."

She was so frightened of him. He spun words around and around her so rapidly that she had no point of balance. He was capable of killing her in so many ways. She could not argue with his madness. Perhaps she was crazy too. That thought made her dizzy again.

"Look around us." His voice was low and steady. There was something wrong with her heart. Too fast. Staggered beats that dragged and then tumbled out of sync.

"We are in paradise. We have been through hell, and we

1 7 7

have been rewarded with paradise. God created the world in six days—the whole world. Were those six days of our time or six days that each lasted a century? Do we know what time it is? Can we believe absolutely that there is still a world beyond what we know now, today, this minute, this place? Is there anything on the other side of those trees and behind those hills? Maybe there's nothing more—maybe the rest of the world has died."

"But you said you'd take me out tomorrow. You promised me."

"I did, and I will. But you must not grieve for anything or anyone while we still have all this. We can only know that we have been blessed."

"I can't be certain of anything. It is very, very difficult for me to think."

"I will think for you."

"I have no choice, have I?"

"You can leave me at any time."

She did not believe him, but she had no strength to argue. She was so tired. She could not form long sentences and her thoughts fragmented before they came together.

"You can leave me. But it isn't going to happen. You would die without me. We've come through the worst of it. Eat this."

She stared suspiciously at the brownish lumps and liquid he held out to her in the bisected metal pan. It tasted of tin and cheap TV dinners and she ate it mechanically.

The meadow was already darkening, closing her in with him for another night. She shuddered and he noted her movement although he seemed to be looking away from her.

"You're cold."

"A little."

He moved to drape a sleeping bag around her shoulders, his hands touching her impersonally. What did she remember about his hands?

She did not want to talk to him, but having no one at all to talk to was the worst thing; the quiet let her mind rove freely to pick at fragments of the horror. She saw Danny's face, his dead eyes beseeching her, his dead mouth calling to her before it filled with a fountain of blood. And she fought to keep the food she'd just eaten from rising in her gorge.

"I have to go into the woods again," she said faintly.

"I'll go with you."

She didn't argue. Her body and all of its functions didn't matter any longer. He had taken it, erasing something she had guarded carefully all her life.

She squatted near a stump and turned her head away, but she felt him watch her. He turned back toward the clearing, their little camp visible now only by the molehill of yellow embers lighting the black.

He tossed more logs on the fire and it billowed high, a circle of warmth against the true cold around them. The smoke choked the air on the downwind side of the flames and she was forced to sit beside him, but she held her sleeping bag around her like armor, dreading his hands.

He had raped her; she was sure of that now, but she could not remember how many times. He was like an animal in rut. She had heard Doss say that a ram could do it dozens of times in a single day, and there was that kind of energy about the red man.

She spoke very carefully. "I need to know what happened to my husband. I think—if you could tell me everything—that I could cope with it. I am having a great deal of difficulty. I imagine things. I see terrible pictures because I don't know what really happened."

He was quiet for a long time. "If I thought it would help you, I would tell you, but it wouldn't help you. I told you that it was sudden, that he didn't feel pain, and that's enough for now. When it's time, and when there isn't so much danger around us, I will answer everything you ask. Not now. And we won't have sex tonight . . . ."

She felt a wave of relief. No. It was probably one of his tricks.

"We can talk, but there are rules. You have to take the part of life that cannot be dealt with and shut it off. Talk about anything that happened before we came together, or talk about what will happen tomorrow or next week. But we will not talk of anything in between."

"That's impossible."

"No. Think this: that you and I are riding on a train through the night. We're going somewhere we want to go, and you're a nice pretty woman, and I'm not such a bad guy, and we have a long way to go together. So we talk to each other and we pass the time, and we leave behind us everything that we don't want to think about, and everything ahead of us is under my control."

"But nobody can control the future."

"*Yes.* Yes, it can be shaped and painted the way we choose. Now, look at the fire and keep staring at it. See the lights in the houses along the track? Hear the whistle blowing? Hear how the wheels go clackety-clackety-clackety underneath us, bumping over the tracks."

"No. I hear a loon crying."

His hand grasped her arm so tightly that his fingers hurt. "That's *not* a loon; that's a whistle. You have to listen."

"I'll try."

"Clackety-clackety-clackety-clack." His voice was so deep that it vibrated oddly in her bones. She shifted so that her arm slipped away from his hand and he let her go easily.

"How old are you?"

"That doesn't matter. That's only part of time."

"I don't know how to talk. I'll break your rules."

"You're soft and gentle, like my mother was. You even look like her."

"Where is she now?"

"Gone."

She waited for him to say more, but he fell silent, staring into the fire.

"I remember everything, you know. Do you believe that I can?"

"Yes." She would not disagree, afraid to set off some spark that would trigger his crazy side.

"We weren't town people like you were. We were with the carnivals—because that was the only thing she knew. My mother was very young, but everything she did was for me, and she was with me every minute she could be."

POSSESSION

He paused as if he expected her to deny that, but she said nothing.

"She danced and she was good; she could have danced anywhere, but she was afraid to try. I remember she wore this little pink costume with shiny things on it, little beads—whatchacallit—sequins. She looked like a princess. And her hair was like yours, but longer." His voice changed, anger sliding into it; she tensed, but he talked on, remembering. "We never had shit. Nothing. We lived in a crummy little bus-trailer thing, cold in winter, an oven in the summer, and the tires always blowing. I'd wake up in the night and we'd be stopped somewhere along some road and she'd be crying because we'd been left behind and she couldn't find anyone to get us going. Unless you've lived like that, you don't understand. Town kids used to laugh at me when I tried to play with them. Their mothers would come out and tell me to go away.

"So, anyway, I always wanted a bicycle. Fuck, she couldn't afford to feed us. She had these silver shoes with different colored bows to match her costumes, and they were all cracked on the sides and so thin on the bottom that she got slivers from the stage, and she couldn't afford new ones because she was trying to feed me. I'll bet you've never been hungry in your life, have you? Did you ever eat cornmeal mush and boiled potatoes for a whole month running?"

"No."

"So a bicycle was out of the question. I could ride one when I was four. Some bratty town kid came by and he had his bright red bike and I got on it and I rode that sucker and he started screaming and crying and saying I stole it. I just got on it and rode it. First time. That was *free*. The wind swishing by my ears and my legs pumping and I knew I could go anywhere I wanted, only his daddy comes running up and grabs the handlebars and says, 'Give it back, you little bastard,' and the kid's standing there and grinning like a monkey and sticking his tongue out.

"Lureen, she tried to explain I was only trying it out, and

1 8 1

I remember that prick town-daddy reached out and patted her on the breast as though she didn't deserve any respect, and he said, 'You keep your little bastard-trash kid off my son's bike.'"

"You must have hated him."

"I showed them. They were sorry."

"You were just a little boy. How could you—"

"Oh, I was a smart little fucker. I watched them go back to their car once, and they had their stupid dog with them— shut up in the car with the windows rolled down a little bit because it was hot. I just waited until they went back on the midway, and then I tried the doors. They weren't locked, so I rolled up every window really tight. They had a nasty surprise when they found it."

She felt a wave of nausea and fought not to let him know. But he kept talking.

"I got a bike later. Some kid left it with a flat tire, and I took it before he got back. The geek patched the tire and it was good as new."

"What's a geek?"

"Some old alky that bites the heads off live chickens."

". . . why?"

"Because it brings the rubes in. They go for sick stuff, like pickled babies."

"You don't like people."

"Some. Most of the time there's not much to like. Everybody's out for himself."

He was so violent. Every subject that came up seemed to draw some awful story from him, as if there was nothing inside him beyond hate. She tried to think of something gentler to talk about. "Where is your mother—Lureen?"

"Haven't you figured that out yet?"

"No."

"She died. That's the only way she ever would have left me, the only way. She was going into town one night in— hell, it doesn't matter—Texas, Oklahoma maybe. This cowboy was driving and she was sitting in the front seat, and he ran his convertible right up the back of a truck loaded with telephone poles. He saw it coming—damn him—and he ducked, but one of the poles came through the windshield and it took her head off."

"Oh!" It hit her bluntly and she could not stop the gasp, although his voice remained steady and matter of fact.

"I was about five, and I waited and waited for her to come back. They put me in the fat lady's truck and they just moved on out of town. I used to worry that she wouldn't be able to find us when she came back. I used to go write my name on the outside of that truck, so she'd know I was in there. Then I started writing it on billboards in different towns and putting down where we were headed next. So finally they told me she wouldn't be back. They just said she had gone away, but I heard them talking about the poles one night, and what happened to her head, and I knew she was gone for good and I quit leaving messages for her."

"Didn't your father try to find you?"

He laughed harshly. "We have to sleep. I've got to get you down the mountain tomorrow."

She picked up her sleeping bag and started to spread it out on the other side of the failing embers.

"No. Over here."

She was afraid. "Why?"

"Because I have to know where you are." He led her to a spot beside his sleeping pallet and drew a length of rope from his pack.

"Lie down, but don't zip up your bag."

"I'll freeze."

"You can zip it part way. Hold out your right ankle."

He looped the rope around her calf and then cinched it around her ankle, tight enough so that she couldn't get it off, but not so tightly that it cut off her circulation. He tied the other end around his own leg, binding them together with the foot-long hobble.

"You don't have to do that," she protested. "There's nowhere I can go at night. I promise I won't try to get away. Don't you trust me?"

"Why should I?" His voice was close, so soft that she

could barely hear its muted whisper, but she could not see his face. "You tried to kill me this morning. You were going to splatter my brains with a boulder."

She could scarcely remember it, but if it had happened—if she had held the stone above his face—it had been a long time ago, a week, maybe more. They had been in the meadow for days. She was quite sure of that.

16

On Wednesday Sam called the farm phone six times in an hour, had the operator check the line, found it in working order, and then forced himself to stay off his own phone so that it wouldn't be busy when Danny called. If they'd taken an extra day, they'd be in soon.

Waiting, he confronted the possibility that Danny's constraint during their last conversation in his trailer had been more than embarrassment over his own confessions of loneliness. He had blundered into Danny's personal boundaries, intruded into a marriage, and Danny had begun to shut him out. Their travel plans were their own business. Let them stay away on their private journey. Let them come back when they damn well pleased. It was Danny's responsibility if he failed to show up for shift tonight. It was *his* night off, and let Danny cover his own ass.

He switched on the five o'clock news and watched it without interest as he lit one cigarette after another. After an hour, he grabbed the phone again and dialed information and asked for the number for the North Cascades Lodge in Stehekin.

"The only listing we have, sir, is a number in Chelan."

"Give me that, then."

After a dozen rings, a young man's voice answered. No, there were no passenger lists. No reservations on *The Lady of the Lake*—you bought your ticket, you rode up, you rode back, nobody checked you in or out.

POSSESSION

He hung up, dialed Walt Kluznewski's number and that too rang empty. He called the Chelan number back.

"Son," he said, pushing authority into his words. "This is Deputy Clinton at the Natchitat County Sheriff's Office. You have a parking lot up there for your passengers?"

"Yessir—for the overnighters and longer."

"Give it a quick look-see and tell me if there's a 1979 GMC pickup—red with Natchitat County plates—lemme see—here: TLL-687 or 876 still parked there. No. I'll wait."

He heard Willie Nelson wailing over the boat office radio. Twenty seconds later, the phone was picked up again.

"Deputy?"

"Yes."

"It's here. Looks like it hasn't been moved for a long time. Can't see through the windshield for dust."

"Don't touch it. Leave it alone until I get up there. You got a boat to Stehekin tonight?"

"No sir. One trip up every day at 8:30 A.M. One trip back."

"Any other way to go uplake?"

"Yessir. Ernie Gibson'll fly you up in his seaplane. He can make Stehekin in about twenty or twenty-five minutes— been doin' it every day for over thirty years except in deep winter. Or you got you a power boat, they go up. Chelan County's got a sheriff's boat out there. Why don'tcha call them?"

Sam hung up without thanking the kid and sat staring at the phone. If he were to go charging up to Stehekin to find Danny and Joanne enjoying themselves, safe, they'd be pissed. More than pissed; he'd interfered enough in their lives.

He cracked a beer and turned the television up, trying to quash the niggle of alarm that wouldn't go away. When the phone rang, he jerked so forcibly that he splashed beer over his coffee table, and cracked his shin in his leap toward the ringing.

But the voice was a woman's voice, familiar and faintly querulous.

"Mr. Clinton?"

"Yes, ma'am." It registered: Elizabeth Crowder, Joanne's

185

mother. He tried to keep the disappointment out of his voice.

"I'm feeling some concern, Mr. Clinton. I have heard nothing from my daughter and son-in-law. They were to be back Monday night. Did you know that?"

"Yes, ma'am, I know they intended that, but I wouldn't worry if I were you. I'm sure they'll be in this evening."

Mrs. Crowder began to weep. "I drove out there, and nobody's home, and I drove over to Sonia's—Mrs. Kluznewski's—and they haven't heard anything either. I'm so concerned, Mr. Clinton. Joanne is the type of person who always calls, even if she's only going to be fifteen minutes late—"

He felt sweat bead the back of his neck. "There's no telephones up there, ma'am. She wouldn't be able to call you."

"I didn't want her to go."

"I'm sure everything is just fine. I'll tell you what, if they call me first, I'll get right back to you, and if they call you, you give me a jingle. How about that?"

"Yes, yes. We'd better keep the lines clear. It's just—Mr. Clinton—it's just that they're all I have—"

He stripped as he walked through the trailer, pulled on jeans and an old flannel shirt, dug through the dust under the bed in the back room for the fatigue boots they'd issued him for the Tact Squad in the riots in Seattle, and cursed the rotting laces when they snapped. He was on his way out the door when he remembered Pistol. He opened five cans of cat food and set them on the counter, dumped some dry food in the sink; the cat always drank out of the toilet anyway. He propped open the bedroom window above the wall marked with a trail of claw marks, and saw that Pistol had eaten his way through one tin of shrimp and tuna already and was working on another.

"Make it last, kid, or you'll have to work for a living. And keep your eyes on the valuables."

He didn't bother calling the office. If he wasn't back, he wasn't back. And Fewell could like it or lump it.

* * *

POSSESSION

They lifted off the south end of the lake at dawn in one of Ernie Gibson's seaplanes, the DeHaviland left over from World War II. Sam, riding copilot in the six-seater, noted there was still a knob marked *bomb release* on the instrument panel, and speculated on the craft's history. He saw himself at eighteen, the gung-ho sailor who never saw anything of the war outside of Great Lakes Naval Station. Ernie Gibson had. You could tell by the way he flew, as easily as if he and the plane had welded into one form four decades before. He glanced sideways and saw the pilot, ageless—but he had to go sixty or more. Tight weathered skin over aquiline features, his concentration focused on whatever tune played through his earphones, his whole mien so relaxed he seemed to be napping. That was O.K. Sam wasn't up to small talk.

They flew over orchards, farmhouses, and bright aqua swimming pools, and then over the lake itself, between the dark mountains. Twenty-five minutes later, the DeHaviland settled on the water in front of the lodge as gracefully as a gull pouncing on a bit of bread, and Gibson was out and tying them up before Sam could react. They walked up the creaking dock toward the smell of coffee and bacon from the lodge, and Sam felt a moment of regret that he had no time to talk to Gibson or know him. Another time, another place, they would have been friends. Now Ernie headed toward the restaurant's steamed-up glass door and Sam walked toward the ranger's office, grateful that he'd worn his down jacket; the air here whispered of frost even while the zinnias and petunias still bloomed along the walkway. What had been summer here was gone, and the feeling was one of closing up and closing in.

The Forest Service Office was warm and comfortably familiar, and the ranger in charge smiled broadly and held out his hand. "Deputy. Glad to know you. Must have been one of your guys through here last week."

"That's why I'm here. My partner and his wife were headed up here, and they're late getting home. Thought I'd check in with you and see what's up."

The ranger frowned slightly and pulled a ledger toward

1 8 7

him. "That so? Let's see what they wrote down here. We keep track of people—follow some of them all up and down the Pacific Trail. Lindstrom? Right?"

"Right."

The ranger ran his finger down a column of names, turned the page, and repeated the motion, stopping halfway down the list. "Here it is. I talked to them last Friday; they stayed that night in the lodge. They signed out for Rainbow Lake, and your buddy talked about going on over to pick up the North Cascades Highway instead of coming back here. When they weren't back Monday, we figured that's what they'd done. Seemed to be experienced hikers—had plenty of gear."

"Yeah. Well—he hasn't called in. How far would it be for them to go over the other side?"

"From the lake? Ohh, five, six hours. Once they got out to the North Cascades Highway, they wouldn't have had any trouble getting to a phone. We figured they'd decided to go over Bowan Mountain, and pick up the highway and catch a bus from Winthrop back to pick up their vehicle in Chelan."

Sam shook his head. "Their truck's still back there at the boat dock. If you'll point out the trail to me—the one up to Rainbow Lake—I'll hike on up there and have a look. They're probably just having such a good time they decided to stretch out their vacation."

"You want me to come along?"

"Thanks, but I'll be fine."

"Grade's fairly steep. You in shape?"

The ranger was nudging fifty too, and Sam grinned. "As much as any of us old guys. Do me good to sweat a little."

"O.K. Here's your map—pretty basic."

"Do you want me to leave crumbs behind so you can find me?"

"Just stay on the trails. You'll probably bump into them coming down."

"Most likely."

For half an hour, Sam climbed without stopping on a surge of false energy, but it could not last. His hip sent first a

POSSESSION

twinge of pain when he put his right foot down too solidly, and then it sprouted a steady ache that was like a girdle radiating from his lower back. He tried to ignore it, but it would not go away. His muscles knotted in spasm until his entire back was rigid. Too many years of sitting. Too many years period. He tried to pace himself, stopping and resting too often. His lungs would not expand the way they had—how many years ago? Ten? Twenty? Thirty, probably. He panted and grunted like an old woman.

At the first meadow he eased his treacherous body down and lay on his back, feeling his right leg twitch by itself. He could see why they shuffled most cops off the street before they were fifty; he couldn't chase a one-legged blind man and expect to catch him.

He stretched, and the spasms lessened their hold, but only partially. He knew if he lay too long, he'd never walk again, and if he started climbing too soon, they'd have to come get him with a litter.

He was sure he'd made three miles, but when he checked the map, he found he'd gone just under two. He wanted a cold beer more than he'd ever wanted anything, and he remembered the perfect rows of Olympia that waited back in his trailer. It hadn't occurred to him to bring any. He'd thrown two cans of franks and beans into his jacket pockets and bought some beef jerky at a 7-11 in Chelan. What the hell could you expect from a city cop?

He groaned and hit it again. The trail was obviously designed for mountain goats. The switchbacks were a maze. Once he was on the zig-zag path that led higher and higher, there was no stopping, no place to sit, and sure as hell no place to lie down.

His tension—the steady hum of concern that had seen him through the night's drive where nothing existed beyond the two yellow funnels of his headlights—shaded gradually until it became anger. Anger at himself because he was a fool. Anger at Danny for somehow summoning him to this mountainside, and, only slightly diminished, anger at Joanne for thinking of the whole fucking mess in the first place.

He crossed the creek on the plank bridge and lay on his belly to drink the icy water that, miraculously, tasted better than beer. The air was warm now, and the sun deceived him into thinking he had found summer. With the heat, a faint suggestion of well-being crept over him.

A mile further on, at least by his shirttail reckoning, he came to a camping area. Five campsites, and none with the look of recent occupancy. A scrabbly, blighted area with no view of anything. The little can of franks and beans opened with a tab that made him think of beer. He had had no supper or breakfast, and the food, cold and gelatinous as it was, restored his energy.

He lit a cigarette and sensed at the moment he slipped his lighter back into his shirtpocket that he wasn't alone. The presence was to his left, and he turned his head slowly—ready to speak until his eyes met the flat lidded yellow orbs staring at him with lazy interest. The rattler, thick as his wrist, lay stretched across the rock pile three feet away.

Sam blew out the smoke that swelled forgotten in his throat and lowered his hand very slowly. The snake watched him but made no attempt to coil. Its forked tongue flashed and the wedged head followed his movements. He inhaled again, trying to match his arm motion to the snake's torpor.

"Want a puff?"

The eyes blinked; the tongue shot out.

"No? Nasty habit, anyway. Get much traffic through here?"

Gone fucking crazy. Talking to rattlers.

He'd be damned if he was going to move first—not until he'd finished the cigarette. He took his time, watching for a sudden change in the serpent's position, but it moved nothing but its head. He searched the ground where he sat for other snakes, but there were none; then he ground the butt out under his heel. He wouldn't know until he tried just how much agility remained in his bad hip. He rolled to his right, away from the rattler, balanced for an instant on his boots and fingertips, and then was on his feet and out of striking range. When he looked back at the rock pile, the snake was gone.

17

She knew that they had been in the same meadow for a long time, but she was not sure how long. She forgot things very quickly and it was so hard to call them back. One morning—it might have been the second or the third, she wasn't sure—they couldn't leave because a thick fog made the trees vanish and he'd said they would fall off the mountain if they tried to move down. Remembering the drop so dangerous even in clear air, she knew he was right. The next day, or maybe some other day, there was a reason to stay. What was it? She couldn't remember. Sometimes it seemed as if the light lasted so long that night would never come, and at other times, the periods between day and night and day again flittered by in minutes. He liked it when she sat quietly and listened to him talk, but there was often a sudden panic that demanded that she move. When that happened, she found she could lessen the terror by action. She circled the meadow's boundaries then, hurrying faster and faster to leave the crawling feeling behind. He always made her stop before she was entirely free of it and led her back to their little camp. She tried not to cry because it seemed to annoy him, no—infuriate him. Sometimes in the night she had to cry because her tears choked up in her throat and she couldn't breathe, but she learned to do it softly. Even so, he caught her at it, his thick fingers finding the tears on her face.

And once he had touched her he would not let her go until he had touched her all over, exciting himself and finally plunging into her. She had learned to lie still and accept him passively so that he wouldn't hurt her, and afterward he was nicer and calmer and left her alone. In the blackness and especially in the fog—when she thought she had died—his hands defining her were proof that she was still alive. When

191

she didn't fight him, he was almost gentle with her. He let her breathe, and he allowed her to live.

In the daytime, when she could see his face, he looked at her so strangely sometimes as if there were something she should know. Once in a while, when he came, he cried out some name or some word that sounded like "Reen" or "Reenee," but she didn't know what it meant.

When he talked, she didn't have to think or remember and she could let her mind rest. And when he talked, he would not fondle her—as long as she responded correctly. When his voice made her drowsy with the deep buzzing cadence it could have, she had to balance her answers carefully. Most of the time, he only wanted her to listen and to look at him.

". . . some souls never die." He was staring at her again with his questioning look.

"No. They go to be with God."

"There is no God. There is only a continuum of particular, special souls. Special people—the rest are only reflections of the best and they die like cows. I am a special one. So are you. We will never die."

Hadn't he talked about God? She was sure it was the red man who was talking about God a long time ago.

"What cannot be seen by fools is truth. Do you agree?"

"Yes."

"She died when you were ten years old and became part of you. Do you remember?" he asked.

"I—"

"Say you remember!" He was angry, demanding an answer.

"I remember."

"I always knew you. All the times we were together, you always needed me. When I had to leave you, you died. But when you left me, I was stronger. I was always stronger because you belonged to me, and I possessed your soul. I never let it go, but you hurt me when you went away."

"I'm sorry." His stories were so confusing. They made her feel dreamy, tumbling along the tunnels he formed, trying to understand.

POSSESSION

"I forgave you. I always forgave you because you were weak. Do you remember who we were?"

"I don't understand—"

"Don't make me angry. You said you remembered when you started to be Lureen."

". . . oh, yes." Maybe she did remember. He was so sure of it, and she was no longer positive of who it was that she was now. There were no mirrors here, only his eyes, and he seemed to recognize her.

"I went to libraries and I saw our pictures in old books. We had different names, but our eyes stay the same. That's how you can be sure—by the eyes. I knew you when I saw your eyes. Did you know me?"

"I—yes, I knew you." She couldn't seem to pull her gaze away from his, and she could truly see her image in them. She finally looked away because they made her so dizzy.

"Would you like to sing?"

"*What?*"

"You always liked to sing—Elvis's songs. Love me tender. . . ."

She joined in because it seemed important to him. They had sung at their other camp. . . . No. Not with him. She had sung with someone. With Danny, maybe, but she couldn't remember.

All she could remember was that she had been safe then—and happy—and the thought of it made her want to cry again. But she sang with the red man for a long time because it seemed to calm him. When he was calm, because she pleased him, he seemed almost nice. He didn't frighten her then. She only had to remember not to talk about things that bothered him. There were so many things she had to keep track of. To keep from dying.

They had stayed in the meadow far too long, and he railed at himself for that. It had been so perfect, having her with him, belonging so totally to him, that he had not wanted to end it. But the days had run on, and they had only come four miles from the lake. He had seen no one, but there could conceivably be searchers. He couldn't be sure because

193

she didn't remember when her vacation was supposed to end. When he asked her, she would say "Monday" one time, and another time she said "In time for graduation." He should have questioned her earlier. He was pleased by the vague hazy way her mind was—it made her sweeter. Physically, she was doing well; she ate and slept when he told her to, and she complained only rarely of nausea. She let him make love to her, and she allowed him to hold her at night and fit himself around her to keep her warm.

But they had to leave now, and he was ill; his body had suddenly betrayed him. He was certain it would pass, but his mind was dulled by a stubborn fever. His body responded slowly to what he asked of it. He could work his way around the pain by blocking it out, but his swollen arm got in his way, and the burning in his head expanded and made it impossible to concentrate.

The damned arm had wakened him Monday night. He thought at first that she had pulled on her hobble and was trying to leave him, but she lay asleep beside him. It was not his leg, but the arm that felt oddly tight as if its skin had shrunk and could no longer accommodate his flesh and muscle. He could not tell what it was then, not by the quartering moon and the remnants of fire. It itched and hurt when he scratched it and was full of unhealthy heat.

He finally found sleep again just before dawn by letting the swollen arm rest outside his sleeping bag and pretending it was not part of him. When he awoke, he saw the arm swollen from his wrist to his armpit where the lymph nodes bulged like walnuts. The scratches and the marks left by her teeth gleamed a bright, unnatural color.

She didn't know. He'd kept his sleeves rolled down, and the new coldness in the air made that seem reasonable. But the arm seemed almost alien now, a heavy, throbbing weight. He tried to throw it out in a wide gesture to end the song, and she looked at him sharply when he could not.

"What's the matter with you? What's wrong with your arm?"

"Nothing. I got scratched when—you remember, I told you. The grizzly ripped up my arm some. It's kind of sore."

POSSESSION

"Let me see it." She reached for his arm and he drew back.

"It's nothing. It's beginning to feel better now."

"You're moving funny, and you've been dropping things."

He shrugged and rolled up his sleeve, holding the arm out.

"Oh my God!"

He followed her stare and was startled to see the arm, swollen and darkened so that it looked sausagelike. The tracks were spread apart and oozing pus. Her teeth marks looked worse. He shivered.

"Why didn't you tell me you were hurt? You've let it get infected. What happened to you? What did this?"

"You've forgotten again."

She turned his hand in hers, gently pressed the tooth marks. "What's this? What bit you?"

"You did."

"I couldn't have!"

"When we were in the tree."

Her face was stricken. "I'm sorry. I'm so sorry. You were hitting my head—"

"You were hysterical; I had to keep you from slipping down. You didn't mean to. It doesn't matter now."

"No. I wouldn't have done that to anyone deliberately." She turned away and started pawing through her pack. She looked back at him. "Are you allergic to penicillin?"

"I don't know. I never had it."

"What about when you were a child? You never had it for a sore throat? You must have."

He stared back at her, wondering at the vast blank spaces in her recollection. She seemed truly to have forgotten.

"No. Never. I always got better eventually—even that time with my ears."

She dug a brown plastic tube out of her pack and shook two round white tablets out. "Take these. I'll get the canteen. Just take them. I have enough for four days—that should help. I always bring them just in case."

"What if I'm allergic?"

195

"We can't think about that; we don't have a choice. You're not allergic to bee stings, are you?"

"No."

"Then it will be all right, I think." She carried a silver tube with a paper label with her and reached for his arm. "Neosporin. We'll put that on too. You should have told me before, though."

And it had helped some. His arm still bothered him, but the infection seemed static, neither retreating nor accelerating, only smoldering with chronic pain. He liked having her take care of him, and what he had viewed as a setback seemed actually to be a blessing. During the time she fussed over him, she seemed serene; nurturing seemed a comfortable role for her. It was only when she had nothing to do that she grew restive.

She was afraid he was going to die, and that she would have caused it. She could not remember that she had tried to kill him before; she only knew that if he died, she would be all alone. He told her that often, reminding her that it was her teeth that had sent the deadly spores into his bloodstream, and then he cried when he talked about what would happen to her without him. He slept, or seemed to sleep, much of the time, and she had to keep the fire going and fix food to make him stronger. But he would not eat, and he grew weaker.

He had promised her he would take care of her and he had done that. She didn't know where Danny had gone, but Danny had left her on the mountain and something bad had happened to her. But she couldn't recall what it was. She could not remember beyond yesterday. When he touched her, he had given her life; he had willed her to live. She remembered that. Alone, even standing alone in the meadow, she was afraid. She needed some human thing to touch and hold on to because the air around her was empty. Caring for him was the most important thing. Women took care.

Sometime, sometime when there were walls to lean against and secure space with a roof and doors, she would sort it out. Unless he died and left her behind even though he had assured her he wouldn't. If he died, there would be no one left to see her. She would not belong to anyone, and she would cease to exist.

She had misjudged him, thought he had deliberately kept her in the meadow. And that was wrong. As sick as he was, he kept rousing from his delirium and telling her they had to leave. Of course, she could not let him do that. When she pushed him carefully back to his sleeping pallet, his muscles were still as heavy and strong but they seemed not to be able to work efficiently. He looked at her, but he seemed not to see her, and still he let her gentle him.

Someone—or something—had frightened her but she did not know who it was. She belonged to the sick man, and she knew that because he had explained it to her so many times. If she belonged to him and let him die, nobody would forgive her.

She watched him. He moaned in his sleep, but he would not talk to her, no matter how often she called out to him.

When he opened his eyes and saw her and she knew he knew her, she was grateful. He seemed to be in terrible pain still, but she thought her medicine was helping.

"Tell me the stories," she pleaded, and he talked to her again, in a voice not so deep, but steady.

"You won't leave me, will you?" she asked.

"I will never leave you. I possess you. I am part of you."

And she felt alive again.

"I have to know how protected we are," he explained. "You must go out into the woods and show me. I have to know if something could sneak up on us. Try to surprise me. Go far enough away so that I can't see you, and then try to fool me. I'll close my eyes. When I hear you, I'll shout 'Bingo.'"

She was rather good at it, but he always heard her; she betrayed herself with a crackling branch or a rustle of leaves when she was closer to him than a hundred yards or so. Even when he drowsed in his fever, he heard her. It made her feel safe.

When she was finished with her games, she came back to

him and lay down beside him. He was far too ill and weak to make love to her, but he felt her against him. The tension that had been there was gone. She lay beside him as easily as a lover, no longer a captive. He had sent her out of his sight deliberately, and she had come back. He was too sick to hobble her, but it didn't matter. She would not leave.

18

The fork in the trail was clearly marked, and Sam could see the arrow to the left reading Rainbow Lake and the one to the right indicating McAlester Pass. Five and a half miles to go now until he found them. The trail seemed easier for the moment, deceiving him into believing he had conquered the worst of it, falling downward beneath his feet to Rainbow Creek. He crossed a jerry-built bridge and filled his canteen, feeling more confident. The old man wasn't doing so bad after all.

But beyond the creek the trail became a maze of switchbacks, steeper than those he'd already climbed, and his lungs sucked up dusted air. At the top of each ramp of dry ground there was another and another—a labyrinth—as he trudged 1,200 feet higher on the sere breast of the mountain. He could not imagine anyone's deliberately seeking out such agony for recreation.

Five miles. He drank the last of his water grimly and started up one more switchback. His throat was dry as baked gravel as soon as he turned the corner.

And then there was water again, and the trail grudgingly flattened to negotiable planes. He mistrusted the mountain now and the mirage of meadowland sheltered by peaks on every side, but the hike was easy for more than a mile, the land lush and bespeckled with flowers again. His breathing eased and his body ached less. With the slackening of physical pain his sense of isolation grew strong and made him eager for the moment he would walk into their camp.

POSSESSION

Danny was going to whoop and clap him on the back for surviving this ordeal.

And he was starving. He hallucinated food odors on the wind. Steak and fish frying, whatever else Joanne might be cooking up only a mile ahead. Danny was going to devil him about being out of shape. Joanne would smile and tell her husband to shut up, and the three of them would sit around the campfire and fill each other in on their days spent apart. Where they waited was as fixed in his mind as if he really could see beyond the top of the trail; he held the picture as the path started upward again—not fooling him this time, but made bearable by the waterfall close by. What the hell. So he'd missed them; that was no crime.

He looked at his watch. Almost six-thirty. The ranger had said five and a half hours to the lake. It had taken him a little more than six, not too bad for an old man fueled on beans and water and no sleep.

He saw the lake, green water surrounded by a horseshoe of crags and spires, looking like a goddamned picture postcard. They would be down there hidden in the trees. He shouted a "Halloooo!" that startled him as it burst from his throat. He waited.

There was no answer.

He was probably beyond shouting distance; he would continue calling as he drew closer until he reached a spot where the woods wouldn't swallow his voice. He would not sneak up on them. He knew better than to surprise a cop. He kept shouting at regular intervals, stopping each time to listen. If they were in there screwing, he was going to feel like an ass.

"Come out, come out wherever you are . . . Uncle Sammy's come for supper . . ."

He listened. There was some answer. And then he realized it was his own echo mimicking him. Tree limbs sighed and groaned around him too, and a flight of tiny birds rose from the ground and circled over his head before they disappeared deep in the forest.

The smell at first was only a trickle of an odor. The rancid sweetness resembled the skunk cabbage stench that lay over sodden lowlands around Seattle in March. Cloying perfumed air, urging the uninitiated to pick an armful of the greenish-yellow hooded lilies. Once in drunken romanticism, he'd picked Nina a mass of them, and then been sorry; at the first bruise, they'd bled their pungent stink over everything.

But he knew what the smell really was; he had encountered it more than most men. He would not acknowledge it.

It grew stronger with every step toward the lake, and he held his breath. When he opened his lips to shout again, it rushed in and filled his lungs. Rotten air. He lit a cigarette and gulped the smoke, but the miasma choked out burning tobacco.

It was decaying flesh, something long dead that surely rested off the right side of the trail, close by now, fouling the air. He did not want to walk toward the slope of land that sheltered the dead thing.

But his feet took him to the edge and he bent his head slowly to look down through the underbrush and narrow-trunked saplings. There was a roaring in his head and then no sound at all as if he had slammed full-tilt into a wall and died. And yet, there was no surprise. He had known it for a long time, days—all those days of pretending and manufacturing explanations while the man below him had never moved at all.

The corpse lay on its face next to a deadfall, one dead hand lightly curled around a rock, its knees drawn under the swollen belly. There was no life in it; even its hair looked spiked and false, the scalp beneath it dull white.

Sam stared down for a long time before he could unlock his knees and side-step through the underbrush, down and down and down. He began to slide and saw the previously hidden ravine twenty feet beyond the corpse. He did not will himself to stop or make any effort at all to stop. He thought for a moment that it would be easy to go with the momentum and drop heavily on the rocks below—easier than greeting the dead man.

He did not go over; the ground cropped out just at the end of his descent and held him fast. A great lassitude filled him,

POSSESSION

and he lay alongside the precipice for a time and looked up and back now at the body, trying to make it unfamiliar.

Something or someone had dragged the corpse downhill by its boots; the arms reached back toward the trail, the plaid shirt was bunched up beneath the armpits, exposing a wide band of visible flesh, striated with purpling lividity along the belly portion and leached of blood on the back. He could see no blood stains on the jeans or the flannel shirt, nothing on the back of the head. He could not see the face at all.

He did not want to see the face. He longed to run away, back down the eleven miles of mountain to Stehekin. If he had not come, he would have had what? Maybe three or four more days of not knowing. It seemed an important block of time to hang onto, but it was too late; he had rushed to this place to find what he could not endure.

He gulped air and found that the smell was not as awful as it had been up above. The dog men always said that and he'd never believed them—that death odor rises in the woods, leaving the corpse oddly pure of scent. He'd seen dogs circling and howling at treetops and still hadn't believed it, but it was true.

His legs could not support him. He crawled on his hands and knees until he was four feet from the faceless, ruined man. The boots were nondescript, the jeans were Levi's, the shirt looked like all plaid shirts.

It could be any man.

His damn teeth were chattering. He crawled closer and allowed himself to look more carefully. He reached out and touched the left hand, finding it cold, its skin slippage already begun. The first layer would slip off like a glove if the skin was severed at the wrist. He unbuttoned the taut band of flannel with his own dead fingers and tugged the material back.

The tattoo—Danny's dumb home-made heart—crept into view, expanded now, stretched along with the bloated arm until it spread out grotesquely like something in a funhouse mirror. The D and J were there in the center of it, distorted too.

"Oh pard, oh pard, oh pard, oh pard," he was not aware that he spoke out loud. "What happened to you, Danny?"

He could not keep a partner; it was as simple as that. He sat back on his heels and let out a sound, a howl. Rage and grief, a primitive lament common to all tongues. It sent a hundred wild creatures scuttling for shelter, terrorized.

And then he worked rapidly with some icy deftness, racing the sun that had begun to sink toward the western ridges. He felt a curiosity, an obsession to know, coupled with a dull conviction that knowing would change nothing.

Danny was heavier than anything he'd ever tried to lift, and he struggled to turn the corpse over. Rigor had come and gone; what had happened had occurred days before. All that time, Danny had lain moldering through sunrise and sunset and sunrise again, unattended. An unattended death had to be the loneliest death of all.

He fought to think objectively. This was just another dead body, like the dozens of others he'd worked over. He could manage it in time-sets. For fifteen minutes he would not remember that this was Danny. He checked his watch and saw that it was only seven o'clock, not hours since he'd slid toward the rocky edge.

The eyes rolled into view, open and staring, their pupils clouded over with opaque circles. He did not recognize them. He did not recognize the face either. Purple as wine. He noted what he was supposed to note; the body had lain prone since death—it had not been moved or the lividity pattern would not be so classic.

Sam jotted findings on an imaginary pad. Cause of death?

The right cheek was scratched deeply with four parallel lacerations—bloodless. Why bloodless? An animal's claws maybe, but why bloodless? Post mortem. Mutilated after death. But why?

The blood was along the shirt front, pints of it spilled there, staining the blue and white plaid so completely that only black lines remained, framing neat squares of red now. The gore had sluiced down over the blue jeans and left them stiff. He lifted the shirt and saw puncture wounds, sucking wounds, over the heart and lungs, the skin around them already putrescent, green going black. Stab wounds? Bite wounds?

Eleven minutes to go.

Danny's—*no, the corpse's*—right arm flopped loosely, its humerus wrenched from the shoulder socket. Oh God, the power. What power? What creature?

The gun was there, lying in the crushed foliage where Danny's body had been. Danny's battered .38 that had belonged to the old man, to Doss. Sam picked it up by the checkered grips where fingerprints never clung, released the cylinder cautiously, and saw that every chamber was full. Danny had not fired it. He had carried it with him to this dying place, but why had he waited too long to use it? Neither of them had ever had to shoot bullets into a human being; they both knew what all cops knew—that any cop forced to shoot a man is himself maimed by the experience. Seattle P.D. or Natchitat County Sheriff's Office—the officers forced to shoot had all retired early on "mentals" that were called other things. It was one of the silent axioms of law enforcement: don't shoot or the bullet will eventually hurt you worse.

But killing an animal was different. Danny hunted; most cops fished and hunted, perhaps to find some acceptable channel for the hours of required marksmanship. Danny should have fired, emptied the damn cylinder. Sam shuddered and lay the weapon down, terribly puzzled.

He was not thinking well. There was something else he should be remembering, something of vital importance. He was not afraid; that wasn't it, although he visualized some animal, a bear probably. They were six feet, eight feet, when erect. Razor teeth. Five hundred pounds, a thousand— maybe more. He would relish the sight of the creature and the chance to destroy it. His pistol would be a pea- shooter—unless he could put out its eyes, but it scarcely mattered. There was nobody left to grieve over him. He could die up here and be absolved of guilt for having killed yet another partner.

Then he remembered. *Joanne. Where was Joanne?*

He scrambled through the saplings to the trail, shouting

her name. He called until he was hoarse, listening each time for her answer, and then unable to stand the mocking quiet, shouted again.

He thought he heard something near the lake, a woman crying, some muted sobbing. When he reached the water, a dark jade now in the gloaming, the sound stopped. He could hear it again, this time behind him on the left of the trail—wailing and pleading—but when he pushed deep into the trees there, the sound had moved back into the meadow from where he'd just come.

"Joanne! It's Sam," he shouted. "Wait for me. Stay where you are—I'm coming!"

Now the crying woman seemed to answer from high in the trees. He wondered if he really heard her at all.

He grew frantic in his search; she would be so frightened, perhaps even afraid to come out where *he* could see her. She had waited far too long for help, all alone. Danny had lain dead beside this lonely trail for at least three days, and she had been alone all that time. Frightened? God no, she would be terrified.

If it occurred to him that she too might be dead, he never let the thought bubble up. The worst had happened. There could be nothing more. He talked to himself unaware, "I'll find her, pard—don't worry. I'll find her and take care of her. She's in here someplace, pard, and she'll be O.K. Don't you worry about that."

He saw her then, her back to him, leaning against a log in the small clearing near the lake, motionless.

He ran now, unconscious of the pain in his back and thighs. Closer, he could see their little camp, the burned-out fire with the coffeepot resting on gray ashes, but even as he reached out to touch her, he saw that the figure he had been so sure was a woman with lowered head was only a sleeping bag, left propped against a log. Danny's old surplus khaki sleeping bag.

They had camped here, but there was no one here now, nothing but shadows. He looked up and saw something suspended from the trees and felt sick, afraid to go nearer and find that she had hanged herself in despair. When he drew near the swinging thing, he saw that it was only a duffel bag of spoiled food twisting in the wind and bumping against the pine.

The tree's bark was scuffed and he could see the broken branches where someone had crawled frantically upward. He saw even the crusted mounds of dried vomit on the ground. Someone *had* hidden here, someone in the grip of nauseous horror. He expected to find blood on the ground. She was no longer in the tree, so she had either come down of her own volition or she had been dragged down.

He was relieved to find no blood, no claw marks on the foodbag, nothing at all in the abandoned camp itself that indicated the bear had found her. Her sleeping bag was not here nor was her backpack, although he found Danny's pack behind a log. She had to be alive, but he could not imagine where in this morass of wilderness she crouched hidden—or how much longer she could survive.

The cold came with sunset, and he was aware of his body again. He gathered wood mechanically and lit the fire, but only for her, a signal she could see and know that it was safe to come out from her hiding place. He watched it burn and tried to work through the complexities of what had happened.

She had been in this camp, and she had tried to hide from . . . something . . . in the tree. There was physical evidence of that. Danny had been a few hundred yards away, but for what fucking purpose? He wasn't hunting; he wasn't armed for hunting. If he'd been fishing, he'd have gone toward the lake—not the trail out. If he'd foreseen trouble, he wouldn't have left Joanne alone.

Danny's death scene spun around in his head, a film reel playing over and over, but he could never get a fix on a frame that made sense. He could not keep the two separate: the dead man with the livid, swollen face and the live Danny—laughing, waving goodbye to him.

And he grasped only one thought. Nothing would ever be the way it had been again.

He had not meant to sleep, but exhaustion crept over him where he sat and his head dropped on his chest.

When he woke, it was dawn and nothing had changed. No one had come seeking the fire's warmth. He called for her for hours, until the answering silence was so heavy with futility that he knew he had to seek help.

He took nothing with him but his canteen as he headed downtrail. He looked straight ahead as he caught the corpse odor from below the path, and concentrated on putting one foot ahead of the other until the air grew fresh again. He called out to her occasionally, knowing that the chance she could hear him grew less and less as he neared the fork in the trail and turned down the last route to the ranger's station. She would surely understand when he came back with help that he had not been able to find her by himself, alone.

He drove himself without let-up, feeling no jolt or shock when he slid and fell with the loose shale on the downward inclines, unaware of the tears that coursed through the deep crevices of his face.

19

He was not sleeping well. She thought that he was recovering, but almost as soon as the sun disappeared, he had stopped answering her questions and slept, his bad arm held gingerly away from him. She was careful not to bump it; even the wind across it made him whimper in his sleep. She tried to sleep too, but his groaning and tossing woke her again and again. During the stealthy games he had been all right, but now he was delirious.

She wanted to say his name to comfort him and found it so odd that she did not know what it was. She had known his name, and now she didn't. She wet a rag from her canteen and stroked his forehead, and his eyes opened but they would not look at her.

"Are you O.K.?"

POSSESSION

His good hand darted out and gripped her shoulder, hurting her.

"Damn it. Damn it, you bitch. You're trying to kill me."

"No . . . oh no—you're sick."

"Open the window. There's no air in here."

"We're outside. There are no windows. You have a fever."

"I said open the window or I'll—"

His head dropped back and he seemed to sleep again, but his hand held her shoulder fast and she could not pry herself loose of him. She touched his face and his skin was hot, taut, and papery.

She didn't know what to do.

"Listen!"

"What?"

"They're coming to kill us again. Lock the door, Reenie."

"There is no door . . ."

"I said *lock it!*"

"All right."

"You brought them here on purpose. You've been fucking around with all of them and I told you and told you—"

"No. I didn't—"

"You lying bitch." His sick arm rose up, and then fell back onto the ground and he cried out. "You're so fucking dumb, Reenie. Now, you've gone and killed us."

His fingers slipped to her breast and clutched there and she thought she would faint from the pain. She began to cry.

"Don't cry, Reenie. I forgive you. I always forgave you. I won't let you die forever. I'll find you. You belong to me. I own you."

She could not remember what she had done that had to be forgiven, or why he called her the other name, but she knew she had done something despicable, and that she had killed him—them. No, just him. She poked at the fire, trying to make it warmer; he thought he was burning up, but it was really so cold.

And she tried to think. It was like building a bridge without enough lumber to go across, but she searched her mind for the pieces she was sure of. She knew they were on a mountain, but she did not know where it was. She had come up here with someone, not him, but someone else, *Who?* Danny. Thinking about Danny made her feel sad, because Danny had left her. Then *he* had come to take care of her. Because she belonged to him, because he knew her, because they were meant to be together. He could have killed her. *Why?* Why would he kill her? She couldn't remember why she had been afraid that he would. But he hadn't. She was grateful for that. Since she knew he possessed her life and that he had chosen to allow her to breathe and to live, she was very grateful.

He knew that she was someplace near him, but the fever drugged him and kept him in his deep sleep where the nightbirds' cries echoed down fiery corridors and he could not hold onto her. It took tremendous concentration to waken. He was weaker than he thought possible, his blood clattering through his veins, hot as steam pipes, his infected arm throbbing almost rhythmically.

He closed his eyes and dove under the pain again, asleep but not resting.

She caressed him awake, her hands cool on his penis. Too late. She had come to him of her own accord just as he had known that she would, asking for it without any prompting, and it was too late. He was too goddamned sick.

He watched her, naked over him in the first daylight. Her breasts swung close to his mouth, and her fingers were insistent on his cock. He was incapable of any response beyond his hard-on.

"What should I do? Tell me what to do."

"Kiss it."

He had ordered her to kiss his cock before, and she'd turned away, gagging. She'd told him she'd never gone down on a man. Now she bent over him eagerly and took him deep into her mouth. He was the first. She was his.

He could trust her completely now. She would not jar his arm or humiliate him or leave him behind. She mounted him and slid herself so gently onto him. He could feel that she was like oiled silk, so moist and cool where he burned. She moved herself back and forth over him, and he possessed her, this butterfly caught on his shaft.

He left the pain behind, or perhaps it vanished inside her. He rose to meet her climax and clutched at her shoulders with both of his hands, pressing her down against him so that her breasts and belly flattened on his chest.

He came in a shattering spasm that submerged everything else, and he did not feel the bursting in his hand, the stretched skin opening over its thinnest points. Neither of them felt the viscous stuff that poured out.

A long time later, they looked at his hand and saw that it had spilled its poison, leaving a pale torn glove of a hand, but no longer deadly. She brought water and washed herself and then him. She watched over hi   while he slept the morning away, his face serene.

She heard nothing, not the slightest fragmented sound in the thin air washing down from the other side of the peak. She heard no one call her name.

20

The head ranger, his brother who ran the lodge, and both their wives sat with Sam in the restaurant section of the bigger building at a table next to the window, their coffee cups on the red-checked oilcloth sending plumes of steam onto the glass and obscuring the view of the dock beyond. One of the women was cooking behind the counter, cooking for him because he needed to eat, although he wondered if he could. They were all nice people, really nice people, quiet now in shock and sympathy for him, but Sam found it impossible to speak more than an occasional word now and then, and they were silent too. Waiting. Waiting for the Explorer Scouts and the Chelan County Sheriff's deputies, and Ernie Gibson, who was flying dogs in as soon as he could locate containers. Hopefully, too, a helicopter from Chelan County. All of them summoned via solar-powered radio to deal with disaster in paradise. From time to time, the door opened and someone stepped in and whispered to the ranger or his brother, the college kids in their last week of temporary forest service, or one of the pretty girls who cleaned the cabins.

Sam sensed they found him inappropriately cold and contained in the face of the loss of his best friend. He had barked out his orders of who to send for, what he wanted done, and when—"immediately." He had accepted coffee, a shower, a change of clothing from the tall, lanky college boy from Indiana, and a shot of whiskey from the ranger's brother, but he discouraged any sympathy or small talk. His face and neck ached from the strain of remaining expressionless.

He reached for a cigarette and found the pack empty already. Before he could move to the counter to buy another, the ranger's wife placed a pack in front of him.

"Thanks." He looked at the blank window and rubbed at it with his hand, exposing a circle of view. The boardwalks were empty of people, the lake and the mountains beyond all the same metal gray, the show for the tourists over and the serious business of winter begun. Sam tried to remember the heat in Natchitat only—when? Yesterday. The day before maybe. He hated it, but now he wished it existed here; it would help to keep Joanne alive until they found her.

He spoke to no one in particular. "Saw a rattler yesterday."

"That so." The ranger looked up, obviously eager to encourage any thread of conversation to lift the pall. "Big one?"

"Maybe four, five feet. Maybe he just seemed that big."

"Pacific rattlers don't usually run much over three feet. It takes them a while to coil. They can't jump and they strike less than their own length."

"The guy seemed amiable enough."

POSSESSION

The ranger chuckled, a strange sound in their long quiet wait. "I wouldn't call any snake amiable. Probably getting too cold for him to feel frisky. I still wouldn't try to shake hands with one."

"The bear——" Sam said it aloud for the first time in an hour. He plunged on. "You think it could have been a grizzly?"

"I won't say absolutely that it couldn't be——but, like I said, the last verified sighting around here was in 1965. It's not like Glacier Park. Grizzlies were wiped out here a long time ago. It's possible that one could have come down from Canada, but I can't figure it, nobody catching even a peek of one all summer. We had thousands of hikers this year."

"They didn't see any bears?"

"Sure, some black bear in the upper valley. The usual stuff——trying to make off with food, pestering. One sighting of a she-bear and her cub up by High Bridge at Coon Lake in July. Woman tripped over the cub and the she-bear reared up and growled, but she didn't attack; she let the hiker take off and she skedaddled up the trail. You just about have to corner them before they'll attack."

"It had to have been something huge. He didn't shoot. His wounds were . . . terrible."

"It was pretty dark last night. You might not have seen everything clearly."

"No, I saw."

The ranger reddened and looked away. "You'd know best."

For the first time, Sam could identify with the "220s" he'd hauled in to Harborview Hospital in Seattle to be locked away on the fifth floor. The woman who lived in her car with twelve cats, the old men who refused to be moved from condemned buildings, the black girl who screamed obscenities on the corner of Third and James, and Herbert Pyms and his daughter, Violet, who crashed every society party in Seattle in their matching outfits Violet sewed of funeral ribbons and T-shirts. In their world, in their minds, they made perfect sense. Well, he had seen what he had

211

seen, and it didn't compute with what was supposed to be. He was going to raise hell until he found out what was wrong.

He thought of Joanne's little hands and the way she hunched her shoulders when she felt threatened, remembered her kitchen and the jars of jam waiting for her to put away, and felt a stab of pain behind his eyes.

"How the hell long does it take them to get up here?" he demanded.

The ranger looked at his watch. "An hour and a half. They'll be rounding that last bend in the lake any minute. The kids here have got a crew started up already, and Ernie's bringing in two bloodhounds."

"I want the helicopter. I want to bring her down right away and get her to Wenatchee to the hospital."

The ranger looked down.

"What's the matter?"

"Deputy—Sam—you've got to be prepared that . . . she might have . . ."

"What?"

"If we've got a renegade bear up there . . ."

"You do! Dammit. I told you it killed my partner."

"She might be gone, too, Sam. She may be dead."

"No. I'm going to bring her down."

"You're exhausted. Let the search party go up."

"I'm going with them."

"O.K. But eat that. It's going to be a long night."

He looked at the plate before him. Steak and eggs and hashbrowns, the meat rare and bleeding into yellow yolk. His stomach balked, but he dug into it, wanting to ask for beer instead. They wouldn't let him pay for the meal.

The food hit the bottom of his stomach and bounced, but it stayed down. He didn't feel exhausted; he felt steely anger and frustration at the wait for the Chelan County deputies who seemed to be taking their sweet time responding. By noon he had made up his mind to head up alone when he heard the distant buzz of a motor, growing louder until the launch appeared. Just behind it, Ernie Gibson's

POSSESSION

DeHaviland dropped gracefully from the leaden sky and touched down.

The deputies were young, kids in their twenties. He had grown impatient with young men. They either knew nothing and pretended to know something, or they knew unnecessary things and flaunted their superfluous knowledge. They moved too slowly now and pointlessly, tying their cruiser up with agonizing care. They listened to the ranger explain something out of Sam's hearing, nodded, looked back at him, nodded again. He watched them from the dock as they shrugged on coveralls.

The tall kid walked toward him first, empty handed, and Sam frowned. "Where's your gear?"

"Sir?"

"Not sir—Sam Clinton, deputy from Natchitat. You'll need your death kit."

"Ranger said it was a bear attack."

"That's hearsay. *I* said it. You assume that everything you hear is true? How many deaths have you investigated? You always just write down what somebody tells you?"

The kid turned on his heel and walked back to his boat. Sam could see him whisper to the other deputy, a stocky man not more than a year or two older. They rolled their eyes and laughed, quickly turning away from him. The stocky man reached into the launch and brought out a small attaché case. Sam relaxed for the moment, still doubting that they had any idea at all what they were doing. When they walked back toward him, their faces were bland and watchful.

The older man stuck out his hand. "Dean McKay. Sergeant out of Chelan. Pleased to meet you, sir."

Sergeant? He wasn't thirty yet. Sam shook his hand and felt no confidence. "Clinton."

"This is Rusty Blais. You goin' up with us?"

"Let's go."

Yesterday's empty trail was crowded now, full of men and dogs, all of them more fleet of foot and gifted with stamina that left Sam and the ranger far behind. The older men climbed with stoicism, stopping by tacit agreement when their lungs were pumped out. They could hear shouts and bursts of laughter far ahead of them, but they seldom caught a glimpse of the young, disappearing backs.

At the last meadow, the ranger stopped and sat down, panting. "Wait up, Clinton. We made it. Sit for a minute."

Begrudging the delay, Sam rested.

"Don't mind when they laugh. They mean no disrespect."

"Hell, I know that. I've done it. The M.E.'s deputies dropped a corpse once—over in Seattle. Didn't belt it tight enough and it kind of bounced down the steps. Thank God, the widow was over at the neighbors and didn't see it, because it struck us funny—weird funny. My partner started to laugh, and then I did, and then the M.E.'s guys caught it and there we were, four grown men, giggling like maniacs while the deceased sits on the bottom step looking confused. You can't cry over every stranger's tragedy or you crack up—but—"

"I know. When it's one of your own people—you gonna be O.K.?"

"Hell. I don't know. Maybe not. I loved that man."

"He was a nice guy. Her too. She was—she seemed like a nice person."

"She *is* a nice person. Scared of the dark though." He stood up. "I've got to go. We have to find her before the sun goes down again."

"They're looking now. It's a good crew. They grid search, using the dogs. Ernie's up there flying over. If she's in there, we'll find her. What color were their backpacks? I can't remember."

"Khaki, damn it. 'Chubby and Tubby'—surplus specials. His is still up by the lake. I guess I told you that. Of course, she's in there. Where else could she be?"

The ranger shook his head and then drew his breath in sharply as he caught a whiff of death. The two men were silent as they left the trail and slid down to where Blais and McKay stood, nostrils pinched, lips tight together.

"What do you think?" Sam asked, not caring what they thought.

POSSESSION

"Seems like a bear."

"*Seems* like? He's a brother. You owe him the full treatment." They weren't going to like him. He didn't care about that either. "Give me some of your baggies. You have baggies, haven't you?"

"Yessir." They handed him several and stood back, watching him suspiciously.

He worked alone, dismissing them, barely aware of their presence. He filled the plastic envelopes with bloodstained leaves, dirt, a broken button, and labeled each with a grease pencil, marking his initials and the date. He had trouble for a moment remembering the date. September 11. Friday. One week since he had seen Danny and Joanne alive and smiling and happy and—

He thought he smelled cigar smoke, and turned his head, half-expecting to see Danny sitting up, alive, the joke on Sam. McKay, the sergeant, sat on a log twenty feet away, puffing on the brown stub. Blais teetered back and forth on his heels, hands in his back pocket. Even as he hated them, he was aware that they had done nothing really to pull his rage; they were guilty only of easy assumption. If they weren't cops, it could be forgiven.

He could not forgive them. Respect must be paid.

He lifted one of Danny's softened hands and slipped a baggie over it, held his own hand out like a surgeon's and was only slightly gratified to feel McKay slip a wide rubber band into it. He secured the plastic covering and repeated the process with Danny's other hand.

McKay hunkered next to him. "Fingernail scrapings? You think there might be any?"

"I don't know. I want to know why he didn't fire his gun. I want to know why he didn't fight back."

"He didn't fire?" McKay whistled in amazement. "Shit, I would have emptied it into that mother."

"The gun's there. *Don't touch it!* Cylinder's full, chamber too."

"Maybe she jumped him from behind?"

"Not him."

He finished his work. He longed to be done with this

2 1 5

ruined Danny who was no part of the real Danny. He would not be until after the post mortem was accomplished. And he could not now conceive how he would manage that process. He turned to McKay. "Who'll be doing the post?"

McKay looked surprised again. "The post?"

Sam spoke evenly. "The autopsy. You do autopsies up here in the toolies, don't you?"

"Hey, man . . ." McKay reddened with irritation, but checked himself.

"Who'll be doing it?"

"If they have one, it will probably be Doc Hastings. Albro's on vacation."

"You have a suspicious death here, deputy. You don't really know what happened, and neither do I. You have sucking chest wounds; you have deep facial lacerations; you have an unfired weapon, and you fucking well better be scheduling an autopsy."

"It's not up to me."

"That's a relief."

Blais muttered something, and Sam heard a faint "asshole."

"You got something to say, kid?"

"No sir."

"Then shut your fucking mouth." He turned away, and crawled up the bank, carrying his baggies full of evidence with him. He had no time for inept idiots.

Sam clung to his anger, warming himself with it; it was vital that he keep it aglow. Without it, the icy core inside him would expand and immobilize him. It was no longer necessary that anybody like him or find him a good old boy.

The helicopter settled over the meadow, its backwash flooding the long grass with air. Blais and McKay emerged from the brush with the same apparently deliberate languor and strolled toward the craft. Sam watched them silently and wondered why the whole world seemed to move in slow motion, heedless of the lowering sun and the terrible necessity for action. By conscious force of will he kept himself from directing the removal of Danny's body. He had worked Danny's death scene and worked it as meticulously as any he had encountered. They wouldn't be able to goof it up now—unless they dumped the bird in Lake Chelan.

Blais and McKay disappeared into the woods with the rubberized body bag and struggled up finally, carrying Danny's shrouded body. He watched them strap the bag onto the helicopter and wave it away as the plane rose up and disappeared into the clouds. He felt his throat close up on him and walked quickly away toward the deserted camp. When they followed him, they saw him scrape the vomit beneath the tree into a baggie and nodded at each other.

The old cop *was* crazy and best left alone.

21

Sam did not pretend to be a woodsman; all his searching skill had been honed in cities. Spin him around three times in Seattle and send him into an alley full of human rejects, and he could find his man nine times out of ten. He knew the wilderness of the city, all the dark, inaccessible places that gave shelter to derelicts and innocents and predators. But he was no use at all up on this mountain and he knew it. If he plunged into the brush beyond the green lake to call Joanne out, he too would be lost.

He waited alone near the fire, ignored by the occasional pair of searchers who broke off from the pack to warm themselves by the flames he kept replenished. He caught something in their manner, something he recognized. Like the deputies, none of them moved with the purpose or energy that suggested urgency. They did not expect to find her—or, they assumed, if they found her, she would be dead too.

He moved into the brush to take a leak, and heard voices carrying clearly through the chill air.

"Whatta you think?"

He stood and slowly buttoned his fly, listening.

"Negative."

"How long did they say the man's been dead?"

"Five . . . six days."

"Then I don't know what the hell we're breaking our butts for; them dogs are just circling around like turkeys. Can't find their own assholes."

"You think the bear got her too?"

"No. I think a bunny rabbit ate her. The guy was armed and look what happened to him. *Shit.*"

"I never heard of a bear actually attacking anyone up here."

"Happens every twenty years or so, and then people forget about it. They get to thinking they're just big teddy bears and they go and try to feed them. Tourists. You can have 'em."

Sam froze, breathing shallowly, feeling rage fill his chest again. The older man was enjoying himself, playing big-shot for the young guy.

"They messed with a she-bear. Grizzly maybe. The only choice you got when you meet you a grizzly is to lie down and play dead. If you're lucky, they'll only chaw on you a little. We ain't never gonna find nothing of that woman but some left-over pieces. That sow's probably dragged her off somewheres to eat off her slow . . ."

Sam's figure rose out of the brush and loomed over them, his face a contorted mask in the firelight. The bloodhounds leapt at him, snarling, and then reached the end of their leashes and gagged.

The dog men stared at him open-mouthed. The dogs howled, their hoarse baying bringing more men into the firelight, all of them watching Sam cautiously.

"If that was your wife out there, you wouldn't be so quick to find her a pile of bloody lumps," his voice shook.

The dog man studied him, realized who he was, and sat back, stroking his hound self-consciously. "Didn't see you out there."

POSSESSION

"I guess not."

"Hey—I'm sorry. We get to talking rough sometimes. Don't mean nothing."

Sam's shoulders sagged and he felt weak as the adrenalin dissipated. He moved to his watching place by the fire, chilled from even the short foray into the brush. "Nothing?" he asked.

"She might be up a tree out there," the younger man said quickly, glancing back at his partner. "It's easier for our dogs at night. Be better now. The skin 'rafts'—sweat and bacteria—come up with night moisture. Bloodhounds' old ears just sweep smells up like brooms—right into their snouts. Dogs are amazing. We'll find her."

The old guy held out a flask. "Have a hummer?"

The liquor went down with a jolt and sang in him. He took a second hit and then a third before he handed it back. He wanted to believe the young man, but the conversation overheard smacked more of truth.

"What's the longest you ever looked for somebody up here—and found them—O.K.?"

Lies came, and he swallowed them whole because he needed them.

"Oh, lessee. Three weeks, probably. Two—three weeks. People can be resourceful when they get pushed to it." He turned to the young man. "Remember that guy from Wenatchee back in '72—'73? Must have been missing that long. Right?"

"Right. Yeah, at least that. Kind of skinny when we come on him—but O.K." He lied glibly. Not mean men, either of them.

Sam slept again, his second night huddled against the logs that defined Danny's and Joanne's last camp. He heard only faintly the shouts in the woods and the heavy feet of men who filled the circle of bodies around the fire. The dogs snuffled and groaned in the night, twisting and turning on their leashes, and the searchers talked in voices so deep that their words were only rumbles. He dreamed of her, that she had come back through the trees alone and stood outside the cluster of sleeping men crying to be let in to the warmth. When he held out his hand and reached for her, she disappeared.

It snowed in the night, dainty flakes at first, and then fat snow that dropped on his cheek and melted there. His hip pressed against the ground and ached, but he slept on, unaware of the white mantle that covered all of them. When he woke finally, he found them up before him and he felt guilty that he could have given in to the warmth of the sleeping bag so easily, when she still waited somewhere alone for help to come for her.

It was barely seven and daylight only beginning to wash over the shallow snow pack. He felt stronger, less likely to go off half-cocked at the men around him. They were doing their jobs, unfettered by personal involvement—just as he always had.

He forced himself to make small talk with the searchers as they sipped coffee. He could not hurry them.

"Don't let the snow scare you." The ranger was talking to him.

"It looks bad to me. Will it just keep on piling on now until spring?"

"Naw. It's only fake winter. We always have snow above 4,000 feet the first week or so of September. I guess the mountain wants to warn us of what's coming. It'll melt off in a day or two and then we'll get three, maybe four weeks of Indian Summer. The snow might make it easier—give us tracks to follow."

But what if the tracks were only their own? Sam didn't press him.

"Did anybody find anything last night?" He knew no one had, or the ranger would have mentioned it.

"No—but they got started late. None of her gear's turned up—and that's good, I think. She did have a pack *and* a sleeping bag? You're sure?"

"Positive. I saw them packing up their truck."

"Good. That's a good sign."

How many times had he placated families with such

empty words? He was tainted by his own experience, and he had no guile to fool himself.

But she lived. Just as he had known that Danny no longer lived—long before that awful instant of discovery—he knew that Joanne was alive.

There was something about the tree. When they left him alone again, he walked around and around it, studying the broken limbs, the bare spots where pine needles had been skinned off. The scuff along the trunk had come from something wide and flat—a human shoe, not claws. Someone had climbed, fifteen to twenty feet high, and clung there.

And then come down. Not fallen down. Sidled down with handholds of needles, sliding feet cracking branches, sliding further.

He found a place to start and climbed upward through the trunks and limbs slippery with wet snow. He had not climbed a tree in forty years, but he inched higher until he found a place where the marks on the pine stopped. He looked down and saw the spot where he'd retrieved the vomitus, a straight line below. He knew that it had been Joanne who had hidden here, terrorized into nausea.

It was an old technique. You put yourself in the victim's place and tried to see. He'd never gone as far as the dick in Seattle who talked to corpses in a conversational tone all the while he did a crime scene—but it was a way of going to the source. She had stood here. What was happening when she did?

He turned his head to look downtrail to where Danny had been, everything blanketed with white now. But the spot was hidden by a jutting back of the path. She might have heard the struggle, but she could not have seen it.

He turned too quickly the other way and felt a stinging scratch against his neck. A sharp little nubbin of forked wood and, in it—*caught in it*—two long strands of fine dark hair. It was hers; he knew he could put it under a scanning electron microscope and isolate it almost absolutely as hers. The top of her head would have extended to the twig that scratched him. Her head came exactly to the point of his shoulder.

He leaned back against the thicker spur of the bisected "school marm" tree and tried to think. The branches directly in front of him blurred as he focused beyond them into the woods, catching a glimpse now and then of the searchers moving arms' length apart, their feet shuffling for something that might lie beneath the snow.

He blinked and his focus changed to close up. And he saw it. Green and black, so close to the tree's color that it was almost lost in protective coloration. An impaled triangle of fabric, checked, its threads drifting lazily in the wind.

He reached for it, mesmerized. He had never seen it before. That was the important thing. *He had never seen it before.* He had never seen the garment it had come from. Danny would not wear green; he found it unlucky. And it was a man's fabric, nothing that Joanne would have worn.

She had not been in this tree alone.

The baggies were below on the ground, stashed in his gear. He braced his back against the trunk so that both his hands were freed, and slid his pack of Marlboros loose from his inside pocket. He slipped the green plaid between the cellophane and paper pack on one side, and the strands of her hair on the other, and climbed down.

She wasn't here any longer, nowhere within the range of the men who searched, but if he told them that, they wouldn't believe him. He was not sure himself how he knew, so how could he convince them with a few strands of hair and a bit of rag?

Danny knew the answer. Somewhere in his disintegrating flesh lay the key to the puzzle.

Sam did not want to leave the mountain, but he could not stay. Danny lay waiting for him. He had no use here; he was the only observer who would know what to look for when they cut into Danny, and how to sort out the false truths.

Sam went down with the ranger in the helicopter, and the snow beneath them disappeared as they left the high elevations, making the winter wilderness scene seem something he had only imagined.

While he waited for Ernie to pick him up in the seaplane, Sam paced the Forest Service office.

"You talked to them the day they hiked in?" he asked the ranger, although he suspected he had asked it before.

"Not that morning. The day before when they got off the boat."

"You talk to anyone else that day?"

"A lot of people. Let's see—that was the fourth. Right?"

"Yeah—the Friday before the Labor Day weekend. How many people hiked in that day? No, let's look at the whole week before and through the weekend."

The ranger slid the ledger across the counter and Sam studied it, pages of unfamiliar names scrawled in a variety of handwriting, some of it almost illegible. The routes varied: Purple Creek Trail, Boulder Creek, War Creek, Rainbow Creek *via* McAlester, Rainbow Lake, and next to all but a very few of them, the check mark to show that the hiking parties had returned and signed in.

"What if somebody just took off and didn't sign in?"

"That happens. We don't like that because if somebody got into trouble, they'd be out of luck."

"But it happens?"

"I'm sure it does. We can't stand by the trailheads and stamp their hands."

"Can I have a sheet of paper?"

The ranger handed him a tablet, and looked at him sharply. "What are you looking for?"

"I don't know." He ran his finger down the pages and copied the names with no check beside them. "Vincent party?"

"Oh—them. Let's see. Went up Boulder, transversed south and came back down Purple—over here. They come up once a month maybe."

"O.K. Dr. Bonathan and son? No check here."

"I know them too. They came back in Sunday night. Had dinner in the Lodge. Forgot to check in."

"Steven Curry?"

"He was going over to pick up the Pacific Trail. Young fellow, hippie type, looked like he could do it easily. Working his way up from California to Canada."

"What did he look like?"

"Little guy. Blond beard. Stocky. Smelled like a horse barn."

"David Dwain?"

"I don't know. What does it say?"

"Rainbow Lake. Did you sign him in?"

"Lemme see. No, that's Ralph Boston's writing. One of the summer hires."

"Can I talk to him?"

"He left Wednesday to go back east to start school."

"You never saw Dwain?"

"Nope. What are you thinking about?"

Sam equivocated. "He went up there Friday night. My friends went up on Saturday. He might have seen them—might know something."

"He probably went on over Bridge Creek and into Twisp before they got there. You have a party leaving here even a half hour ahead of another party and they never see each other."

"I suppose so." Sam folded the sheet from the tablet and slipped it into his jacket pocket. "I'm going down to Wenatchee. Will you let me know the minute they find her? If you hear anything from Curry or Dwain or—anything—would you give a holler down to the sheriff's office in Wenatchee? I don't know where I'll be staying but I'll leave word there. You've got radio contact with them?"

"Yes." The ranger paused. "Is there anyone else I should notify? Any family of—of the Lindstroms?"

Shit. He'd forgotten Elizabeth Crowder. Waiting by her phone in Natchitat, pacing and calling and calling and calling for three days. He hadn't thought of her. He hadn't even thought of calling the office.

"He's got nobody. She's got a mother. I'll call her from Wenatchee."

22

Joanne heard the thick lub-lub-lub of the helicopter's rotor blades long before Duane did. Submerged in his dense, healing sleep, he had seemed to drift in and out of awareness for most of the day, and she had watched over him. She was concerned that he might chill again; he slept so deeply, scarcely moving. She covered him with her own sleeping bag and fashioned a kind of windbreak of their packs between the boulders that already sheltered him. She was awkward with fires, not able to bring back the coals that had guttered and died during the long, long time they had made love, but it wouldn't matter until dusk. The sun was a steady heat in the pewter sky.

She could not get enough of touching him, and she found reasons to place her hands on him; she stroked his forehead free of wrinkles, and held his uninjured hand, her own so small by comparison, so pale against his callused brown palm. She was quite content to stay quietly beside him oblivious of the passage of hours, although she longed to have him waken again and respond to her. The time between dawn and full morning had seemed only minutes as they rolled and heaved together, moving without any definite stopping place from the first climax to the second and, for her, a third. She was tender inside from his thrusting, but hardly satiated. Her desire had seemed to grow with each consummation of the act, and she would have kept him inside her all of the day and into the night if she could have.

She had walked along the narrowed precipice over death, felt it actually crumbling beneath her feet, and he had pulled her back. And now she had saved him, and she would keep him safe. She could not imagine that she had doubted him. He had almost died for her. *He had almost died for her.*

She rubbed his chest gently, but he didn't wake. She

rolled on her side and moved her thigh until it covered his. He smiled in his sleep and she traced his mouth with her finger. She couldn't tell if he was awake or gone someplace away from her; she was jealous, even of his sleeping, and lonely. She touched him and felt his penis flaccid and defenseless, a soft tube of flesh in her curled hand. She wanted him again. She stroked him, kneaded him, and felt him swell in her hand. He groaned, but his eyes were still shut away from her.

The sound of the helicopter brought her back to the present. She listened with stopped breath until she recognized what the noise was. He had never told her exactly what it was that threatened their existence. But there was something. Some reason that he'd trained her to crawl on her belly through the weeds, something that demanded their stealth and cunning. Something evil intent on destroying them. He'd promised he would teach her how to shoot the guns. That would make her feel safer, and it proved that he had forgiven her and that he trusted her.

She thought that she didn't deserve to be trusted, but it was only a feeling. Because she could not remember what she could not remember (and on and on into the black vortex), she had to move very carefully around the edges of it and ask no questions. He would insulate her from any memory that might torment her. He always had, but sometimes—and so queerly too—when she was the happiest, the most greedy in tasting of him, she was afraid and had to pull away from him until her terror eased.

There were several things that she could be totally sure of now. No one else had ever loved her this much. No one else would ever love her this much. He would never leave her. He had told her those truths over and over and over until his words made a little rhyming hum, and she could hear melody behind them.

And whenever she grew frightened, he told her again.

She could not, of course, allow any harm to come to him.

She lay beside him and heard the enemy in the sky looking for them. She put her hand over his mouth so that he could not cry out and give them away before he was fully awake, and then she placed her lips against his ear.

"Wake up."

His eyes snapped open and she felt his lungs expand and hold open against her breast.

"What is it?" His words were so muted that she read his lips more than heard.

"Something. A helicopter, I think. Listen."

"Did you see it?"

"No. The clouds came over just before I heard it. I think it's back on the other side—where we were—before."

"We'll have to leave. We've stayed too long here."

"Yes."

"We'll have to be in the forest again when it's dark; we can't wait until tomorrow. Are you afraid?"

She kept her mouth against his ear. "I am never afraid with you. Are *you* O.K.? Do you feel strong enough to hike out now?"

He lifted her on top of him effortlessly, and she felt him still erect against her as he kissed her mouth. He *was* strong again, reassuring her with his penis and his hands and his mouth of his capacity to survive all things. They made love in the shadows of the rocks and clouds, their coverings blended into the landscape, the dead fire incapable of signaling their location to the intruders who walked the forest on the other side of the pass.

When they had finished and lay, still joined, they heard the craft again, its rotors roaring through the thin air miles away. They could not see it lifting off into the clouds, but they knew it would come again. He explained the new heaviness in the sky meant the clouds were full of snow. They had no choice but to head down away from the threats behind and above them.

Within fifteen minutes they had packed everything, and their meadow was as it had been before, save for the ashes of their fire which could have been left behind by any camper.

"Where will we go?" She looked so small under her burden of gear.

"Does it matter?"

"No, not really. We're together."

"We'll stay together. We have always been together, and we will always be together. Do you realize that?"

"Yes—but I—get afraid—not for myself—but for you. I get afraid that they'll try to separate us, that they might hurt you."

"Why should they hurt me?"

"I don't know. The—the people who are looking for you. You've never told me why they're following us. The games we play—wasn't that because someone's looking for us?"

"You don't have to worry about that. I will take care of you. All you have to do is obey me. If I tell you to do something, you will have to do it without question."

"Yes."

"Come here."

She walked over to him, and he took her hand. He slipped his cat's eye ring from his own finger and held it out to her. She saw there was a wedding ring still on her left hand and was surprised. She twisted it off so that her finger would be ready for his ring. His eyes reflected the bleeding sun on the horizon.

"With this ring, I thee wed. I did not exist before you and you did not exist before me. Separated, we no longer live. Do you believe that?"

"I believe that."

"If I die, you will no longer exist. If you should die, I would not exist. We are entwined, flesh together, blood together, bone together, throughout eternity."

"Together."

"I would kill for you. And you would kill for me."

She shivered.

"You would kill for me."

". . . and I would kill for you."

"And if we should die together, here on this mountain, we would be glad."

She bent her head against his chest, and he could see the

slenderness of her neck, tender and fair where her hair fell away. "We would be very glad."

"Very, very glad."

She looked up at him, and he saw himself in her pupils. He regretted that they had to leave.

"I want to say a few words for him," he said finally.

"For who?"

"For Danny."

"Oh." She looked away, back toward the mountain behind them, and he could sense that she seemed distracted. He spoke quickly. "Give me the ring—the one you took off."

She handed it to him absently and watched as he snapped three white daisies from the ground and slipped the wedding band over their stems. He lay the flowered ring on the large boulder and bent his head, his eyes open and watching her, "In memory of Daniel—was it Daniel or Danny?"

"Either. But he hated *Daniel.* Say *Danny.*"

"In memory of Danny Lindstrom. Ashes to ashes . . . dust to dust."

He could see that she no longer really remembered who Danny was.

The rock turned black as the sun sank lower and they shouldered their packs again and walked away into the forest. The trees closed in behind them as the trail fell away, down steeply. She kept her hand hooked into his belt, afraid of losing him.

23

"I know who you are. What puzzles the hell out of me is what you were doing messing around one of *my* scenes? You really threw your weight on my men. You're not going to sit on me, buster."

Captain Rex Moutscher glared at Sam, letting him stand

at the counter like a citizen making a lost dog complaint, obviously unwelcome in the Chelan County Sheriff's Office.

"Can I come in?"

"You're asking permission now? That's a pleasant change. Clinton, the big shot. This is my county. This is my office. I don't care if you're governor of Washington. You don't fuck up my scenes. And you don't order my men around. If you've got any ideas about playing God, here, you can turn your ass around and find the door out."

"I lost my partner. I needed to know why."

Moutscher softened only slightly. "I'm aware of that. And I'm sorry. But that's no license for what you did—not in my book. What do you want here?"

Sam leaned his elbows on the counter, monumentally fatigued. "I've been up in the mountains for three days. I flew down in a little-bitty plane through a snow storm, and then I drove from Chelan here. And I'm out of cigarettes."

Moutscher held out a pack and Sam took one, waiting.

"That all you want? A smoke?"

"I came for the post. I want to attend the post."

"I haven't decided if we need one."

Sam fought to hold his tongue.

"Come on in." Moutscher held the pass-through door open. "Sit down there and keep your hands in your lap."

"I'm not here to grab your follow-ups and run."

"You bet your sweet ass you're not. You used to be with Seattle, didn't you?"

Sam sighed. "Seventeen years, until 1977."

"How come you vested with three years to go?"

"Personal reasons."

"I heard you blew it over there. I know a lot of those guys."

"What did they say?"

Moutscher looked away. "Said you hit the sauce."

"That was nice of them. You got on the phone right away, didn't you?"

"Look, Clinton. You were up there doing a very, very accurate impersonation of a 220. I expected you to show up here—why else do you think I'd be sitting here on Saturday night? I wanted to know what to expect."

"And here I am. Two heads. Breathing fire. Loony-Tunes."

Moutscher grunted. "Why do you want an autopsy?"

"I don't believe grizzly now. I don't believe any kind of bear. I don't believe any of it."

"You're fighting the obvious. Why?"

"I knew him. I knew how he reacted, and he reacted fast and he wouldn't go down without tearing up the landscape and himself. Not with her up there too."

"They find any sign of her?"

"They didn't call down here yet?"

Moutscher shook his head. "They won't find her alive. Face it."

"You're a real bleeding-heart, aren't you, Captain?"

"I'm a realist." Moutscher looked away from Sam and stared out over the trees that surrounded the old courthouse down toward the Wenatchee River. "You're wrong about no bear. The way Lindstrom looked—I saw him, and I don't agree with you. Have you ever seen somebody a bear was into?"

Sam shook his head slightly.

"Well, I have. And he looked familiar. I'll tell you what— I'll make you a deal so's we both come out of this with our feathers battened down. You turn over all that physical evidence you withheld from my team, and I'll have Doc Hastings meet us tomorrow morning at seven. You can have your post."

"I thought we might give Doc Reay a call in Seattle. I know him; he'd fly over. You've got a coroner system here. I want a medical examiner."

"Clinton, if you think the coast is the only part of the state of Washington able to handle for-en-sic sci-ence, why didn't you stay there? You see this file? You see here? We've had eight homicides this year. And we've had eight convictions. They match that over there? Not on their butts they can't. They're lucky if they do 75 percent. So don't you go sticking your nose up at us. I've been to Louisville. I've been to the FBI Academy in Quantico. And I've been around. Take it or leave it."

Sam knew better than to remind Moutscher that his 100 percent on eight had undoubtedly been Mama-Kills-Papa or Papa-Kills-Mama-and-Mama's-Lover homicides—messy to mop up, but easy to solve. The dicks on the coast had strangers killing strangers, nut cases killing strangers, druggies killing each other with no mourners, and murderers with a lot more room to hide. Given that, 75 percent was damn good. He looked at Moutscher and let the argument go.

"I'll take it."

"Where's my baggies full of stuff?"

"In my car."

"Then you go get them now—as security—and I'll call Hastings."

"Where's Albro?"

"In Dallas."

Moutscher had him by the short hairs, and Moutscher didn't like him. He had broken all the rules of getting along with a fellow officer, and Moutscher was never going to like him even if he reached across the desk and gave him a kiss and a hug. Fuck it.

He turned over the baggies, but he kept the long, dark hairs and the green plaid. They didn't know about that, and they weren't going to; they'd probably throw them away.

Sam left his truck where it was, lonely on the street behind the looming courthouse, and walked downhill to the Cascadian Hotel where he lost himself in the lounge full of Saturday night cowboys and their girls.

He sat at the bar and listened to the jukebox. He ordered Glenlivet and had downed three doubles before he realized someone was playing the same damn song over and over and over: "Woman" by John Lennon. After three hours of Lennon and drinking, listening to a dead man sing of improbable, impossible, true love, the bartender pulled the plug and the jukebox blinked off and died too. The woman at the jukebox turned to Sam and tried to focus on his face.

POSSESSION

"Doesn't that just want to make you puke it's so sad?"

"Almost everything does, ma'am."

"You want to go upstairs with me?"

He considered it and remembered with a dull jolt where he would be in less than five hours. He lifted her hand, turned it over, and kissed her palm. "No thank you, ma'am—I'm driving."

It seemed to make sense to her. She got up gravely and maneuvered her way to the exit, still wiping her eyes. The bartender washed her glass and winked at Sam. "Don't blame you. She's a pig."

"So am I."

"Have it your way, ace."

He remembered that he hadn't called Elizabeth Crowder or Fletch, or Fewell, or anyone. Maybe Moutscher had. There was no point in getting a room; he couldn't remember when he'd slept in a bed. He couldn't remember when he'd slept.

He threw twenty dollars on the bar and walked out into the cold air of Wenatchee. He slept in the back of his truck with Lennon's song going round in his head.

He woke with an unbelievable pain behind his eyes and a pounding in his ears. Moutscher was banging on his truck and Hastings was waiting for him.

Sam washed up in the lavatory on the first floor of the courthouse, the cavernous, high-ceilinged room unchanged since the building went up decades before, grandiose with marble floors and golden oak cubicles. He wondered idly where they'd gotten the money for such a fancy outhouse. The radiators buzzed on and filled the room with the smell of layers of baking paint, but there was no hot water and he sluiced his face with cold water in the vain hope he could wash away the scotch that still fogged his brain. Moutscher watched him silently, puffing on a pipe.

Sam turned with a grin that didn't work. "You got a breath mint?"

"Don't bother. You smell like a distillery. I smelled you

2 3 3

when you crawled out of your truck, and Doc Hastings can't smell anything but formaldehyde. Fewell puts up with your kind of drinking?"

"I don't drink with Walker; I don't socialize with Walker, and Walker has no jurisdiction over what I do off-duty."

Moutscher said nothing; maybe he knew Walker Fewell.

Sam stared into the mirror and had difficulty recognizing the image he hadn't seen in five days. An old man looked back at him, the pouches around his eyes creased with dark new gouges, the eyes themselves sunk in their sockets and branched with red. He had needed a shave for days, and his beard was gray. He had never seen it gray before. He brushed his sandy hair back with his hands in lieu of a comb. No wonder Moutscher thought he was a derelict. He was a derelict.

But Hastings, as it turned out, was older. "This is Dr. Wilfred Hastings. Sam Clinton, Doctor."

Sam took the pathologist's veined hand and felt the bones beneath the thin skin, the tremor there. Hastings looked at him from behind trifocals, his pale blue eyes huge and vague. Sam guessed seventy-five—no, eighty-five.

"Doc Hastings was coroner here—when was it, Doc? 1945?"

"1936 to 1962."

God. It was a joke.

It wasn't a joke.

The room was too bright, the slick tiled walls reflecting the lights that dangled over the sheeted mound in the middle of the room. Sam inhaled formaldehyde and refrigerated death, and the floor slid downhill beneath his feet. He shut his eyes, aware that they were staring at him—the fat detective captain in his white socks and the old man. He concentrated then on the framed sign on the wall:

> All Who Lay Here Before You Were Once Loved;
> Respect and Dignity For the Dead
> Will Be Maintained At All Times.
> As He Is, You Will Be—As You Are, He Was.

234

POSSESSION

And beneath the words in very small print, "Courtesy, East Wenatchee Sign Co." The thing was printed, apparently mass printed. How much call would there be for such homilies? Every home should have one?

A flash of light pierced the brightness, and Sam turned to see Moutscher winding the film sprocket of his Yashica. The first frame would show Danny's shrouded body, awaiting Dr. Hastings' ministrations.

The sheet was whipped off and it began.

As he is, you will be; as you are, he was. I hope the hell not, Sam thought, staring at the felt pen scrawl on Danny's thigh—the coroner's reference number.

Something on the body moved. Maggots, tumbling over themselves, gray-white and fat in the black chest wounds. Sam's hand darted out and closed around the container of ether. He sprayed the parasites and saw them stiffen and roll onto the table, dead. His gorge rose and he swallowed the acid that had been expensive scotch, turning his head toward Moutscher.

"The container. Give me the container."

"Let them be! Knock them on the floor!"

"I want the goddamned box."

Moutscher passed a thin plastic vial over, and Sam scraped a clot of maggots into it, capped it, labeled it, and finally was able to breathe.

"I want to know when he died. The flies come and they lay their dirty little eggs and they hatch and they crawl and they fly and they lay eggs and they never change their timetable. Those goddam grubs can tell us something."

Moutscher seemed about to argue, and then his face changed. Sam recognized the expression. *Don't argue with a maniac.*

"You ready to go ahead?" Hastings was ignoring Sam completely, looking to Moutscher for permission to cut. Moutscher took four angles in his lens, snapped, again, again, and then nodded.

"Wait," Sam blurted.

"Now what?"

"Could you cover his face?"

"Why don't you wait outside?"

"I have to be here. Could you cover his face?"

Moutscher turned to the old man. "Put a drape over his face." And to Sam. "It's not going to hurt him any more." Sam could not isolate the emphasis in the words. Sympathy? Empathy? Scorn? The words lay flat.

With Danny's blackened features hidden, it was not all right, but it was bearable. He concentrated on the old doctor's hand, saw it pick up the scalpel, saw the hand and cutting tool shake, and then plunge with remembered deftness as it cut obliquely down from each shoulder to the midline, leaving the skin flayed open in a wide V. Again, Hastings cut—straight down the midline from sternum to pubis, forming an elongated Y opening.

Sam roared, and the old man jumped back with alarm.

"You cut through one of the fucking wounds! Can't you see what the hell you're doing?"

"Shut up!" Moutscher bellowed so loud that his words bounced off the tiled walls. "You say anything else and your ass is going to be out in the hall! Go ahead, Doc."

Apparently oblivious that he had just contaminated much of what he had to work with, Hastings bumbled ahead. Rib snips cut through the chest cage, and Sam heard the snap of bones giving. The ribs and flesh folded back like wings, and the soggy lungs and dull red heart came into view.

Sam could see the damage, a familiar destruction. There were two—perhaps three—penetrating wounds that had gone through the chest wall, through the third intercostal space, perforating the lingula of the upper lobe of the left lung, the pericardial sac, and on into the heart at the left ventricular wall. The wounds seemed directed left to right, front to back, and angulated slightly downward, administered certainly by someone taller than Danny—and Danny had stood six feet two. The track was at least four inches deep, but the width of the weapon would be impossible to determine now, given the extent of decomposition. One thing was clear; it *had* been a weapon, a knife, a dagger even—but never a tooth. The wounds were separate things that he could concentrate on without personal involvement. Sam glanced at Hastings, who seemed confused.

"Bear, you say?" Hastings focused obtusely on Moutscher, who nodded.

"Looks like a bear, sure as hell."

Hastings nodded. Sam turned to Moutscher to protest, and then looked back into the open body cavity. Before he could prevent it, Hastings had lifted the heart out and was cutting through the pericardial sac *into*—NO!—*into* the heart, exposing the valves with their leaflets. *The damn old fool had destroyed the tracks of two more wounds!*

"You didn't even put a probe in, you idiot! Will you open your eyes and look before you cut any more? You've just fucked up all three wounds."

Hastings looked to Moutscher for assistance, stricken.

"He knows what he's doing, Clinton. You open your mouth one more time and I personally will take you out."

"He *doesn't* know what he's doing."

"You going to shut up?"

It was too late to save it. He was dealing with incompetents; there was no way to put it back together. He felt vaguely sorry for the old man and knew that Hastings was too late aware of what he had done. He sighed and waved him on, this parody of a postmortem. "Go ahead."

The room was choked with death stink, clouds of it bursting from the decaying organs. He ignored them, his right hand skimming incessantly over his yellow pad, recording only his own observations, denying most of what Hastings perceived. Even as he wrote, he knew that his view had no credence, would never have credence—but it was all he had left.

He saw Hastings's hand emerge holding Danny's stomach, saw the scalpel flick it open. Hastings sniffed. The old man might have been good in his day; he seemed to slip in and out of proper procedure. Sharp now. Fading away again.

"Stomach contents." Hastings's voice was reedy, high as an adolescent boy's. "Undigested eggs, vegetable matter, probably potato. Animal protein, perhaps ham or bacon.

Subject succumbed within fifteen minutes, half hour of eating."

Good, doctor. Really important. Now that you've obliterated the vital wounds. Sam wrote it down anyway.

One by one the organs that had kept Danny alive were lifted out: liver, lungs, heart, spleen, kidneys, bladder. Each was sliced and examined. All normal. *Danny, if you hadn't died, you would have lived to be one hundred.*

Sam could feel a presence in the room. The two of them were together, laughing at the travesty. He could almost feel Danny nudge him and say, "Pard, they don't know any better." He chuckled, and the other living men in the chamber looked up startled. Then they looked at each other and shrugged knowingly. He let it go.

Hastings piled the lacerated organs back in the body cavity willy-nilly. Later, somebody would stitch up the gaping T with thick black thread. No fine surgeon's hand needed now.

Sam felt as if he watched from a distance, curious. When he spoke, his voice echoed from the vantage point where he observed. Good. He was handling it.

Even when the drape was tugged off the corpse's face, it was still O.K. The face wasn't Danny's.

"Looks like bear all right," Hastings mouthed from a long way off. "See where the claws ripped down. Bear."

Moutscher's face nodded. It was hard to hear his voice; he shrunk in his distant perspective.

"It didn't bleed." Sam's own voice seemed too loud.

"Postmortem. She must have mauled at the body some. Won't bleed after you're dead."

Hastings's scalpel scored the skin at the back of the neck, and then he loosened the scalp from its moorings and peeled it back until the face was hidden again by the inverted scalp. The saw burred along the skull and the hot smell of burning bone rose into the air. Sam watched the skull cap lift off with wonderful detachment.

"You want a stool?" Moutscher's voice was almost too faint to understand.

POSSESSION

Sam was not aware that he had answered, but felt the solidness of a wooden stool beneath him, and thought it remarkable that it was there just as his knees declined to bear his weight. There was a continuous buzzing in his head. He assumed Hastings was still sawing away at the skull, but when he looked, the freckled, blue-veined hands were empty.

"Brain's liquid," Hastings muttered.

"Let it go then." Moutscher's voice, coming back down the tunnel where it had been.

Sam meant to say no, but his own voice eluded him.

"You O.K.?"

"Who?"

The voice, much louder now. *"You O.K.? Clinton?"*

His head snapped up and the room spun.

"Get out of here for a while." Moutscher again.

He made the door, walking uphill along the floor that had suddenly tilted up at him, and he was grateful that the heavy metal door pushed outward. The air was better—not good air, but better, full of dust and floor wax and no death. The alley exit was a long way down, and his stomach betrayed him even as his head cleared. He vomited up the scotch, oblivious to the stares of a Sunday morning cleaning crew unloading their van. It came up for a long time, seeming to strip some of his stomach lining with it. But when he was done retching, he felt better. Not good. It was unlikely he would ever feel good again, but the red foam behind his eyes had dissipated and he could think.

Moutscher looked up, surprised, when Sam walked back into the tile room and reclaimed his perch on the stool.

"Everything fits, Clinton. The right humerus has got a spiral break, pulled completely out of the socket. It's a bear kind of injury. I'm satisfied."

"I'm not."

"Then it was a Sasquatch. You try to convince somebody of that. Our prosecutor will laugh you out of his office. You don't need that. You've had enough. Give it up. Go home. Let it go."

Danny's hands still rested in their plastic casings. Sam turned away from Moutscher and loosened the bindings from the left hand. Danny's wedding ring shone under the lights, its tracing of entwined hearts grotesque against the loosened flesh. Moutscher assumed it was the ring he wanted.

"Take it. You might as well take that and the watch while you're here."

"I want nail scrapings."

"Shit. Go ahead. Take it all. I'll give you your other stuff back too, but I can't see that any of it will be any use. I'm clearing it accidental."

Sam said nothing, bending to his work, sliding an orange stick beneath the long, ridged nails, loosened now on their beds. The other men watched him, looked at each other, and shook their heads.

It was over. When he walked away from Moutscher, he carried his gleanings from the mountainside, the envelopes and tubes and vials from the autopsy—all of it jammed into a cardboard box that said "Friskies" on the side. The sum total of what was left of four years with Danny. Danny wasn't the body that awaited delivery to the double rear doors of Phelps's Funeral Home in Natchitat. Danny was in the Friskies box.

Sam got a motel room, but only after producing every piece of identification he had; the clerk studied the neat cards with their official seals, looked at Sam suspiciously, and finally agreed to take his fifteen bucks.

The physical evidence that Moutscher had believed in so little that he had given it away was still cold, straight from the morgue's refrigeration. It was not as perishable as ice cream—but close, its useful life wholly dependent on time and temperature. Sam set the white box full of vials and bags in the square refrigerator that other motel guests utilized for beer and headed out to find a Fred Meyer store. He was startled to find that he had no more cash, but his MasterCharge bought him styrofoam pellets and cotton batting, brown paper, and strapping tape.

POSSESSION

Back in his room he arranged his bits and pieces as tenderly as a mother sending cookies to her son in college, finally satisfied that nothing would break or roll or crush in the journey ahead.

He had, of course, no proper forms for lab requests, but he knew the language. The motel stationery featured the Holiday Inn logo, and he crossed it out, and printed "Natchitat County Sheriff's Office" below it. Beneath that, his listed exhibits: twenty-seven samples; twenty-seven questions. Not professional in appearance, but correct. The answers would come back to him neatly typed on thin yellow and pink and green sheets. With great good luck, they might neutralize the damage done by Hastings and Moutscher. He figured he had four hours safe time before all of it disintegrated. Not a prayer of getting it to D.C. and the FBI Lab, or to Rockville, Maryland, and the ATF Lab, but they were not his first choice anyway. They would leave his treasures to wait their turn. He wanted the Western Washington Crime Lab to ferret out what lay hidden among the white pellets.

He debated how to send it and settled for Greyhound. The dog-bus would get it to Seattle as quick as a plane would by the time you considered all the messing around at the airport.

He ducked into a phone booth at the bus station, took a deep breath, and hoped his voice was going to come out official and uncrazy. He dialed the Crime Lab, charged the call to Natchitat County, and asked for the director.

"The director doesn't come in on Sunday," a woman's voice replied.

Sunday. How the hell did it get to be Sunday?

"This is Detective Sam Clinton of Natchitat County. Our office is sending a package of evidence via Greyhound. It should arrive at the Eighth and Stewart Station in Seattle at—let's see—at 4:02 P.M. I'll need a police courier to pick it up. It's very important. Can you do that?"

"Well—" She sounded annoyed.

"*Very* important. Perishable material. Must be refrigerated by 5 P.M."

"All right. I'll send someone."

"Tell the director I'll phone him tomorrow morning."

"O.K."

"You've got that?"

The phone was dead. He had no more change, not even enough to dial the operator.

He thought of his motel room, and he thought of driving home, and neither seemed possible. He thought of Moutscher home watching football on his television, drinking beer and surrounded by his family. He could not think of Joanne and the mountain and whoever had worn the plaid shirt. He understood now why street people crawled under their cardboard blankets and shut out the world. Without his magic plastic card, he would do the same. With it, he could walk into the Cascadian and find Nirvana in a glass.

He stared at the antique apple crate labels displayed behind the bar as he downed the first double and realized with dread that it had lost its power. It took three before he felt the warmth. After six doubles, he found the lounge as comforting and soft as a mother's breast. After eight, he didn't have to think about anything at all.

Sam dreamed of Moutscher's voice shouting in his ear. He smelled disinfectant and urine, and a harsh fabric scratched his face. Something tugged at his shoulder and shook him like a rag doll baby. He opened his eyes a slit and saw Moutscher's florid face bending over him and yelling so loud that spittle spattered on Sam's cheek. *Go away Moutscher.*

Moutscher would not go away, and Sam painfully separated his eyelids from one another and saw where he was. In jail. Not his own, but jail; it was unfamiliar-familiar. He looked beyond the Chelan County captain and saw that the yellow-painted metal squares in the door didn't match up, that the cell door wasn't closed.

"If you weren't a cop, you'd be in here for a month, you damned fool." Moutscher's words fell into place and made a sentence. "It's Monday morning; you've slept it off. We don't owe you anything else. Now get your ass off that bunk and take it home."

". . . It's Monday?"

"Eleven in the morning. You drank up the bar at the hotel, you tried to deck the bartender, and you vomited all over our patrol unit. Clinton, you are a fuck-up and I don't care to spend the whole day babysitting you."

"Go to hell."

He hated Moutscher, and it felt amazingly good, this strong, cleansing rage. If Moutscher wasn't the enemy, he would do for the moment. Sam got up, folded the army-green blanket neatly, hitched up his pants and headed for the opening in the cell door. By the time he was in the corridor, he remembered where his truck was, waiting for him parked beneath the maple trees.

"I called Fewell and told him where you were. He wants to see you—pronto."

Moutscher had little tiny piggy eyes; Sam wondered that he hadn't noticed that before. And hairs growing out of his nostrils. And a gut that hung over his silver belt buckle.

Sam turned to leave, turned back, and severed all good will.

"And you sir, my good captain, have a brain as tiny as your pecker."

24

It was dusk on their second Sunday together when Duane looked at the forest and then at the slope of the land and knew he had made a mistake. The route down below Bowan Mountain had appeared the easiest of all those he'd considered. If he had not been so sure of it, he would never have let them linger so long in the meadow. But he had been weak, and it had been too easy to feel secure knowing that they were only a few miles from the highway that could carry them swiftly to the Canadian border, to the beginning of their new life.

While his arm hampered him from other movement, he had worked over the Forest Service map for hours and found it rudimentary; the Pacific Crest Trail would lead them in two—or at the most, three—days to Slate Peak, and then into the Pasayten Wilderness where no motorized rig could venture. Their food would last a week or even two without supplement from his hunting and fishing. He could build them shelter before the heavy snows came.

He had planned to tell her where they were going when they actually crossed over into the Pasayten, and he was annoyed that she broke his concentration with questions as he focused on leading them down the mountain. It was neither cold—they had left the thin snow layer behind them—nor was it dark; the moon had swollen now to three-quarters of its face. Once their eyes adjusted to the dim light, they could maneuver the trail. But what would have taken them four hours in daylight required double that at night. Even draining of its poison, his arm still ached and the aching distracted too. Her hand hooked in his belt did not seem enough to assure her that he would not leave her behind. She talked to him continually.

"Are you there?"

"You're touching me. You know I'm here."

"Talk to me."

"I'm trying to find the way."

"Then tell me what you're thinking. Think out loud so I can hear your voice."

"I can't think out loud."

"Then sing."

"If we sing, we can't hear . . . things."

That frightened her. "Then talk to me."

He made no reply.

They reached Bridge Creek at dawn, but he allowed them to rest for only a few minutes. They were an hour's walk from the highway, too exposed to other hikers. She started

POSSESSION

to protest when he ordered her to follow him again, but she obeyed.

An hour later, he missed the turn-off at Fireweed Camp. They had gone on for almost two hours before he felt the first niggling of doubt, so involved in hiding them that he had misjudged the simplest turn they came upon. When he put his finger on the pleated map, he saw the problem at once—but it was not easily corrected. He had gone east at Fireweed instead of obliquely north. If he backtracked, she would know that they were lost. It was a matter of pride and he continued, thinking that they could rest in the meadow he saw ahead and then go back on a circuitous route she would not detect.

One fly and then a dozen of them landed on his seeping hand and he batted them away, hurrying further along to a place where he could rethink their route.

He was very tired now, and the flies that buzzed and stung at him aggravated the pain in his arm until he found it almost too heavy to carry. When he held it over his chest, it threw his balance askew; when he let it hang down, the blood fell into it and pressed his nerves.

They climbed north along rock cairns to a ridge, and then the trail was clearer. There had been a look-out site, but he relaxed when he saw that it seemed long deserted—only weather-scored, broken timbers remained of whatever building men had tried to place here. No one had come here recently.

He led her along a scrabble trail that seemed to be easterly and was rewarded. A splendid, tiny plateau of meadow lay below and beyond that he could see a lake and a few narrow streams—a place meant for them, surrounded by flaming larches, protected by rocky peaks.

She was enthralled. He pretended that he had meant to bring her here all along. When he was really well, he would find their way into the Pasayten, but until then, he was quite content to stay where they were. He was sure that they had been led here by some design.

"Where are we?" She lay on her back in the grass and

245

spread her arms, tumbling in the greenness of it. "It's wonderful. How did you find it?"

He looked at his map. "Stiletto Meadows. I chose it for you."

"I never want to leave. Can we stay here forever?"

"Forever," he lied.

25

Sam let the dusty truck decide, allowed the steering wheel to whirl lightly in his open hands, and it headed for the barn: Natchitat. There was no reason to go back, but there was nowhere else to go. He was not welcome in Wenatchee. Alone, he was of no earthly use in Stehekin. He still coaxed the delusion that Danny and Joanne somehow lived in Natchitat, a crazy hope that he had endured a terrible alcoholic nightmare that would dissipate in daylight. It allowed him to maneuver his vehicle through the traffic on this bright blue and yellow Wenatchee noon, despite the steady thumping in his head. He would have preferred to simply cut and run to a place where memory could not follow him, but he'd already exercised that option when he bolted from Seattle. A man could do that only once in his lifetime. A second blind flight would stamp him a bum for whom there could be no redemption. He had no plan, but he trusted that one would take form as his head cleared because there was a powerful urgency in him. Wherever she was, Joanne waited for rescue.

He drove faster, although he had no good reason for going home. *Home.* Home meant dealing with Fewell, explaining what could not be explained to Elizabeth Crowder, and a starving cat. He passed his hand across his forehead and felt cold sweat.

The taverns beside the road, their windows shuttered but their blue neon "Open" signs beckoning, called to him seductively. He longed to let the truck turn in, to find shelter himself inside one of the bars where the air was icy and the sunshine was lost behind thick walls and translucent colored glass.

He could not run. He could not hide. He apparently was not going to die; his heart had got him up the mountain and down and up again, and he could not depend on a medium-grade hangover to kill him.

He crossed the Natchitat County line, still forty miles from town, the highway skirting the reservation, and rounded the long curve past the quarry. Two lean hogs dashed across the center line, stopped and gazed placidly at his approaching truck. He hit the brake and slid onto the shoulder, swearing.

He had seen the signs a thousand times: Max Ling's faded totem pole beside a tree studded with advertisements for himself. It drove Walker Fewell into quiet rage because he had no dominion over Max's enterprises, protected as he was by treaties drawn in another era.

In descending order, the signs read:

Puppies: Bird dogs. Watch dogs. Pets.
Cigarettes: No tax—all brands.
Dahlias—Cut Flowers for Weddings, Funerals. Tubers.
Honey.
Used Cars: Classics
Antique Bottles
SEARCH

and a new sign, bigger than all the rest, its paint so fresh that it appeared still wet: DMSO HERE NOW!

Sam and Danny had been at Max's place a time or two, sent out by Fewell to confiscate cigarettes, and to sniff for untaxed liquor. They'd always had to return the cigarettes because Max had an attorney who knew tribal law and federal treaties a hell of a lot better than Walker Fewell did—and Sam had been delighted to bring back the evidence. He liked Ling, although he had always found it a little hard to believe in a blue-eyed Indian.

His eyes ran down the signs again, and stopped at

"SEARCH," and he could hear Danny's voice laughing, "That little blue-eyed chief can track anything—if it interests him. Runs circles around dogs and white men and any goddamned scientific gear you can name."

At this moment Sam could not remember anything that Max had found, could not be sure that Danny hadn't been pulling his leg, teasing the old flatlander cop. One thing was clear; almost anybody could track better than Sam himself could.

He wheeled his rig through the opening in the poplar trees that cut Ling's operation off from the highway, into a jungle of Max's peculiar collectibles.

The field on the right side of the dirt lane was full of vehicles, heat devils shimmering from their baked metal. Packards, Terraplanes, an Edsel, a half-dozen Hudson Hornets, and the overturned-bathtub Nashes of the early fifties. What Ling considered "classic" had always amused Sam. Max never seemed to sell any of the rusting hulks, only added to his graveyard of Detroit's embarrassments.

Dahlias dominated the left side of the property, in full bloom now, their red, yellow, white, maroon, and salmon flowers so brilliant that they hurt Sam's eyes. Between the dahlia patch and the three-storied, asbestos-shingled house, bees hovered and soared over their white hives, fifty, sixty of the square bee-homes, lined up with precision.

The dogs, the ugliest dogs Sam had ever seen—liver-colored dogs of no particular lineage—ran beside his truck and barked in hoarse whoops. There were a dozen of them. He could not imagine that anyone ever bought "Puppies," and assumed that Max must breed them only to add to the guard that protected his empire from unfriendly visitors. He braked the truck and they sat back on their haunches, waiting for him to make a move.

He waited for someone to emerge from the house, although it was impossible to tell if anyone was inside, the front of the residence was so camouflaged with trellises, awnings, honeysuckle, wisteria, and the odd piece of auto body left there when its intended purpose was forgotten. The dogs had always liked Danny—but Danny had liked and trusted dogs. Sam was a cat man and he wondered if they knew that. He hit the horn and listened; the house remained silent while the dogs smiled at him with their teeth bared and their tongues lolling. A bee flew in his side window and danced over his nose. Something was going to bite him or sting him no matter what he did.

He slid out of the cab and headed for the door that looked most likely of the four fronting on the long porch, the killer dogs jostling each other for a chance to lick his hand. They waited with him as he rang a bell that didn't ring and then knocked. When there was no response, he sheltered his eyes with his hand and peered through the screen. He could see a woman inside the living room, a space so aqua from its shades that it appeared to be under water. She sat with her back to him, watching a huge, tavern-sized television screen.

He knocked again and she didn't move. He pounded on the wall beside the door and she flinched, looked around, and strode like a graceful dancer toward him. She held open the screen door and smiled at him; he found her one of the most beautiful women he had ever seen in his life. An Indian, surely, but not a Northwest Indian, her features delicate and Caucasian, her skin the color of almonds. She was at least six feet tall, full breasts suspended in a white lace halter, long brown legs emerging from denim cut-offs. She turned away from him and looked back toward a darkened area beyond the living room and her straight black hair, which reached to the top of her thighs, brushed his hand. He felt the slightest surge of masculine appreciation for her excellence. A small thing but wondrous in its displacement of nothingness. He spoke to her as she was looking away from him.

"Max here?"

She didn't answer.

"I said, is Max at home?"

She turned back toward him and stared at his mouth, waiting. And then her hands moved across each other like brown birds. He saw instantly that she could not speak or hear.

He enunciated slowly and she read his lips, nodding and smiling. She moved her hands again, her fingers so rapid that they blurred.

He shook his head and touched her shoulder lightly, then pointed at his own lips: "I don't understand. I cannot speak the language."

She took his hand lightly and led him through the shadowed room. Ling's house was a series of additions, each one built either a little higher than the next, or sunken—so that no threshold matched another. Sam stepped carefully, his pupils still contracted from his long drive in the sun. One room was lined with narrow shelves full of bottles— blue, aqua, amethyst, white—their glass flawed and thickened, lips applied awkwardly, bases marked with pottles where some glass blower had sealed off their melted substance before the century turned. All of them valuable now, when they had once been somebody's garbage.

The next room was clearly the woman's studio. Canvasses with paintings of wild flowers and studies of hands. Hands folded; hands held out in supplication; some graceful; some gnarled. Hands would be important to her. He touched her elbow and inclined his head toward the paintings and smiled. She nodded.

They moved into the last room, the kitchen. Max Ling, bare to the waist above painters' pants, siphoned clear liquid from a gallon container into what looked like mayonnaise jars. He recognized Sam and grimaced, but his hands were steady at his task. He spoke not to Sam, but to the woman—in her tongue—when he had finished pouring. His hands moved and she answered, their eyes catching one another's. Max pointed to Sam and said something in finger talk. Her face grew solemn and she looked at Sam, alarmed.

"Tell her I come in peace."

Max laughed. "You don't have to talk Indian. She can't hear you."

"I know. Tell her I'm not here officially."

Max put his arm on Sam's shoulder in a gesture of friendship and the tall woman relaxed. "Sam, this is Marcella, my wife. Marcella (he spoke directly to her and she studied his lips gravely), this is Sam Clinton, a good friend of mine. He says he didn't come from the Sheriff. Not today. It's O.K."

She smiled again, her face magical, forgiving him for whatever she had assumed, and walked away, leaving them alone.

"Damn it, Sam. I've got a right to sell this stuff. They've been selling it for months down on the Nisqually Reservation. I just put that sign up yesterday. Your undersheriff must have smelled it."

The jars had plain black and white labels: "DMSO, Solvent" and Sam was confused; he had no idea what Max was talking about.

"You've lost me. What is it?"

"What *is* it? This is an elixir to cure all the ills of mankind. Bruises, cuts, sprains, arthritis, rheumatism, sore throat, burns—probably even herpes. Some M.D. down in Portland was on 'Sixty Minutes' talking about it, and he's got patients lined up all the way across the Columbia River Bridge, fighting to get some. And here it is, $11.95 a pint. Cheaper than aspirin."

"Solvent?"

"To appease the law, my friend. What my customers do with it is not my concern. They buy it as solvent. That's O.K. with me, and it should be enough to placate your Mr. Fewell. It comes from the trees, all those trees that belonged to my blood brothers and stolen by yours. A heretofore useless by-product. A natural remedy." Max looked sharply at Sam. "Which it would appear you are in need of. You look like something no tomcat would piss on."

"Thanks."

"Seriously. Let me give you a sample. You have any spots that hurt, any arthritis due to your advanced age and life of excess?"

"Pick a spot. Name it; it hurts."

"Lower back. Lower back is the first to go. Turn around and lift up your shirt."

"Come on, Max. I didn't come to arrest you or haul off your merchandise—or to see the medicine man."

"Lift your shirt."

Sam let Max daub some of the oily, clear liquid along his spine. It burned within seconds and he jumped away. He tasted garlic and oysters in his mouth and spat. "What the hell is that?"

"DMSO. Put that on three times a day and you'll walk again."

"*God*. But nobody is likely to kiss me. That's disgusting!"

"Taste it? That shows how quickly it moves through your system. The big drug companies are fighting it. It's too effective and too cheap. Scares the shit out of them—but all the big leagues use it. Whole damn Kingdome stinks of it, but those athletes stop hurting."

"I hope it sells better than your fleet of classy cars. They don't seem to be moving."

"They will." Max's clear blue eyes leveled on Sam's. "Where's your partner? Where's old Danny?"

He could not say it again. Not yet. He tucked his shirt into his jeans, feeling the sandpaper burn of the solvent on his back. "I still don't believe you're an Indian, Max. I think your name's really Abraham Stein, and you're hiding here on the reservation from three previous wives in New Jersey."

"My father's name was Blum. Morris Blum. Ahh, but my mother was Mary Toohoolzote Ling, a Coeur d'Alene, once removed. That's enough. An eighth, a sixteenth, is enough. You've decimated us. The Jews don't need me; the tribe does. Now, Marcella's a Tuscarora. Niagara Falls. Beautiful people."

"She is that."

Max Ling was a good six inches shorter than his wife, compact to the point of squareness, muscled like a wrestler. Sam had no idea how old he was. He could be anywhere from twenty to forty, and his hair was Indian black and fine in startling contrast to the pale eyes. "A lot prettier than you are."

"Where's Danny?" Max would not allow him to change the subject again.

"Dead."

POSSESSION

Max screwed the top on the jar of solvent and did not speak for so long that the word hung on the air, bounced around the room, and came back to Sam full-blown. Finally, the little Indian looked up, his face quite bland but his eyes darkening.

"Was *that* him? There was something on the radio this morning, but I only caught part of it—something about some deputy who died up at Stehekin. I figured it was somebody from Chelan County."

"That was him."

"He was O.K. I always liked him better than . . . the rest of you."

"Everybody did."

"What happened?"

"I can tell you what I think happened, and I can tell you what the searchers and the rangers and the Chelan County Sheriff's Office said happened, but I don't believe that either version is completely accurate. I'm prejudiced in favor of mine."

"So tell."

"What makes you think she's alive?" Ling's voice betrayed no doubt, only listening.

"I've answered that before and nobody believed my reasoning."

"But what?"

"Some things I can explain—some I can't. Danny was stabbed. I saw the wounds before the coroner destroyed them. Joanne's gone, and so are her sleeping bag and her backpack. And . . . she's not alone. I found the piece of a shirt in a tree up there that wasn't hers and wasn't Danny's. Somebody's got her. There was no damned bear, except in some fools' imaginations."

Ling looked thoughtful. "So what do you want with me?"

"Your sign says SEARCH. Danny said you could find things. And frankly, you're about my last chance. Chelan County ran me out this morning on a rail. I'm probably going to get canned here because I took off without permission. I'm what you call a person with very low credibility, and I am strictly no-talent in the wilderness. I cannot find my way from Point A to Point B."

"I believe *that.*"

"I want you to go with me."

"You got any money?"

Sam looked up sharply. "You don't strike me as a mercenary."

Ling laughed. "Look around you. Look at everything for sale and tell me I'm not a mercenary."

"Are you?"

"In this case, no, but you just told me you are not exactly sanctioned by your fellow piggies. That means that it's unlikely that any county is going to loan you a helicopter or any other gear we might need. So have you got any money?"

"I've got about two thousand dollars in savings."

"You'll put that up?"

"Hell yes, I'll put that up."

"Do you believe that I can find her?"

"I'm not sure."

Ling slapped his hand on the table in front of Sam, the splat of it making Sam jump back. "For that, I'm charging you my standard rate as an Indian guide, $100 a day, payable when we find her. You know why my fee just went up? Because if I don't charge you an arm and a leg, you're not gonna believe in me. If you have to pay me, you'll think you got somebody *exceptional.*"

Sam winced. "I believe in you."

"Too late. Doubting me cost you. You bet your ass you believe in me. Every time you get all wishy-washy, my price goes up another $25 a day. Dragging you along isn't going to be easy. You are not exactly what I call fit."

"I'll hack it. If I die going uphill, you can cover me with pine cones and call the meat wagon—or the meat sled, or whatever. And sue my estate, you little fucker, for your consulting fee."

"You can't drink up there."

"What makes you think I drink?"

POSSESSION

"When you came in you smelled like a week of firewater; now you smell like stale booze, garlic, and oysters."

"That's so you won't keep trying to hug me."

"It's even possible you have a few cogs missing."

"Several."

"Marcella's not going to like it. She doesn't like to have me leave her."

"And you aren't going to like to leave her. Will she be safe here by herself?"

"The dogs won't let anybody close to her."

"They let me in."

"Sheriff Sam. Believe it or not, that's one of the main reasons I'm throwing in with you. Those hounds like about one sucker out of a hundred. They evidently saw something in you that your own mother wouldn't recognize anymore. I was watching you when you drove up, and I saw those dogs laughing and bouncing and licking your hand. I trust dogs."

"Then you've never had your ass bit."

Max stood up. "Nope. When did you eat?"

"What day is it?"

"Monday."

"Friday. Maybe Saturday. I can't remember."

"Then you're going to eat and you're going to keep eating." He strode to the stove and lifted the lid on a pot simmering there. "Voilà! Chicken soup."

"You're kidding."

Max laughed. "It's really lamb stew."

"I have to make some phone calls."

"After you eat. I'm going to tell Marcella that we're taking off this afternoon. She may not forgive you soon, but she'll forgive you."

While Sam spooned up food, he could see them together, through the several doorways, framed silently in the underwater parlor. Max leaned over the couch where she sat, his hands tender on her face, soothing. She shook her head and Max lay one finger on her lips. Then he spoke to her with both his hands. After what seemed a long time of mute conversation, she nodded and bent her head.

255

Marcella rose and walked down the corridor of doorways toward him, and Sam looked up and smiled at her. She did not acknowledge him. Her face was troubled as she turned into her studio. When he walked past her room toward the phone in the living room a few minutes later, he saw her at her easel, filling the canvas with white daisies against a purple-black sweep of rugged peaks. It jarred him in its familiarity. She must have begun it long before he came into her house; she could not have painted so much in a few minutes.

Fletch's voice on the other end of the line was chastened with shock and sorrow with no hint of his raucous humor and Sam felt a somber returning of loss. He listened to Fletch's disbelief, to his questions that had no clean answers, and tried not to let the emotions touch him. He had called Fletch at home, allowing himself harbor for a while longer from Fewell's wrath, and he could hear Mary Jean in the background, whispering questions for Fletch to pass on. Then shushing, quiet, and more questions.

"They brought him back here this morning," Fletch said in the same hushed tone. "Mrs. Crowder's taking care of the arrangements. Then she's going up to that place—the lodge place in Stehekin—with Sonia Kluznewski."

"She can't do any good up there!" He was angry, and then softened. Elizabeth Crowder deserved her own chance at futile vigil.

"We're not going to set the date for the services—until, until—they find Joanne."

"Yeah, that's good. She'd want to be there."

There was a painful pause on the other end of the line.

"Geez, Sam. I thought she was de—, er, gone too."

"We don't know that, Fletch. There is no evidence at all that she's not going to be found alive."

He could not convince Fletch of something he could not truly convince himself of.

"Fletch, there are some things I want you to do for me. And I don't want anyone else to know about it—nobody—especially not Fewell. Have you got a piece of paper?"

POSSESSION

Fletcher sounded better, given something to do. "Gotcha. No problem with confidentiality. Shoot."

"First, I sent some evidence over to Seattle, to the Crime Lab. I want you to watch for any response on that. When it comes, you take it home and keep it. I'll check in with you. Second, I've got two names here—let's see—I want you to run them on the computers—NCIC, WASIC, and SEA-KING. Whatever hits you get, clear the machine after you write down the info. Then, I want you to take these two names and—this is a little tedious, Fletch—I want you to go through all the FIRs in the county since August first and look for a match. If you don't get an exact match on names or vehicles, I want you to look for 'sounds like,' or similarities. Make me a packet of anything you find. Don't even tell Mary Jean."

Fletcher was transparent as cellophane; his voice lowered confidentially as he whispered, "O.K. Our secret." Immediately Mary Jean's voice rose suspiciously behind him. He could hear Fletch cover the receiver and say something to placate her. Then he was back on the line.

"Fewell say anything about me?"

"Oh, Sam—he's raving. He's frothing. Your butt is in a sling; he wants you like a baby wants milk. Some brass from Chelan got him on the horn. What'd you do up there?"

"Nothing important. I'll tell you when I see you."

"Where are you?"

"No place where I'll be for long. You ready for the names?"

"Lay them on me."

"O.K. Number one: Steven or Stephen Curry. Birthdate roughly 1958 to 1963. White male adult. Five feet six to nine. Blond. No eye color. Possible birthplace, California."

"The computer won't do much with no firm birthdate."

"It can scan a couple of years in either direction. Give it a shot. Next: David Dwain. No birthdate. Address, Portland, Oregon."

"Shit, Sam. You're dreaming."

"Try it. Try the FIRs. Maybe you'll get more that you can put into the computer."

"O.K. What do you want this for?"

"I'm not sure I can tell you. A hunch. Maybe nothing."

"Good luck. You want anything else?"

"Yeah. Feed my cat."

26

Duane had never expected to be angry with her. In their perfect companionship, there were to have been no negative emotions. No anger, no jealousy, no doubt, no rejection, no annoyance. She had opened up her mind finally and allowed him to slip into it. And he had drawn her back into his. She was in him and of him and part of him.

But she had lost the goddamned map.

It had to have been her fault. It had been next to his hand. He could still place it there in his memory, feel it rustling against his wrist when he fell asleep. And now, it was gone.

"Don't cry. Try to think. Try to remember what you did with it."

"I can't. I didn't have it." She began to cry again.

"But you saw what it looked like? It was a big sheet, all folded up, blue and green and red."

"I remember that, but I don't know what happened to it."

"You can remember anything if you clear your mind and concentrate. Close your eyes and try to picture it."

She closed her eyes. "I can't see it."

"Think. Dammit!"

"You're mad at me."

She was a child. She had always been a child-woman. He reached out to touch her shoulder and she flinched and pulled away from him. He should not have trusted anything important with her. But he was still so easily fatigued, slipping suddenly into naps, each of which he expected to reward him with the return of his usual vigor. Any renewals were short-lived. He had slept most of the day away, his

POSSESSION

blood sluggish in his veins and seeming to carry no oxygen. And they had made love again all during the night until he finally slept only fitfully toward dawn. She was draining the life out of him.

"Are we lost?" She sounded like some other woman now.

"No."

"Are you sure? I look back and it looks the same as any other direction. Everything looks the same. Rocks and mountains and trees. It would be easy to get lost up here."

"We're not lost. I simply need the map to pick the best way out."

"I feel lost."

"You're with me. You cannot be lost."

He closed his eyes and saw the map in his mind, all the trails spread across its face, arteries and veins of escape. He remembered Copper Pass, and Stiletto Peak, and Twisp, and something else—McAlester Pass. But they would not fall into place; they twisted like snakes, doubling back into a maze. Without the map he would have to make forays himself and construct a new one.

She moved close to him and massaged his neck, her fingertips sliding gently around the cartilage of his ear, her breasts pressing against his shoulder. She made it difficult for him to think.

"I made the fire," she whispered. "I didn't want you to wake up and be cold. It's so warm and sunny all day. And then it gets cold all of a sudden."

"That's nic—" Before the words were out, he felt a terrible premonition. He sat up, tumbling her away from him, and strode to the fire that licked blue and orange around blackened limbs. He stared at its edges and drew his breath in sharply. There was a small triangle of paper caught under the uncharred end of a branch. It had white borders and what he could see of the rest was blue shaded to green.

She cried out as he kicked the fire apart, sending chunks of flaming wood spinning into the grass. He was on his hands and knees then, pawing through what could be

259

touched without searing his flesh. Finally he turned to her with a look she had never seen before, the man vanished, the boy gone, both of them destroyed by the twisted animal rage on his face. She thought, "red man," could not remember who that was, and waited, hopelessly, to see what she had done that was so awful.

"You burned the map. You burned the goddam map."

She deserved punishment. He left her beside the ruined fire and crashed into the woods while she wailed behind him, begging him not to leave her alone. *She* had left him enough times. Let her get a taste of what alone could be. He knew she wouldn't follow him; she was too frightened of the woods at night.

The way out might be quite obvious; he could do it without the map, but he had to hurry before the sun went down again. He would stand on the ridge and look down and find the way. Then he might forgive her. The scrabbly trail fought his foothold and mosquitos settled over him in clouds so thick that their drone maddened him and shut out her distant voice.

He became aware of something watching him, although he could hear no sound above the bugs. He stopped and looked behind him. She had not followed him; there was only the dark trail that seemed to disappear in the sky. Ahead it was the same. He was suspended on a thin wall of rock with no beginning and no end except air. Still, something prickled the back of his neck and the feel of it made him so dizzy that he dropped to one knee to stop himself from catapulting into space.

He saw them then—first their eyes, eight orbs of fluorescent gold, unblinking. Big cats. Cougars. Their faces were as gentle as kittens' faces, but their tails wound down and around, six feet long and as thick as his arm, their shoulders muscled thickly. They stared at him with interest and he knew they could be upon him in two, maybe three, bounds. He waited in his half-crouch for minutes and the cats never moved.

He should not have left her. After what seemed a very

long time, his shaking legs steadied and he stood cautiously. The cougars seemed stuffed and lifeless. And then he saw pale membranes slide over yellow eyes. They were real.

When he turned and made his way back toward where he'd left her, he thought he heard them padding behind him, imagined their breath on his neck. He reached the end of the ridge and turned back, ready to shoot if he had to— and there was nothing. The rocks where the yellow cats had perched were empty.

He would kill her himself before he let an animal have her. He would kill her himself before he let anything or anyone else have her. She was his own possession, and neither cats nor men would take her. He could see her near the rebuilt fire, huddled in misery, long before she heard him approach. Waiting for him.

The thought of killing her seemed to be part of him, the last exchange between them. Not like with the others. They had died because they were false, because they had proved early on that they didn't recognize him. He was quite sure that she knew him now, but even as she proved herself, memories came back to him. Bad things. If they had time and freedom, he might be able to forgive her. He wished passionately that she didn't have to die. She had pledged to kill for him and he for her, but she had not understood what that might mean.

27

The chartered copter circled over Rainbow Lake and Sam peered down, seeing again the green expanse whose color seemed to change like a lying woman's eyes. Today, it was an innocent bright green, reflecting the sun, and the scene of searchers huddled in the cold was only a dull memory. The weather and the landscape changed continually up here and he trusted none of it.

He glanced at Ling's profile and wondered why he trusted Ling, or perhaps more puzzling, why Ling had thrown in with *him*. Hell, he was having a hard enough time convincing himself. Neither "Curry" nor "Dwain" had drawn a hit on the computers, and Fletch seemed lackadaisical about searching through the FIR's for something more. Sam wondered what Moutscher had insinuated when he called Fewell. If he'd hinted that Sam had cracked up, that would be enough to scare Fletch. If there was one thing that alienated cops, it was craziness. *Because we're all half-sure that we'll catch it from being exposed so often.*

He hated helicopters. Once in Seattle, he'd been sent out to photograph the decapitated uniformed bodies and burned fuselage of a crashed police helicopter. Air I all in ashes. He breathed easier as the rotors lowered the pod they sat in onto the ground and he could feel solid land beneath his feet.

"Watch your head!" Ling shouted above the cyclone of noise and Sam bent double as he trotted clear.

The pilot promised to fly over areas designated by Ling each afternoon until they signaled him they were ready to be picked up. Sam doubted that Joanne would be able to walk out when they found her.

It was very quiet when the craft's rotors faded in the distance, all of the searchers dissipated. They had left their mark, bright ribbons on trees and bushes where they'd shown sections already combed, electric blue plastic streamers flowing in the wind, mocking and empty.

Ling paced back and forth along the lake edge, lost in a reverie of his own. Sam watched him silently, smoked a cigarette, put it out, smoked another, and was lighting a third when Ling padded back toward him.

"They're not here now," he said finally.

"I'd say that was taken for granted."

"They might have come back—after the searchers left. But they didn't."

"You're saying 'they.' Why? Because of what I told you? Forget what I told you."

POSSESSION

"I have." Ling squatted in front of him and his nostrils twitched. "I smell two people."

"Come off it, Max. How can you *smell* anyone?"

"Because if I said 'feel,' you'd go all antsy on me. Nobody understands my methods. You'll have to trust me. We've got layers of human spoor through here. Men and dogs clomping around and smashing hell out of everything. Right?"

"Right. Is it too late?"

Ling shook his head and started pacing again, his head cocked in a listening stance. "The search team showed us where they've been, so we toss that out. We go deeper. You tell me the woman had never been up here before. Say, she was alone—she's scared shitless. She would never have made it farther than the perimeter of those ribbons. And they didn't find diddley. So we assume she did go farther, but not alone. You with me?"

"I always assumed that."

"If she'd gone downtrail, you would have met up with her."

"Yes."

"So she went uptrail. I can't see her running into the brush of her own accord and no matter what those guys told you, bears don't drag their victims very far from the point of attack. They lose interest when the essence leaves after death. Bears kill for the same reasons humans do—out of fear, frustration, to protect their young, or because they think they're trapped."

"But not out of jealousy or for financial gain."

Ling grinned. "Bears are a little nicer than your average man on the street. Your woman wouldn't have been much of a threat to any bear."

"No."

"Tell me what she looks like."

"Why?"

"It helps if I have a picture of who I'm looking for. Just tell me about her."

Sam sighed. "Shit. Ling, I never could describe women."

"Give it a shot. How tall?"

"Little. Not real little, but—maybe five foot, two or three, hundred-fifteen maybe. Dark hair, blue eyes."

"Pretty?"

"I guess so. Yeah, she's a real pretty woman."

"What color is she?"

"She's Caucasian."

Ling snorted. "I don't want a cop description. I'm trying to get a total picture. Everybody gives off a color. You—you're kind of a burnt sienna. I'm dark green. Marcella's pale lavender . . ."

"Ling . . ." Sam's exasperation burgeoned.

"We're playing by my rules. What color?"

". . . rose, very pale rose."

Ling looked at him and whistled. "You have the hots for her, don't you?"

"No! Damn it, Ling. You asked a ridiculous question. I come up with an equally ridiculous answer—to pacify you—and you start playing Dr. Freud. She's my partner's wife."

"Whatever you say." Ling walked to the hiding tree, although Sam had not told him where it was, and circled it. "Look at it this way, deputy. You have certain talents; I have certain talents. You don't believe in my hocus-pocus, which, by the way, is only part of what I'm good at. But you've told me there are at least three dozen sensible men who don't agree with your assumptions. Part of what's burning a hole in you comes from what you've picked out of the air. You've got vibrations too. You combine that with physical evidence. Isn't that the way it goes on TV?"

"Yeah."

"And in real black and white life too?"

"I guess so."

"O.K. Pretty soon I'm going to show you what I can see in dirt and leaves and broken branches. That's my physical evidence. The other is my gut stuff. We put those together with yours, and we'll find your rosy little woman." He looked up into the pine boughs. "She was up here, wasn't she?"

POSSESSION

"I think she was. I think she was up there with someone—not Danny."

"A man. A big man. Twice as big as I am. Bigger than you are."

"How do you know that?"

"I can't tell you. I just know."

Sam laughed without humor. "What color is he?"

But Ling took him seriously and reached out to touch the tree trunk. "Hot. A hot color."

"Ling," Sam said suddenly. "Where's your weapon? You brought a gun, didn't you? You're talking the Incredible Hulk here, and . . ."

"I don't own a gun," Ling said quietly. "I couldn't shoot one if I had one. I'm what you call nonviolent."

"Shit."

"Let's start with the part we can see, Deputy. Give me your foot."

"What for?"

Ling pulled a buck knife out of his belt and bent over Sam's boot sole. "I'm gonna mark you, Sam." He cut a diagonal line across one heel, reached for the other foot and marked that. "If I'm following somebody, I don't want it to turn out to be you. This way, I'll know you. Now, do mine."

Sam took the knife and scored tattoos on the tracker's boots. That made a lot more sense to him than personal colors. He relaxed a little.

"Whose stuff is this around the campsite?"

"The coffeepot and skillet and junk was theirs—Danny's and Joanne's. The beer bottles—I don't know."

"Where'd you find him?"

"Down trail."

"Can I see it?"

"There's nothing there now."

"You say."

"Hell, come on."

They walked along the trail so dry that it was impossible to remember that snow had covered everything only three days before; it had evaporated like seafoam under the sun as hot as August's. The blue plastic banners were tangled in the trees where Danny had lain, slim snippets of color there too. The leaves that had been crushed under Danny's body had all blown away, leaving the forest floor unmarked—at least to Sam. Ling, however, walked immediately to the body perimeters next to the fallen log, an outline emblazoned in Sam's mind if not in his sight now. Ling noted tiny bony twigs still pressed into the moldering mulch of other seasons, flattened leaves from this autumn pressed too tightly to the earth.

"He was here?" It was more a statement than a question, and Sam's estimation of the little tracker's expertise was enhanced again.

"Right there."

Ling padded over the body site, touching, listening, searching—but he found nothing more.

"You were right, deputy. You do know what you're doing. There's nothing left here except for the place he fell."

They walked back to the lake camp in silence. Ling seemed given to spells of introspection—or perhaps concentration—where he shut out all conversation. He would not respond to Sam's agitation to do *something*. Despite the deceptive heat of the day, twilight was closer than he had thought.

"The trail's gone; isn't it?" Ling had reassured him before that it was not, but he took Ling's taciturnity for the same lack of purpose he'd sensed in the first searchers. "They blew it for us, didn't they?"

Ling looked at him, annoyed at his distraction. "I am trying to find my starting point. I'd rather search the right ten feet perfectly than crash all over to hell and gone half-assed. Nobody ever has the smarts to bring a tracker in first. I'm used to working with a whole bunch of shit that has to be eliminated before I can move. I'm a sign-cutter; you know what that means?"

Sam shook his head.

"That means that we're going to pick out the most likely direction, and then we're going to find our signs on the ground that make us believe we picked right. Isn't that what you detectives do?"

POSSESSION

"Yeah. Like the green plaid I found."

"Exactly. Sam, you're already trained for this. Just close off your blind side and question more. Look at everything twice and when something doesn't look quite right, give a holler. Deputy, I think you're a natural. You wheeze some, and you've got a hitch in your getalong, but I'm going to consider you a blood brother. I'm even getting to like you." Ling grinned. "Although I'm not known for my taste. You're going to look for signs until your eyeballs get dusty. If I say go back and do it again, you're going to do it. Don't expect to find footprints leading us right to her. We don't have snow, and we don't have sand, and we don't have mud. We'll be lucky if we find a piece of a print anywhere. Pick a trail."

Sam sighed and stared into the jungle of trees and vegetation. "O.K. I'll start rudimentary. She didn't—I *think* she didn't—double back, so that means she, or they, went ahead."

"Seems fair."

"So what the hell constitutes *ahead?* It all looks the same to me."

Ling unfolded the map from the National Park Service. On the side it carried a banner headline, "Touch the Wilderness Gently," and the other was swirled in concentric circles that reminded Sam of the whorls and ridges of fingerprints—all of it a far cry from the Texaco maps he was accustomed to. Max ran his finger along a thin red line of ink and stopped, tapping.

"Over Bowan Mountain—here. That's maybe six miles to the Pacific Crest Trail or on out to the North Cascades Highway. And there ain't no way we're going to make it before dark. I'm good, but not that good."

"We'll lose them."

"That's another twenty-five bucks a day." Ling folded the map. "If you feel that way, we've already lost them. They have—what?—nine days start on us? But they didn't come out on the other side yet, did they? And if *I* can't move in the dark, they can't move in the dark. And if you keep pissing and moaning, you aren't going to see what you're supposed to see. We pack our butts out of here at dawn. In between, we eat; we sleep a little. You with me?"

"I better be—I can't afford your rate hikes. You know, Ling, you must be really insecure, you don't handle rejection well." Sam laughed.

"My mother abandoned me. I was raised by wolves in Spokane and they never understood me. Go build me a fire."

Sam woke in the deepest part of the night, used now to having to orient himself to where he was. He had slept in the woods, in his truck, in jail, in Ling's house, and—he remembered—now in the woods again. He lay unmoving, trying to figure out what had wakened him; he listened to the sound of Ling's snoring next to him, a shudder of wind in the quaking aspens, an owl—and something more. There was another presence.

He listened and tried to see into the darkness beyond their own outlines without moving his head. The sound came again, a stealthy murmur that seemed human and then not human. A soft whistling of air drawn into heavy lungs, followed by a grunt of displeasure. It was not Max's labored snoring; the snores continued in a counterpoint to the alien noises.

It scared the hell out of Sam as he realized that something moved fifteen or twenty feet away, some live thing watching him while he lay swaddled and damn near helpless. He eased one arm free, and then the other, still unable to see what thing had come upon them as they slept. The thing was heavy. A padding, thudding noise—feet, booted feet, stomping on the turf—emanated from somewhere near the pine tree where Ling had hung their food.

Sam felt his pistol in his hand and he cocked it and pointed it toward the coal black nothing in front of him, waiting for his pupils to adjust so that he could see some outline. And even as he did, he was sure he heard something coming up from behind, through the line of trees. His shoulders tensed and he braced for the blow.

It did not come. The thing was still in front of him as his

eyes adjusted to the dark and the moon's cloud cover shifted.

He saw the pack jounce on its rope and then begin to swing back and forth as if something batted it. And then he saw the animal on its hind legs, one foreleg outstretched. A dark pelted mound of muscle. He moved slightly and a twig cracked beneath him. The creature froze and turned its head toward where they lay. He saw its eye-whites and a yellow blob that was its nose. And in that instant, saw that he had been wrong. All wrong. A damn, stubborn fool. There *was* a bear.

He nudged Ling who came awake immediately and made no sound at all. He turned Ling's head with his hand, and Ling's breathing seemed to stop when he saw the bear. The little man's hand snaked out of his sleeping bag and Sam heard the whisper of the zipper, loud in the night.

And then, before he realized what Ling was about to do, the tracker was on his feet, grabbing for the mess kit that lay beside the dead embers of their recent fire. The clang of metal beaten against metal was louder than a gunshot as Ling ran suicidally toward the bear.

Sam's zipper stuck and he tugged at it frantically, finally giving it up and shucking himself out like a corn cob. When he was finally on his feet in the frosted air, he heard a new sound: Ling laughing.

The Indian walked toward him and Sam saw that the tree space was empty, the pack still swinging lazily on its ropes.

"Old bear liked to peed himself," Ling chuckled.

"You're nuts," Sam muttered. "I could have gotten a shot off if you hadn't spooked him."

"No, my friend," Ling said. "I thought *you* were nuts. I swear I wasn't really positive about you. Thought maybe there really was a grizzly up here. You know what that was? That was a plain old, soft-living, beggar black bear. Not even full-growed. Ain't no man—or small girl for that matter—couldn't have scared him off by shouting."

"How did you know that when you started out after it?"

"I could see it was only a yearling or so bear."

"It looked big to me."

"White man is chicken, ain't he? Woods full of varmints and all. Sam, that little black bear wouldn't come in here if there was a mammoth grizzly around."

"So now you believe me. What'd you come up here for if you didn't believe me, you little fucker?"

Ling slid into his sleeping bag. "Because you're so damned pretty, deputy. I couldn't resist you. Go to sleep. In the morning I'm going to make a sign cutter out of you."

28

He had not had any penicillin for days, and each morning he felt another layer of fever, a thin hotness that weakened him and made him sweat inside his sleeping bag. His hand and arm had ceased to heal, the wounds once again edged in pus. He bathed them often, sinking his arm in the tiny lake they had found, letting the frigid water numb and cleanse it, but the throbbing always came back as his injured arm warmed. He was at first impatient with it, annoyed that it had defied him and would not mend itself—and then frightened when he counted the days that he had not recovered but had only grown steadily weaker. He thought of being in a clean bed in a clean motel room, safe between ironed white sheets that would cool him. And at night when the air became icy and he could not get warm, he dreamed of a fireplace full of solid logs that would not burn out. He had been uncomfortable many times in his life, sleeping in fields and airports and bus stations, but he had always come to it with a strong body and a clear mind to find a solution. Now he felt trapped.

The more the woman clung to him physically, the more her attention struck him as sticky and cloying, and the thread of communication between their minds slowly unraveled. She talked at him when she should be listening.

He could not build anything in this meadow. The first serious winds would whip any shelter off the mountain and into the chasms beneath them, and most of the trees were dwarfs, blighted by the altitude, able to give only minimal shelter from storms. Worse, they were isolated but not safe from intruders. He could not be confident that some party of climbers wasn't going to stumble upon them.

And there were the cougars. He had gone downtrail three times to search for the passage through into the Pasayten Wilderness and each time the big cats had blocked him. Sometimes one or two of them, and once half a dozen. They watched him boldly and he had even heard them purr.

He was phobic about cats, all cats. Lureen had left him alone in the trailer one summer day with a big old tomcat she'd picked up off the road. And the thing had gone wild as the trailer heated up, snarling and hissing and leaping from counter to ice box, and ending, finally and horribly, a frothing monster in his crib. He could not remember if it had bitten him, but he did remember screaming until he was mute, alone with it for hours before anyone came and took the thing away. Somebody with greasy, hairy hands had strangled the cat right in the doorway of their trailer while he watched, still fighting for breath himself. After that, he had always skirted the cage full of bobcats although he'd been unafraid of the rest of the mangy menagerie that was part of the Hungarian's gig. In his adult life he seldom encountered cats of any kind but when he did, the old terror came back.

He knew the cougars smelled his fear and that they rejoiced in it.

He argued with her on Wednesday morning.

"What did you just do?" he asked her sharply, and saw her too familiar look of alarm.

"What?"

"You just poured half a day's food away. We could have eaten it later."

"It's hot out—the sun would have spoiled it. Besides, you haven't eaten anything since yesterday. You don't like anything I fix."

"We don't have endless supplies. We can't run down to

271

the supermarket. You've wasted more than we've eaten."
He plunged his hands into his pack and came up with only
four envelopes, staring at them in shock. "Where's the rest
of it?"

"That's all that's left. Some of them were torn and I
thought they might have gone bad, so I threw them away.
You said you could hunt." She smiled. "I found some
berries—a whole lot of berries."

He said nothing.

"I'm sorry, but I'm so tired of powdered food. Couldn't
you find us a fish or a wild turkey or something?"

He mimicked her sarcastically. "Couldn't you find us a
wild turkey or something? I'm tired, and there aren't any
wild turkeys." *Shut up. Shut up. Shut up.*

"You're sick again, aren't you? Why didn't you tell me
you were sick?"

"I'm not sick; I'm only tired." He forced himself to hold
out his arms, and she moved into them and let herself be
petted and stroked. "You make things so difficult."

She shook her head against his chest and he held it still
with one spread hand so that she couldn't move.

"You have to listen to me. You remember how it was—a
long, long time ago when you were my mother? You made
things difficult then because you never could understand
anything. You tried to do it your way and it didn't work out
and they took you away from me."

She managed to pull away from him and she stared back
at him without comprehension. "I don't know what you
mean. I never knew you. I wasn't your mo—"

"You remember. Tell me you remember."

"You're scaring me."

"You knew me when you saw me. I know you recognized
me. You were afraid to say anything, but you knew me."

She couldn't remember the first time she had seen him.
She thought that she had been with him for several months,
and she loved him, but he made no sense to her. His games
were so bewildering, but he was so urgent about them.

"You did know me, didn't you?" His hand around hers
had begun to hurt her, the vise tightening.

"Yes," she lied. "I knew you."

He relaxed and let her go. "That's better. You must never tease me like that."

"I'm trying to be what you want me to be." She thought she perceived an opening, a calm place where she could tell him what she had been thinking of continually. She massaged his thigh, making circles with her fingernail. "You know what?"

"What?"

"I want to go home."

He froze; she felt the muscles beneath the jeans tense. "We can't go home. We have no home."

"I want to be in a house. I want a roof and walls."

"You're trying to get away from me. You always tried to get away from me."

"No!" She tried to pull his head onto her shoulder and felt his rigid neck. "No. I want to be with you. You said we could have a place for us and that's what I want too, but I'm cold and I'm getting hungry, and I need a bath, and people to talk to."

"You have me to talk to. You don't need anyone else."

"That's true, but wouldn't you like a warm place to sleep? Couldn't we go down the mountain now, and find some place? We've never made love in a bed. We could make love all day and all night, and I would bring you food when you were hungry and we could take a shower together. Would you like that?"

She had not changed. He felt his heart a cold stone beneath his ribs and his throat constrict with the horror of it. She had let him think she believed, weakened him with her constant craving for sex, and all the time she'd been planning how she could abandon him again. He had always known that he would find her some day. He had found her. *And she did not love him.*

"Honey?"

He turned to look at her, his green eyes quite calm. "What?"

"Do it to me now."

"It's too hot."

"In the lake. It's cool in the lake."

"Whatever you say. Whatever makes you happy."

He followed her to the pebbly edge of the water, and she laughed because she thought she had won. He let her undress him and toss his shirt and jeans into the shallows where tiny fish nibbled at them. She nibbled at him and drew blood into his penis, wizened and soft in the cold water and then engorged when he looked down and saw how wantonly she serviced him. They stood in the water further out, waist deep, and he lifted her onto him. Their hips' undulating changed the lake's wave pattern, and he felt exultation when she was impaled on his penis. But with his ejaculation, he lost the sense of power. Even before he slipped out of her, he remembered that he could not trust her any longer, that she mated with him simply because there was no one else. If another male came, she would betray him. She had always betrayed him. If he allowed her to live, she would turn on him.

She followed him back to their camp, unaware that he had seen through her. She chattered at him while she cooked the last of their food. When the sun began to slide down the sky, he knew that it had to be their last night together. The fever was suffocating him, blunting his strength until he knew he could not keep her if someone came to take her away. He would much prefer to have her dead. Dead, she would still belong to him, and he could find her again when he was well. This time, she had been almost perfect, but she had slipped back into being a slut, just as all the others had.

"Dance for me," he ordered.

"I'm tired. I'll dance for you tomorrow."

"I said I wanted you to dance—like you used to for the others."

"I don't understand you—"

"Damn you. You do understand. Don't make me angry."

She moved slowly near the fire, swaying awkwardly, teasing him.

"Not that way. Take your clothes off."

"I'm cold."

POSSESSION

He didn't believe her, but he wouldn't argue with her. "Take your damned clothes off and do it for me—just for me this time."

She slipped out of her jeans and shirt and waited for him to tell her what to do, pretending that she had forgotten.

"You need music, don't you? I'll hum it for you so you can shake it up." He hummed "The Steel Guitar Rag" and beat a stick against the log with his good hand to give her the rhythm. "Dance."

But she only shuffled her feet and her hands covered her breasts.

"Let me see them. You sure as hell showed them to everybody else. Roll them like you used to, and wiggle your ass. Come on now. Da da-da *dah*. Da da-da-da *dah!*"

She seemed to get it then, slipping back into the old nasty bumps and grinds, thrusting her pussy at him and then snapping it back.

"Roll them."

"Roll what?"

"Your tits. They're standing up real nice. Roll them for me."

She jiggled and bounced them, but she wouldn't roll them the way she once had, making them seem as if they were alive. She was deliberately holding back and it made him angry.

He sang faster, beat the rhythm faster, and she whirled and stomped, but she had grown clumsy, or more likely, she was being deliberately clumsy. She wanted the whole damned bunch of rubes out there, panting and clapping for her. He wasn't enough. His tentative hard-on shrunk, reversed by his rage.

"How many of those cops did you sleep with, you filthy cunt?"

She stopped moving and covered herself with her arms. *"What?"*

"All those horny cops back there in town. You slept with all of them, didn't you? The young ones, and the fat ones, and even the tall one—the old one, that Sam—didn't you?"

"That's ugly. Don't say that."

2 7 5

"You did, didn't you?"

"I only slept with my husband. You know that. I only slept with you."

"Liar. Put your clothes on. I don't want to see you dance any longer. You make me want to puke."

She cried and cried, long after the sun was gone. She begged him for forgiveness, and a long time later he let her creep next to him, although he lay rigid and unbending while she tried to fit herself into the spaces around his body.

"I love you. You know I love you. I don't know what I did that made you angry."

There would be no more nights, and only part of tomorrow. His arm was dead already. He could feel the infection where it crept into his chest and the nodes of his neck. She had drained him, well-nigh killed him, and he would be almost relieved to be rid of her.

The control he had left, the only choice that remained to him, was to pick which hour of the day he would destroy her. He thought that he might go with her this time and disappear from the treacherous sun that promised life and gave no life. They could fall together into the black void that had to be traversed before they could begin again.

29

Sam found Ling an undemanding teacher. Like most men of special skill, Ling required perfection of himself, but he was confident enough of his own ability that he had no need to criticize other men. Sam could sense a certain impatience when he bumbled, but that was quickly quelled. And he realized that it was his own inner screaming to make haste that caused him to plunge ahead too rapidly. He had managed to keep a fragile lid over his anxiety for days, simply because there had been so many steps to take and so many miles to retrace before he could expect to find Joanne.

POSSESSION

Now that they were relatively close, with the possibility of coming upon her with each turn along the trail, the shackled foreboding had broken free. He remembered all the searches of his life where discovery had been barely—but effectively—too late. Children crumpled in abandoned refrigerators with air only just exhausted. Old men who had lain too long under bushes and died a scant fifty feet from busy thoroughfares; old women in sad little rooms who could not call for help while their hearts beat more and more faintly. Young women, their veins full of killing dope. All of them salvageable—if someone had come in time. He could not remember his rescues; he wondered if there had been any rescues, and recalled only those he had lost. In retrospect, it was clear that he should have found them, and he had not.

"Patience. Patience," Ling was muttering at him. "You must allow your conscious mind to focus clearly on what your eyes already see."

"But how the fuck do I know what's right and what's not?"

"O.K. Start with what you are trained to look for—cigarette butts, paper, buttons, old shoelaces, anything that people throw away or that falls off of them. That should be easier up here because this is wild land. They blocked this whole area off to hikers during the search, so nobody's gone beyond those blue streamers except the ones we're looking for. If they dropped something, it will be fresh. Right?"

"Right, I guess."

"That's fifty dollars extra a day, dep."

"O.K. Dammit. Right. Right. Right. You are all-seeing and all-knowing, you little bastard."

"So we look for little pieces of them."

"You could phrase it a little better, Ling. But I take your meaning."

"After that, we look for what the mountain shows us, where twigs are snapped, where leaves are crushed, where grass is flattened . . ."

"How are we going to know if it's been people or animals?"

2 7 7

"If it was deer or goats, you can hardly see where they've been—their hooves are cleft; they don't smash the way humans do." He walked along a sandy spot of trail and then into the brush, demonstrating. "Look now. See the positives? See those little segments of prints where you can spot where you cut my boot? See the angle where the buck brush gave and didn't quite snap back up? We're going to be working this in no more than fifteen foot segments. If you go more than fifteen feet and you don't see a positive, you've lost it, and you back up and hit it again."

"Fifteen feet! They're miles ahead of us!"

"Fifteen feet at a time, but if we work it well, we can do it at a trot."

"You trot—I'll walk."

"Make up your mind." Ling grinned. "You're not as stove-in as you pretend, dep. You've even got roses in your cheeks. When we get going, you're going to cut—you're going ahead, and I'll be behind you with my nose in the ground and my ass to heaven. When we run out of positives, that will mean we've either lost them or we've got them boxed in. Now, leave me for a couple of minutes. I need to meditate."

Ling turned his face up to the sun and closed his eyes, as if he was drawing from some psychic source, pulling something from the air that was completely incomprehensible to Sam.

What the hell.

The climb was rugged and Sam envied Ling his close-to-the-ground construction, the low center of gravity that let him climb so easily, and yet his own endurance seemed to have extended itself, and he experienced little of the fatigue and muscle ache he'd noticed before. He didn't deserve it; he had treated his body as a vessel to be filled with poison: booze and cigarettes. But the booze was gone; Ling allowed him little time to smoke and made him eat.

They were rewarded early on with many signs, so many that the task ahead seemed child's play. The green plaid shirt, its front full of old blood, lay scarcely hidden between two rocks on the way up. Sam folded it carefully and dropped it into an empty pocket of his pack.

The cigarette butt and the crumpled wrapper from a protein bar marked the summit for them, and they slid down and down again through the pines and larch forest. Ling shouted to him regularly as he sign-cut, finding something here—and here—and here that validated their direction.

The meadow itself confirmed the presence, only recently, of more than one person. Wrappings and food packages rested there where the wind had tossed them against a circle of rocks, dried-food pouches, bandages—which made Sam's heart beat faster, although these blood stains seemed not to indicate serious hemorrhage. The ash of the camp-fires was deep; many fires had been built on the coals of previous fires.

He turned to Ling. "They were here for days."

"A long time. They might still be here."

They looked into the blank circle of woods ahead and saw nothing. Sam felt exposed, wished that Ling wasn't such a purist about weapons, and his skin erupted with goose pimples. He looked quickly around, framing consecutive sections of forest in his vision, and still saw no movement beyond wind ripple.

Something bright caught the sun. Probably mica embedded in the boulders or fool's gold. He gazed into the rocks' joining.

"What is it?" Ling said.

"I don't know. Something. Beer tab maybe."

The ring came out of the stone crevice in his reaching hand, the limp daisies still trapped in its circle, and he stared at it, amazed. It was Joanne's; it was the diminutive of the other ring that rested in his shirt pocket along with Danny's watch, forgotten since the moment Moutscher had given them to him. Ling walked over and studied the gold band and the dead flowers.

"Hers?"

"Yeah. Just like his." Sam fished the bigger ring from his pocket and set it beside Joanne's, wondering heavily why he should be in this lost place holding two wedding rings not his. "She must have left it as a marker to let someone know that she was here."

Ling held the flowers in his hand, studying them.

"How long?" Sam asked. "How long?"

"They were picked—maybe three, four days ago. Not longer. Whoever picked them isn't here now, and hasn't been since last weekend. Sam, they could be to hell and gone or to Spokane by now."

"What does your gut tell you?"

"Give me the rings. Let me hold them."

Sam dropped them into Ling's open palm and watched the tracker close his fingers over them, slow his breathing, and disappear someplace into his head. Minutes later, Ling handed the rings back.

"So?"

"His ring is cold—but we know that. Hers is still warm, and she's not far away. Not close, but between here and where the trees end before the highway. And . . ."

"What?"

Ling was silent.

"Say it anyway."

Ling looked into the woods until he spotted the trail. He shouldered his pack. "Her ring is getting cold, and I didn't want to hold it any longer because it made me sick. She's in trouble."

The positives were hard to find, but Ling found them. When they broke out of the trees and into the avalanche slopes, it was still early afternoon. True to his word, the copter pilot found them, circling low until Max waved his arms and signaled with thumb and forefinger. The bird slid sideways along its air channel and disappeared over the woods behind them.

Full dark trapped them at Fireweed Camp. Sam paced the campsite, filled with tension that had no energy behind it. Ling left him alone. It was a drab camp, offering nothing beyond water and wood for their fire.

After a supper of jerky and hardtack, Ling fell asleep at

POSSESSION

once and left Sam gazing into the fire for what seemed like hours. He tried to calculate what day it was, or even what time. There were no days in the wilderness and no time except for day and night. When he could fight it no longer, he slept so solidly that he did not hear Ling's snores or the fire crackling—or even the cougar screams that began an hour after midnight and continued until dawn.

The two men headed out while the sky was still gentian, only slightly streaked with pink, and Sam found Ling strangely subdued as he moved ahead, hurrying more than he had before, but still marking positive signs.

The boot markings that had become familiar appeared on the trail with regularity, and Max Ling turned onto the Stiletto Trail with no hesitation at all. Neither of them spoke. They made the ridge beyond the rock cairns and Max pointed to a pile of feces.

"Cougar."

When Sam's voice finally broke free, it was gravelly. "They attack?"

Ling shook his head. "Naw. Old-time stories about cougars carrying off babies. Never found one that wasn't a made-up scare yarn." He lowered himself onto the rough trail. "Used to be an old look-out here. Burned or blew away, or both. Sam . . ."

"Yeah?" He reached automatically for a cigarette.

"Don't smoke."

"Why?"

"We're close to whatever we're looking for. There were two people going in. Then there are prints of one person—big boots—going out, going in again. But he didn't come all the way out, and she didn't come out at all."

Sam's blood slowed down. He reached for a smoke again, and remembered he could not light it. His hand stayed still in front of him. "What does that mean?"

"I don't know. They're probably still in there."

"Then let's go."

The worst was she was dead, lying ahead of them in some farther meadow. At least he would know. The best? She was alive—injured perhaps, captive possibly—probably—held

2 8 1

by a faceless man who'd worn a bloody green shirt, who was strong enough to tear Danny's arm from its socket, whose boot print measured fourteen inches. He was a cop and he always expected the worst. Danny was dead. He'd known that all along. And Joanne's body was probably waiting for them now.

Ling moved in a crouched trot along a fresh field of green, and Sam tried to bend his own length into a semblance of the Indian's stealth. He did not want to see her body; seeing Danny had been enough. He held his breath unconsciously, fearing the sickly sweet odor that would soon rise up and meet them.

Ling dropped to his belly, and they both crawled then to the stone notch where the larch trees gave a measure of concealment. Then Max looked down onto the plateau below and grunted with astonishment.

"What is it?"

The tracker grunted again, and Sam could make nothing of it. Ling's left hand moved along the ground, signaling Sam to slide up next to him. The last three feet of their search seemed to take him longer than all the rest of it.

He saw, and looked away, stung with a mixture of shock, embarrassment, and disappointment that they had followed the wrong trail, stalked—not Joanne and her captor, but the naked lovers below. Ling had taken him on a wild-goose chase, tracked the wrong quarry.

Ling grunted again, and Sam heard, "Goddam . . ."

Sam looked again. The woman was naked, tanned so darkly that Sam wondered if she were a black. There were no white lines; she had obviously been naked for days. She seemed wild, a wild woman whose hair fell down her back and over her shoulders, full of snarls and electricity and stuck with flowers. She was young and her body was quite good, all of it except her breasts solid with smooth muscle, graceful in a primitive way. He could not see the man except for his shoulders that protruded from the sleeping bag and the back of his head.

Sam turned to Ling and failed to recognize whatever

emotion was written on the Indian's face. "Hell of a long hike for them just to get laid."

Ling only grunted and continued to gaze down.

The brown woman bent over the man on the ground, her breasts swinging free and heavy. While they watched, the man's hand rose up and clasped one breast, stroking it and pinching the nipple. The woman threw her head back and her face was heavy with sensuous pleasure. And then he recognized her.

"Oh my God. Oh my God, Ling . . ."

"Sam?"

Sam pushed his shoulders up, ready to scramble down toward the couple and Ling's fist pounded him flat again, driving his chin into the sharp pebbles that dotted the rock face.

"That bitch!"

"It's *her?*"

"I can't believe it. It can't be her. Look at her. . . ."

"Shut up. Shut your stupid mouth, Sam. They'll hear you."

"That bitch."

"Be quiet. You know him?"

The man peeled out of the sleeping bag and stood up, the light flashing off his red hair. His head swung in their direction and he sniffed the air like an animal sensing danger. But his eyes were blank; he had not seen them.

"You know him?"

Sam looked closely and saw nothing familiar about the tall man, saw that he was huge, so tall that he would not be easily forgotten once seen.

"No. I don't know him. I never saw him before. I'm going down."

He was on his knees and then on his feet before Ling could stop him, sliding on the baked gravel of the path, still shuttered off from them by the trees. He was unaware of the gun in his hand. He had no plan. He had forgotten everything he'd ever known about stealthy approach. He did not hear Max behind him; he was aware only of the man and the woman who stood naked, their eyes turning toward him with a swiftness that seemed lazy because of the roaring in his head.

Joanne recognized him. He could see her eyes widen and the open ring of her mouth. She raised a hand toward him, the palm flattened, and then she fell sidelong, swimming in the grass, away from his line of vision.

He saw the rifle cradled in the red-haired man's arms and rejoiced that he now had a reason to shoot. The man hesitated. He lowered the .22 and swung it away, pointing down into the grass at her, and hesitating again as Sam thudded toward him. All of their movements were in slow motion. Sam was amazed that he had so much time to think, to decide. When the big man turned again toward him and raised the rifle, Sam was crouched in a shooting stance. He could see the flat green eyes, even a thread of spittle on the bastard's lip, and he chose his spot leisurely, unafraid of the barrel of the rifle pointing at his own heart. When he squeezed the .38's trigger, it gave so smoothly that it seemed inoperable.

Noise deafened him. Two reports, then a third, echoing off the rock walls around them. Still in a crouch, he prepared to pull the trigger back again and make it function, and found that his target had disappeared from his view. He swung right and left, and could not find the naked man.

But he saw Joanne and was incredulous. The gun—the registered .38—was completely foreign in her small hands. She could not shoot; she had never picked up a weapon. On her knees, she pointed it toward him with one hand and reached toward the ground with the other.

"No!" It was his own voice roaring. "Joanne! No!"

He knocked her sprawling and the gun slid out of her hand. She came up clawing and kicking, and he struggled to be free of her before the big man had a chance to fire, but she clung to his back and he could not dump her off.

"You've killed him!" Her screams became words that could be understood. "You've killed him."

She tore at his eyes, but her hands were wet with something and slid off his face. With her hand grip gone, her scissored legs let go of him. She came at him again, and he

POSSESSION

wondered how he had recognized her before. She wasn't Joanne; she was some crazed animal, her mouth distorted by screaming. She hit him in the gut with her head, and tried to drive her shoulder into his genitals, but she was weakening, her screams hoarse whispers now.

"You shot him, you bastard. He saved my life. He was trying to help me—and you shot him. You filthy pervert."

He tried to hold her off him with his palms against her shoulders, but she twisted and clawed at him again. He grabbed one wrist and spun her around, pinioning her against him while she sobbed and twisted, spitting out obscenities. When he felt her sag, he let her go and she fell onto the grass, gasping for air.

"You son of a bitch. You lousy, fucking murderer."

She was either unaware that she was naked, that she sprawled in front of him wantonly, or she didn't care. He turned away, prepared to deck her if she came at him again, but she stayed quiet.

He looked for the tall, red-haired man, actually sensed someone just behind him, spun around, and saw no one but Joanne.

"Where is he? Where did he go?"

She began to sob again.

"Where the hell is he?"

"Over there. He's over there. Go see what you did."

He moved behind the boulder that was as high as his waist and saw the prone figure in the long grass. He did not trust it.

"Get up."

The man played possum, keeping his face buried in the turf.

"Get up you asshole!" Sam nudged the knee raised where the red-haired man had stopped crawling. "Game's over."

There was no response and Sam saw that a thin line of ants disappeared into the red hair and then emerged over the visible ear and descended into the hidden face. The guy had a lot of control—they must itch like hell. He touched the knee with his foot again, harder, and the man rose up and rolled over on his back.

285

There was a red furrow along his skull, disappearing behind the right ear. The green eyes stared half-closed into the sun without blinking. The mouth smiled slightly, and the ants dampened their legs in blood that drained into a pool in the ear. The man's left arm was purple and swollen, streaked with gaping peninsulas of pus.

"What's the matter with his arm?"

She didn't answer. She seemed unable to walk, and crawled to the body on her hands and knees, and flung herself on it. He watched her breasts flatten the red, curling hairs on the body's chest and overcame a terrible compulsion to pick her up and throw her off the precipice just beyond them.

"Get dressed," he said finally. "Go put some goddamn clothes on."

Sam walked slowly back to where Max waited, ashamed that Ling had had to see what Joanne was. He could not see the sleek black head on the rock where they'd waited. When he shouted, there was no reply.

"Ling! It's over. You can come down now."

Sam called again and waited for the crackling in the trees where Max hid.

He thought first that the little gurgling sound had come from her, but the source of it was too close for that. He looked down and was surprised to see how small Ling really was, all curled up with his hands clasped around his knees, made into a ball so that he could not be seen.

Ling breathed very badly, taking in air and some liquid so that his breaths were bubbles and whistles. Sam knelt beside him and carefully pried arms and legs apart, expecting blood again, feeling that every human he came in contact with had begun to leak red fluid, burst from veins where it belonged.

He found no blood. There seemed to be no wound. He loosened the shirt buttons one at a time, letting Ling rest between, talking steadily and with some reassurance—enough so that Ling's eyes followed him without doubt.

He could not understand where the hole in Max's armpit

had come from—from which gun. It didn't bleed externally, but it sucked in air when the Indian's chest flared, and Sam clapped his hand over it automatically, shutting out the sound. Closed, the hole was not as formidable, and Ling breathed easier.

"You're O.K., kid. You're going to be fine."

Ling's eyes closed and he shook his head.

"Hardly a scratch," Sam lied.

". . . scratch."

"Does it hurt?"

Ling grinned faintly. "It smarts."

"I'll get you down."

". . . bird coming."

Sam looked up, expecting to see some mythic winged creature, and remembered the helicopter. If it could find them, and if it came in time, and if Max wasn't drowning in blood quietly and efficiently, he might be able to keep his promise to Marcella. He had kept no other promises.

He carried Max, as light as a woman, all muscle slackened by shock, down into the flat. She looked at them without interest or compassion. She sat next to the corpse and held its good hand. Clothed, she resembled Joanne more—but she no longer smelled of flowers and soap; she smelled warm and musky—unhealthy, like the hookers on Pike Street who bathed less than they perfumed.

He could not take his hand from Max's axillary; if he kept it there, he could form a barrier of his own flesh, sealing the air out, forbidding the wound to suck and flatten the lung. She watched him listlessly.

"Sam?"

He turned to stare at her, surprised that she had remembered his name. "What?"

"He's dead."

"So is Danny. You're not very concerned over Danny, are you?"

"Danny's dead." It was not a question, and it was not a statement. "Is Danny dead?" That was not really a question either, because her voice dropped, and her eyes slid out of focus.

"Does it matter?"

"Don't tell Danny."

"Don't tell him what? How could I tell him anything?"

"Just don't tell him."

She's crazy, he thought.

"Are you mad at me?"

There was no way to give an answer with dignity. He stopped his ears to her and watched Ling's face, gray green under the dark first layer of skin. Sam thought he heard the rotors buppering a long way off, and he watched the clouds, willing the helicopter to find them.

Sam was not sure how long they waited. He watched to see if Max still breathed, and he concentrated on willing the brown chest to rise and fall. She moved somewhere behind him. He heard her pacing the grass shelf. She wasn't a threat; her gun rested where he'd flung it, lost in the weeds. The dead man's weapon was beneath his leg; she could not lift her red-haired lover and roll him off it. She talked to herself, nonsense words, from which Sam could draw nothing. He preferred not to look at her.

Her movement stopped and he heard her whisper so faintly that he barely heard her. He held his palm tighter over Max's wound.

Something touched his shoulder, a light touch he easily shrugged off. And then it touched again.

"Go away, Joanne. Just go away."

He heard her say something, sounding far back in the meadow, the sound all out of sync because of the altitude. He spoke again without turning to look at her. "Please stay away. Just be quiet and leave me alone."

The rifle butt caught him just at the base of his skull and threw him sideways, tearing his hand from Ling's wound. Sam looked up, prepared to knock her away from them again, not yet connected to the pain in his head. And saw . . .

The green eyes were wide open and the dead man towered over him, his face a twisted mask of rage and blood.

Sam rolled away from Max, felt thundering noise in his

own head, and focused on the man above him. One arm hung dead, and he realized his attacker could not shoot; there was a fogging, a blindness in the eyes.

The rifle butt swung down at him again, and he ducked and rolled away, closer to the edge of the precipice. Too close. He detected a lack of balance in the giant, but the rifle swung again and thudded against his shoulder. He grabbed it with both hands before it could be pulled back, and put his weight behind it.

The red-headed man seemed about to fall heavily on top of him and he braced for the impact, and then saw that the big man was going over him. The bloody face was above his for a second and then gone. His attacker made no cry as his face and useful arm slid into the rocks above the ravine, as the purple arm was crushed under him, no last roar of protest or fear as he slid slowly and then faster down the meadow's lip and disappeared into the air beyond it. It seemed an inordinately long time before Sam heard the sharp clatter of the .22 on the rocks below, and then a heavier, hollow thud.

He did not look down. His head still jangled with pain and dizziness as he fought to find a handhold to stop himself from going over too. He caught something and held on. He pulled up a little, found another safe thickness of weeds, and used them like rope to crawl farther from the edge. He remembered now that if he could not get back to Max, Max would have no air.

Sam's head began to clear, and he saw that Max still breathed very lightly, and that his eyelids still fluttered. The big man had not been dead, only an ox felled with a stunning blow—but he was sure as hell dead now. Sam sealed Ling's wound again, even knowing it had been uncovered too long.

He watched Joanne now because he did not trust her. She had seen her lover creep up on him, and she had made no cry to warn Sam. If he let her get behind them, she might try to kill him herself.

She seemed not to be aware of anyone beyond the dead man below. She paced along the ravine's edge, trying to find some way to climb down—testing here and there and only pulling away when her movements sent showers of rocks plummeting down.

"Come away from there. You'll fall."

She didn't answer him. When she found no way down, she stretched herself along the edge on her stomach, and held out one arm—crazily, as if she could somehow grasp her dead lover and pull him up to her.

She would not move from that spot. She would not respond to his warnings that she would fall. She gave no sign that she heard his voice at all. He let her be.

Max died so quietly that Sam did not hear him slip away; his breathing had only slowed and gentled until there was no breath at all. Sam heard a heartbeat when he pressed his ear to Max's chest, but it was only his own drumming in his ear. He could not bring himself to pound the little Indian's chest or to force breath into the slack mouth. Ling had spoken of essence, of soul and spirit, and he knew that Max had gone away, so much more swiftly than Jake or Danny had. There was no use to try. And still, Sam held the shell that had been Max, his hand tight over the bloodless wound.

When the helicopter found them, he carried Ling to it, so used to his burden that he felt strangely light when he let go of it. The pilot looked at Max, shook his head at Sam futilely, but strapped the little Indian into the seat when Sam insisted.

When the pilot held his hand out to Joanne, all of her languor and madness seemed to vanish. She turned toward Sam, and when she spoke her voice was cold and rational and utterly calm.

"Killer. You killed for no reason. I saw it all, and I will see that you pay. I hate you and I will always hate you. Murderer. . . ."

Part 3

WENATCHEE
September 17, 1981

30

CHELAN COUNTY SHERIFF'S OFFICE

FORM 927

INCIDENT NUMBER

81-1157

CSS 2187 REV 5 78

DATE 9-20-81   **TIME** 0930 Hrs   **PLACE** Deaconess Hospital

STATEMENT OF: Joanne C. Lindstrom

My name is Joanne Crowder Lindstrom. I live at 16103 Old Orchard Road, Natchitat, Washington. My date of birth is January 29, 1949.

On Friday, September 4, 1981, my husband, Daniel, and I arrived in Stehekin, Washington to begin a four day hiking vacation. On Saturday evening, September 5, we were camped at Rainbow Lake. We were joined by David Duane Demich who was also hiking. He informed us of the presence of a grizzly bear in the area, and we made camp together that night. Mr. Demich hiked out the next morning, but returned to tell us that the animal had threatened him. My husband and Mr. Demich helped me climb a tree, and they went to see about the bear. Within a short period—about ten minutes—I heard sounds of a struggle and a shot. I think several shots. I looked toward the area where they had gone and saw a very large animal in the brush. I heard a scream. I think it was my husband. Mr. Demich was wrestling with the bear. Mr. Demich returned to where I was and told me that my husband was dead. He told me that he would take care of me and see that I got off the mountain safely. We waited in the tree for several hours, and then Mr. Demich led me over a mountain pass. Because he had been injured in his arm, we had to stay in a meadow for several days. After we left the meadow, we became lost. Mr. Demich was quite ill. We were planning to try to find our way out. On the last morning. I'm sorry—I cannot tell you the date—a man I know as Sam Clinton burst into our camp. I told him that Mr. Demich had saved me and I screamed at him not to shoot, but he shot Mr. Demich. At no time did Mr. Demich threaten Sam Clinton or me with a weapon. Mr. Demich was unconscious for a while, and during that time, Sam Clinton attempted to rape me. I would like to say that Sam Clinton has made suggestive remarks to me in the past and that, on two occasions has attempted to put his hands on my body. (I had told my husband about this and he said he would speak to Mr. Clinton.) I attempted to aid Mr. Demich, and he did regain consciousness. When Sam saw that Mr. Demich was alive, he struggled with him and threw him off a cliff. There was a man with Sam Clinton, a man I do not know. He was injured but I don't know how. Mr. Clinton continued to make suggestive remarks to me until the helicopter came to rescue us. I fear for my safety if Sam Clinton should be released on bail. I will testify to the above in a court of law. The above is true to the best of my recollection. No promises or inducements have been made to me.

STATEMENT TAKEN BY: *Capt. Rex Nbatchee, 9271*   **SIGNED:** *Joanne Lindstrom*

WITNESS: *Lenore Skala*   **WITNESS:**

PAGE 1 OF 1

Sam read the Xeroxed sheets for the third time and then turned them face down and stared at the tan wall of the interview room. The public defender shuffled papers and sighed. He was a kid, a kid dressed in what had to be his daddy's Sunday suit.

"They autopsied him, I suppose?" Sam spoke without looking at the young lawyer. He came free; that was about all you could say for him—provided by the public's taxes for indigent defendants.

The lawyer pawed through his papers and drew forth a sheaf of yellow sheets stapled together. He seemed not to be familiar with the contents. "Yeah. It took them three days to bring him out of the canyon. Let's see—'Bullet entered just above the right ear, traveled beneath the skin transversely along the skull without penetration and exited above the occiput two centimeters right of midline. Bullet not retrieved. Nonfatal wound.'"

"Lucky bastard. It should have blown his brain apart."

"Mr. Clinton—I hope you won't make a comment like that to anyone other than me?"

"I wasn't thinking of calling the papers. What killed him?"

"Broken neck—at the—ah—C-3 and C-4."

"They think I did that too?"

"No. Dr. Albro attributed that to the fall."

"Albro? Where was he when I needed him? A guy falls sixty feet on his head, and even Hastings could have figured it out."

The public defender cleared his throat. "It's Mrs. Lindstrom's statement that disturbs me the most . . ."

"Disturbs *you?*" Sam stood and paced the six feet to the other wall, back and forth, back and forth, and fought the impulse to put his fist through the wall. "It bothers me just a jot too. That woman is nuts, and she's a liar. She was up there playing kissy-face—and worse—with Demich. They were getting ready to screw when we walked in on them."

Sam did not want to ask about Ling's postmortem, but he had to know. "What was the scoop on Max?"

POSSESSION

The shuffling of paper again. The lack of emotion. "Hemopneumothorax. Both lungs. The bullet tore out—"

"O.K. That's enough. I know what it means." The wall in front of him blurred. "What's your name again?"

"Mark Nelson. You ask me every time I come in here."

"I think somebody better get another statement from Joanne—because you could walk out of here, find your nearest asylum, go up to the first patient you ran into, ask him—or her—to give you a statement, and you'd have something just as relevant as hers is. He pulled the rifle on me. He was ready to fire. I shot in self-defense. I shot in *her* defense. Check the bullet that came out of—out of Max, and you'll see what Demich was up to—"

Nelson squirmed in his chair. "The bullet that killed Ling was a .38—it shattered on impact and the fragments indicate jacketed, probably hollow point—110 grains."

"That's what I use."

". . . yeah." Nelson brightened slightly. "But the .38 you said she had—they found that down in the canyon. Same kind of ammo."

Sam shook his head, disturbed. "No .22 bullet at all?"

"They didn't find it. But they found the rifle down on a ledge. It had been fired recently."

"That's no help. I fired. He fired. She fi—. Naw, I can't remember if she fired. I can't imagine that she would."

"The thing is," Nelson said quietly, "it's your word against hers. There's no way to show that the debris in their guns didn't come from a couple of days earlier. Without a .22 bullet at the scene, there's no way to prove he fired at you. And everybody's believing her statement."

"I suppose they think I deliberately shot Ling too?"

"Moutscher's willing to stipulate that Ling got caught in the crossfire. Your gun had three empty cylinders; hers had only one."

"I don't know *how* many times I fired. Somebody's got all the marbles, and it sure ain't me. Have you followed up on checking for a rap sheet on Demich?"

"I'll get right on that—"

"I told you to do it yesterday."

"Sam—even if he's got a rap sheet as thick as a brick, it won't change the charge against you. There are plenty of guys in Walla Walla who went up for shooting one of their felon buddies."

"I still want to know who he was."

"I've got a case load that simply isn't workable, and . . ."

"If I'm keeping you, I apologize. You probably have other clients who are more grateful. Kindly shoplifters and maybe a rapist or two who needs a little understanding?"

Sam watched the pink flush turn red and creep up Nelson's neck and over his ears; he knew he'd better shut up. He didn't dislike Nelson. Hell, maybe he did—but not Nelson himself. He was only one of the junior boy scouts who seemed to have taken over law enforcement and the legal process, all of them inexperienced and inept, posturing little devils, and Nelson the worst because he was dealing with a charity case.

"This statement. Where she says you made advances to her. Made obscene suggestions?"

"Where does it say *obscene?*"

"Well, suggestive remarks. Did you ever—ever—kind of kid her, or anything? Did you ever touch her?"

"Sure. Of course I did. Just like you're always messing with your partner's wife—or do you have a partner? Every chance I got, I whispered filth at her while my partner wasn't listening. Damn it, Nelson. Use your head. I've got almost twenty years on the woman. I liked her; I respected her, but I was never so hard up that I'd go sniffing around my own partner's wife. She said she'd see that I paid because Demich died. She's crazy like a fox. *I* don't know what happened. I have lain here night after night trying to figure out why she went off with that man, whether she had it all planned out before, why she was running around bare-assed with him like they were Adam and Eve—and I can't come up with any explanation at all. I've been a cop for over twenty-five years, and I have never, never, *never* come across anything that left me pole-axed like this. If I didn't know better, I'd begin to think *I* was crazy . . ."

"That's one way," Nelson cut in quickly.

POSSESSION

"What's one way?"

"You could plead diminished capacity—only temporary insanity . . . shock over your partner's de—" The moment the words were out, Nelson saw his mistake. "It would be difficult—under M'Naughton. It's just one way . . . to consider . . ."

"Get the fuck out of here!" Sam's right hand smacked the wall.

Nelson picked up the brown accordion file and clutched it to his chest, expecting that he was about to be hit. Backing toward the door, he forced confidence into his voice. "We're looking at second degree murder. We're looking at twenty years. We've got an appealing prosecution witness who says you're guilty as hell, and the state will make the physical evidence substantiate what she says. I'm just trying to find a way—"

"Just get out of here, Nelson. If I weren't so angry, I'd laugh. Even a raving loonie can't beat M'Naughton. You know that, and I know that. Don't come back unless you can generate the tiniest spark of belief in your client's integrity and defend me on the facts."

Nelson looked longingly at the closed door, but stood resolute. "Mr. Clinton, I cannot help you if you refuse to cooperate with me. I am not an errand boy. I am a member of the bar of this state. I'll come back when you send for me, and you're not so combative. In the meantime, I will do whatever I can on your behalf."

"Go away, kid. Just go away."

"If that's what you want."

"What I want seems to have ceased to matter. Go get your shoplifters off. Give 'em hell."

Sam found his box of a cell vaguely comforting. He was alone of course; put an ex-cop in the general jail population and you have a dead ex-cop. His likeness had graced the pages of the *Wenatchee Daily World* and the *Natchitat Eagle-Observer*, even the *Seattle Times* and *Post-Intelligencer*, and the Spokane *Spokesman-Review* every day for a week. The most illiterate felon who shared space in the

Chelan County Jail knew who he was. They called to him in the night, hooting and laughing until the jailers came to shut them up. If he went to prison—and he could not conceive of it despite Mark Nelson's dire warnings—they would have to give him a new name and send him to a federal joint. He'd known of rogue cops who'd been convicted and vanished into anonymity in prisons in Indiana or Illinois, and who'd been scared shitless that one day somebody would blow their cover.

He had felt such desperation for haste while he searched for Joanne, and he had found her, only to realize in one blinding instant that she needed no saving. With that shock he had been rendered powerless. He was glad Demich was dead. Whatever came next, Danny at least was avenged and had been spared the awful vision he himself had witnessed. What Joanne had come to was his own burden.

He tried not to think of Max or of the way Marcella had stared at him when he took her husband away. Cossetted in the hot, airless cell, he slept or read the dog-eared western adventure paperbacks the jailers brought him. Sometimes he thought about Pistol and longed for the heaviness of fur purring against his chest, the only creature who might now miss him.

In the time after lights-out, a woman in the female section sang jail songs—"Detour" and "500 Miles From My Home"—in a rough, sad-sweet voice, and then it was quiet except for coughing and the occasional muffled sound of crying that was neither male nor female.

And then he slept again.

31

They told her she had been in the hospital for nine days, but she was not convinced it had been that long a time, or that short a time. They told her there was nothing really wrong with her—only shock and exhaustion and a too rapid weight loss—and that she would be fine. She did not believe them because their smiles were painted on and they whispered to one another outside her room, but she ate because they insisted and because they called her "a good girl" and stopped nagging at her. When she tried to sit up or walk to the bathroom, the room spun, probably from all the little blue and yellow pills they made her take.

They told her he was dead. She could not bear to remember that. It made her cry and turn her face into the pillow so that she couldn't hear them. They would not let her read the newspapers; they would only bring her vases and vases of mums and carnations that suffocated her with their fragrance. But she smiled and said thank you. And that made them smile their false smiles again.

Her mother was there, sitting beside her bed everytime she woke. So strong. Just like the nurses. Solid, thick women with strong heavy legs in white stockings. All of them seemed so large, and she felt so small and weak, as if she were an infant resting in a huge bed.

The policeman was big too, with a great belly. When he pulled up a chair and sat close to her, the smell of pipe tobacco that clung to him made her nauseous. She did not want to have him near her, but she wanted to tell him what had happened. She owed that much to the man who was dead, to the man who had loved her so much that he had died for her.

Rex Moutscher blamed himself. He had misjudged just how crazy Clinton was. It had never occurred to him that the damn fool was going to go back uplake and take matters into his own hands. He should have seen how obsessed Clinton was with the woman. She was a pretty little thing but nobody to drive a man around the bend. But then you couldn't figure sex. He'd seen men go crazy over women too many times; they stalked and waited and eventually managed to strangle or shoot or burn up women who didn't want them anymore. Or didn't want them in the first place. Clinton had had a thing for Lindstrom's wife—but he'd sure managed to cover it up.

He asked her again, "Clinton bothered you before, Mrs. Lindstrom?"

"Sam?" She picked at the spread over her and looked out the window. "Yes. Yes. All the time. I was afraid to be alone with him."

"He knew you were going up to Stehekin?"

"It was his idea. My husband didn't want to go."

"Had you ever seen Duane Demich before?"

"Who?"

Moutscher waited a long time for her to answer.

"He said—that . . . No, I don't think so. He was just there, and he saved my life and he was kind to me and he said that nothing bad would happen to me because he wouldn't allow it to happen to me and he was going to take me out to a safe place that morning but he was sick."

She spoke with no expression and Moutscher figured it had to be the tranquilizers they gave her.

"Sam killed him, you know. Just came up there and shot him and threw him over the edge and I tried to get to him and he was dead way way down below."

She started to sob, and Moutscher had to wait for her. The nurse, Lenore Skabo, made a sound of disapproval. He'd forgotten she was there, witnessing. He hoped she would keep her mouth shut. Some of these nurses worked faster than Western Union with gossip.

"Now, tell me again, Mrs. Lindstrom. When did you first see Sam Clinton? Where was it?"

"Up there. In the meadow. In the trees. Coming at us with a gun."

"Which meadow? The one where the helicopter found you?"

"Yes."

"Or the one when you camped with your husband?"

"Yes."

"Your husband was already . . . dead when Sam went up there, wasn't he?"

"I'm sorry. Of course. I didn't understand your question. It was in that last meadow, the one with the big cliff. I'm very tired, Mr. Moutscher. Could we—"

POSSESSION

"Of course. You get some rest."

It occurred to Moutscher as he rode down in the elevator that Clinton might have killed Lindstrom too. Wanted the wife. Sent them up there. He called down to Fewell's office, but Fewell said that Clinton had been on duty in Natchitat the whole weekend, seen by good witnesses day and night. Trust Walker to think of checking. It was a long shot anyway.

Ling had no record of violence. The guys in the Natchitat office were sure that he and Clinton hadn't buddied up before. The wife said that too, after Moutscher got a finger-talker to ask her. Ling was just a patsy who ended up dead.

He fed the info on Demich into the NCIC computer, going through WASIC first, and waited for the dull green screen to come alive.

> Demich, Duane Elvis . . . D.O.B. 5–23–57
> 832 Larrabee, L.A., Cal. DL8X30P2–EXP5 23 83
> WMA [White Male Adult] Rd-Gr., 6–5, 220.

That was him, all right. He waited and another paragraph appeared, a warrant number: WASP–D00012–789633, 6–13–82.

He checked Seattle P.D.—Illegal use of bank card machine. No more information. No contact with suspect.

The FBI rap sheet was on his desk, and he tore open the yellow envelope from the Bureau.

PD, Denver, Colo.	Demich, Duane E. #27081	1–19–81	Fraud	Dism.
SO, Alameda Co., Cal.	Davis, Darryl E. AKA Demich, D. E. #11143	3–11–81	Bunco	6 mo. C.J. dism.
PD, Salem, Ore.	Demich, Darin E. #62191	9–2–81	Vag. Narc. GL 1st	Disch.

Demich was no angel, a con man with a lot of luck—until now. But all of it was Mickey Mouse stuff, and no convictions. No morals arrests, nothing in the crimes-against-persons area. A traveling man and slippery, but not violent. Seeing the woman, how helpless she was, Moutscher could understand why Demich would have wanted to help her off the mountain, and knowing Stehekin, he could see why they'd gotten lost.

Given a choice between Clinton's story and Joanne Lindstrom's version, it was no contest. Clinton was lying in his teeth.

Moutscher slipped the rap sheet back in its envelope, punched three holes in it, and slipped it into the case file. He was a little nervous, remembering that he'd let Clinton take away physical evidence from the Lindstrom scene. If that came out, he would look bad. But the stuff was basically only shit that Clinton had picked up himself and had no intrinsic value. He still had the autopsy report and Blais and McKay's follow-ups. If push came to shove, he would go on record that Clinton had taken the stuff without his permission or knowledge. Hastings would back him up because Clinton had made the old man look like a fool and the doc hadn't appreciated it.

Put Joanne Lindstrom and Rex Moutscher up against an alcoholic cop and ask anybody who a jury would believe.

Joanne lay in her bedroom at home, the shades pulled down so tightly that they made a dim twilight of the afternoon. She was awake after sleeping a long time, but if she needed to sleep again, she had only to cry out and they would bring her the little bottle of smooth blue pills, talking to her all the time in hushed voices. Her mother was somewhere in the house and so was Sonia. Who was taking care of Sonia's children? Everyone was so kind. Everyone took care of her. They brought her trays of food with fresh flowers in little vases, and begged her to eat. Yesterday—was it yesterday?—Sonia had bathed her face with cool water and helped her change into a clean gown. Sonia was so subdued and quiet now; before she had always been boisterous and sure of everything. Sonia careful in choosing her words—it frightened Joanne.

She knew that a great deal of time had passed since she had last lain in this room, but she was not sure how much and she was afraid to ask. What month was it? The light seemed weaker, but that might be the shades. She was surprised to find that the songs on the radio in the kitchen were the same songs that she had liked in August.

A certain instinct told her she must not talk to any of them about the things that mattered. They spoke to her, but very cautiously, about Danny and of what "Danny would have wanted." That confused her. Danny had been dead for such a long time that she thought they should not mention him so much. They barely mentioned *him,* David—no, Duane—at all. When she thought about him, she sobbed quietly into her pillow, so muffling her tears that the women who waited in the kitchen could not hear her.

She remembered the time at the cemetery strangely. Color. Blue and red lights flashing on top of a line of cars. A whole sea of red that turned out to be the tunics on the mounties who came down from Vancouver. Why? Black stripes across silver badges. White faces and flushed faces and gray faces bending down to speak to her. She had no idea which of her lovers had been hidden inside the coffin. No one had told her and she had not asked. She thought it was probably Duane. Of course, it was Duane. But then why had there been so many policemen? Duane hadn't liked policemen, but he'd had good reason; policemen had made most of his life miserable. Maybe the police escort had been for her—because she'd been married to Danny once. She had wanted to throw herself into the grave with Duane.

Sometimes she could close her eyes and smell the way his skin was when the sun had baked it all day. Sometimes she could see him above her, and the way his mouth changed—softened—when he was just about to make love to her. She tried to hold onto that image and always found it swept away by the terrible image on the mountain. She saw Duane struggling to save her from Sam, the odd slowness of movement as he moved behind Sam—as if his arms and legs could not move smoothly together—and then Sam's face looking around when Duane hit him with the rifle. She had tried to scream a warning to Duane and been completely voiceless. Duane had floated off the mountain; he hadn't even called out a farewell to her. Maybe he had been voiceless too.

One thing she could not forgive herself. That she had not gone over with him. It should have been so easy, but she couldn't do it. She had been unable to follow him down through the air between the rocks, even though she willed her body to go over. Just as her voice wouldn't work, her body had failed to obey her mind's commands. She had only reached out to him as if she could summon him back up from the pale rocks that glistened red with his blood, as if she could lift and touch him and make him whole.

He had been so strong—so powerful that she still could not really believe that he was finally and utterly dead. Sometimes in the night when the wind made the forsythia's branches scratch against the bedroom windows, she thought it was Duane. She believed—if only for a little while—that he had come back for her, that she could slip away with him through her window before her mother or Sonia could stop her.

Without him there was no point in eating, or sleeping, or getting well. If he was dead, she did not exist. He had told her that so many times. "Separated, we no longer live . . . Entwined. Flesh together. Blood together. Bone together. Throughout eternity . . ." If he did not come back for her, she would evaporate. They would come to wake her one morning and find no one.

The food did her no good. It only exacerbated the nausea that seemed to grow in intensity with each day. It was worse in the mornings, coming piggyback on the anxiety that shook her awake. She vomited then until she had nothing more to bring up, her retching sounds masked because she always had the cunning to turn on the shower before she bent over the stool. The workings of her body, its refusal to exist without Duane, without Duane's body to make it live, were no business of her mother's or of Sonia's. Now that she was away from the hospital, no one could force her to live. She welcomed the nausea; she took it for a sign that she would not live. No matter how much nourishment they coaxed her to ingest, she could get rid of it and they would never know until it was too late.

She didn't blame her mother and Sonia. It was more that she was on a plane that they could not imagine. They were part of her old life, part of the time when she had lived with Danny. They had never known the absolute, final, and convincing joy that she had known with Duane. Since they could not conceive of that rapture, they could not understand. She had loved them once, and she still did, but in a far-off way, in a time that was gone.

When she slept, she dreamed continually. She dreamed on different levels, and her dreams bewildered her. The top layer of dreaming was about Duane. He was there beside her again and he made love to her. His touch was so insistent and real that she came close to orgasm but never actually climaxed. She woke too soon, and she wept because she had not.

Deep, deep in the soundness of her drugged sleep, she dreamed of Danny. Those were not dreams but nightmares. She heard a man scream—so loudly and terribly that she thought the whole house would wake. She woke drenched in sweat, her heart beating chaotically, and knew only that something in the dark had terrorized her and she could not name it.

Joanne came to dread the moon. When she was a child, she had believed that the moon belonged to her alone. Because it followed her everywhere, she thought it was her moon—that all children had their own moons. When she was very small, warm in the back seat of Doss's old car, she had watched the moon through the little triangle window next to her. No matter how far they drove, even over to Seattle, the moon—*her* moon—had tagged along. It was friendly then, protective, its man-face smiling down at her.

That moon had died. The one that had emerged to take

its place was evil, staring down at her while she slept. Her mother or Sonia—one of them—crept into her bedroom while she slept and raised the shades, opened the window to let in air, and exposed her to the flat, dead-white moon with its craters and mountains forming a malevolent presence. She had no idea why it watched her.

The night air was cold. It smelled of no season. The wind came at night too, whipping the sunflower heads so that they thumped and woke her. The soft breeze before had come, somehow, from *him*. The shaking vicious wind— cold as if it had whistled down through ice tunnels—was something else. Some*one* else—trying to make her remember what she would not.

At first, she had taken more pills when she woke in the night, but then they must have counted them and found her out. Her mother took the pills into the kitchen and now she had to ask for them.

So in the dying hours of the morning, long before daylight, Joanne lay awake and shook with an unremembered fear. She always fell asleep before dawn to wake to new terror. She could not tell them about it. She did not know why. They told her she was being very brave, for Danny, and they left her alone.

Joanne wanted only one thing before she died. She wanted to see Sam Clinton punished. She had told the fat detective in Wenatchee exactly what had happened, told him how Sam murdered Duane, let him tape her words, write down her words, and she had signed the paper. No matter what happened to her, that paper existed.

Duane would be proud of her.

She kept no track of time. She thought it might be March. Sometimes she looked at her hands to see if they had blue veins and wrinkles, thinking she might have grown old and not known it. They looked smooth and taut, and they had small white lines where her scratches had healed.

She could not remember when she had last had a period. She didn't think of her body except to hope that it was dying. When her breasts seemed heavier and when the nipples grew tender, she thought that it must be because she had been in bed so long that she had crushed her breasts into the mattress and irritated them.

32

On the few occasions when Mark Nelson arrived at the jail to talk with him, Sam was led past the single clear window prisoners ever had access to. He was startled to look down upon Wenatchee and see that the season had changed, the old trees lining the courthouse lawn gone golden and russet now, the light slanted differently, hurting his eyes. He hungered to be one of the vagrants who drowsed in the midday glow that turned the fading grass bright again, a dozen of them lounging on the benches below and desultorily watching those who had business in the courthouse. He had always felt sorry for bums before because they seemed to have no purpose and no joy—but he envied them now. They were free.

He was not—nor was he likely to be. The chance that he might walk away from the tower that held him captive seemed more and more remote. Whatever Nelson did on his behalf was done with excruciating slowness and with veiled petulance. He had not gone down to Natchitat and contacted Fletch until the first week in October, and when he came back with the crime lab reports, he looked grim.

"Here're your reports, but I can't see where they'll help us. And I might as well tell you that Moutscher's got into them too. Your little friend got intimidated by your undersheriff. The lab sent a follow-up letter about something; it came in on Fletcher's day off. Fewell saw it and started sniffing around. Fletcher had to turn the stuff over to him—but he made copies first."

"That was considerate."

"Look, Sam. His job was on the line. That little man was scared. It took a lot for him to sneak copies out."

Sam sighed. "I guess you're right. Let's see what you got."

Nelson handed over a thin stack of white sheets, the printed material barely readable. The copy machine wasn't very good.

"Blood samples. Lindstrom's blood was O positive. The blood on all the clothing samples was O positive. A small sample found on the leaves was from a human, AB negative."

"That's what Demich was. Right?"

"Yeah. But she said he was wounded in the fight with the bear . . ."

"There was no bear!"

"All right. She said his arm was hurt when he came back for her. So it fits with their theory that he was wounded and he bled some."

"Where's your animal blood? She says he told her he knifed the bear. Where's your bear blood? That big hero said he spilled bear blood, and there isn't any, is there?"

"No."

"What's the timetable on the maggots?"

Davis thumbed through the thin sheets. "Here. Life-cycle projection is eggs were laid six days before autopsy."

"Shit."

"Yeah. Just like she said. Lindstrom died either Sunday or early Monday. Just corroborates what the prosecution says again."

"Danny's fingernail scrapings? What's the poop on those?"

"That's kind of interesting."

"What?"

"Epidermis . . . human. Traces of AB negative, not enough blood to reduce to enzyme characteristics . . ."

"There! Try to tell me there were twenty-seven guys up there with AB negative blood—twenty-seven guys who got scratched in a fight. You know how rare that blood is? Maybe 5 to 7 percent of the population. If Demich was trying to help Danny, how come Danny scratched him deep enough to take off a layer of skin?"

"You're reaching. You know what the state will do with that? They'll paint a picture of two guys fighting off a bear, arms and legs all entangled, say Lindstrom was hitting out at the grizzly and Demich got in the way."

"Let's see the rest of that." Sam reached for the remaining blurred copies and flipped through them. He paused finally and looked up triumphantly at Nelson.

"Got him! Try to explain this away. Three cigarette butts. Benson and Hedges. Found—*I* found them beside Danny's body. Saliva traces from an AB negative secretor. Danny never smoked cigarettes, and he sure as hell didn't puff away on one while he was fighting your mythical grizzly. Besides he's O—not AB negative. So you got your hero—hurrying back to save the damsel in the tree. Only he lets her stay there scared to death while he has him three cigarettes. He's done what he set out to do. He's stabbed Danny—killed him—and he wants her good and scared; so he takes his time. He sits there and he has him several smokes. He's so damned terrified of that bear coming back and he waits around and smokes? No way."

"That is kind of peculiar. It might be of some help."

"*Some?* It gives you the whole picture."

"I don't know."

"Well then, what can you do about her testimony? How come she remembers so clearly what she couldn't have seen? She doesn't remember. She's lying."

"It would seem so, but she's convincing everybody."

"Why don't you go on down to Natchitat and talk to her?"

"I tried, but her mother won't let anybody close to her, and her doctor says she can't talk to me."

"So every door we knock on gets slammed in our faces—and you won't pound to get let in?"

"For the moment. It won't look too good if we push a sick woman."

"I'm going to trial the week after Thanksgiving. You

remember that? I'd like to go in there with more than three cigarette butts and my good reputation which ain't so shiny anymore. Did Fletch find anything in the FIR's in Natchitat—anything that shows Demich was down there? They had to have known each other before. I can't believe she'd lie down so easy for a stranger. She wasn't that kind of woman."

"Maybe you didn't know her."

"If there's anything I know, it's women. I may not have been so good at keeping a relationship going with one myself, but I understand them. Something's hinky. She didn't chippy on Danny—at least almost until the last, if she did. They were arguing some before they took off."

"About what?"

"It doesn't seem to matter now. If it looks like it might, I'll tell you. I don't want to have to unless it's absolutely necessary."

"You don't owe her anything, for God's sake—and it won't matter to him anymore."

"It does to me."

"Anybody ever tell you you had a self-destructive streak?"

"Often." Sam stood up and signaled to the jail guard watching through the small window in the door. "I'll take these sheets if you don't mind. You can come get them in a day or two. It'll give you time to work your case load without thinking about me."

33

Sometime in the night a revelation came to Joanne, wrenching her out of sleep violently. It was a truth so awful that she could not share it with anyone. As reality rushed back, she wished that she had remained mad.

She remembered the red man.

His name was Duane. His eyes were green and smoldering and they had no bottom to them at all and they never blinked. He was the worst thing . . . yes . . . thing—not person—she had ever known. She had been so terribly afraid of him.

She gagged and the rest of the memory came tumbling out of her brain like vomit from her throat. Unstoppable and putrid. She was not imagining this. My God. Ohmy-God. She had let him touch her. No—not just touch her. She had allowed him into her body with his penis and his fingers and his tongue. Wait, that was a lie she was telling herself. Not just allowed him. She had begged him to do it. All soft, she had been, and burning for him.

It had happened. She did not know why.

Her skin crawled, remembering, and she looked to see if her flesh was truly black and scaled from his touch. It felt so defiled. The red man. The hideous, disgusting red man.

Shame rolled over her and she was consumed by it. She had crept to him on her knees and her belly and asked him to do those things to her. Worse. It kept getting worse, no matter how hard she tried to stop remembering. She had done things to him too.

She needed to scream, but she dared not do that. She shuddered and lifted her shaking hands to her mouth so that she would make no sound. She forced herself to breathe slowly. She remembered hating him. And she remembered wanting to kill him. She had *tried* to kill him and failed because she was a coward. She remembered terror and revulsion. But she could not grasp why she had come to accept him and desire him . . . *lust* for him.

It was incomprehensible, and it was too much for her to face without going crazy again. Crazy was safer than where she was now, but she could not guarantee where she would go if she slipped back. It could be worse. If there was more to remember, she did not want to know.

She switched on the bedside light and saw that her room was the same. She paced quietly, afraid of waking her mother. When she was exhausted, she read and when she could not read any longer, she counted the holes in the ceiling tile and prayed—although she did not deserve to be heard by a Higher Presence.

And then she slept, and her deepest dreams burst forth full-blown with horror. *Danny.* Danny came back to her, his hands held out, his face so sweet and good, and so full of shock at her betrayal. Danny was mute. She begged him to shout at her and damn her with his rage, but he would not. He only stared at her beseechingly and his dead lips mouthed "Why?"

She didn't know why. She tried to tell him that and woke saying it aloud. But he would not listen.

She had pictured Danny dead. She had imagined him injured so she could care for him. And then he was dead.

In this bed, to turn herself on, she had done it. And she had killed him.

And then she had clung to another man, had rolled and rutted with a stranger when Danny was scarcely cold. When Danny was not even buried. It was so awful because she didn't know where Danny was now, or if he was buried at all. She could not ask, because she could not tell. *If anyone knew . . .* If anyone ever found out what she was, what she had done . . . She could not tell.

She had lied to everyone. She was a bad woman, a worthless woman, a whore, and a liar.

When the truth came, it was demanding, sucking up every particle of knowledge that she had buried within herself. She prayed for dawn to come but the night hours stretched and widened.

She had refused to acknowledge something else too—her nausea, and the darkening nipples that ached like boils. She crept into the bathroom and flipped the calendar back and found no mark after the middle of August. Even though she had no idea what month it was now, she knew it was not August. She hadn't bled at all, not even a spotting. What a cruel practical joke God had played on her.

She had no clue whose child it was. If it was Danny's baby, she did not deserve it. She had betrayed him in as many ways as a woman could, and she would surely betray his child, come to a day when it would ask about its father and look at her with clear, trusting eyes—Danny's eyes. If it was *his,* then part of the devil—a fetal demon—even now pulled her blood into itself. She did not want it; she would not bear it, and she would not suckle it. She would dash out its brains before she would raise the child of the red man.

She would run. That would jar it loose from her. She would run until her heart began to falter, and take her blood away from the monster inside, pound and pound with her feet until it could no longer cling to her womb.

When they woke in the morning and brought her her pills and her breakfast, she did not let them know what she had remembered. They were fooled and thought that she was better because she said she wanted to get dressed and come out into the other rooms and be with them. She could no longer bear to be alone.

The days were shorter than the nights, and she bought time, day by day, allowing herself more of it when she truly wanted none of it. She sat with Sonia while her mother taught—or rushed to find something to can, paring and dicing and blanching to keep her hands from shaking. She sat with her mother through the evenings and she did not scream out loud. She let them take her to see Doc because she had no more excuses, but she lied and gave false dates of periods that had never been. She let him examine her and asked no questions about what he found. When he tried to talk with her, she turned away and said, "I think perhaps I would not like to talk about anything until next week."

She saw something in his face, and then it was quickly replaced by a professional mask. He knew about the fetus; he had to know—but he said nothing.

There seemed to be something about her that stopped them all from confronting her, as if they expected that she would fly into a thousand fragments if they pushed her too far. They did not know that she was leaden, too diminished and tight to explode. She saw that people were born with a certain portion of hope that belonged to them. Life took hope and goodness away like cupfuls of flour from a bin. If you were lucky, you still had some left when you were old. If you weren't, there was no reason to go on after your bin was empty. There was no way to replace hope. When it was gone, it was gone—and her luck had dwindled to a thin layer of white, so few grains that no amount of yeast could make it double and redouble again. A breeze could blow it away.

She had harmed Sam, but he was strong. She had no strength or courage left to save him. She wished that she could, but it always came down to the fact that she could not tell. She *could* not tell.

It was the last thought she held before she finally slept from sheer exhaustion. The bad dreams came immediately, and she woke with the same terrible mazes to be worked through until she came to the final question. And knew not what the solution was.

34

Sam heard footsteps approaching, and then the face of Noteboom, the day shift jailer, loomed beyond the bars of his cell.

"Lawyer's here, Sam." Noteboom grinned as if he had a secret.

Noteboom stopped outside the interview room and gestured grandly with one beefy arm. "I'll be back in half an hour to see if you're finished."

Sam walked into the little room, expecting to see Mark Nelson. Instead, a woman stood there, her back to him, her head bent toward the file folder on the table. The scent of her filled the room, a scent so familiar that his stomach turned over. Yardley soap and linen and English cigarettes. Nina's smell.

He absorbed her image in a second; the long hair was gone, replaced by a rough shag cut. The suit—beige and well cut, the long slender legs in low-heeled, plain brown leather pumps. Nina.

POSSESSION

He turned and tried the door. Locked, of course. No way to get out without buzzing for a jailer.

He had thought he would never see her again. For five years, he had done without her. Done badly, done so-so, and finally, done well. He had thought of her and dreamed of her and gone without loving anyone but her.

Until this moment.

She turned and stared at him without smiling, searching silently with her brown eyes. She held out her hand and he stepped forward and took it; there was nothing else he could do.

"Sam."

"Nina."

"Sit down. Talk to me."

The five years had not been particularly kind to her. She had been a youngish woman, a woman who could have been anywhere between thirty and forty. She was not youngish now. Her skin stretched too tightly across her cheekbones, thin dry skin that ages badly. There were tiny lines around her eyes and the corners of her mouth, and her neck was no longer the taut smooth column he remembered. Still, she was lovely.

She watched him watching her and picked up on his thoughts as if he had spoken them out loud.

"Time got to the old broad, huh?"

Caught, he stammered. "You look well. You look wealthy and successful—like a rich lady lawyer."

"I am. Rich and successful—and well. You won't believe this, but I haven't had a drink of anything stronger than tea for four years. But I know how I look. My dance card is empty. The men I meet are old fools and young guys who could be my sons. How about you?"

"Me?" He grinned slowly and reached for her hand again. "Old fools and young guys too. None of them come on to me. I guess I've lost my charm."

"I meant do you still drink like it's going out of style?"

"Not lately. They don't serve much in here. Not that much before—before it happened. Beer mostly. What are you doing here?"

"You fucked up, Sammie."

"That depends on how you look at it. You didn't answer my question."

"I came because I read about you in the papers. I saw you on the six o'clock news and the eleven o'clock news. After a while, it occurred to me that you needed a good attorney, and you always said I was the best working lawyer you knew."

"This embarrasses the hell out of me. I suppose you know that. Anyway, I've got an attorney."

"I met your attorney. When his ears dry out, in about ten years, he might make a criminal defense attorney. You deserve better than that."

"Maybe, but I'm broke, babe. I spent my entire life savings renting helicopters and a peerless Indian guide—who I managed to get killed. I am what you legal types refer to as indigent."

She looked away. He felt her hand cold in his.

"I'm not for hire. You're a famous defendant, and we big-time criminal defense attorneys thrive on patsies like you. Me and F. Lee and Melvin B. lust after defendants who'll bring us headlines. You're money in the bank."

"That's not why you're here."

"You haven't seen me for five years. How could you know why I do things? You didn't even know me then."

"I tried."

"You did that. Like they say, Sammie—if only I'd met you ten years earlier." She pulled her hand away from him, and opened her file. "I dismissed Nelson."

"The hell you did."

"He was glad to go. He told me he was 'terribly overloaded.' Actually, I think you frightened him. I assume you didn't want a defense attorney who could be scared off so easily. In your situation, you need a tough guy."

"You're a tough guy, are you?"

"You bet your sweet ass I am. I'm the Iron Maiden—well, maybe the Iron Matron now—and you're stuck with me representing you. Unless you say no."

"How could I say no to such a proposition?"

POSSESSION

"How's Pistol? Did he survive the exodus as well as you have or has he gone to the great kittyland in the sky?"

"He's fine—the last I heard. He asked for you often."

"He never. He used to sit at the window and watch for you to come ho— . . . to show up." She stuffed her handful of papers back into the brown file, and reached for the handsome attaché case beside her on the floor. "Let's go see him. We can work over these later."

"They get real funny about prisoners walking out of here—something about maximum security. And we're having macaroni and cheese for lunch. It's my favorite."

She laughed, an unnatural sound. "You'll have to forgo that. I bailed you out."

"You're kidding."

"I never kid. I never, never kid. You should know that."

"That's $5,000 on the barrelhead. You have that kind of money?"

"That—and more. I'm very good at what I do. I told you that. You're not going to skip on me, are you? I'll get it back. You can pay me 18 percent interest if you like, and we'll be square. Why don't you push that buzzer and go and pack your gear? I'll wait for you outside. I'll be the lady in the silver Mazda. The sun is shining; the leaves are what they call a riot of fall color. We'll go get a steak and you can tell me what really happened. Then we'll go see Pistol and Joanne Lindstrom and we'll rearrange the pieces of this odd puzzle until they fit the way they're supposed to."

"I don't have to tell you that's the best offer I've had today."

"No."

". . . and how grateful I am."

"Wait until you have something to be grateful about." She held the file and briefcase against her chest. "And Sam . . ."

"Yeah."

"Nothing's changed. I'm in a comfortable place now. I don't want to lose hold of it. I like my life. Do you understand?"

"Gotcha."

He rang, and Noteboom let them out.
The air outside smelled wonderful.

Nina drove well, if too fast. The wind through the driver's side window picked at her hair and ruffled it, and he wished that she had not cut it, wanting to see it whipping behind her as he remembered it. He was too aware of the movement of her right thigh as she accelerated and braked, of her elbow inches from his hand as she shifted down. He had not thought of sex in jail, where all men are said to be obsessed with it, but she brought all of his libido back.

The silver car left Wenatchee behind, skirting the rolling bare hills and plunging past miles and miles of orchards and their windbreaks of poplars, the fruit trees so pregnant now that they seemed to creak under their burden of red and yellow delicious apples.

Sam experienced again the sense that the seasons had accelerated and telescoped upon themselves—heat and then frost and then snow, and heat, and now it was fall again. The apple smell filled the wind and drifted into her car.

She turned south and the Mazda took the foothills approaching Blewett Pass, its engine a throaty purr. He remembered his truck and wondered idly what had become of it. He'd left it in the cruise ships' parking lot in Chelan during one of the spells of summer, and it probably waited someplace in an impound lot, had, perhaps, even been sold at auction by now. She picked up on his thoughts as she always had.

"What do you think of my jalopy? Beats your truck, huh?"

"Anything would. What happened to your Volkswagen? I always liked your bug."

"Somebody pushed it into Lake Union in—oh, probably 1978. I found it sitting there underwater one morning. We had a funeral for it and a dock party, threw flowers in, and said words over it. It's still there. The crawfish use it for a condo."

He shivered involuntarily, remembering cars with bodies in them that he'd seen winched out of Puget Sound. He thought often of death now, dismissing calm memories and going straight for the macabre. She looked younger—not young, but younger; the fluorescent lights of the interview room had not been kind.

"Are you happy?" He hadn't meant to ask it and was surprised to hear himself speak the words.

"Was I ever?" There was neither gloom nor lightness in her inflection.

"I guess I meant to ask how things were going with you—beyond the obvious. Private practice has certainly raised your standard of living."

"Sammie, you'd pee your pants if you saw my houseboat now. Nothing's left but the flotation. Cedar shakes, skylights, a greenhouse window, a sleeping loft—it's two stories now, honest to God. I've even got a cleaning lady. I drive her nuts."

He smiled. "I would imagine she'd find you confusing. You *seem* happy."

"That was always so important to you—being happy. Hardly anybody is. I finally found the formula for—what would I call it? Equilibrium. No big highs; no more excruciating lows. I juggle. I've got my career. I've made some friends on the dock. No lie. You may not believe it, but I have. And I have young lovers . . ."

She looked quickly at him, saw nothing on his face, and looked back at the road. "Nothing heavy. Their bodies are nice, and they're enthusiastic in bed and they haven't grown up enough to think deeply enough to interest me. When one leaves, there's always another one. All of it is like walking barefoot on a hot sidewalk. When one foot starts to burn, you jump onto the other one. If one part of my life disappoints me, I concentrate on another part. I never dwell on the hurting part, so I don't feel it."

"What if you run out of places to jump to? Your anesthesia might wear off."

"I'll find something else. When I told you I was comfortable, I meant it. I'm O.K."

"Am I someplace you jumped to because your sidewalk got too hot?"

She was quiet for a full minute, shifting into lower gear as the incline rose ahead of them. "Not you yourself, although I do care what happens to you, even if you find it hard to believe. What you are, *where* you are, and what they're trying to do to you represents a challenge."

"Maybe you should have left me where I was—like your bug. The challenge may get sticky."

"No." She laughed her mirthless laugh. "The bug will stay down, and it's quite content underwater. You're such a stubborn bastard, you'll always try to surface. Now reach into my purse and light me a cigarette and let's get down to business. Tell me what happened . . . every little detail you can remember. When you've finished, I'm going to want to hear it again—and again—and again, until you get so sick of going over it that you'll want to strangle me."

"What about your young man? Won't he get tired of waiting while you play nursemaid to an impossible defense?"

"If he does, I can always find another."

Before they rolled into Natchitat, he had told her all of it three times over.

He could not tell if she believed him.

Sam watched Nina, saw her sitting on his couch in his trailer, her stockinged feet tucked under her, her thin arms bare in her sleeveless blouse. He had visualized her in the little trailer a million times the first year, twenty thousand the next, and finally, not at all. He was thankful he'd cleaned up the hulk and bought furniture after he'd seen Danny's shock at the mess that last day; she looked out of place enough as it was, too rich for his blood, his salary, his taste. All of her energy was channeled into listening to him. He felt glad to be able to talk freely to someone he not only trusted in the ways of the law, but someone who might be able to grasp and understand what he could not.

Pistol clung to him, a matted lump of gray fur, scrawny but not starved, purring ferociously. The old cat had forgotten to be sullen and full of rebuke and had leapt at him the moment he crawled out of her car. Only after he had licked Sam's face had the cat allowed Nina to hold him. She looked at them now, man and cat, and said solemnly, "See, he always liked you best."

"Tomcats cling together."

"No they don't. They walk by themselves. You're both pussycats. Make me another cup of that disgusting stale tea and get me a sheet of paper and a pen. Let's see what we have."

He moved to refill her cup, still carrying the cat draped on his shoulder.

"This time dust the cup out."

When he passed the window over the sink, he felt rather than saw the eyes outside watching them. He knew Rhodes, the manager, and probably half of the park were out there beyond in the cold dark, staring from darkened mobile homes so that they wouldn't be seen. He suspected that Rhodes was plotting at this very moment how to break his lease. Killers in the park certainly were even less desirable than sick old men who didn't mow their grass or haul their garbage. Sam raised his right hand, the middle finger extended and waved it toward Rhodes's triple-wide. He pulled another beer from the refrigerator—only his second; it didn't taste as good as he'd imagined.

"So what do you think? We gonna blow them out of the courtroom and leave it a disaster area?"

She grimaced and ran her hand through her hair, revealing her pale, high forehead, unfreckled like the rest of her skin was. "We might only make them a little nervous with what we have here. There's nothing that will make the prosecutor foul his trousers."

"She said she saw the bear attack Danny."

"So . . ."

"She couldn't have. She was in the tree. She admits that. I was in the same tree. You can't see from there to where she says the struggle happened, to where I found Danny. The trail turns back on itself there; there's no visibility at all from where she was—all you can see is rock wall."

"Then why would she say that?"

"Nina, it's obvious. She had something going with

Demich right here in Natchitat. She coaxes and pleads with Danny to go off someplace where her lover boy can fake a death. Then she covers for him."

"From what you've told me about her—and your perceptions were always reasonable, even when you weren't—I can't see her participating in that kind of treachery. She doesn't sound devious. She sounds like a rather simple, naive, dependent woman."

"I thought she was."

She lit another cigarette. "Suppose she didn't know Demich before . . ."

"Then she wouldn't have been so willing to kill me to save him, would she? She wouldn't have been rolling around in the grass naked with him when I found them. Even sluts have loyalty, and she wasn't a slut. She loved Danny. Shit, Nina, I used to envy him she loved him so much."

"Did you now?"

"Not her—just the situation. Why would any woman change partners so easily? I *saw* her. She was nuts about Demich."

"What? Say that again."

"She was nuts about Demich."

"Again."

"Come on, Nina. All right. *She was nuts about Demich.*"

She stood up and paced, hampered by the confines of the narrow trailer.

"That's all we have, Sam. A mind."

"A *mind?*"

"You've been concentrating on physical evidence. That's what you do best, and God knows, we need all of it we can get our hands on. You know where I think our real evidence is? It's locked up in a mind that's not working the way it should. I think what we need is inside her head. She may not even know it's there . . ."

"I must have made your tea too strong. Look, she's lying, so I guess that means that she holds the key to why it happened. If you want to get fancy and say it's inside her head, that's fine with me."

POSSESSION

She stopped walking and pulled the hassock up so close to him that her knees touched his.

"Let me tell you a story. We had a case. I went to court with it. The victim was a hitchhiker—seventeen, maybe eighteen, kind of a plain, stubby little girl. A runaway. Nobody wanted her. Mother took off with stepdaddy number four. Father was supposed to be in California; so she figures she'll hitch a ride and go find him and say, 'Hi there. I'm your long-lost kid.' She started out from Bellingham, and she made it to the southern limits of Seattle when this creep picked her up. He had no intention of taking her to Portland. He got off the freeway someplace south of Tukwila and drove into a gravel pit. The usual stuff. He screwed her. He made her blow him. And then he screwed her again. That tired him out; so he tied her up and put her in the back seat while he slept. In the morning, he repeated the whole process."

"That's almost your average American rape scene—"

"Shut up. O.K., you're right. A nice average rape. Well, it went on for three days. Forced sex. Bondage. Isolation. No hope of surviving for her—at least in her mind. On the fourth day, he finishes with her, and he remembers he's supposed to be in Vancouver, and what's he going to do with her? So he shoots her. Not once. Not twice. He shoots her three times, and any reasonable victim would have lain down and died. She certainly seemed to be dead. Blood all over, eyes closed, breathing so shallow he thinks he's gotten rid of a complaining witness. He takes off."

"I can't see how . . ."

"*Please* shut up. O.K. This little girl is made of tough stuff. She's got a .22 slug in her arm, and one in her hip, and one in her neck, only—get this—the one in her neck is stuck neatly in her carotid artery. If it had gone through, she would have died right away. If it stays there, her brain will die. *But,* if they take it out proper, they can stop the bleeding and she might live. She can't know that, of course. Her organism only wants to live. She comes to, and lover boy is gone, and she's hurting like hell; so she crawls, *crawls,* up to the road and lies down there. She probably crawled three hundred yards a little bit at a time, and she leaves a trail of red behind her. Somebody comes along, sees her, scoops her up, and gets her into Harborview Emergency. They operate, see that slug that stopped her from bleeding to death, and didn't quite kill her, and they take it out and sew the carotid together neat as you please. She lives. She not only lives, she eventually walks and talks."

"Babe, if you just want to trade war stories, I can match you horror for horror. I can invite the neighbors in and make popcorn."

Nina shook her head impatiently. "She gives a statement when she's in the hospital, while she's maybe not quite rational—but the county dicks figure out what happened to her; they find a gas credit slip with his license number on it, and they pick him up in Camas and charge him attempted murder, rape, sodomy, kidnapping. They match the gun he had with the slugs that came out of her. They find somebody who saw her get in his car, but you know what happens when they go to see her about testifying against him?"

"What?"

"She starts to cry. She refuses to testify against him. She says she wants to marry him."

Sam stared at Nina. "She what?"

"She loves him. There was nothing the dicks could do, nothing *I* could do. That girl was totally entranced, totally in love with the bastard who almost killed her, who left her bleeding inside and out. He went to prison—but without her testimony. *She married him* before he went to Walla Walla."

"*Why?*"

"Right. *Why?*"

"She must have been nuts."

"Right again. No particular argument on that. Which brings us back to where we started. There's something here, I think—something that matches what I just told you. The shrinks kept mumbling about isolation . . . and fear. Let's think about it overnight and see where Joanne fits into it."

Nina moved toward the couch where her suit jacket lay,

and he stepped aside, too conscious of the small space with only the two of them in it. She bent over to pick up the jacket, poised in mid-movement without moving at all, and then she turned back to him, her hands empty.

"Oh, hell Sam. I'm not going. I have a forty-five-dollar motel room downtown, all reserved and paid for, and I can't go."

He thought he knew what she was saying, but he stuttered like a schoolboy. *"You want me to go through it again?"*

"No."

"What then?"

"I want you to fuck me." She would not lift her eyes to his face, but kept them focused at his chest level. "I want to be here with you tonight when the wind out there picks up and rocks this trailer, and feel Pistol on the bed between us, scratching fleas and being annoying. I want to feel your old bones next to my old bones."

His arms were awkward, but she moved into them easily, fitting against him just as she always had.

"You think it won't get too hot, too uncomfortable?" he whispered. "You won't have to find a cool place, some stalwart young man who doesn't have one foot on a banana peel and the other in the joint?"

"Not tonight. All I want is tonight."

"All you ever wanted was tonight."

"Don't talk. Don't ask for a goddamn commitment."

He heard her undressing behind him while he unfolded his new hideabed. And remembered he was a loser. Maybe he would fail at this too.

She was thinner; her expensive suit had hidden a new boniness, flesh gone from her hips and breasts. It didn't seem to matter. Even knowing the risk, he responded to her completely, recalling in his loins their exceeding joy in one another. The ache went out of him when he was at last inside of her, and just before he came, he thought that it was quite wonderful that he should be here, locked with her, instead of lying on his jail bunk in Wenatchee.

He fell asleep on top of her, too exhausted and too consumed to move away from her. He kissed the damp hair at her temples, and remembered nothing more all night long.

She was gone when he woke, chilled under the single blanket, the cat purring against his chest. He thought that he had dreamed her there. And then he saw the sheet of paper pinned to the hideabed arm, a yellow legal sheet with her square printing on it.

S.—
Will call later. Gone to see Joanne.
N.—

35

Nina had found the element of surprise wise in her first contact with Sam in five years; she now considered it essential in getting close to Joanne Lindstrom. Mark Nelson had tried the proper channels and had been rebuffed by Elizabeth Crowder, and the welcome wouldn't be any warmer for her. None of them were going to give anything to Sam. She had no doubt that they had been warned to avoid the defense, told they did not have to face Sam Clinton outside the courtroom. Well, Mark Nelson was forthright to a fault—at least a fault in a defense attorney—gifted with no slyness and precious little ingenuity. Nina imagined him, hat in hand, announcing who and what he was and asking to see Joanne.

She had left Sam's bed at six and driven to the Holiday Inn to claim her suite, take a shower, and dress again in something that did not label her "professional woman." In jeans and a red-checked shirt, boots that had cost three hundred dollars but didn't look it, she could have been the wife of a well-to-do Natchitat rancher.

She found the Lindstrom farm easily enough. She was good at directions, and she was lucky. She was invariably

POSSESSION

lucky for other people—unless they depended on her for something more than she could give. Just before she drew up to the lane to the farm, she saw a perfectly maintained 1972 Plymouth emerge from the narrow road and turn toward town. The driver had to be Elizabeth Crowder, an older woman sitting bolt upright behind the wheel. Nina slowed and satisfied herself that the Plymouth had disappeared around the first curve in the gravel road before she turned her Mazda toward the farm. Bumping over the last rutted hillock, she saw that there were no vehicles parked in the yard or in the shed, that the curtained windows shut any occupant off from a view of her.

She rapped sharply on the back door and waited. There was no answer. She rapped again and heard some sound in the house beyond, but no one came. A door slammed inside; music rose and then stopped as if someone had turned the volume knob of a radio or television up when they'd meant to turn it off. She knocked again, and called, "Joanne!"

No answer.

"Joanne! I have to talk to you."

A figure moved toward her from the far end of the kitchen, and she thought at first that it was an old woman, the movement so tentative. The woman inside peered at Nina at a disadvantage as her eyes tried to focus into the sunlight of the back yard.

"Joanne?" Nina called loud enough to be heard through the glass.

The door opened slowly and Joanne Lindstrom stood before her, so pale that her skin seemed translucent.

"Yes."

"I came to talk with you."

"There's no one here."

Nina stepped inside as if she had been invited, and Joanne moved aside, her back against the edge of the counter. "There's no one here now."

Nina smiled and drew no response. "You're here. You're the one I want to see."

"I'm afraid I don't remember you. I . . ."

"We haven't met."

"Then I don't understand. I've been ill."

"I know, and I'm sorry for the trouble you've been through. My name is Nina Armitage." She held out her hand and saw that Joanne was confused, only belatedly lifting her own fingers. "I'm a friend of Sam Clinton's."

The reaction was immediate and full of panic. Joanne slid around her and moved frantically to the other side of the room, using the long table as protection. "No. No, I can't talk to you. I'm not supposed to talk to anyone who . . ."

"Who what?"

"Anyone who knows Sam. Anything like that."

"Sam bears you no ill will. He asked me to tell you that. He wondered how you were."

"I'm . . . I'm all right."

"You look upset. Does my coming here upset you?"

"No! Yes. It's only that I haven't seen anyone. I've had to rest, and my mother has talked to—people."

Nina studied Joanne without seeming to do so, and she noted her sunken eyes, the lines in her face that had not been there—at least not in the pictures she'd seen. Joanne Lindstrom's hands trembled; she looked down at them, saw the tremor, and grasped the back of a chair to quiet them. She looked near collapse. Her arms were thin as sticks and her jeans bagged around her hips, the line of her jaw so bony that it had the harshness older women who diet obsessively attain.

But there was something else. Joanne Lindstrom wore a T-shirt that hung over her jeans, and the flesh beneath it was not wasted as the rest of her body was. Her waistline had thickened and the material over her breasts was drawn taut. Joanne saw Nina studying her, and stood up straighter, sucking her stomach in. But the thickness remained, and Nina recognized it for what it was.

Joanne Lindstrom was pregnant.

"Could I sit down?" Nina asked quietly. "Could we have a cup of coffee and talk?"

"But there's no one here."

"You're here. We'll be talking in the courtroom in a little

over three weeks now. It might be easier for all of us if we could talk now instead."

"What do you mean? What do you mean about the courtroom?"

"I'm Sam's friend, but I'm also his lawyer. I came over from Seattle to represent him."

"You lied to me!" Joanne was poised for flight, but she seemed not to know where to go or how to get Nina out of her kitchen. "You lied."

"No. I didn't tell you all of the truth, but I didn't lie. Are you positive—absolutely positive—that you want to go on with this? Do you really want Sam to go to prison?"

"I want you to leave. I shouldn't be talking to you. Could you please go away?"

"You didn't answer my question. Do you really believe that Sam did you any harm?"

"He made you come here to get me all confused."

"He didn't know I was coming here. He's too kind for that. I came on my own."

"How is he? Is he terribly unhappy in jail?"

"He's all right. He's not happy, and he's not in jail anymore. He's back home."

"Oh." Joanne smiled, but it was not a real smile, only a vague mimicry. "That's good. Tell him 'Hi' for me?"

"Tell him Hi? *Tell him Hi?* You could do a lot more for him. You could tell the truth, Joanne, and there wouldn't be any trial. People's lives are involved. Your life is involved. Joanne, do you know what the truth is? Do you realize what you're about to do to that man? What you've already done?"

The bright kitchen was quiet. Joanne moved one hand slowly and brushed a strand of dull hair away from her face. She looked at Nina as if she could not remember who she was or why she was there. Then her eyes shifted and she was panicked again. "Go away."

"I'll go away now, but I will have to come back again. Will you talk to me again?" She started to go and then asked suddenly, "Do you have bad dreams?"

"I don't know . . . just please go away."

Joanne disappeared down the hall. Nina waited to see if she would come back and heard the sound of a television blare from somewhere far back in the farmhouse. The kitchen phone rang but no one answered it.

As Nina drove back toward town, she knew what it would come down to. If Sam was to survive, Joanne would have to be driven into the ground, all her deceptions exposed, broken so badly that she might never again function with any degree of sanity. Nina wasn't sorry. The strong survive and the weak perish. That was the first law. All the others came after.

36

Joanne stayed in her bedroom for two hours, afraid to look into the kitchen to see if the woman was gone. She had been foolish to open the door. Her mother would be angry with her, and so would Mr. Moutscher and the lawyers. She stared at the portable TV without seeing anything but a jumble of color, and she scarcely heard the sound. She was afraid to pull the shades aside to see if the thin woman's car was gone. She was afraid to answer the phone. Her mother should not have left her alone.

After a long time, she turned the volume knob down and listened. There was nothing. She heard only crows calling outside her window. It took all she had to raise the blind and look. She saw no vehicle, no one at all outside except for the big black birds that perched in the elm tree and stared down at her. One of them broke away and flew toward her with its clumsy, jagged wings barely moving. At the last moment, it veered off and avoided her window. She could hear claws scratching on the roof overhang above the window and knew it was waiting for her.

She took the black bird for a sign.

The thin, sure woman *knew*. Joanne had expected the day

would come when someone would accuse her, but she had also expected more time, tender forgetful time—a long tunnel of it—through which she might miraculously emerge with a solution to what was insoluble. She had contrived to put the trial out of her mind as an event that was far, far in the future. Rex Moutscher had told her that long trials—and Sam's promised to be protracted—were almost invariably postponed when they were scheduled during the holidays. She had managed not to ask, "What holiday?" Her mother talked about getting a turkey and who would make the pies and she knew that it must be either Thanksgiving or Christmas. There was a calendar in the kitchen but that was for 1981—the year Danny died—so that was no use to her. She looked at the calendar in her bathroom, and saw with amazement that it was a 1981 calendar too. She had only looked at the days before. Was it possible that time had stood still—that so much had happened in a matter of three months? Moutscher had dictated the dates when she made her statement to him, but she had not been listening.

That woman—Nina—had seen that she was pregnant; Joanne had caught it in her cool glance.

They weren't going to leave her anyplace to hide. And they'd seen to it that she couldn't run away. Both the truck and her car were gone. Where were they parked? She could ask Sonia. No. Sonia would tell her mother. They were all lost to her now. Every single person she used to count on. Danny. Sam. Sonia. Her mother. Doss. It made her cry to think about Doss. He would have helped her. Would he? Or would he be as disgusted with her as everyone else would? Nobody left. Nobodynobodynobodynobody . . .

Fletch had retrieved Sam's truck from the impound lot—possibly an act of contrition—and parked it behind the sheriff's office, but Nina refused to ride in it. They took her car again, although Sam would have much preferred to drive. He arranged his bony knees beneath the Mazda's dashboard as Nina headed back toward town.

"Did you see Joanne?"

"I saw her."

"Well, *what?* How is she?"

"Have you eaten?"

He felt his stomach growl. "I guess I haven't."

"I saw a Cakes-N-Steak place down the road. Let's have a cup of coffee and talk it over."

"How are you this morning?" Sam glanced at Nina as he spoke and thought she looked, again, younger—dressed in jeans and a shirt, sunglasses covering any wrinkles around her eyes, wrinkles that he might only have imagined. "You look chipper."

"I'm fine."

He waited to see if she would say more, acknowledge in some way what had happened between them in the night.

She didn't.

He would have chosen to talk to her in a private place, away from the frank stares of Saturday diners. He appeared to be a most recognizable commodity, so much so that he almost expected that they would be asked to leave, but the young waitress slapped place mats and silverware down in front of them; her jaws busy with chewing gum and her eyes blank behind her smile.

When the girl left, he repeated the same question he'd asked before.

"You did see her?"

"Easy as pie. She was alone out there. Mama Hen passed me going into town."

"So how was she?"

"Funny. She asked the same thing about you. She said to say 'Hi.'"

"You're not serious."

"Quite. I, of course, didn't know her before, but the woman I saw this morning is not playing with a full deck. I could have been talking to a child, somebody who wasn't supposed to answer the door while her mother was gone. Very, very frightened. So full of denial that you couldn't believe her if she said the sky was blue and the grass was green. She was terrified when I told her who I was. And she looks like hell."

Sam sighed and made grooves in the place mat with his fork.

"Don't act like it's your fault, Sam. For God's sake, the woman is trying to destroy you. You can be such an ass."

"What do you want me to say? That I'm happy she's cracking up?"

"Joanne's pregnant. You should have mentioned that. A widow on the witness stand is bad enough—but a pregnant widow . . ."

"No."

"No what?"

"She couldn't be pregnant."

"She looked fecund enough to me, perfect maternal soil. What makes you think she couldn't be pregnant?"

"Well. Well, she had a period just before they left. They were trying to have a baby."

"She really shared everything with you, didn't she?"

"She didn't; he did." Sam stopped talking while the waitress put their food down, her eyes sliding toward him now; someone in the kitchen had apparently filled her in on his notoriety. When she walked away, his voice lowered to a whisper. "Shit, Nina, they were spending half their time down at Doc's, having tests, taking their temperatures. I don't know what all."

"And what were the results?"

"I don't know. I never wanted to get involved in it in the first place. I hate to talk about it now." He sighed. "O.K. Danny said he was going to have to take a semen sample in to the Doc to have a sperm count or something. He was planning to do that just before they took off. He didn't tell her because he was—shit, he was worried that something was wrong with him."

"Maybe there was. How long were they married?"

"Thirteen, fourteen years, I guess."

"And she never got knocked up before?"

"You still talk as delicately as ever, don't you babe? I guess not. It seemed to be what they both wanted. They weren't holding back on a family on purpose."

"And now she's pregnant. Isn't that a coincidence? She

said she was only 'good friends' with Demich, never even held hands probably. It must have been something in the wind."

Sam looked at the stack of hotcakes in front of him and knew he had no appetite. "What's she going to do? Are you sure? It seems awfully soon to tell."

Nina shook her head. "You are a constant puzzle to me, Clinton. No, I guess you're not. What she's going to do is not your concern, and nobody declared you the White Knight. She is definitely pregnant. She's one of those dainty, short-waisted women who blow up like a balloon the minute the seed's planted—or almost. I would say she's about ten weeks gone. Due date would be about the first of June. They'll put your trial off until the middle of January because of Christmas, and you'll have a witness sitting up there with her round little tummy under a smock and you'll look like the meanest son-of-a-bitching defendant a jury ever saw. Unless we can show it's Demich's, not Lindstrom's."

"Isn't there another way?"

"Not that I can see now. Look, if it bothers you, think about something else. Think about spending the rest of your life in jail."

He looked down at his plate again and pushed it away.

The primary medical care personnel in Natchitat itself included three osteopaths, two chiropractors, a podiatrist, and Doctor Will Massie, Jr. Massie, the son of a doctor, had grown up in Natchitat and was known as Little Doc from the time he was ten. When Big Doc retired, he became plain Doc, and at thirty-eight was treated with all the respect the only M.D. in town reserved. A burly, competent man, given to practical jokes when he was away from the office, he stood four inches taller than Sam.

His staff of two slim, blonde nurses looked at Sam with surprise, but passed him back to Doc's office ahead of the full waiting room.

Massie's handshake was firm, and his smile seemed sincere. Sam wondered if he would spend the rest of his days wondering what people really thought of him, if there would be no final vindication—ever. He appreciated the doctor's tact in asking nothing and offering no regrets. Even "Nice to see you back" would have hit a nerve.

"Sit down, Sam." Massie waved one fat forearm. "Take a load off."

"You're busy. I won't stay long."

"I'm always busy. I need a break. You don't look sick. Are you?"

"Probably should be—but I'm not. I've been eating all that balanced, nutritious jail food—"

Doc Massie looked down, and Sam detected embarrassment. That was it. He was either embarrassed or annoyed with his presence. He hurried ahead and damned Nina for forcing him to do what he was about to do.

"Doc, I've spent a lot of time lately asking for information that doesn't seem easy to get, and isn't easy to ask for. This may be the worst."

"Shoot."

"I have been charged with the murder of a man whom the prosecution paints as a kindly stranger, a veritable Samaritan. I have reason to believe the guy was a good deal less than that. Joanne Lindstrom's statement makes him look like a saint and makes me look like a monster. Her perceptions may be less than accurate."

"You never struck me as a slavering beast. Something of a wise-ass, maybe."

"Thanks."

A furnace cut in someplace in the long, flat clinic, and the blast of hot air tickled the toes of a skeleton behind Massie's desk and set it dancing in lazy turns. Sam stared at it, trying to pick the right phrases.

"Danny told me he was coming in here before they left on vacation."

Doc Massie said nothing.

"It was none of my business—but we were close and he was shook up. Hell, Doc, the thing was he was going to have a fertility test. He expected to get the results when he came back—only he didn't . . ."

Massie waited and Sam could detect no reaction on his face.

"I know your patient files are privileged information, but the shitty thing is that once you're dead, you lose your rights to privacy. I don't want to force you into anything—"

"What you're asking me is whether Danny could have fathered a child."

"Yeah. Damn it. Yes, that's what I'm asking."

"Sam, you understand that I cannot tell you anything about any *living* patient. That the rules still hold true . . . as far as that goes?"

"I do. I'm not asking anything about anyone else."

Massie whirled in his chair and pulled open a metal file drawer, fished through the tabbed dividers, and drew forth a thick file.

"Danny's been coming in here since he was two years old. My dad took care of him. Small towns, huh?"

"Yeah." Sam waited, although he sensed that Massie had already made up his mind. "Damn few secrets in a small town when it comes down to it."

The doctor read from the last entry in the file. "Daniel Lindstrom. September 2, 1981. Semen specimen presented. Lab report: September 9, 1981. Specimen indicates a disproportionate number of nonmotile spermatozoa. Five million viable sperm per cubic centimeter."

"Five million! Then he was O.K.?"

Massie shook his head. "That means that Danny could not, would not, have been able to father a child. Anything below 20 million—forget it. The chances were that he never would have been able to. I was dreading having to break that news."

"And you never had to."

"No. I never did. No specific reason for it. He was healthy as a horse."

"If it came down to it—and I hope to God it doesn't—we might have to subpoena that file. You understand that?"

Massie stood up and the visit was over. "Have at it. But Sam—"

"Yeah."

POSSESSION

"Don't ask me any more questions. Don't even ask me to surmise that something else might be true, because I won't tell you. I won't tell you if what you're thinking is correct, or if it could possibly be correct, or how I think it might have occurred. You know what I'm saying?"

"That's a given."

Massie shook his hand again. "Sam, when your neck is on the chopping block, you do what you have to—and I understand. But if there's another way, a way that will work for you, take it. O.K.?"

"I'm with you Doc. I'm with you all the way on that one."

37

Joanne's Sunday began before five, long before a flat, dull sun lit the tenebrous sky in the east. She knelt at her window and saw that all the elms and oaks and cottonwoods had gone quite bare of their leaves, that their limbs and twigs seemed charred against the horizon. The crows, sleeping in silhouette, sensed her in the window and woke to mock her.

"Whore! Whore! Whore!"

Even beneath the covers again with her pillow over her head and pressed against her ears, she could hear the black birds' cries. Like all the night sounds that had made her feel protected and cozy when Danny was alive—wind and rain and the whistle of the Union Pacific headed for Spokane—now the crows' cawing only reminded her that there was no hiding place.

She crept back to the window and listened for the river. It was still there, and she could concentrate on its roar and drown out the wicked birds. So close behind the farm property, the river rose high now between the walls of its rock channel after the rain and rain and rain, its current frothing white water over the deep green. She listened to it and smelled its clean, faintly salty smell until she began to shiver in the cold. She pulled on her robe in the dark and walked softly to the kitchen. Her mother appeared almost immediately, pretending she had not been able to sleep either.

"Can I get you something, dear?"

"My pills—I can't find them. I need to sleep."

"Oh . . . Joanne. It's not good for you to take so many pills. I think they just depress you more. Why don't you wait a while?"

"Never mind. It doesn't matter. What time is it?"

"Almost seven. Why don't you go back to bed for a while? Reverend Schuller's coming on at nine—or would you rather watch Oral Roberts?"

"It doesn't matter. Whichever you want."

It didn't matter. She watched her mother move stiffly in the harsh kitchen light and saw that she was old and tired, frail after all the years of being so strong. She should try to be pleasant but the air in the room was heavy and it was so difficult even to talk. The best thing she could do for her mother would be to just go away.

Surely she had been meant to perish on the mountain, and she was suddenly angry that she had not. Each of them—Danny and Duane—had promised her that she was to be with them always. Danny because of love and the other man for a reason she could no longer remember, and each of them had betrayed her. Her life was only left over, a mistake.

"You should get dressed, Joanne, if you can't sleep. Put on something bright and a little lipstick. Someone might come over later."

"Who?"

"Don't jump like that. Only Sonia or one of the girls from the bank, or Mr. Fletcher and, what's her name—the nurse—Mary Jean. They all ask about you."

"I don't want to see anyone but Sonia. Don't let anyone else come. I'm not ready."

Her mother sighed and rose to clear away their coffee cups. "All right, dear. But one of these days—"

POSSESSION

"One of these days, I'll be ready to talk to people. I promise you."

I promise you something easier, Mother. And you would thank me one day, if you understood why.

38

Chelan County's senior deputy prosecutor—Martin Malloy—had watched Nina Armitage in action and under other, more benign, circumstances would have welcomed the chance to confer with her. At present, he was aghast to learn that she—and not Mark Nelson—would be handling Sam Clinton's defense. He had never shared Moutscher's steamroller confidence that they would convict. Moutscher had left too many crevices in the case unchinked; the structure was not as sound as it might be. Even as Malloy stood with wary graciousness and urged Nina to sit down, his hand hovered over the ballistics reports he'd been perusing when her visit was announced. If she didn't have the same reports now, she would demand them soon enough. If he didn't give them to her, she'd scream "Failure to Disclose" and make a jury wonder what he was hiding.

The bullet fragments they'd scooped out of Ling were .38's, jacketed hollow points—police type—but there was no law that stopped civilians from buying them. No lands. No grooves. No firing pin marks. They could have come from either of the .38 pistols recovered, and Armitage would know that and go with it.

He smiled at her and slid the reports into his desk drawer. "Counselor, this is a pleasure."

"My pleasure, Mr. Malloy."

She was relaxed, and that bothered the hell out of him. She seemed already to view him as dead in the water. Why? She was too solicitous, too complimentary about the prestige of his law school, and the unexceptional decor of his county office.

339

"What can I help you with, Ms. Armitage?"

"I thought we might communicate better if I came in person to tell you I've taken over the case."

"Is that all?"

"I see you have the ballistics report there."

Shit! He slid the ballistics sheets out of his desk and handed them to her, and met her head-on, his voice studiously casual. "Minor consideration, you'll see. A toss-up. Only bullet recovered was in little, tiny pieces."

She read the report without expression, and then smiled at him. "I already have this, but thanks. Ling was *behind* Sam all the time. Sam was firing toward the canyon. Demich had a .22. It looks like the lady may have got a shot off. Amazing, isn't it? She seems such a delicate woman, and from what I've been able to find out, she was terrified of guns. That she could react so quickly, so accurately. What's the pull on a .38? Fourteen pounds, isn't it?"

"That's double-action."

"Of course."

"Single action would be only five to seven."

"You know your stuff, counselor. But you think a mere child could fire a .38 and hit a bull's eye fifty feet away? That puzzles me. It almost seems that someone gave her a crash course, prepared her in case of attack."

"Lindstrom might have. Up there in the woods, he might have shown her how to fire."

"Sam says he tried many times, Mr. Malloy. She wouldn't touch a weapon."

"Clinton is not my most reliable source of information."

"Perhaps not."

She shook a cigarette from her pack, held one out to him and he shook his head. She lit one and inhaled deeply.

"You don't smoke. That's admirable in this business. I suppose you play racquet-ball and lift weights too?"

"Squash." He reddened. The woman was what—ten—fifteen years older than he was, and she made him feel like a gawky student, stuttering before a teacher.

"Have you met Mrs. Lindstrom? Have you talked with her, Mr. Malloy?"

POSSESSION

"Rex Moutscher has. My staff members have, and I will. She has been through quite an ordeal, and I . . ."

"What about a polygraph? Voice stress analysis? Did you run her on any of those magic boxes? No? Have you ever considered that it was possible she'd blow ink all over the walls—that she could talk into a PSE and make a lovely line of telling domes? But then, you do have the perfect witness. She's the All-American Beauty, the little heroine, McDonald's, and the Lutheran Church, and . . ."

All her jousting about ballistics had been cat-and-mouse. Malloy saw that she was rolling now, but could not see her direction clearly.

"The tests occurred to us, but it seemed kind of nasty to subject her to all of that when her statement was so straight-forward."

"A little like putting the Virgin Mary on the lie-box? It's all right to ask hookers and gypsies if they're telling the truth, but not the kind of girl every man wants to bring home to Mama?"

"We all make value judgments, Ms. Armitage. Any attorney, any detective, has to depend on his—his instinctive sense. My choices are based upon the physical evidence, on Mrs. Lindstrom's statement, on the medical evidence, and on Moutscher's opinions."

She laughed, almost a happy sound.

"Rex Moutscher can't tell a rat's ass from a primrose. Rex Moutscher let half of the physical evidence slip between his clumsy fingers, and I think, Martin—if I may call you Martin—that his ambition might just possibly exceed yours and mine, and we both admit that we're greedy as hell."

"You coin a poetic phrase, Nina—if I may call you Nina?"

"Of course. I'm only a woman, really, and it's difficult to believe I do what I do, isn't it? A pale flower of a woman cast into the path of ruthless men. Not unlike your little witness."

He leaned back and grinned, but she caught him before his tilted chair hit the substance of the wall.

"Did you know Joanne Lindstrom was pregnant?"

He bounced back with a jolt. Before he could respond, she skewered him.

"Did you know that the late Daniel Lindstrom didn't have enough motile spermatozoa to impregnate a female—not even if they froze thirty ejaculations and stockpiled them? Did you know he was sterile?"

". . . no. That I did not know." Barracuda. Armitage was a barracuda.

"We have the medical records to prove that. Unless you're anxious to explain to a jury that an immaculate conception took place up there in the greenery, that Joanne is even now carrying the next Messiah, you might be interested in a compromise."

"Fuck!"

"You speak with a certain lyric quality yourself, counselor."

Malloy sighed and she felt a moment of empathy for him, remembering her own losses when victory had seemed so close. Resignation hung heavy over his slumped shoulders. "You're sure about the pregnancy, and the other?"

"Absolutely sure. Funny, isn't it—how many of our efforts come down to the birds and the bees?"

"What do you want? When you speak of a compromise, what would you want from me?"

"Surrender with honor."

"Given the alternative, that seems generous of you. What could you possibly gain from preserving my honor? Your reputation has preceded you, Nina. You've left a lot of opponents twisting in the wind."

"It's not for me. I'm a cut-throat; my client is a man of some compassion. Sam would prefer that the woman not be held up to public ridicule. I don't agree, and I don't really fathom why he isn't itching for revenge. But there you go. For me—for you too—there might be an interesting phenomenon. A defense we could use in the future. I've promised I won't use it this time, but it's happened before and it will happen again. Something weird happened to Joanne Lindstrom and left her brain scrambled; when Moutscher talked to her, she didn't *know* if it was Sam

Clinton or Godzilla who shot Demich. I think she may have gotten some of it back by now, and I'm fascinated with the process."

Malloy listlessly arranged paper clips across his desk; he had no enthusiasm for Nina Armitage's psychiatric research, coming as it did on top of the shambles of his best, most glorious, and, yes, most longed-for murder case.

"So then. What do you want?"

"I'm going back to Natchitat. I'd like to take you and Moutscher with me—and we'll arrange a meeting with your witness."

He thought of Moutscher, the outraged disbelief on his face. "Rex is not going to like this at all."

"It might be good for him. Better than a 4.6 deposition from your witness, anyway. From what I've heard, he is a man of little imagination."

"You might say he doesn't know the meaning of the word. He's a cop. What do you expect from cops?"

"I won't tell him you said that. Counselor, we feed off cops. They bring us all their treasures neatly labeled and initialed, and their theories, and their gut reactions, and we make something intelligent out of it. They're our raw material any way you look at it. From your seat, you need them. From mine—and one day you'll be a defense attorney too because you want the money; you're only here for experience—from *mine,* I get my jollies out of pointing out their overweening stupidity. For now, Moutscher is your cross to bear."

She stood up and smiled again, and he thought he liked her very little. "One thing. Sam Clinton is a cut above them all. If he had had the good fortune to be born meaner, a little quicker on his feet, and a little hungrier, he could have been one of us."

"Is that how he got you for his attorney?"

"That's a long, tired, pathetic story, unfit and uninteresting for your ears." She handed him her card with the Holiday Inn number scribbled on the back. "Can you and Moutscher get down to Natchitat by three or four?"

He reached for his desk phone. "I'll call him now."

"Wait until I leave. I don't want to gloat. We'll look for you by four. And Martin . . . don't call Joanne first. If she spooks, we'll both be up shit creek."

"You're so damned smug," he said, a bite in his voice that he hadn't meant to betray. "You keep ordering me around and I'll balk. I may just decide to go for a tussle in court. You've got a right to all my paper, but you don't know my battle plan. You could be whistling in the dark, Nina."

"I could be. If today doesn't convince you, then we go ahead into trial. You'll still have your zingers and I'll still have mine. If you do see what I think you will, then we can ask the judge for a 4.9 pretrial conference—clandestinely, as it were, without the press—and we work it out to our mutual satisfaction."

"You've got a deal."

"You don't sound that certain, but I'll shake on it." She held out her hand, and he took it, and found it was only a woman's hand, thin and bony and crushable in his.

"One more thing, counselor—"

"Yes. What else?"

"Do you fool around?"

He laughed and dropped her hand. "With you, my dear, only with the greatest of care."

39

Joanne had kissed her mother before Elizabeth left for her day of teaching.

"I love you, Mama."

Her mother could not say it back. "Take care of yourself today. Is Sonia coming over?"

"Maybe. Maybe this afternoon."

"Well, that's good. Try to keep busy."

"I will."

"You're a good daughter."

She heard the car door slam, the whisper of tires moving

away over the frosted lane, and then the vast promising silence that meant she was entirely alone.

She was no longer afraid. There was such calmness in her and so much relief that it should be that way. She moved in cool fluidity where nothing or no one could harm. It seemed as if the river already flowed over her, gently forgiving.

She suspected there would be nothing beyond. If there was a God, if the God of her Sunday school days in whom she had believed without questioning still endured, He would not have allowed the red man to have her. It was quite simple. There had been no God to save her, and there was no God waiting now to punish her.

She no longer resented the child. It deserved only the small kindness of dying in her womb before it could be thrust into a world that promised nothing to it.

She had control at last. She had chosen never to be older than thirty-two. She had chosen this day, this last cold Monday, for her own, and she had hours of it.

She did her mother's breakfast dishes, wiped the counter clean, and, not satisfied, sprayed kitchen wax and polished the Formica until it glowed. She swept the floor; it was important not to leave a dirty house behind. The effort exhausted her and she slept until two.

When she woke, she took a very long, very hot bath, and felt clean. Really clean, at last.

If she left a note, then Sam would be O.K. They would let him go, and he would forgive her. But she couldn't leave a note. Everyone would know about her. Even when she was dead, she couldn't bear to have them know.

She chose her garments for her own pleasure—if not for pleasure, because pleasure seemed an excessive word, then to her own liking. White. All white. A light cotton skirt that she had not worn for years, and a blouse, long-sleeved and full of lace at the neck. The shoes were her wedding shoes, retrieved from the furthest corner of her closet, and still with a grain of rice clinging to one outdated, pointed toe. A bride rushing to meet no bridegroom.

She wanted something of Danny's, some last garment that had belonged to him, and she found a silk scarf, white too, a gift from her mother that he had worn once to be polite. She twisted it around her and found that it covered the place where she could not fasten the skirt at her waist. She thought she had caught the faintest wafting of Danny's odor when she shook the scarf out.

Joanne had not looked directly at her own face in a mirror since Elizabeth had driven her carefully home from the hospital. She gazed at her image and saw a strange woman with pale lips and lost, faded eyes, such sallow, yellowish skin. She touched her cheek in wonder, and traced the sunken places beneath her eyes.

She brought herself back—the self that she remembered —with an application of liquid foundation, Erace under her eyes, and heavy dusting of Indian Earth blusher. And because it was part of an old ritual, she sprayed her throat and wrists with cologne.

When she was ready, she left the house without looking back. The wind was blowing off the river and she could smell the water the moment she shut the back door behind her.

She looked up at the sound of a heavy footfall and saw them coming toward her. The woman and Sam and Captain Moutscher and the other man that she didn't recognize.

And knew she was trapped. The terror rushed back in as if her body was a shell surrounding a vacuum.

They were staring at her, not surprised, but only curious, perhaps, to find her dressed and coiffed and smelling of roses and on her way to nowhere.

40

"Could we go inside, Mrs. Lindstrom?" Moutscher broke the silence, and Sam saw that Moutscher's hand reaching out to touch Joanne made her shrink back in something very close to panic.

"What?"

POSSESSION

"I asked if we could go inside—where we could talk. We're sorry to interrupt you, but something has come up. You look very nice. Were you expecting someone?"

"No . . . no one." She made no move to welcome them in, only stared beyond them toward the river path.

"Then you have a little time for us?"

"My mother isn't home."

Nina's voice cut in, washed of its imperious edge, and Sam breathed more easily. "We know that, Joanne. If you like, you could call your mother and have her come home. We could wait for that—"

"No!" Joanne moved away from the door and held her arm out in an odd wooden motion, seeming to indicate they could enter.

Sam ducked his head at the back door and stepped into the kitchen, and wished instantly that they had chosen some other place for the confrontation that must come. He had been welcome here and was not now. The room was the same still, and he saw ghosts sitting in the empty chairs. He was relieved when Joanne led them into the living room; they had never sat in the "parlor" together. Only at the long kitchen table where Joanne had laughed at them, and with them, and fed them, and rarely spoken beyond her gentle counterpoint to their voices.

She seemed to be aware of his presence in the group, although she had not yet looked directly at him. He could not tell if she was frightened of him or ashamed to face him. She looked like herself now and yet unlike the Joanne he remembered, more uncertain and somehow disjointed. He studied her covertly, this tired, thin girl in white, tried to superimpose the image upon that of the wild brown woman on the mountain and could not.

". . . coffee?" Joanne's voice was so slight that the ticking clock overrode it. "Would you all like coffee?"

"No thank you," Nina answered. "We've all just had coffee."

And enlightenment and a lot of discussion on how you lied and how they can trap you, Joanne. Joanne looked at Sam, startled, as if she had read his mind. He looked away.

"Does having Mr. Clinton here upset you, Mrs. Lindstrom?" Malloy asked.

Joanne looked at the prosecutor. "I—I didn't want to see him anymore. Excuse me, but I don't know who you are."

"I'm sorry. My name is Martin Malloy. I'm the chief criminal deputy prosecutor from Chelan County. You might say I was your attorney."

"Is this something official?" Joanne started to rise from her chair, as if to take flight, saw that her way was barred, and sat down again. "I need to know if this is official."

"Not really official, Mrs. Lindstrom," Malloy said smoothly. "It's in the nature of a conference—all interested parties meeting by mutual agreement. Is that all right with you?"

"I don't know."

"You would—(Nina caught the word *would* instead of *will* and smiled faintly at Malloy's gaffe)—have to see Mr. Clinton at the trial. A defendant has the right to confront his accuser. That's the law. We all thought it might be easier—talking here in your own home."

"I don't understand." Joanne sat stiffly, her ankles crossed neatly, but her twisting hands in her lap betrayed her. "I thought I would just go to the trial . . . and testify."

"Are you afraid of Sam?" Nina asked bluntly. "Is this room too small? Is he too close to you?"

"No."

"But you were afraid of him before? You were afraid for your life, as I understand your charges?"

Joanne looked toward Sam and made a half-nodding, half-shaking movement with her head.

"Ms. Armitage," Malloy interrupted. "I think—and Captain Moutscher agrees—that we should go at this in some kind of order. I'll speak with Mrs. Lindstrom, go over her statement with her, and then, if you like, you can ask questions. And Mrs. Lindstrom, of course, you may ask questions whenever you like. Would you be comfortable with that procedure?"

Joanne nodded. "Then you're on my side, Mr. Malloy?"

Malloy had the grace to flush as he nodded. "Technically,

yes. I represent the state, and you are the state's prime witness."

"And Miss Armitage is on Sam's side?"

"She represents Mr. Clinton, yes." Malloy reached into his sleek attaché case and pulled forth Joanne Lindstrom's statement. "We'll begin at the beginning, as they say, Mrs. Lindstrom."

Don't smile like that, you slippery bastard. Sam looked away from Malloy out over the fields beyond the window, down to the poplars bending in the wind. He did not want to see Joanne's face. He was no innocent sitting in on this massacre; he had agreed to it—to keep himself out of prison. He accepted that, and the guilt that went with it, but he hoped the questioning would not be protracted—that the kill would be quick.

"Mrs. Lindstrom, you stated that you and your husband—Daniel—arrived in Stehekin in September. What date was that?"

"I'm not sure. It was right before Labor Day, 1979."

"You mean 1981, don't you?"

"Yes. 1981."

"Was it on September 4—let's see here, the Friday before Labor Day?"

"Yes."

"And how did you happen to meet Duane Demich?"

"Duane?"

"Yes."

"Duane came into our camp one night. I think the first night—no, it might have been the second night. It was dark, and he sort of loomed up out of the woods and he said a bear had tried to get him, or he'd seen a bear, or something like that. He was a policeman . . ."

"He was *what?*"

"He told Danny he was a policeman in Oregon, and they kind of sat there and talked about people they knew and things like that."

"Why didn't you mention that when Captain Moutscher talked to you before?"

"He didn't ask about that. And Duane wasn't really a

policeman. I don't know why he said that. It might have been a joke."

"How did you feel about him? Had you ever seen him before that night?"

Sam listened closely, but kept his head averted.

"Duane? No. I'd never seen him before."

"He was never in Natchitat?"

"Oh no, Mr. Malloy. He hadn't ever been to Natchitat—he told me that."

"How did you feel when he walked into your camp? Were you glad to see him?"

"Danny liked him."

Sam suppressed a groan.

"*Danny* liked him. How did *you* feel?"

". . . he made me dizzy."

"I don't understand."

"He was a red man."

"A *red* man. I'm sorry. You'll have to explain that to me. Do you mean you thought he was an Indian?"

"He was awfully large. Very, very tall and big, and everything about him seemed to glow or burn or something. It's hard to say—but I was af . . . startled. His hair was red and his skin and eyes were red in the firelight. I guess at first, I thought he wasn't real—or something like that."

"But he *was* real?"

"Yes."

"And he camped with you that night?"

"No. He camped someplace down by the lake, and he was gone in the morning."

"Were you disappointed?"

"What? No. I was glad. I was relieved."

"Why?"

"Because we went up there to be alone, and he was a stranger."

"But he came back again?"

"He came back in the morning. He said there was a grizzly bear on the trail, and that he needed Danny to help him do something—get rid of it, or scare it away, maybe kill it. I don't know."

POSSESSION

"You say Duane Demich was a big man. And strong. Were there other trails he could have taken?"

"I don't know. There were trails, I think—but I never knew where I was. He seemed to be very upset."

"Did Mr. Demich have any weapons?"

"He had a rifle, and a pistol, or a revolver, or something like that—something you hold in your hand. And he had a knife in a leather holder."

"But he was afraid of the grizzly bear?"

"He seemed to be."

"What did your husband do?"

Joanne bent her head and stared at her hands.

"Do you want a drink of water?" Nina asked.

"No. I'm all right. I'm trying to remember how it was. I have—kind of cloudy places. It gets black, like black smoke in front of my eyes."

"What did your husband do?" Malloy's voice was a drone, no inflection, no insistence.

"Danny went with him. They pushed me up in a tree. They wouldn't let me go."

"What happened while you were in the tree?"

"The birds came."

"What birds?"

"Little women birds. They waited with me, and it seems as though they talked to me. No. That sounds wrong, doesn't it? I'm sorry—it's not clear. I was very frightened."

"How long were you in the tree?"

"I don't know."

"What happened to your husband and Duane Demich while you were in the tree?"

"I don't know."

"You told Captain Moutscher you saw them fighting with a bear—with a grizzly bear."

"No . . . Did I? I can't remember."

Sam's head came up at that, and Moutscher stood up and strode to the window, turning his back on them. Nina seemed perfectly calm.

"Do you remember anything about the bear?" Malloy probed.

3 5 1

"Duane said it was awful. He said it was the most horrible thing that he had ever seen. He tried to kill it. I think maybe he did kill it. No, something was following us so—so it must have been alive, but there were terrible scratches on his arm when he came back."

"So you remember telling Captain Moutscher about the bear?"

"I must have. I must have forgotten." She bowed her head and stared at her shoes, lined the toes up and waited. The room was too quiet. Her hands flew to her ears. "Ohhh . . . Danny screamed. Somebody screamed."

Nina struck a match and everyone in the room but Joanne looked at her.

Malloy tried another tack. "Why did you tell Captain Moutscher that you saw the bear?"

"I must have. I wouldn't have said that if I hadn't seen it; I just can't remember it now. It's so hard to explain how you can get clouds in your head like this. You try and try to clear them away so you can see, but—"

"O.K. Let's leave that behind for a moment. What happened later? Did someone get you out of the tree? Did someone come back for you?"

"He saved me."

"Who saved you?"

"Duane. Duane came back and saved me." There was something odd in the way she spoke; she lapsed into a kind of sing-song. "I would have died. I would have died if he hadn't saved me."

Moutscher turned around and stared at Joanne, shaking his head faintly.

"How long after you heard the screaming? When did he come back?"

"I don't know. I can see the part where he was in the tree with me. He held me tight so I couldn't fall. I bit his hand."

"You *what?*"

"I bit his hand. I don't know why, but I left teeth marks in his hand, and it made him sick. But he didn't blame me. He forgave me."

POSSESSION

"How did you get out of the tree?"

The clock in the corner chimed four times, and then another in the kitchen answered. When they stopped, the silence in the room seemed heavier.

"Joanne." Malloy tapped her knee lightly to get her attention. "How did you get out of the tree?"

"I don't know. The next thing I can remember is being in a meadow—with a rock. I was holding a rock over my head and—"

"Why? What were you doing?"

"I can't remember."

"A little rock? A big rock?"

"A big rock to smash—"

"What? Were you using it as a weapon—or to cook—or—"

"To smash his eyes."

Nina looked across at Malloy, but he would not meet her eyes. His voice was softer when he spoke to Joanne again.

"Joanne, were you afraid of Duane Demich? Did he attack you?"

"Attack me?"

"Did he—interfere with you sexually?"

"NO!"

"Nothing like that. You're sure?"

"I was married to Danny. I wouldn't let anyone—any man—do that to me."

"Your husband was dead. Didn't he tell you Danny was dead?"

She lifted her head and looked at Malloy. "If he did, I don't remember it. I was all alone. Everyone was gone, and I was lost. He said he would help me—us—get out, and I believed that he would. Don't you see? I—"

"You liked him then. You came to like him?"

She tensed, as if she suspected a trap. "There was nobody else. It wasn't that I liked him or didn't like him. He was all there was. I thought I was going to die. Sometimes it seems as though I wanted to die."

"But he wouldn't let you die?"

353

"No. He saved me."

Sam heard the same odd cadence in her voice, as if certain phrases she spoke were by rote, like a child mouthes poems. It made the hair stand up on his neck. Malloy had become quite gentle with Joanne. Moutscher sat on the window seat and stared at the floor, fidgeting with his socks. Only Nina seemed unmoved and placid.

"Do you know how long you were up there on the mountain?" Malloy asked. "How many days?"

"A month. A couple of months. It's hard to measure time. It was most of the spring."

"Spring? What months? Do you know the months?"

"April. May." She seemed confused. "No, it wasn't spring. There were yellow trees; their leaves were changing, and it snowed some of the time. Didn't it snow?"

"I wasn't there, Joanne."

Joanne looked across the room at Sam and spoke to him for the first time since they'd come into the farmhouse. "Didn't it snow, Sam?"

Malloy shook his head in warning at Sam, but Sam ignored him. "It snowed, Joanne," Sam said softly. "It was autumn."

"Yes. It was autumn. It was October and November."

"What is the date today, Joanne?"

"Could I look at a calendar?"

"Just give us your best guess."

"It's almost Thanksgiving."

"That's right."

"Then it's November."

She was trembling, so faintly that Sam looked again and saw the lacy bow at her neck flutter. It was going on so long. Why didn't Malloy just come out and ask his heavy questions and be done with it? He pulled away from the leather chair and felt his shirt cling to his back, soaked in sweat.

"If it's November now, you must have been home for a long time. What year were you lost?"

"1977."

Moutscher choked and slapped the window seat with his hand.

POSSESSION

"After you were in the meadow, what happened?" Malloy plodded on, as if at any moment the pieces of his case would magically come together again. "Was Mr. Demich . . . let me rephrase that: Did Mr. Demich continue to make you feel—'dizzy'? Were you afraid of him?"

"No."

"Did you like him?"

"He was sick. He needed somebody to look after him. Nobody ever had looked after him. He was like a little boy when he was sick, and I think he was frightened."

"So you began to like him?"

"I guess so."

"Did he attempt to rape you, or, let's say did he try to have sex with you?"

"No. I told you he didn't. I don't like that question, Mr. Malloy. His arm was all infected, and it was very hard for us. I thought he was going to die and leave me up there alone."

"But he didn't?"

"No. I had some penicillin which I gave to him, and he got better for a while. We had to hide."

"Hide from who?"

"People. People following us."

"What people?"

"I don't know."

"Sam Clinton?"

"I don't know."

"You were very frightened?"

"I was always frightened."

"Let's skip ahead. Let's think about when Mr. Clinton found you."

"Do we have to do that?"

"I think so. When did you see Sam Clinton? What was he doing?"

"Could I see my statement?"

"Try to remember, if you can."

"Sam was angry."

"And . . ."

"He was holding a gun."

"Did Duane Demich have a gun?"

"I wasn't looking at him."

"He might have held a gun?"

"He might. He told me that he wouldn't let anything happen to me."

"Did you have a gun?"

"No. I don't think I did."

"Do you know how to fire a gun?"

"Duane showed me how to. In case someone came, someone who was trying to hurt us."

"What happened then?"

"Sam shot Danny." Tears rolled down Joanne's cheeks, although she was seemingly unaware of them. "He shot him and he fell down, and I tried to help him."

"You said Sam shot Danny. Did you mean he shot Duane?"

"Yes. He shot Duane. I meant Duane."

"Do you know why he would do that?"

"No—I guess—no. I guess it was a mistake."

"Did you see another man up there? Did you see Max Ling?"

"I saw him later. After Duane fell over the edge. He was bleeding."

"Who was bleeding?"

"Everybody was bleeding. Duane was bleeding, and the little man was bleeding, and Sam was bleeding."

"What was the matter with Sam?"

"His head was hurt in the back. Somebo—something hit him. Mr. Malloy, I would rather not talk about this now."

"We have to go through this before we go into court, Joanne. We could stop for a while if you need to."

"I feel sick."

"Do you want to stop for a while?"

"No, but that's all there is. There isn't anything else to tell."

Nina had sat so quietly that Sam had almost forgotten she was in the room. She rose and touched Malloy on the shoulder, and he moved over on the couch and Nina took his place. She set her attaché case in front of her and smiled at Joanne.

"Joanne, I have a few questions. Is that all right with you?"

"I guess so."

"Nina," Sam spoke out loud, and they all jerked their heads around to stare at him. "She said she felt sick. Maybe, we should wait, and—"

"No. Sit down, Sam. Let me handle this."

Moutscher was looking at him. Puzzled maybe, not angry, not even annoyed as he would have expected. Sam sat down and looked away from the two women.

"Joanne, let's sum up a little. You've been talking to Mr. Malloy for a long time. O.K.?"

"Yes."

"A very bad thing happened to you, a shocking thing. You lost your husband very suddenly. Very violently."

"Yes."

"And you were all alone with Mr. Demich, and you were terribly frightened?"

"Wouldn't you have been?"

"Of course." But her voice was brusque. "Of course. And you were so confused and things got all mixed up and jumbled around and it's hard to remember."

"I guess so. Yes."

"But you remember when I was here before, when we talked in the kitchen?"

"Yes."

"You asked me how Sam was, didn't you? You asked me to say 'Hi' to him? Why would you care about Sam Clinton—if he did all these things you're accusing him of?"

"He's a person."

"Yes. You care about people, do you?"

"I try to."

"You cared about Duane Demich. You took care of him when he got sick in the mountains."

"I had to. Because—because he was the one who could save me."

"Who told you that?"

"Who?"

"Yes, who told you he would save you?"

"He told me."

"Did he talk to you a lot?"

"Some."

"Didn't he tell you what to think, and what to-do, and—"
Nina stood up and moved her face close to Joanne's. *"Why were you going to smash his eyes?"*

"BecauseIcouldn'tlookawayfromthem!" Joanne clapped her hand over her mouth, to stop the words that were out of her control.

Nina moved back, satisfied for the moment, and lowered her voice. "What color were his eyes?"

"Green."

"Always?"

"They were red in the fire."

Malloy's voice cut in, "Ms. Armitage, I don't see how the color of Demich's eyes has anything to do with—"

"My turn, Mr. Malloy." Malloy opened his mouth to protest, thought better of it, and remained silent.

"You called him—what was it?—'the red man.' Why was that?"

"At first he was."

"But later, later he wasn't?"

"No. He saved my life. I would have died if—"

Nina held up one hand wearily. "You've told us that before. Did he tell you to say that?"

". . . no. I don't know . . ."

"Did you love him?"

Joanne was as white as milk, her face so chalky that her white clothes had gone gray in contrast. She swayed visibly, caught in the force of each question. "No. No. That's not true. I was grateful."

"How grateful?"

"I don't know what you mean."

"You do know what I mean. You listened to him, and listened to him, and you began to believe everything he told you. It got very easy, didn't it? It was easier than you thought it would be. It was even easy to have sex with him . . ."

". . . no . . ."

"It was easy to fuck him, wasn't it?"

"Nina!" Sam's voice bounced off the walls and Moutscher jumped. Nina looked at Sam with an angry shake of her head.

Joanne's arms had risen slowly until they crossed over her midsection, covering, hiding. She stared into Nina's eyes, and seemed to have forgotten the men were in the room.

"Please don't say that."

"All right," Nina said. "All right, you don't have to answer that now. Joanne, do you have any children?"

"No."

"How long were you married to Danny?"

"Fourteen years."

"You didn't want children?"

"Oh . . . yes, we always wanted children, right from the start. Always."

"But you never had any children?"

". . . no . . ."

"Did you wonder why?"

"We were trying to find out why . . . when . . ."

"You're pregnant now, aren't you?"

Joanne didn't answer, but her arms drew up tighter around her waist.

"You are pregnant now. I'm a woman. I've been pregnant, and I can see that you are. Why don't you just say it?"

Damn her, damn her, damn me. Sam had asked Nina not to do this. A man could not have done it.

"It seems a bitter thing, doesn't it—to have to go through this pregnancy alone when you both waited so long for it? But then, maybe it's a blessing. Maybe it gives you something to occupy your mind. Did Danny know about the baby?"

Joanne was rigid, a deer caught in the crosshairs, unable to move out of the line of fire. Transfixed.

"Did Danny know you were pregnant?"

"Of course not—no . . ."

"You say 'of course not.' Why?"

"It—it was too soon to tell."

"Oh. Really? How soon was it?"

Malloy and Moutscher looked uncomfortable, more than uncomfortable, aware that they had been led along in something even they had no stomach for. They relaxed slightly when Nina moved physically away from Joanne, striding now in the stance Sam had admired so many years before, moving across the quiet room easily. She seemed to have forgotten that Joanne hadn't answered her question. More likely, she knew she'd made her point. But Sam knew she'd come back to it—bore in until . . .

"Let's go back again to the tree, Joanne. You were high up, holding on for dear life, weren't you?"

"Yes."

"Let's go through it again."

"Please—I'm so tired."

"You can do it. Mr. Malloy, could I borrow your copy of Mrs. Lindstrom's statement? Thank you. 'I looked toward the area where they had gone and saw a very large animal in the brush. I heard a scream. I think it was my husband. Mr. Demich was wrestling with the bear . . .' I wonder how you could have seen that. From that tree, down along the trail, one naturally comes to a wall of rock. You must have amazing vision, Joanne. Can you see around—or through—rock?"

". . . no . . ."

Nina reached into her attaché case and drew forth an eight-by-ten sheet, turned it carefully against her thigh. *"Do you remember anything, Joanne? What did the red man look like?"*

"Oh . . . please. I can't—"

Sam saw what Nina was about to do. It had not occurred to him that she could be so cruel, so willing to destroy. He started to move, but it was too late. Nina turned over the glossy sheet in her hand and thrust the morgue shot of Demich—in full color, eyes open, his long body white against the swollen purple arm—in front of Joanne.

"Is this him? Is this your hero?"

POSSESSION

Joanne screamed, a terrible high-pitched monotone sound that had nothing human behind it. The scream went on interminably.

Moutscher jumped between Nina and Joanne, and Malloy grabbed for the photograph and tore it away. And then Joanne slid from her chair as if she had no bones at all and crawled across the carpet, making gibbery noises that struck Sam as far worse than the screaming.

She crawled to Sam, inching along the floor until she could grasp his knees and hide behind them. He lifted her and carried her to the couch. She clung to him, burrowing against him, her face tight against his chest. He looked over her head and saw Nina holding half of a torn picture.

She was still smiling.

"Over there is your rapist and your killer, counselor. You notice that Joanne didn't run to either of you or to me? She went straight to Sam because she's always known he wouldn't hurt her, no matter what she tried to do to him."

"Lady," Malloy said slowly. "You'd eat your own young to win. I'm amazed that you denied yourself the pleasure of doing this in a courtroom."

"That wasn't necessary."

"Neither was this. You made your point a long time ago." Malloy looked down at Joanne. "Is she O.K.?"

Sam shook his head. "Call Doc Massie. He's in the book."

The other men welcomed an excuse to leave the room. Nina stood next to Sam as if she expected him to say something to her, but there was nothing to say; all his energy was focused on Joanne. Nina shrugged and left them alone.

Sam held Joanne closely and rocked her. He could hear voices in the kitchen, muffled conversation with no meaning. Nina's mocking laugh rose and stopped half-born when Moutscher and Malloy didn't respond. He wondered for a moment what she could possibly find to laugh about, and then realized that she had won and so had he. That he was now a free man seemed a hollow conquest. The means had soiled the end, and the devastation seemed irreparable.

Joanne clung to him as if he really could save her, and he

stroked her hair and whispered, "It's all right now. You're safe. Sam's here. Sam's here. It's all right. It's all over. You're safe. Sam's here." The words he had meant to say on the mountain.

He heard a car door slam and the sound of a car leaving. He was alone with Joanne for a long time, waiting for Doc to come. He heard Elizabeth Crowder's voice, and then Sonia Kluznewski's, but neither of the women ventured beyond the doorway. He kept talking, and Joanne gradually stopped whimpering against his chest. She breathed so shallowly that he was alarmed, but her eyes were open and blinking occasionally. His bad hip demanded a change of position, but even slight movement set off her trembling, and he stayed still, stroking and holding and whispering with his face against her hair.

When Doc walked in, the two of them together could not unlock Joanne's arms from Sam. He carried her to Doc's car, held her against the night while Doc drove too fast into town, and then carried her into the hospital, and laid her on a bed. She would not let go of his hand.

Doc Massie shut the door against the hovering nurses and filled a syringe.

Sam held his free hand out and stopped Doc's wrist. "What is that?"

"A sedative. She's not going to let loose of you until we sedate her."

"What if she's pregnant? Would that hurt the baby?"

Doc pulled the syringe stopper back and turned away from Sam. "Did I say she was pregnant?"

"No. And I'm not asking you. I said I wouldn't ask you."

Doc turned back and winked, a solemn wink with no humor behind it. "On the off-chance that she's pregnant, that she's carrying Danny's kid, I've got something in there that won't harm it. Nothing I've given her so far would harm it."

"That she's carrying *Danny's* . . ."

"Who else's? And who would know, and who would tell?"

Joanne's features relaxed, her eyes finally closed, and her hand slipped out of Sam's and lay open.

POSSESSION

When he was sure that she was really asleep, he walked down the stairway and away from the hospital. The night smelled of chrysanthemums and smoke and apples. His truck was still parked behind the sheriff's office. He drove past the high school and saw the stadium lights were on for night practice.

He drove past the Safeway and went home to feed his cat.

Epilogue

NATCHITAT
Spring, 1982

People forgot. The scandal had burst upon Natchitat already blooming, scarlet flowers budding and fading prematurely; like most gossip, the roots were shallow. It could not survive—at least not with its original glory—the hard winter. Those who knew the truth would not speak of it, and even the most dedicated tale carriers gave up after a while. Without a definite hero (or heroine), or a certain villain, it was too difficult to draw battle lines. In small towns where one can hear each neighbor breathe and laugh and cry, and sometimes in the act of adultery, new transgressions rush in to fill the void. Whatever peculiar secret thing it was that had prevented a trial became part of the folklore of Natchitat, scarcely examined except by old women with nothing better to do, and nobody listened to them anyway.

The winter was bad, full of blizzard and drift, the snows muffling everything and quieting life. The volcano down at St. Helens rumbled and stirred long before spring and threatened to suffocate Natchitat for a second time with eerie and perhaps deadly gray ash. The economy faltered. They closed down the lumber mill and one of the apple packing plants, and people worried far more about running out of unemployment compensation than they did about sin and the possibility of unavenged murder. Jobless, depressed men fought with each other and with their wives in taverns and houses, and when blood is drawn and property threatened, no one looks closely at the deputy who comes to the rescue.

Walker Fewell had to take Sam back into his department, a bitter pill to swallow. Under the law and according to civil service guidelines, Sam was without blemish. The rest of the deputies clapped him on the back and made loud, awkward conversation, and then everything was the same as it had been—except that Danny was gone. Sam refused all partners at first, patrolling alone on day watch, but then he accepted the new man, a kid not over twenty-five, who needed a mentor if he was going to make it. And, if the truth were known, Sam was lonely.

Joanne. Joanne went away in a quiet caravan of cars with Doc and her mother and Sonia. They came back without her, leaving her in a gray, quiet, and terribly expensive private sanatorium on the other side of the Cascades. When she came back, she remembered what she had forgotten and understood what she remembered. Except for certain times when the air was a familiar color or when the night was very dark and the wind tore at the moon, she was well. Not wonderfully well, but as well as most.

She came home in January and was welcomed tenderly, all the more tenderly when they saw that she carried her dead husband's child. The women at the church gave her a surprise shower, and she went to natural childbirth classes with Sonia who was pregnant again herself. When Doc Massie saw Joanne for monthly check-ups, he always referred to the unborn child as "Danny's kid," and she gave no sign that she might believe otherwise.

The child within her was active early on, and she stared at her white belly when she bathed and saw its elbows and knees making little bumps there. She was glad that it was healthy.

Sam passed her one day as he patrolled along the Old Orchard Road. She stood at the mailbox and waved him down as he wondered if he should stop. She looked beautiful again, more beautiful, standing there in one of Danny's blue plaid wool shirts, bundled up against the snow. She smiled at him happily and there seemed no reason not to drive her up the lane and sit in the kitchen and drink coffee with her.

It was easy then—more than easy—for him to stop daily. By tacit agreement, they never spoke of the summer or of the trouble in the fall. They were comfortable together. She needed someone to talk to; she was as serene as he had ever known her to be—worried only, she confided, at being alone at night because the snowstorms so often broke the thin black power lines. She would not go to her mother's house in town; she was quite determined about that. He was concerned enough so that he began to sit with her through the long evenings until she was tired enough to sleep. They watched television and talked, and he hugged her when he left, feeling paternal or telling himself that he felt paternal toward her.

It seemed reasonable and mutually beneficial that he accept her offer when Rhodes caught Pistol fouling the laundry room once too often and told Sam to get his trailer out of the park. He moved it to the lower part of the farm property, hooked into the water and electricity lines, and became a sentry at the beginning of the lane. Hidden as the trailer was behind the poplar screen, it was weeks before any passerby noticed it was there. And since he was so close now, it would have been ridiculous for them to cook separately; so he bought the groceries and she cooked for them.

Sam found himself more and more anxious to hurry "home" to Joanne, and she began to listen for the sound of his truck coming up the lane. She had some memory, some old recollection that might not be real, of being safe in his arms.

Three things occurred on the 14th of April, apparently unrelated.

Nina Armitage's bill for "Interest on $5,000.00 loan: $900.00" reached Sam's post office box. He wrote a check immediately, enclosed it in a sweet, flowered thank you card, and mailed it.

The ground in Chelan County thawed, and Duane Demich's body—which had remained unclaimed—was removed from its vault and buried without ceremony in an unmarked grave in a cemetery outside Wenatchee.

And, although the moon was only three quarters full and she had been very careful, Joanne Lindstrom went into hard labor and was delivered of a premature son. Despite his shortened gestation, the baby boy weighed over seven pounds and came into the world with a full head of burnished red hair.

Joanne nursed the infant and rocked it, and carried it close to her wherever she was. He did not have the dull blue eyes common to newborns; his were full of light and intelligence. He clung to her and would have none of Sam at the beginning. But Sam persevered, fascinated by the baby's vulnerability, determined to let this child know that he would not harm it. Gradually it relaxed in his arms as he sat, dwarfing the rocker with his heavy shoulders, and sang to it in a gravelly voice that made Joanne laugh.

Joanne named the baby Danny. Hearing her say the name so often first made Sam wince, but he agreed that it was the only choice.

In May, when the apple trees were dotted with pink and white blossoms, they carried Danny outside and laid him on a blanket in the bright green grass so that he could reach out for the blossoms.

"Look at him, Sam. Watch him. He seems so wise the way he stares at us—as if he knows everything and would tell us if he could only talk."

"All babies do that."

"No, he's special. He's really special."

He could not argue with her because she was so happy, and it was good to see her smile again. "Maybe he is. You never can tell."

"I'll love him so much; he'll grow up perfect. You believe that, don't you?"

He looked away from her for a moment, toward the river, and when he turned back her face was suddenly grave.

"You do believe that, don't you?"

He took her hand and lied, "I believe that."

He thought of Nina, who believed in nothing, and he finally let her go. He was not sure what it was that he believed. But the sky was clear above them, and the grass was sweet, and the child too. And there was, after all, only this one place where they were. Only this day.

Look for these other classic
bestsellers by

ANN RULE

...AND NEVER LET HER GO

BITTER HARVEST

EVERYTHING SHE EVER WANTED

IF YOU REALLY LOVED ME

DEAD BY SUNSET

and her #1 *New York Times*
bestselling novel
POSSESSION

POCKET BOOKS
A VIACOM COMPANY

3022

THE #1 *NEW YORK TIMES* BESTSELLING AUTHOR

ANN RULE

IN THE NAME OF LOVE

and Other True Cases

Ann Rule's Crime Files: Vol. 4

FROM POCKET BOOKS

POCKET
B O O K S

1391

Jerry Bauer

ANN RULE is a former Seattle policewoman and the author of twenty-one *New York Times* bestsellers, including nine Crime Files volumes: *Kiss Me, Kill Me; Last Dance, Last Chance; Empty Promises; A Rage to Kill; The End of the Dream; In the Name of Love; A Fever in the Heart; You Belong to Me;* and *A Rose for Her Grave.* Cases from this acclaimed series were anthologized by Ann Rule in *Without Pity.* She is also the author of *Green River, Running Red,* a revelatory account of the infamous Gary Leon Ridgway serial murders; *Every Breath You Take,* the only true-crime book written at the request of the murder victim; *. . . And Never Let Her Go,* the nationally renowned case of deadly seducer Thomas Capano, which was made into a CBS miniseries; and *Bitter Harvest,* which unravels the shattering case of Debora Green, a doctor and loving mother driven to lethal acts of vengeance. Her other bestsellers include *If You Really Loved Me, Everything She Ever Wanted, Small Sacrifices, Dead by Sunset, The Want-Ad Killer, The I-5 Killer, Lust Killer;* and her classic *The Stranger Beside Me,* the unnerving chronicle of Rule's dawning horror as she realized her friend and coworker, Ted Bundy, was a serial killer. She has also written a #1 *New York Times* bestselling novel, *Possession.*

Ann Rule has testified before the U.S. Senate Judiciary Subcommittee and often presents seminars to law enforcement agencies, including the FBI Academy, as well as district attorneys and victim support groups. She served on the U.S. Justice Department task force that set up VICAP (the Violent Criminal Apprehension Program now in place at FBI headquarters) to track and trap serial killers. She lives near Seattle. For more information, visit her website at www.annrules.com.

CPSIA information can be obtained at www.ICGtesting.com
Printed in the USA
LVOW07s1607151014

408902LV00001B/111/P